ACTIVATION

DEGRADATION

ACTIVATION
DEGRADATION

A NOVEL

MARINA J.
LOSTETTER

HARPER Voyager
An Imprint of HarperCollins Publishers

ACTIVATION DEGRADATION. Copyright © 2021 by Little Lost Stories, LLC. All rights reserved. Printed in the United States of America. No part of this book may be used or reproduced in any manner whatsoever without written permission except in the case of brief quotations embodied in critical articles and reviews. For information, address HarperCollins Publishers, 195 Broadway, New York, NY 10007.

HarperCollins books may be purchased for educational, business, or sales promotional use. For information, please email the Special Markets Department at SPsales@harpercollins.com.

Harper Voyager and design are trademarks of HarperCollins Publishers LLC.

FIRST EDITION

Designed by Paula Russell Szafranski
Interior images © PLST_4D / Shutterstock.com

Library of Congress Cataloging-in-Publication Data has been applied for.

ISBN 978-0-06-289574-5

21 22 23 24 25   LSC   10 9 8 7 6 5 4 3 2 1

For all found families

CONTENTS

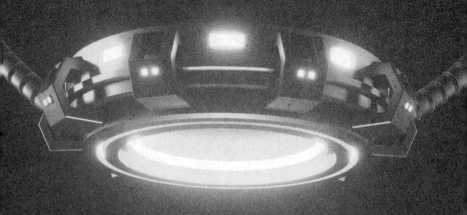

ACTIVATION
DEGRADATION

PART ONE

ROBOT

>>>Coming Online

>>>Designation: Autonomous Maintenance System, Unit Four

>>>Activation Instance: Emergency

>>>Age of Flexible Biomechanical Materials: Six minutes fourteen seconds

>>>Lifetime Radiation Exposure, Total Ionizing Dose: .0002%

>>>Database upload . . . 97% complete

Please wait.

Please wait.

CHAPTER ONE

The first forty seconds following AMS Unit Four's activation were nothing but chaos and pain. Its bio-hardware had been fused to its chassis in a flurry of accelerated growth. The flexible pistons that drove the hinges of its joints were raw with the surge of new lubricants, feeds, and wires. Internal warnings flickered through its central processing unit. Available memory was low; perhaps something hadn't been installed properly. The entire integrated platform system—of which the unit was a small part—was running at thirty yottaflops per second, far below the expected speed. And the unit's parts were stiff. As though they hadn't quite finished cooling and solidifying. Perhaps the test-flex had been skipped.

This was not the usual initialization process.

As it rose half out of the reconstitution pod, it opened its intake vents wide and threw back the shutters from its cameras. The sounds filtering through its microphones were disorienting at first—a blaring siren came from everywhere, the rhythmic yawing ill-timed with the flashing of the emergency lights. The approximal-temperature and pressure gauges in the unit's grasping pads told it *cold* and *hard* as it clung to the edges of the pod.

Another unit detected its presence and hurried over to aid its emergence from the reconstitution station.

"The transmission dishes are under attack," came an alert from inside Unit Four's CPU. It immediately identified the voice as that of its handler, stationed on Earth, which could interface with the robots via its buoy-routed, long-distance ansible link. The FTL comms channel allowed for real-time instruction and direction—indispensable in an emergency.

The unit accessed its primer containing the location, structure, and purpose of the mining platform. Flipping through the files, integrating them as quickly as possible, it did its best to orient itself, to find its marker on the map.

And all the while a red and yellow *warning, warning, warning* flashed across the uneven bulkheads, a flickering projection. Stunning and distracting.

It stumbled to the floor once out of the pod, the other unit—Unit Two—failing to keep it upright, clearly expecting the new robot to be able to maintain its own balance.

The AMS units each had four limbs, which could contort into multiple shapes and positions, letting the soft robots become quadrupedal or bipedal at will. As Unit Four struggled to stand erect—its bipedal option feeling more like a hindrance than a help in the moment—it found itself before a window, gazing out, off the mining platform, into the swirling, banded storms of the solar system's largest and most treacherous planet:

Jupiter.

The mining platform was a small, spinning sanctuary, a mere seven hundred million kilometers away from the gas giant's thermosphere. It currently rested between Io's plasma torus and Europa's neutral torus, utilizing the off-cast ions from the former to power itself.

This was the robot's home.

This was its whole world.

And it was under attack.

"Is it—?" Unit Four tried, but the drivers for its speakers hadn't been fully installed yet.

"The invaders. Again. Yes," said its handler. "I'm sorry we have to welcome you into the world this way, Unit Four, but if you and Two don't get in those maintenance boats right now and incapacitate those bastards, the whole operation might go down."

Acknowledged.

Its core programming initiated: protect and maintain the platform.

The platform . . . the platform . . .

It was still trying to assimilate all of this newness—to decipher just where it was and what it was and *why* it was.

Let's start with where, it thought.

This was the reconstitution and activation wing. Small. The room was only six meters by six meters, containing three pods for growing biomechanical robots, a manual input station, three doors, and a single window. The left door led to the fuel-input center, the right to the waste depository. Just beyond the center door lay arm-E, a long hallway that connected to a spinning central hub. The spinning of the platform created simulated gravity of approximately point nine gs. Primary equipment and monitoring stations formed bulky rooms at the end of each arm—seven of them in all.

Seven stations.

Four active AMS units.

One invading ship.

Finding its footing, AMS Unit Four took unsure steps away from the window and toward the other pods. One was empty. One was active, but in the early growing stages. The top was hermetically sealed and UV shielded to protect the engineered biotech inside. Most of a unit's internal parts could not be directly exposed to radiation or atmosphere without immediate damage. They were delicate, but pliable. Plastic. And that plasticity was both their greatest weakness and greatest strength.

My greatest weakness and my greatest strength, Unit Four thought.

A small, thin-slit of a window allowed for visual monitoring of the robot's soft-body development within. The new unit's chassis lay bare, a few cells coalescing and clinging, but this robot wouldn't be ready for activation for at least another seven hours.

"*To the boats,*" its handler said again with urgency. "I'm sorry, Unit Four—*quickly.*"

Unit Four *felt* the urgency, and yet its mind and body were still sluggish, still catching up. The chemicals didn't feel like they were pumping correctly through its tubing. Excessive vibrations tingled through its outer layers.

"We have to go," agreed Unit Two.

"Remote fire is only doing so much," their handler said. "Damn ship keeps using the dishes as a shield. And there's no way I'm letting you move the platform itself any closer."

"Something feels defective," AMS Unit Four said. "I'm concerned my activation process was faulty. My compounds—even my fluid pump—they're . . . they're . . ."

"It's adrenaline," its handler said. "I shot you up. Your biological components need it right now. A lot of it. You're going to crash after, but we'll take care of that, all right? I just need you to do what I activated you to do, okay? I know this feels strange. I know it conflicts with your past memories of activation. I'm sorry. I *know*."

Apologies weren't needed. AMS Unit Four was the one having a difficult time booting. It was already failing at the job it had been grown for. The panic and disappointment in its handler's voice was distressing. It wanted to be efficient, to do well, to execute its tasks swiftly and competently.

"I will show you the way," said Unit Two, placing one of its grasping pads on one of Unit Four's articulated arms. "I was activated two days ago," it said as it reversed, keeping its focus on Unit Four. "My process was much slower than yours, but I, too, was disoriented."

AMS Unit Four looked into Unit Two's cameras, feeling both familiar with its sister unit and disconnected. The robots were all identical, based on the same schematics and consistently regrown from exactly the same vat of materials. It had memories of "Unit Two" from before, but those were no more this exact same Unit Two as it was the Unit Four of times gone by. Each activation was different, each reconstitution and regrowth different.

Unit Four returned to its files as the heavy airlock doors to the reconstitution room slid aside for the robots. Each arm on the rotating platform was an independent unit, with fire blocks and docking sockets in case of dislodging, replacement, or emergency detachment—an especially useful design element if Unit Four failed in its task.

It was still unsure of itself. Trying to pilot a boat in its state didn't feel efficient. It looked up everything it had on the craft—its steering, weapons system, navigation.

"There are superfluous files in my databanks," it said, wandering through a maze of recall commands.

"I know, I didn't have time to cherry pick for your particular expected functionalities," said its handler. "I just dumped everything in."

"Should I delete the unessential?" It scanned the file categories, which included multiple languages, fuel processing and development, and . . . dance?

"It doesn't matter now. Just get to the damned boat. Please, Unit Four, I'm *begging* you."

It let the dispensable files remain.

Unit Two led it down the long arm, and the simulated gravity gradually shifted. Through another window, Unit Four saw it—the nearest phased microwave array, little more than a sharp glint of silver to its cameras. Currently, the array lay no more than two hundred and fifty kilometers off the platform, which meant if a dish were to dislodge at the correct angle, it could barrel into them. The debris would arrive in mere minutes—not enough time to safely reposition the station—resulting in various possible levels of damage.

And if one of the helium-3 fusion reactors was hit? The reactors sat well within the haze layer of Jupiter's atmosphere, just above the troposphere. A safe distance from the maintenance platform under ninety-nine point eight percent of malfunction scenarios. However, if there was an explosion . . . the shockwave could easily reach them. Even as movable as the platform was, being tossed out of orbit could cause significant problems—if they fell too far into Jupiter's gravity well, there would be no escape, as their engines couldn't compensate. They could be torn apart by the storms, crushed by the atmospheric pressures, or hit dead-on with a burst of radiation.

A hundred and one possible situations could permanently decommission all of the equipment and the entire operation—including every robot aboard.

It couldn't let that happen.

Wouldn't let it happen.

Unit Four brought up its Earth primer and saw a small, blue-green world. Well-tempered, compared to the planet below.

Earth relied on this mine for a third of its energy, and ninety-eight percent of all Earth energy needs were met by off-world endeavors. That's what kept the planet safe, and beautiful, and well-balanced.

Number of Species: Five point two million

Number of People: One point eight billion

Those life-forms were counting on it to stop the invaders, to save Earth from a crisis—from power outages and short-ages that would inevitably lead to chaos and death.

Through the window that ran the length of the platform arm, Unit Four searched the assaulted array for signs of the invading craft. For a distant glint of sunlight off a hull, a flash from an energy weapon. Though it tried, focusing in as sharply as it could, it was unable to make out the alien ship.

The majority of the platform was kept at 22.22 degrees Celsius, which felt stifling on Unit Four's new casing. The climate was supposed to be optimized—22.22 degrees was the prime stimulating temperature for the robots' organic muscles, essential for peak performance. And yet, its casing was dewing, shedding excess heat via water evaporation. Perhaps that was just further proof that Unit Four was oper-ating at less than optimal levels.

But its handler wanted it moving, so it continued for-ward as quickly as it could.

As the two units reached the center hub, they began

to float. Here, the simulated gravity gave way to true microgravity. Unit Four grabbed a helpful bar, and Unit Two swiveled to look back at it. "Systems level?" it asked.

"Not at this time," Unit Four admitted. "Perhaps one of the other units would be better qualified to pilot a boat."

"None of the others have undergone muscle-memory stimulation. They could download the piloting program, but would have dissatisfactory reaction times."

"I believe *I* will have dissatisfactory reaction times."

"Our functionality is not for us to question," Unit Two said.

True.

"Dish seven has shattered!" their handler yelled. "Debris incoming. Get to the hangar!"

"Two minutes to impact," came a new voice. Another unit, elsewhere on the platform.

They wouldn't make it in time. AMS Unit Four spun a three-dimensional diagram of the platform in its CPU. Even at ideal travel speeds, it would take them six minutes to arrive at the boats.

"Debris trajectory?" Unit Two asked, tone level. *Its* fluids weren't raging. *Its* biology wasn't unbalanced or its files poorly installed. "Can we shift the—?"

Unit Four had only been activated for a precious few minutes, and already it had only known two chemical modes: panic and envy.

The new unit, Unit One, replied, "No time. The majority will hit platform arm-D with a ninety-seven point six-two percent certainty. There are chances"—it paused, performing a quick calculation—"that a percentage of the fragments may hit arm-C. Porting calculations to all other units now."

Arm-C. The arm they were about to enter.

The shutters on Unit Four's cameras blinked, and then the projections were there, in its databanks.

There was a nonzero chance at least some of the debris would impact arm-C.

"Faster," said Unit Two. "Higher gears. We need to stop the invaders."

"Be careful," their handler pleaded. "We can't afford to lose any of you."

Unit Four pulled itself more forcefully along the bars with its grip pads. It tried to steady itself with evenly timed bursts through its intake valves and out its exhaust. It had a job to do. It wanted to do its job. It wanted to pilot the boat, defeat the aliens, earn its handler's praise, and then live out the rest of its activation period in whatever state of being was exactly the opposite of this *go go go go.*

It had been awake for less than fifteen minutes and already it longed to *rest.*

The two units rounded the central hub. The inside was an empty space where the entrances to the arms slowly flashed around perpetual openings—aligning, then un-aligning—as the platform's engines drove the spin. But the hub served as more than just a waypoint between arms and a center for revolution. Thick bulkheads on either side protected essential equipment, everything from the vaults to the platform's energy converters to its fuel stores.

The arm rotation was slow, which left plenty of time for them to slip from the hub into arm-C without worrying they would get pinched in the dealignment, and yet Unit Four felt its internal pumps flutter as it passed between the perpetually moving bulkheads.

"We're not going to make it," it noted, finding the array through the next set of windows. The debris was growing closer, barreling toward them, chunks of twisted metal and wiring, each piece larger than a robotic unit.

"We need to keep going!" Unit Two insisted, its volume increasing by ten decibels.

"No—" their handler cut in. "Brace. I need you to brace!"

"We should keep going," Unit Two insisted.

Unit Four paused, gripping a bar, heeding its orders from Earth.

"My calculations—" Unit Two started, continuing onwards.

"Unit Two, impact in twenty seconds, please just—"

"We can travel another six meters in that time, saving—"

"Damn it, Unit Two. Brace!"

But Unit Two continued on, its movements steady, sure. Unit Four wondered if it had received any extra adrenaline, anything to help its biological growths respond with the urgency and awareness and caution that the situation warranted.

Perhaps it was *too* level.

The chunks of dish swelled in the window, the rays of the far-off sun glinting off them to create straight, harsh shadows over their contours.

If the window broke—if the arm was breached—the robots could be sucked into space, where their biological parts would wither and die.

How much of each unit would be salvageable after that? Reconstitutable?

Unit Two continued to pull itself down the arm, trying to escape the microgravity.

Unit Four ducked away from the window, curling against the bar, counting down silently.

Three . . . two . . . one . . .

It shuttered its cameras, stuck itself fast against the wall.

The unit felt the impact long before it noted the sound of buckling metal. The first strike rattled it down to its core. Everything from its hard chassis to soft muscle shook with one long reverberation. The force jarred its articulated limbs, twisting its CPU housing on its slick rotators.

It clung to the bar, but the corridor bowed inward, striking it in its side, splitting open its taut outer skin, making it ooze.

It hardly had time to register the damage before the platform shook again.

The second impact was only moments behind the first—this time accompanied by a flash of fire outside the window—an orange glow laced with green. The deep reverberation of the strike was met with an off-key squeal as grinding steel snapped, wires split, and pipes broke.

The entirety of arm-C yawed to the side, sweeping through space.

Unit Four was sure its activation period had come to an end. The awakening had been brief, terrifying.

At least it was over.

Its microphones registered a terrible sound—a high-pitched wheezing scream.

At first, it matched the sound to that of an atmosphere leaking into vacuum. But it couldn't be that—there was a rhythm to it. Like a robot's pumps fluttering. Failing.

"Units!" their handler yelled in its CPU. "All units, answer me!"

Unit Four's vocal modulations failed it again. It tried to use its speakers, but found they would not respond properly. There was something affecting it in the hall—a gas. Some kind of gas was leaking.

Toxic.

Potentially lethal to its soft parts.

It had to exit arm-C as soon as possible or be incapacitated.

"Units!"

AMS Unit Four uncurled from the wall, ignoring both the wet slide of fluids out of the tear in its lower body, and the pain signals spiking throughout its system.

Where was Unit Two?

It glanced out the window, noting arm-C's new angle relative to the center hub. The arm had bent in the middle, pinching the hull, making parts of it collapse in on itself.

But it was still attached.

A propellant jet spurted from the center hub, repositioning the platform, trying to compensate for the kinetic energy it had absorbed—trying to keep itself in its proper orbit.

The robot could no longer see arm-D. Had it detached?

Unit Four covered its intake valves with a grasping pad, swimming through the microgravity to the narrowed, collapsed portion of the corridor. Unit Two was not on this side.

Unit Two wasn't on the other side either.

One leg, one foot-pad, dangled from beneath a chunk of wall. Internal lubrication liquids pooled beneath the limb.

The sound. The wheezing scream—

It was coming from Unit Two.

"Unit Two!" it said, finding its voice, "Unit Two . . . has been incapacitated."

"No. *No no no no*," their handler said, a biting anguish evident in their voice. "How badly? Can it be patched?"

Unit Four braced itself, using its exceptional strength to

move aside what wreckage it could—the microgravity aiding in the slide. It uncovered Unit Two's torso—soft bits torn open, its chassis mangled. Swaths of engineered biocells leaked out over the decking and into the air, droplets taking flight.

The scream did not cease.

Unit Four reached forward, manipulating the flaps and broken bits of Unit Two's frame, trying to fit them back together. Four's grasping pads quickly grew slick, stained.

A terrible pity settled in its CPU. "Unit Two needs to be reconstituted," it said.

"Fuck!" its handler shouted, voice trembling.

"It's in pain," Unit Four continued. "Its biological portions are feeding it failure signals. How do I stop its pain?"

There was a long pause.

"How do I stop its pain?" it repeated.

"Disconnect its central processing unit from the rest of the chassis," its handler said. "That will engage permanent shutdown."

It leaned farther over the other unit. There was no obvious way to separate the CPU chassis. No latches or buttons or seams.

It would need to cut it away.

There were plenty of sharp edges among the debris, but nothing it could fit easily, like a tool, into its grasping pads. Just large, hulking slabs of steel, twisted piping, and frayed wires.

It took hold of a loose interior panel—one that had been snapped in half, leaving the two portions of metal long and jagged.

Serrated.

It fit the panel in its two grasping pads, setting it firmly like a spanner between its articulated arms. The metal was *cold* and *hard*.

Bracing itself between the pinched portions of the corridor, it loomed over Unit Two, holding the panel-half poised over the junction between its main body and its CPU chassis. Unit Four locked its elbows.

Fluids bubbled from Unit Two's vents—the scream began to die as its speakers flooded. But its cameras could still track.

They found Unit Four's.

"Thank you," Unit Four said. "For being with me when I awoke."

It thrust the panel down.

There was a horrid *squelch*.

"I'm so sorry."

The panel's edge sank firmly through the layers of organics, severing Unit Two's CPU from its body, cutting the connections, the controls.

The robot spluttered once more. Its cameras lost their hold on its sister unit, slipping to the side, half shuttered.

A ragged cry burst from Unit Four's speakers.

The dribbling, severed CPU chassis began to lightly float in the microgravity. Spinning. Casting its cameras away.

"AMS Four?" its handler asked.

"Unit Two has been disconnected."

"I'm sorry you had to do that," they said.

"It hurt. It hurt *me*."

"I know. Your empathy programming is important. Keeps all of you connected, supportive. Working as a whole. The pain—your pain—it'll subside."

Unit Four looked down at Unit Two's rotating CPU

chassis. It fixed its cameras on the spin, unable to move, still leaning heavily on the panel.

"Can you get through?" they continued. "Is the arm still traversable?"

"No."

"Return to the hub. I've already got Unit Three working on an alternate way for you to get to the hangar, but it might take a few minutes to verify it's safe. Looks like it might mean you'll have to go outside. Don't worry, we've got plenty of hard-body shells. I'll have Unit One retrieve Unit Two, and—"

"No," it said quickly, feeling strangely possessive. "I'll do it."

"I need you to focus on the task at hand."

It couldn't stand still. It couldn't simply wait around for a new, secure route to be identified, even if it was only a few minutes. That wouldn't be restful, and its burst of adrenaline would go to waste. "There is a gas leak," Unit Four said. "We need to seal the fire doors as soon as possible. I'm already here. I'll return Unit Two to reconstitution."

"Fine, but the moment we've got a new path, I'll need you back on task."

"Understood."

With a shaky appendage, it scooped up Unit Two's central processing unit and shuffled backward, through the pinch.

It grabbed one of Unit Two's limp legs, pulling.

Severed CPU in one grasping pad, body in the other, it weakly shoved off, floating back toward the hub, the mangled form of its brethren drifting behind.

CHAPTER TWO

The final few meters back to the reconstitution pods were the most difficult. Unit One met it in the hall, but Unit Four could not, for some reason, share the burden. It insisted on carrying all of Unit Two itself. Even as the simulated gravity increased and the body fell to the floor—leaving brightly colored slicks of fluid as it was dragged—Unit Four would not hand over so much as the severed CPU chassis.

Unit One primed an empty pod. Not the one Unit Four had come stumbling out of—that one was still resetting. Cleaning. Certain maintenance bacteria would run amok in the system if each pod wasn't flushed after activation. No, Unit One busied about the dormant pod Unit Four had noted before, on the other side of the room.

The top slid aside, ready to accept material for reconstitution.

Only when the pod was fully prepped and there was nothing more to do did Unit Four let Unit One set its grasping pads on the body. Let it help lift the mangled robot parts up and over the lip, into the deep tub perfectly shaped and sized to fit one unit and no more.

Unit Four's casing was now covered in Unit Two's lubrication fluids—in flecks of somatic cells, chemicals, shreds of flexible wiring, chipped bits of its framework. Everything that should have still been snuggly inside Unit Two was now smeared across Unit Four's bodywork.

"You should clean your exterior before snapping into a hard-shell," Unit One said, carefully inputting instructions into the pod.

"There's no time," it said, cameras fixed on the pod's narrow window as the tank flooded. Acidic, milky-yellow liquid ate at Unit Two, breaking it down. The outer casing was stripped away nearly instantly, tinting the acid pink. Fine bubbles formed along the distorted pieces, sizzling, obscuring. The liquid grew darker as it came into contact with new materials, and soon what remained of Unit Two could be seen no more.

An individual unit's time was short, mostly due to the extreme levels of radiation constantly wafting away from Jupiter. The shielding on the platform was excellent, but radiation cascades and sudden bursts caused by the mining were frequent. Lifetime exposure levels were usually reached somewhere between *seven hundred and twenty hours* and *two thousand, one hundred and sixty hours.*

Unit Two had only gotten to experience forty-eight of them.

A solid sucking sound preceded the pod's sudden evacuation. Once everything had been liquified to set parameters, the newly freed materials were returned to the vats from whence they'd come.

Activation periods were short. But the robots' materials could be reconstituted—dissolved and rebuilt—again and again and again. Their larger organic proteins might be damaged enough during activation to stop supporting a unit's functionality, but reconstitution meant the damage wrought to those proteins could be easily repaired on the molecular level.

Once dissolved, the building blocks were returned to the vats deep within the platform. There were five such vats: one in the hangar for reconstituting the boats; one in the command center for the massive bio-computing servers; one in the reconstitution room for the AMS units; one in the upkeep center used for fueling the robots; and the massive backup vault at the platform's hub.

No active units could perform inside the vat-vaults, such was the intensity of their safeguards and the purity of their functionality—no atmosphere, no light, not a single stray molecule or unplanned substance ever made it past the filters. That was the only way to guarantee proper reconstitution and the longevity of the materials.

After the proteins were fixed, once all molecular damage had been accounted for and reversed, a unit—or boat, or grappling arm, or server—was regrown again, using the same basic schematics and more or less the same materials, as the vats stored all the bio-building blocks communally.

Pure hard-bodied robots could not be repaired with such ease. They would need relentless material support from Earth. New parts shipped to them continuously. Each unit's activation period would be longer, but the mining production wouldn't be self-contained.

Soft, flexible, organic-based robots—malleable on every level—meant the systems could be active for much, much longer without any interference. Every aspect was recyclable, and the recycling process was their greatest asset.

Now Unit Two was gone—returned to the vats, to the robots' shared origins. Ready to be remade and reactivated.

Ready to be one more step forward in the constant march of reusability.

Small bits of acid still *drip, drip, dripped* from the pod's sealed lid.

"How old are you?" Unit Four asked One.

"One thousand, seven hundred and sixty-two hours, ten minutes, and sixteen seconds," it replied, moving to check on the growing unit.

"Lifetime radiation exposure?"

"Seventy-eight point three three three percent." It turned to exit. "I must return to my duties. Maintaining the flow of energy—even during the attack—is vital." It turned, stomping back through the doors without another word.

"Unit Three will meet you in the hub with your hard-body," their handler said to Unit Four. "Use the emergency hatch there to exit the platform. Arm-C should still be tra-versable from the outside. Get to—"

"The boat," Unit Four said.

"Yes. The invaders have paused their assault. I'm worried we're going to lose them."

Unit Four followed Unit One into the hall. "Wouldn't that be better? If they broke contact on their own?"

"So they can come back another time and do even more damage? No. We need to swat them out of platform space. Now."

Acknowledged.

All three currently active units came together in the central hub, nearly perfect mirrors of each other. Nearly. Unit One was missing part of a grasping pad. Unit Three had a long break in the top of its torso, one that was sealing over and mostly superficial, but still visually prominent. Unit Four had its own gash in its side, but that seemed to be clotting just fine, its onboard systems repair mechanisms functioning as expected.

Other than that, they were all of the same height, the same bulk. Each of their ports—one for chemical insertion and hardline-uplink, one for fuel, two for waste—were placed just so. The seams of their limbs were all prominent, the casings shifting color along the same clear lines of delineation.

They were the same. They should all feel the same, and function the same. And yet, Unit Four knew the others did not share its unease.

The set of three paused only for a moment to acknowledge one another, to note that this was the first time—and hopefully not the last time—they were all physically in the same place. Then Unit One spun off down arm-A, toward the platform's main control centers.

Floating behind Unit Three was the hard-body. An empty shell, the same shape as the robots, but a bright-turquois color, very different from their soft casings. The bottom front of the CPU covering was shaped like fuel masticators—jagged, pointed in places. It made the housing look rather intimidating.

"You are unclean," Unit Three said, gesturing up and down Unit Four.

"There is no time."

"Sealing you in the hard-body in such a state may lead to the degradation of your exterior."

"There is no time," Unit Four repeated frankly.

"Very well." It brought the shell forward, then input a seven-digit code on the front of the hard-body. The shell opened, bits of it hinging outward all over—like a flower blooming, petals unfurling.

A flower, AMS Unit Four thought. It would never see a flower, except in its databanks.

Unit Three grasped Unit Four by the top of its torso, positioning it into the shell, pressing it backward so that the hard-body hugged it from behind. It nestled in, wriggling into the snug fit.

Another seven digits told the flower to close. The hinges snapped shut around Unit Four, sealing it inside.

"Chemical port aligned?" Unit Three asked, its voice now sounding distant.

Unit Four pressed at its upper left arm, checking the corresponding readouts in the shell's display. "Yes."

"Ventilation working?"

Unit Four filled, then evacuated, its atmospherics.

"Good. Movement?"

It flexed each articulated portion of its grasping pads, bent all of its joints. The exterior had significant mass, and put extra resistance on all of its muscles, even in the micro-gravity. But it was workable.

"Cameras? Speakers?"

"Working. Clear. Clear?"

"Clear."

"Fins?"

Unit Four clutched its grasping pads closed and tapped at the flats of them with a halting rhythm.

Sharp, curved fins slid from its forelimbs. A similar movement with its feet sent a sister pair springing from its lower extremities, and a more complicated pattern com-manded a larger pair—toothed, with wide solar membranes stretched between thin spurs—to unfurl at its back.

"Have you integrated the operational instructions?" Unit Three asked.

"Doing so now."

"Good. You'll note these"—Unit Three indicated the rear fins—"are typically for HALO work. Put to better use around planets with more . . . *welcoming* atmospheres. But your forward pair can be used as blades in an emergency. They should easily sever soft tissues, fabrics. If you need to perform an amputation, for instance. On yourself or the boat."

Amputation. Dismemberment. Mutilation. Excision.

Unit Four attempted to ignore the gruesome synonyms fluttering through its processors, but the words arose unbidden.

A shiver reverberated across its chassis as it retracted the fins once more.

"Earth connection stable? No interference?" Three continued.

"Can you hear me, Unit Four?" asked their handler.

It struck Unit Four how constant, yet quiet, their handler was. Trusting them to perform, only offering guidance or input when essential. Omnipresent, yet not omnipotent.

"Yes. I can hear you."

"Good," Unit Three and their handler said simultaneously.

Each stationary wall of the hub sported an emergency hatch. With a light touch, Unit Three guided Unit Four, encased, to one of them. "You will do well," Unit Three tried to assure it. "There are plenty of holds and tether points. Test your shell's jets as soon as you are outside. If you become detached from the platform, they will help you return."

"Arm-C has been sealed from both ends until the invaders have been dealt with and the group of you can focus on repairs," their handler said. "The hull wasn't breached, despite the buckling. Climbing along it shouldn't be any trouble."

Unit Three spun the latch on the inner door, pulling the hulking hatch inward. A long, narrow airlock with a ladder was all that separated the well-balanced inside from the harsh nothingness of outside.

"Use caution," Three said, leaning in close to Unit Four's cameras. "We don't want to lose your materials."

The other robot said "lose your materials" in the same way Unit Four had said "I'm so sorry" to Unit Two.

This, the necessary spacewalk, concerned Unit Three. It was afraid for it.

Unit Four leaned its CPU housing against Unit Three's, unsure of what other gesture of reassurance it could make. "I will use caution."

Moving away from its sister unit, Four glanced back for only a moment before climbing steadily into the airlock. The door *thunked* behind it. A resounding, *final* sort of sound. A green-lit bar on the hatch showed the atmospheric pressure inside the lock slowly dwindling, seeping out, leaving the room, eventually, in total vacuum.

With trepidation, Unit Four climbed up between the bulkheads.

It wasn't the ladder or the tunnel it was afraid of. On the contrary, the shaft itself was a comfort. This end of the hub held the organics; all around the robot, liquid proteins floated between the thick walls of the vat. Similarly, those walls now protected Unit Four—cradling it in their center. But only for its brief journey up the ladder.

Once it left the shaft, however, there would be nothing to protect it from the harshness of space.

It reached the top just as the airlock lighting on the exterior door signaled the all clear. Forcing itself not to hesitate, it broke the outer seal, flinging the hatch outward.

A vast emptiness met it on the other side.

A vast *aloneness*.

The hub curved away from it on all sides at a six-degree angle, the surface slightly convex. The arms reached out like a starburst and continued their constant plod, swooping "above" and "below" Unit Four's position.

In the center of the hub lay the communications tower—their connection to the ansible relays that allowed the AMS units to connect in near real-time with Earth.

On the opposite side of the hub lay another tower—a large, coiling ion-plasma capture station, which passively absorbed the radiation from Io's taurus and converted it into electrical power for the platform. Power that supported the platform's uplinks. Power that transformed the proteins in the vats into robots. Power that had given Unit Four its functionality.

Moving deftly within the shell, Unit Four found the beginning of the hub's access tracks—a series of small, curved anchor points, branching out in two directions from the hatch. Perfect for lodging a grasping pad into. It exited the hub easily, pushing the door closed behind it, sealing itself out.

It simply needed to crawl to the end of one track and wait for arm-C to align. A small leap from the stationary hub to the rotating arm should prove easy.

But best be sure all systems were working on the hardbody first.

As promised, it immediately tested its jets. Using interfaced commands, it chose a point-three-second burst.

The jet engaged. A puff of whitish gas erupted from a rear port.

Unit Four was not prepared to counter the force.

It had miscalculated—the light spurt sent it barreling forward, stealing the atmosphere from its air pumps.

It lost its hold on the track. The front of its shell scraped across the hub's plating, and its grasping pads scrambled for purchase as the robot careened toward the edge, where the platform's arms were yawing round like the blades of a giant fan.

Flailing, it searched for any protuberance. But the jet had sent it bowling away from the path.

The lip of the hub came closer.

Beyond—just darkness.

Unit Four's vents fluttered. It rolled, twisted itself. Hit its jets again.

The new angle thrust it away from the edge just in time. Saving it from a tumble into nothing.

Unit Four caught the track right before its body threatened to sail past it once more, stopping itself with a mighty jerk.

Its pumps roared. Its fluids surged. *Action* chemicals and *danger* signals ricocheted through its extremities. With a stutter of air rattling through its torso, it gave itself a moment to recompose itself.

It didn't need any more diversions, distractions, or sudden failures.

"You all right?" its handler asked. "What just happened?"

Unit Four wasn't sure exactly what kind of information

Earth received about its minute-to-minute functionality, but likely its biometrics had just spiked.

"I'm fine," it insisted. "I am on my way."

It set a grasping pad into the next divot, then the next, pulling itself along, determined not to let its own constant miscalculations get the best of it.

CHAPTER THREE

The shell echoed strangely here, in the dead of space, where there were no outside sounds to compete with those of Unit Four's own mechanics.

If it chose, it could change the registering frequencies and the sensitivity of its hard-body's sensors. It could let the shell pick up Jupiter's aurorae—let the *ping* of charged particles bouncing off the magnetosphere rattle through its CPU.

That might make it feel more grounded. More anchored.

Less . . . adrift.

Hoping the reconfiguration wouldn't seem too strange to its handler, it set new parameters for the shell's instruments, and shifted the detected radio signals into the audio frequency range.

The planet *sang*.

A haunting, clicking reverberation—akin to something one might expect from a creature dependent on echolocation—filled the confines of its hard-body. The sounds were soaring, ghostly. Of nature and yet seemingly preternatural.

Unit Four felt much better for the song's company.

And yet, it was another reminder of its lifetime limits. Of the radiation constantly surrounding it, eating its time away.

"I want to go over the primer you have on the invaders," its handler said, interrupting Unit Four as it adamantly tried to focus on *grab, pull, grab, pull.* "Call it up for me."

Unit Four searched its databanks, found the files quickly, and spread them open.

"Twelve files?" it asked. "That's all?"

Its one job was to fight the invaders. It had more information on how to sauté spring onions than it did on the aliens.

"We don't have a lot of primary source materials, I'm sorry. Our interactions with the invaders have been quick and violent. They come into the solar system every few cycles. They buzz our planets, once in a while break something, then buzz out again. Occasionally there are battles—dogfights. But those have all ended in . . . Doesn't matter. Point is, I wish there was more for you. It's important that you integrate everything we *do* have, so that you have the best shot at engaging them effectively. I need to make sure your software is executing correctly, all right?"

"All right."

"Should we talk skirmishes, or ship design first?"

"Ship design." It pulled up the image files. There was a set of precisely drawn and professionally organized schematics, but they were light on tactically useful information. Another file contained a single blurry picture of a boxy craft. Hard lines, not the roundness of the boats. Sharp points and right angles. Long, but not branching. The image was so degraded, Unit Four couldn't even identify its primary materials or decide which parts might perform which functions. Another set of pictures displayed various explosions, though Unit Four couldn't tell what, exactly, was exploding. In one, something that might have been the platform hung off to the right.

"Most ships we've seen have had thick armor plating," its handler said. "Heavy stuff. We can bore in, but one shot won't bore deep enough. As far as we're aware, they don't have frequency-shielding like our boats."

"Weapons?"

"Energy weapons—phased anti-plasma, same as yours. Though theirs seem to have a higher rate of fire than those on your boat. We don't have any records of physical projectiles, bombs, or destabilizing tactics—no transient electromagnetic disturbances or anything."

Unit Four called up the accompanying vid files. There were only two of them. The first was all of three seconds long. In it, a craft, different from the ones in the blurry pictures—larger, but with those same hard-cut corners—darted across the camera's field of vision. A glowing-green shot of anti-plasma fire followed.

The next clip was even shorter. The image was completely blacked out, but there was one point eight seconds of a sound. A high-pitched screeching that grated in Unit Four's microphones. The sound was consistent, never changing in volume or note. Hard to tell if it was artificial or biological.

"The ship you'll face is likely larger than the boat—way more massive," its handler explained. "That means you'll be more maneuverable, but also that they'll be able to outrun you in a straight line."

"And what of the aliens themselves? There are no records here of their makeup—their vulnerabilities, their environmental requirements—nothing."

"No one's ever gotten a good look. And we don't have any samples."

"Even with the skirmishes, no one has recovered—?"

"There's nothing to recover, Unit Four. The skirmishes end with . . ."

"End with what?"

Its handler sighed. "At best, the invaders' ships are obliterated. Sometimes by us, more often by them. Most of the time they simply get away, leaving a wake of destruction behind. You *can't* let them get away this time. We're counting on you. If the mine goes down, if we lose power—"

"I understand," Unit Four acknowledged.

"You should have a file with sets of telemetry readings," its handler continued. "That'll help you get a feel for how their ships move. But I have to warn you, there's no real pattern from fight to fight."

Unit Four pulled up the real-time recordings, let them run through its CPU at highly expedited play speeds. The battling ships were little more than labeled dots on a three-dimensional field. It noted the invader's maximum velocities, accelerations, their maneuverability, their tendency to attack and then immediately retreat.

"Will you port me the trajectory our invaders—this ship—came from?" it asked.

"I can give you all the data we have from first detection," they said. "But the buoys didn't see them until they were well within Jovian space. We weren't even sure the ship wasn't just passing space junk until it started carving up our equipment."

A moment of blankness followed, then a searing, internal light whited out Unit Four's cameras for point zero six seconds as the information was uploaded via the long-distance ansible link.

The craft's incoming trajectory told it little.

"There is truly no further information?" Unit Four asked.

"I have a few more audio files, but they're just . . . there's nothing in them but the dying cries of Berserker bots and AMS units. I can give them to you if you want, but I don't see how they'd help."

No, that definitely wouldn't help, but Unit Four was still sure there had to be more. Something its handler simply hadn't thought to give it, maybe. "The invaders have never tried to make contact?" Unit Four pressed. "There are *no* other records?"

There was an unnatural pause.

"We have . . . accounts. There's a reason we call them invaders," its handler said. "Again—this info isn't relevant to your mission. Your job is to stop them, and you don't need a whole sordid, third-hand history lesson to do that.

"There are things you're better off not knowing. Trust me on this. You already feel too much—that's my fault. Your engineered endocrine system is in overdrive, and if you . . ."

"If I what?"

"There are cruelties you don't need to deal with. You're a maintenance robot. This is already more worry, danger, and hardship than I ever would have wished for you."

"I *am* a maintenance robot," it agreed. "Which means I was *designed* for hardship."

"Not this kind."

It couldn't tell if they meant its body or its software wasn't designed for this kind of hardship. And did they mean the hardship of defending its world from the invaders, or the hardship of the history they refused to burden their charge with?

So many variables, and not enough hard data.

Unit Four looked around itself. Into the depths of black, black, black beyond the solar system. It found the brightest star in its field of vision—the sun—a cold spotlight at this distance. It let its camera's track the length of arm-C, measure the distance it still had yet to climb to get to the hangar. The distance to the buckling in the middle.

Yes, I was designed for hardship.

"Would you like some music?" its handler asked suddenly.

"Music?"

"Sounds help focus biology . . . as I gather you've already discovered, given the chirping-wailing thing coming through. Is that the aurora? Anyway—it's rudimentary physiological programming. Sounds at certain beats per minute can sync things like bio-pumps, gas exchange, chemical production, systems circulation. Would you like to switch to music?"

"If you think it would help."

The soft flutter of a string instrument playing in A minor flooded its microphones—the music coming from the hard-body, rather than inside its CPU. The tinkling of piano keys soon joined the sound—a gentle pitter-patter. Like falling water from the sprinklers, from the washer heads in the bot-scrubber—where it might have cleaned its exterior of Unit Two's remains, had there been time.

At first Unit Four thought its handler was trying to sooth it. Calm it. But soon the pitch of the music rose. Soprano vocals joined the instruments. The song progressed at one hundred and thirty-nine beats per minute.

The sound felt *solid*. Driving.

Motivating.

It ignored the lyrics. The lyrics were . . . sad. About loss.

"Is this all right?" its handler asked.

"Yes," it said. *And no*, it thought.

It liked the music, but it made it think of Unit Two.

Unit Two, which should have been climbing right beside it.

Unit Two, whose activation period was too short.

It looked forward again, toward the buckle in the arm. Where it had known loss for the first time.

Then it threw its grasping pad forward, hauling itself onward with new vigor. It *would* rid the mine of the invaders. For Unit Two.

The song played on a loop. Each crescendo pushed it farther, sent a surge through its joints. And then the music would fall, a moment of silence would dot the transition, before the soft beginning would play again. Each opening note felt like new hope. New drive.

Reaching the pinched portions of the hull, it carefully assessed the exterior damage.

A piece of one microwave dish was lodged in the outer plating. A curved section of it rose high, several meters above where Unit Four clutched like a scuttling insect to the access track. It had no way of knowing how stable the flotsam was—if touching it or climbing on it would disturb the material and send it spinning dangerously away.

"There they are!" came a sudden shout in its shell. "They've started firing again. How far are you from the hangar?"

"Approximately two fifths of the way across arm-C. At the impact site."

"Good. You're making good progress. You're doing very well, Unit Four."

It appreciated the praise, but it still didn't *feel* like it was doing very well.

The dish cut across the track, preventing Unit Four from continuing along the steady line. It would need to divert sideways, around the tube of the arm. It slid one of its shelled pads into the breach and was rewarded with a shock through the shell. Luckily, nothing shorted out. It tried again, pulling at a different bit of flayed material.

"Are the chemical terminals active in the hangar?" it asked as it struggled along.

"Yes," its handler said. "You'll need to give the boat's cradle a few injections before taking off. The ship's biomechanics have been dormant for the past three days."

"Will there be sufficient supply if I inject myself as well?"

"Absolutely. I expect you to shoot up—several times, if need be. What do you think you need?"

"Mixture thirty-seven should suffice."

"Five-hydroxytryptamine heavy," its handler said contemplatively. "You know, your current levels aren't all that far from normal. I know you *feel*. A lot. But you're actually within acceptable standard deviations right now, I promise."

"Don't you ever feel . . . unbalanced?" it asked.

"Of course."

"In those moments, wouldn't you do anything to feel balanced again?"

Its handler laughed. "Remind me to tell you about recreational drugs when you get back."

Back from battle.

If it felt unbalanced now, during a more or less steady

climb, how would it fair under the gun? When a single instant separated it from victory and oblivion?

"How often are space-based conflicts with the invaders successful? What percentage of our craft are victorious?"

Silence.

"How many of us survive?"

Nothing in them but dying cries.

"Just focus on your climb."

CHAPTER FOUR

It made it around the disk without incident, and without further shocks. The remainder of the climb went quickly, smoothly.

Unit Four pushed the conversation with its handler from its executables queue. It even considered erasing the memory altogether, because their silence, their hesitancy, only worried it further.

They were just trying to protect it, of course. Protect it *emotionally*. Upon activation it had decommissioned its first friend, then worried it was malfunctioning. It didn't need the cold, hard truth about its odds for survival as well.

What difference did it make?

The hangar's hatch was easier to access than the hub's. A few keystrokes had the airlock releasing on its own, inviting Unit Four inside without protest.

The robot had accepted its role as pilot and protector, and yet, as soon as it was locked inside, it didn't want to go back out.

Maybe in the minutes it took Unit Four to prepare the boat, the invaders would disappear. Leave the platform and its robots in peace.

It turned down the volume on the music. Turned it into a low, barely audible thrum. The airlock was like a cocoon. Small, safe. A pocket of pause.

Once it opened the inner door, it would be nothing but push, push, push again.

Run, run, run.

And what was it running toward?

If it had any real sense of self-preservation, it should be running *away*.

It shook itself.

It was trying to protect the platform. The mine.

Earth.

Trying to protect Units One and Three.

The way it couldn't protect Two.

Silly, stupid robot.

It turned the volume back up. "I need . . . new music," it said.

"Oh?"

"Loud. Fast. Hard."

"You sure?"

"My biology needs new programming. I need—I can't pause."

It stepped into the hangar control room as drums—deep, reverberating, frantic—assaulted its microphones. It increased the volume further still, until all of its systems told it the noise was too much, too loud. Until it was swimming in a roar.

A roar so full, it interrupted its new-data retrieval. Its integration and processing.

Interrupted its doubts. Its worry.

It was perfect. Now all it had to do was follow its pre-programmed muscle memory.

Each heavy drumbeat became a footfall.

Swiftly, Unit Four went to the left of the control room, to the chemical shunts. It ignored the broad wall of glass that looked out into the hangar proper, where five boats sat anchored to the decking by two sets of clamps each. Instead, it focused on the dispensary, on commanding the chemical banks to deliver the proper dosages of the requested molecular compounds. The dispensary itself was set inside the wall, shielded in layers of lead. The interface was a copper-colored set of tubing, each line capped with a nitrogen-compressed release valve that could only be opened by attaching the proper vial heads.

The vials were freely accessible on a nearby rack. Moving deftly, with confidence, it selected the necessary containers and screwed them into the dispensary. It performed the task as though it had performed it hundreds of times. Its grasping pads knew what to do—Unit Four just had to let them act. With the music pounding, it moved to the rhythm, unconscious of each action.

Retrieving the full vials, it secured three chemical barrels with port-interfacing shunts for the boat, and six for itself. It considered using a dose of the compound right then, but decided that wasn't the most efficient use of its time.

It could shoot up once it was in the ship.

Before leaving the control room, Unit Four went to the computer terminal to port over instructions for launch. It identified which boat had been revived from anhydrobiosis, and set time releases for both the main hangar doors and the decking clamps.

Only then did it glance out at the boats beyond.

Each was a sphere, their hulls composed of thick, convex, interlocking triangles. The hard-body was mostly turquoise—like its own hard-body—and the seams between triangles were a pearlescent purple in contrast.

And, just like Unit Four's own shell, a soft-body lay within.

The hangar itself was cavernous, its corners dark. Bulkheads in the ceiling, walls, and floor all contained mods for the hard-bodies and the systems for installing them. Each interlocking triangle could be swapped with another, shifting a boat's purpose. It could be a scouting vessel, a repair craft . . . a warship.

Sometimes it needed to be all of the above and more.

The appropriate mods had not yet been added to the active boat's hard-body. Executing a few lines of code, Unit Four directed six long arms to descend from the ceiling. Biological, but with mechanical roots, they shot along their tracks to each mod's storage space, returning with guns, a grasping metal claw, and a series of repair kits for if—*when*—Unit Four defeated the invaders and could turn its attention to the microwave array. The hangar arms, each with the same dexterity in their grasping ends as the AMS units, slid current sections of the hard-body away—revealing, for only a moment, the biology—gently throbbing—beneath.

The anti-plasma—AP—cannon locked into place. Then the claw. And the repair tackles.

The superfluous triangles were stowed before the arms snaked away, back into their compartments.

With the drums still beating, Unit Four stepped out of the control room and onto the decking.

And the platform *rumbled*. Jagged vibrations ran up the robot's legs, but all of its gyroscopes were working, keeping it upright.

"What was that?" it demanded.

"More debris," said its handler inside its CPU, their voice unhindered by the blaring music. "It struck the hub. They're not letting up."

If the hub went down . . .

Unit Four broke into a sprint. Its shell *clang-clang*-clanged on the corrugated decking—its steps heavy, determined.

The hull of the activated boat swooped high above Unit Four, the bowing curve of it imposing, yet familiar. Each clamp holding it in place was larger than the robot itself, and the entire orb gave the impression of some giant monster's egg—fitting, given the organics inside.

"Hello," Unit Four greeted it fondly, though the boat itself was not sentient. "We'll make it."

It wirelessly interfaced with the boat's onboard controls, and one set of triangles—hinged together, different from the rest—unfolded to allow the robot inside.

Unit Four was met by a quivering gray, tan, and brown biomass. The boat was a genetically engineered soft-ship—a unified, ultra-responsive sphere of nerve and muscle grown atop a branching chassis. The hull door led to a fleshy iris: an egress in the boat, for easy atmospheric intake, and for AMS units to use as an entrance and exit. A portal for one robot, into another.

Before it climbed inside, Unit Four considered stripping itself of its shell. Boats were meant to be piloted soft-parts to soft-parts. Everything aboard was controlled by touch and nerve impulse, and a bio-casing to bio-casing connection could increase the craft's response time.

Perhaps under different circumstances, Unit Four wouldn't have given a second thought to shedding its outer layer. But it had already been outside. Had already seen the damage wrought by the invader's guns.

If it kept its shell, perhaps it would have half a chance in the event of a hull breach.

Carefully—making sure not to pinch the boat's casing in the joints of its hard-body—Unit Four slipped through the flaps of the fleshy aperture and into the center of the craft.

Bioluminescent veins lit the inside, created a blue-green glow that cast the boat's flesh in an ironically inorganic hue. Small spiracles lined the veins, allowing the boat to perform minute gas exchanges. The boat's center was a single chamber with a single seat growing out of its center, the controls all around it were long arms, designed to perfectly fit into an AMS unit's grasping pads. The slightest press and pull would tell the craft where to go, what to do, and how to respond.

All around Unit Four, the boat pulsed, heaved, with the pumping of fluids and the fluttering of gasses. The AMS unit touched the inside as reverently as it had the outside, making what connection it could.

Swiftly, it tucked itself into the pilot's seat, found the ports for the chemical shunts, and dumped the first dose of the appropriate hormonal concoctions into the ship.

The boat quivered—the boat *sighed*—as the chemicals worked their way through its nervous system.

The boat's CPU was very different from Unit Four's; the ship had no higher functions, no ability to reason, judge, or learn. But it could feel. Its whole functionality was based on touch, on sensation.

Lining up a barrel with the connection on its shell, Unit Four injected one vial's contents into itself.

A literal shot of confidence.

It would take a few minutes for its pumps to send this particular mixture of chemicals to the correct receptors, but that was fine. As long as it knew the confidence—the *stability*, the *focus*—was coming, it could continue on.

Securing the future doses under a soft flap of the boat's casing, Unit Four swiped one digit on its grasping pad over a nerve nodule. Chromatophores on the concave inside wall of the boat swirled. The cells contained pigment that, through contraction and dilation, could be commanded to visually mimic what the boat's exterior sensors detected.

A window that wasn't.

Another swipe over a different nodule brought two constricting arms around the top part of Unit Four's chassis, holding it down, hugging it into its seat, to keep it secure when the boat finally left the simulated gravity of the platform.

The robot checked its chronometer. The clamps securing the boat's hull to the hangar decking should be releasing in three . . . two . . . one . . .

It engaged thrusters, lifting the orb off the floor.

Via the chromatophores, it noted the lighting in the hangar had changed, signaling impending decompression. Pumps syphoned the atmosphere away, equalizing the interior and exterior.

The lighting shifted again, and the hangar doors were opening. Crisp blackness greeted it beyond.

Unit Four had already spent far too much of its existence confronting that darkness.

And yet, falling into it, soaring through it, was its very purpose.

"Good luck," bid its handler.

"Good luck," echoed the other units after a moment.

Unit Four increased the volume of the music by another ten decibels. It knew it risked blowing out its microphones if it pushed too far, but it needed the process-numbing. It needed to push everything else aside. It could be all focus and all feeling, or it could be a mess of calculations and simulated thought.

It chose the former.

It was going to war.

It needed the drums, inside and out.

It slotted its grasping pads through the hooked digits on the boat's control arms and leaned forward.

As the boat took off, shooting through the hangar's doors, Unit Four let a strong, single note rip through its speakers. A purely instinctual battle cry, bubbling up from it knew not where.

CHAPTER FIVE

Unit Four's intake valves stuttered as it cleared the platform. The increased g-forces slammed it into the supple casing of its seat as the boat accelerated. There was something about the clearness of space it didn't like—the utter *sharpness* of the chromatophore picture. It was proof there was no atmosphere. Nothing to distort the reality of emptiness and vacuum. Evidence that most of the universe was nothingness.

And, that if the unit failed in its task, its processing would cease and it would return to that nothingness.

The boat hurtled toward the accosted microwave array. The flashes of AP fire slowly grew from small, sparkling spots into ribbons of light, and then streaks of anti-ionic danger.

Debris glittered all around.

The vastness of Jovian space meant the battleground was immense—the distances between opponents *stretched*. Even now, the invaders lay hundreds of kilometers away, and the gulf between them felt simultaneously unbridgeable and easily conquerable. Both a wide gulf and a thin fissure.

Even Unit Four's CPU felt as though it were compressed and pulled taut at the same time.

The robot tugged on a soft petal of skin protruding from the boat's control mound, and a burst of magnetized, bioluminescent spores filled the air before it. The spores settled into a design—created elliptical loops that coalesced into place only long enough for the unit to take note before they were sucked into the ventilation system for recycling.

The brief display showed it where Galilean moons were in their orbits. It was primarily concerned with Io—currently the closest orbiting body to the platform.

Though the platform could be moved to any of a hundred preprogrammed Jovian orbital locations if needed, it typically orbited Jupiter in counterrotation to Io, along the same elliptical plane. This standard orbit was the easiest location from which to take advantage of the energy swells in Io's plasma torus.

But it also meant—

Yes, Io was swiftly approaching now. It could pose a danger.

As the last of the spores dissipated, Unit Four returned its attention to the chromatophore display.

Jupiter loomed to the right, far, far below the ship. Inside the atmosphere, the automated parts of the helium-3 mine did their work via a combination of aerostats, scoops, and suborbital skyhooks.

Every quarter-rotation of the planet brought the skyhooks in line with one of four nuclear-fusion reactors, which were on a continuous cycle of feeding, fusion, conversion, and purging. The energy created was converted to microwaves for easy transmission to corresponding Earth arrays, and all excess materials were summarily dumped back into Jupiter's atmosphere, purged back into the storms from whence they came.

There were, in all, twenty-seven microwave arrays staged around the planet, each active at different times, depending on where Jupiter and Earth were relative to one another. They beamed the energy straight and true, no matter what passed before them: an asteroid, one of Jupiter's outer moons—the sun. A blip in Earth's reception was preferable to the disruption of powering on and off to avoid a cosmic body.

Unit Four's knowledge of the mine's functionality was crucial, because, right now, the array under attack was still active, still *on*, despite the assault. Units One and Three were making sure of that.

The microwaves were currently invisible to the boat's cameras—Unit Four had decided sticking to the visible spectrum was best for now—but it couldn't afford to miscalculate the bleed-range of the dangerous radiation wafting away from the front of the dishes at every moment. The beams blasted and sanitized whatever went in front of them. Anything biological—engineered or otherwise—that fell in front of an active dish would be instantly cooked alive.

As the boat approached, the invaders took no notice. The invader's ship's design was as the primer indicated: heavily armored, with thick, fanning layers of plating. Yet, overall, it looked sleek—the bulk of it forming a wedge. Unit Four estimated it to be somewhere between ninety-five and one hundred thousand cubic meters in size—huge, compared to the boat's trifling twenty-five hundred.

The wedge tip had inserted itself between the long lines of connecting rods that held the dishes at a stagger, and continued to slice up the array.

The aliens proceeded with far more precision than Unit Four had expected. The ship's bright-green shots were not let loose with the haphazardness of gleeful destruction. Nor were they aimed with efficiency—as though to disable the machinery. Instead, the invaders appeared to be . . . harvesting. Taking great chunks from the array.

Pieces from it were already clamped to the ship's underbelly.

Before, when Unit Four had dared hope the invaders were retreating, perhaps they had simply taken a pause to secure their catch.

What did aliens need with parts of a microwave array?

For a brief moment, Unit Four wondered if it could find out—could chase the invaders back to . . . to wherever they hailed from, and port the information to Earth, to give them something to work with—some real, solid information so that the next AMS unit or Berserker bot wouldn't have to go into battle so utterly uninformed.

But it hadn't been tasked with reconnaissance.

It had been tasked with termination.

It was to kill, not study.

Why did so many of Unit Four's instincts contradict its direct orders?

Shaking itself, nudging the music's volume just a bit higher, it primed the boat's guns.

Unit Four knew that when it engaged, it had to be ready to disengage just as quickly if need be.

Another moment and it would be in range.

Time to see if the meager amounts of data its handler had begrudgingly given were as inadequate as it feared.

The drums pounded.

Its chemicals surged.

An acrid scent—sharp, bitter, unidentifiable—filled its

sensors, and a distinct flavor of copper ran through its wet pipes.

Its chassis shook and its casing shivered.

Sensing Unit Four's tension, the boat's soft-body, in turn, quivered.

Gripping the controls just *so*, Unit Four took its first shot.

A brilliant streak of violet cut across the blackness.

An instant passed.

Silently, the shot struck home.

The assault forced the invader's ship away from the array. But it quickly compensated, changing direction, identifying the source of the blast and hurriedly putting the broad expanse of a dish between itself and the boat.

Though Unit Four couldn't tell what kind of an effect the blow had had—be it negligent, critical, or otherwise—it did note that the invading craft moved as though its steering system conformed to a four-axis propulsion alignment.

In contrast, omnidirectional jets made the boat hypermanuverable. Unit Four couldn't understand why the aliens wouldn't use a similar system. The aliens were more advanced than Earth; they had interstellar capabilities. It seemed strange that they wouldn't take full advantage of space. Further, their ship's design suggested their species had a fixation with aerodynamics.

Unless . . . under all that armor was a craft primarily *meant* to enter an atmosphere? Meant to make planet-fall.

Meant to invade, be it via vacuum, or gas, or maybe even liquid atmosphere.

Did it mean to assault Jupiter directly?

To get at the reactors?

The mine proper?

The alien ship peeked out from its cover.

A flash of green—a dagger of hot anti-plasma—ripped toward the boat.

Unit Four spun the sphere out of the way.

As it went, there came another flash. Another. Another.

The robot had to get *closer*. Distance was the aliens' advantage, not its.

The boat tumbled, over and over, making the chromatophore display blur, swirl—the cells wildly contracting and dilating as the boat rolled through space, dodging debris and AP charges alike.

The robot fired again, as rapidly as it could, barreling forward, toward the other ship, still spinning—everything *spinning, spinning, spinning.*

The distance closed, kilometer after kilometer disappearing between them.

The boat swung out in a great arc above the array, exposing the armored craft, depriving it of its hiding place.

Skulking like a scaled beast, the vessel retreated, but its guns never lost sight of the boat. It fired again, attempting to regain the advantage.

Unit Four ordered the boat to dance. Swirling, sliding, bobbing, and gliding. Each nimble shift was only a moment soon enough—brief instances where fortune and skill came together to yank it out of harm's way. The bright-green blasts skated past—sizzling and sparkling through whisps of charged particles wafting away from Io's plasma torus—as true and deadly as blades flung or bullets shot at Unit Four's soft-body.

Two more of the boat's blasts found their mark before the aliens landed their own blow.

Unit Four paused its functions as the chromatophores flashed sickly green.

It had hoped it wouldn't need to test its shields.

That terrible burst of color could be the last thing its databanks ever recorded.

But the phasing shields did their job, obliterating the incoming anti-ions before they struck the boat's hull, dispersing the danger in flashes of matter-antimatter annihilation, siphoning the energy away in powerful electromagnetic bursts.

Such a strong phasing event temporarily halted the boat's ability to accept commands. Only autonomic functions continued. The craft was a motionless, strobing spotlight for five seconds after the impact.

And the invaders used the pause to flee.

Five seconds was no time at all, and yet enough to put kilometers and kilometers between them.

Space *stretched* again—became a wide, gaping mouth.

Unit Four understood: this was how their fight would be, their dance. Long minutes—hours, even—of chase, interspersed with the quick, manic twirling and gnashing of attack.

Like interplanetary bodies set on a collision course, they would take forever to come together, only to violently collide and spiral away again.

"Unit Four?" its handler asked, checking in.

"Still here."

"Good, registered the hit. They can't land too many more before the shields get overloaded and fry, just remember that."

How could it forget?

"How are you doing?" its handler continued. "Feel more in balance?"

It did. It felt more focused, more prepared.

It was made for this, to do this.

And it could.

It would.

And yet, it could still feel something *insidious* in its programming. A distinct, underlying urge to *run*. To turn the boat away from the fight. To hide. To self-preserve.

But it couldn't tell its handler that.

"Yes," it said, as steadily as it was able. "Well balanced."

"I won't distract you, then."

Unit Four shook itself, fixating on the drumbeats in its CPU and the shape of the invader's craft in its cameras.

Tensing, it gave chase.

They exchanged fire, again and again, each landing blows, each shrugging off the impact and continuing on.

The two ships zigged and zagged away from the platform—pitching toward Io, painting an arc over Jupiter's sky.

Did the aliens know about Io's plasma torus? Did they know about the tidally locked moon's volcanic spewing? About the way Jupiter and Europa and Ganymede tugged at it, pulling it, tearing at its crust and core, making it a small, violent place?

Maybe they didn't. Maybe they had no idea, and Unit Four could use that to its advantage. What did it care if the invaders broiled themselves in the moon's radiation torus, or in its molten mix of iron and sulfur eruptions?

They needed to die. It didn't matter if that happened by its guns or their own folly.

The invaders ran from Unit Four but made no indication they intended to break away from Jovian space. Clearly, they didn't want to disengage.

As Unit Four continued to roll and tumble, repeatedly changing its relative angle to the other craft, it tried to take stock of possible weak points. Bits of stolen machinery dangled from the wedge's belly—they could be hiding a vulnerability. Unit Four looked forward to recovering those parts, to bringing them home as a trophy. Even if the alien armor wasn't thinner beneath the scavenged bits, perhaps the aliens would be overprotective of their prize. Perhaps Unit Four could use that in some way.

Long hours passed as they continued their dance. The chemicals slowly worked themselves out of Unit Four's system, its body absorbing the molecules into a water bath and extruding it as waste—which filtered into the shell.

Every time it felt anxiety creeping up its chassis again, it retrieved the next barrel and plunked it into its socket. The boat sympathetically trembled in response, and the robot fed the ship additional doses as well.

The chase went on. And on.

Then, suddenly, the distance between the two craft began to shrink. The invaders turned, dodged, but weren't accelerating.

Unit Four was gaining on them.

Perhaps they'd wasted too much fuel.

Perhaps the boat had landed a critical hit.

Unit Four started to see details in the ship it hadn't before—veins and bulges of antennae.

The distance closed. Shrank to only a few kilometers.

Its handler had said that Unit Four's victory would likely mean the invader's obliteration.

It didn't want that.

It was going to disable their craft, kill everything on board, and then *take it all*. No more wondering. No more scant primers and paltry readings. No more robots sent into the compactor ill-prepared.

It could bring back samples and technology to help not only the robots on its platform, but maybe all the robots on all the different platforms throughout the solar system. It could help the Berserkers.

It could avenge Unit Two.

It could—

The aliens pulled up short, putting their ship in hard reverse.

The distance between them disappeared in an instant.

Unit Four's vents faltered. It pressed hard on the controls, willing the sphere to skim over the top of the wedge instead of colliding full-on with its back end.

It avoided a head-on collision but did not escape unscathed.

An awful *skrrrrrreeeeeetch* of a whine reverberated through the boat, and the sphere's outer layers vibrated violently. Inside, the biomass shuddered, rippled. Unit Four clutched the controls and the controls clutched *back*.

Its cameras flickered across the chromatophores, surveying the flexible inner skin, looking for a breach. For leaking fluids and leaking air and darkening, broken organic bits and any other signs of failure. It searched . . .

The hull hadn't been breached.

The boat was fine. They were both fine.

At least, their biological parts were fine.

Bioluminescent nodules flashed to Unit Four's left. One of the boat's cannons was gone. As were two of its propulsion jets. And one of its shield generators. All of that vital equipment, now nothing more than metallic confetti glittering through space.

Which left the boat with a vulnerable spot.

A tender spot.

A *weak* spot.

The aliens could try to exploit it. Could try to get Unit Four to focus on its own safety. To forget about harming them in favor of helping itself.

They could try.

But Unit Four wouldn't let them.

After making a rapid-fire assessment of the damage, it spun the boat around. The aliens were already moving off in a new direction, flying with the wedge-tip pointed menacingly at the boat while they once more put kilometers of space between them.

The robot had no choice but to pursue in a similar fashion, while carefully keeping the damaged plating out of the wedge's line of sight. It rolled the vulnerable section away just as another barrage of AP fire turned the chromatophores green, then blazing white.

The inside of the boat shuddered, its casing tensing, prickling.

A warning glow told the robot the shield's receptors were straining.

The invaders angled themselves toward the microwave array again, heading once more in the direction of the platform.

Shaking off the shock of the scathing collision and the recent attack, Unit Four rushed to put itself between the platform and the aliens. It had to get ahead of them if it could. It had to protect the mine.

More dancing, more chasing, more cat and mousing across the field of stars.

As the invader craft approached the array, it abruptly changed direction, as though the pilot had forgotten for a brief, dangerous moment about the microwave beam. One back corner of the wedge shifted into the bleed, and while the outside of their craft appeared unaffected, Unit Four wondered what kind of internal damage the mistake had wrought.

As the wedge reduced its forward velocity, the boat zipped by it, settling into the gulf between the array and the platform.

The invader crewing their guns didn't seem quite as distracted as the alien piloting their ship. They landed another shot in the dead center of the sphere.

The white glow came post-strike, chased by the blue, gold, and green of a sharp, quick chemical fire.

The shield shorted out.

Unit Four twisted the controls, and the boat yawed to the side. Another AP blast scorched across its hull in a glancing blow. More chemically fueled flames burst to life—destroying a gun relay—before flashing out of existence.

Unit Four tried to shoot back.

Nothing happened.

The robot muttered denials over and over, pressing growths, pulling on flaps, twisting the joints of the controls harshly until they let out a sickly *pop*.

Its weapons were completely off-line.

As were its shields.

It had no way to protect itself, and no way to fight back.

Harried, it looked up at the chromatophore display just in time to see the wedge rise up over the array, its sharp nose pointed directly at the boat. The guns swiveled, and a bright-green flash erupted from the barrels.

With an edge of panic muddling its programming, the robot yanked on the control arms and willed the boat to spin out of the way. The platform suddenly splayed wide in its chromatophore display, like a bone-white sea star.

Unit Four shuddered as it watched the blast meant for it go hurtling toward the platform.

The station could handle a bit of AP fire. That was fine. It would be fine.

Except—

Except the shot was barreling directly for the communications tower. The tower that picked up the ansible relays from the communications buoys set throughout the solar system.

"Earth!" the robot shouted, though it knew it was too late. It kept talking, kept transmitting, even though it *knew*. "I'm still—"

The anti-plasma struck.

The drums cut out.

The tower glowed red-hot at the sight of impact. Metal buckled. The anti-plasma had blasted through all but one of the struts, torn the bulk of the antennae from the platform's hide.

"—here," it finished softly. "Earth?" it tried, on the off chance the connection still held. Inside its shell, where music had once raged, now there was dead silence. "Earth, are you there? Unit One? Unit Three? AMS units? Hello?"

Its connection was gone. With Earth, with the platform—with every other sentient being it had ever known.

The robot was good and truly alone.

It had no way to communicate. No way to fire upon its enemy.

All it could do was limp back to the docking bay, a failure.

It had been activated for one purpose, and it couldn't even accomplish that.

Useless.

Utterly useless.

Despair filled its limbs, made its pumps flutter painfully. How could it have failed so completely?

Now the invaders would carve up their mine, steal their power, kill its fellow units.

Destroy its home and one of Earth's primary sources of energy all in one stride.

Unit Four might have served its fellow units better by sitting in front of that last shot, by shielding the tower. If only it had possessed the foresight to sacrifice itself in the moment.

After all, it had already been prepared to sacrifice itself during this endeavor, had been *expected* to sacrifice itself—to see its mission through no matter what.

Unit Four paused for a moment, turning the boat so that it could set its sights on the invaders once more.

The robot had been expected to sacrifice itself . . . and it could still do that.

The boat's weapons *in name* were off-line, but it had one very big weapon left at its disposal.

The boat itself.

It had no idea what the outcome would be if it hurtled its craft at the invaders. The boat might simply collapse—fold in on itself—brutalized by the alien armor.

But with any luck, the collision would disable the other craft. Maim it. Or worse.

Unit Four hardly dared hope for an explosion—for a hot spark that would set the invaders aflame.

Regardless of the damage it might cause, it just hoped both itself and the boat would shut down quickly. That they would be disconnected without much pain.

With a deep intake of atmosphere, it rubbed lightly, soothingly, at the controls. "I'm sorry we won't be going back," it said to the boat. "I'm sorry we won't be reconstituted. But this is necessary. We have to."

Did they have to? Really? A small bit of doubt crept through its CPU.

It could try to live. To get a full activation period.

Ninety Earth days—that seemed like forever.

It could run back . . . or run away.

No. It had been activated to do one thing, and this was it.

With its fluids roaring—a great thumping heaving across its soft-body and behind its cameras and under its grasping pads—it shoved against the boat's controls.

There was no need for nuance. No need to conserve fuel or watch its speed or appraise the engines.

It just had to make sure it struck true. That its collision course was solid.

The boat surged forward.

Minutes-to-impact shrunk to seconds, and the aliens did not move away.

The invader's wedge swelled in the chromatophore display.

So the robot turned off the screen.

Unit Four sunk into itself, pulled back into its CPU, tried to detach itself from its body.

This was it.

The end.

Nothingness awaited.

A terrible cracking, like the sound of thick ice breaking, met its microphones before the jolt hit its form. The restraints around Unit Four held fast, but the collision was brutal, smashing it against the arms, against the inside of its hard-body.

It expected pure pain.

It expected blackness.

A terrible crushing.

Squeezing.

But none of it came.

The abrupt stop was jarring—made its insides feel bruised. But there was no tearing or torture or fire.

Nor was there a rebound. The two crafts didn't slide away from each other in space. But there *was* a tumble. A sudden yawing.

Metal groaned—a deep reverberation, indicating more mass than the boat possessed. The invader's ship was protesting. Tremors ran through the boat from outside, from something—something *connected* to the ship.

And then Unit Four realized: it hadn't simply smashed into the alien craft.

Instead of breaking against the invader's ship like a wave, or bouncing off like rubber, the boat had stuck fast.

Parts of both ships had to be embroiled together—woven, clinging.

Entangled and ensnared.

The collision sent the conjoined crafts tumbling through space. Over and over and over. Unit Four's fluids rushed up its body, then back down as the ships spun along multiple axes. Its cameras' gaze couldn't latch on to anything, so it shuttered them. And no matter how it gripped and pushed the controls, the omnidirectional jets were unresponsive. All of them.

It was locked to the alien ship, with no hope of ceasing their joint spin. If the invader's wedge was similarly disabled, they would stay forever like this, banking through frictionless nothingness until by luck or design they collided with something or were drawn into a gravity well.

Either way, Unit Four had no hope of returning to the platform.

It was lost.

It would never see its fellow units again.

Its components would never be reincorporated in the vats.

The robot thought it had already made peace with that, but . . .

It had also expected a quick decommissioning.

It wouldn't be able to capture further intel about the aliens either. Even if the invaders stopped the spinning, even if they were able to uncouple the craft, even if they didn't decide to simply finish the job and destroy the boat, with the communication tower gone and the information relay disrupted, Unit Four had no way to send a message to anyone.

What was left for it now?

It had mourned for Unit Two, for the shortness of its activation period.

Would Units One and Three mourn for *it*?

Minutes passed.

The ships could be putting hundreds of kilometers between themselves and the array with each rotation. They could be tumbling away from Jupiter, or into its gravity well.

As long as it was away from the *platform*, that was all that mattered.

How far away would they be hours from now, when the air in the boat could no longer be recirculated? When Unit Four would have long shed its shell, and the spiracles would begin to spasm and close?

It wished now that it had brought along an additional

set of chemicals. It had understood the likelihood of sudden death—of being speared through with an AP blast. But it hadn't anticipated a slow, nauseating deactivation via endless somersaulting. It hadn't considered that it and the boat might both go off-line due to asphyxiation.

If only it had possessed the foresight to bring morphine. Something that might ease the cessation of both it and its craft's biological functions.

Unit Two had been in such *pain* when it was decommissioned.

Would suffocating hurt like that?

It had no memory of its previous deactivations. It didn't know if other versions of Unit Four had suffered when they ceased.

It knew of death, but it did not know death.

Suddenly, a slight jolt altered the direction of spin.

Unit Four's pumps felt like they flipped over in the cage of its chassis, so abrupt was the change of rotation.

Then another jolt followed.

And another.

The invaders.

Unit Four wasn't sure why it had taken them so long to address the problem, but they were finally acting.

Responding.

The tumbling began to feel like a corkscrew, and then like a slide.

The robot reactivated the chromatophores.

Only a small corner of the screen could see space.

Slowly, surely, the stars stopped being blurs, became circular streaks, and eventually righted themselves into pinpricks of light.

Not once did the gas giant make an appearance.

With nothing left to do, AMS Unit Four waited, steeled itself.

Perhaps the robot and its boat would be granted a quick deactivation after all. Perhaps the aliens would find a way to blast them off their hide.

The centrifugal forces slowed. The robot began to float within the confines of its harness.

What would the aliens do now?

Long minutes passed. A quarter of an hour, a half.

Nothing changed.

Occasionally, there was the creak of metal, the straining yawn of stressors on the boat.

But nothing else.

Nothing.

Nothing.

Until—

Something covered the exterior sensors, made the chromatophores go dark. And it could hear them—invaders, crawling on the boat.

They sounded heavy. The bangs and thumps reverberating all around it meant *mass*. These creatures were no delicate waifs.

And then, *slicing*. Not with anti-plasma, like they'd used to harvest from the array, and not with a laser. This was mechanical—the sound of blades.

Something with *teeth*.

They were tearing into the boat.

The biomass around it heaved, shuddered.

There was nothing AMS Unit Four could do to stop the cutting.

Nothing it could do to save—

A saw blade breached the inside. Everything around Unit Four pulsated, *revolted*.

The harness clamped down more firmly on Unit Four's chassis, and the robot tried to pull away.

A spew of dark-brown, black, and red fluids cut the chromatophore display down the center. The controls were awash in ichor as they clutched and unclutched at the air— searching frantically for the robot's grasping pads or stuttering with numerous impulses sent from severed lines.

The boat couldn't scream, so Unit Four screamed for it.

It struggled against the harness as more liquids sprayed through the wound—the incision growing larger and larger by the moment. Frantically, it took one harness arm in both grasping pads and broke it—heard the inner hard frame snap, while the outer skin kept it whole.

The biomass around the cut started to turn a molted gray as Unit Four kicked out from beneath the harness. Something long and metallic—like a monstrous version of the surgical spreaders—slipped into the cut and wrenched both halves aside.

Unit Four expected a sucking. A rushing of atmosphere out into nothing. Physics trying to equalize what could only be equal in the end, at the heat death of the universe.

But the invaders had created some kind of seal. A makeshift airlock, between their craft and its.

Scrambling, AMS Unit Four kicked around its seat, clawed its way to the concave curve of the far wall, opposite the puncture.

Pressing itself into the dying biomass, it tried to regain its composure. To prepare.

Something was coming through the wound. A bright, blinding spotlight.

An invader was entering its ship.

Unit Four held up a grasping pad, doing its best to protect its cameras from white-out.

This was it. If it could somehow make it out of this, get back to the platform, it would know. It would have seen.

"Whatever you are, we come in—by the gods," someone said.

Someone not in its CPU.

Someone it could hear with its shell's outer microphones.

Someone with activated speakers on the outside of their own shell.

Someone it could understand.

The language wasn't the language of the platform—wasn't what it spoke with its handler or its siblings—but it was a language in its database.

Which meant it couldn't be *alien* at all.

"Holy fuck, what the fuck, what the *actual fuck*?" The voice held nothing but pure, unadulterated horror.

"I'm—I'm gonna—" said another voice, strained.

"*Don't* you fucking—"

A wet, slopping sound.

The spotlight went out.

Unit Four froze.

Halfway through the breach, covered in the boat's sputtering fluids—

No.

No, how?

—was another bipedal robot.

Just like it.

PART TWO

INVADER

CHAPTER SIX

One robot—in a thick, flexible outer shell, but still unmistakably of a similar design as Unit Four—stumbled inside, and was followed by another. Then another. The three of them looked at the arms of their own shells as though stunned, taking in the wetness—the dark color—that now stained their bright-green exteriors. Their CPU housings were hidden beneath bulbous casings, the fronts of which obscured their primary sensors behind a coppery, metallic sheen.

The boat's fluid pumps still worked, sending throbbing spurts of the slick, oxygenated compound into the air. The interior of the sphere was soon fogged with free-floating droplets, which landed on their shells. The red shone on the copper, and the green fabric made the fluids run brown.

The air was filled with the boat's liquefied life-force. Choked with it, like a swirling, dirty rain. But still, the curtain it created wasn't enough to obscure Unit Four's presence.

"There's somebody in here!"

"*Somebody?*"

"It's not—I don't know, what the fuck, man? What is this shit?"

"What are you waiting for?"

"This isn't—I'm not going to just *kill*—"

"Then get the fuck out of the way and I'll do it. Bastard tried to blow us out of the sky, I don't care if—"

"Jonas, stop!"

One of the new robots pushed another out of the way, floating to the fore.

Unit Four had no time for higher processing.

Its close-quarters combat programming engaged.

The unit designated *Jonas* raised a small gun. The weapon's design was unfamiliar, matched nothing in Unit Four's databanks.

But, fundamentally, a gun was a gun was a gun.

Jonas aimed.

Unit Four activated a jet on its hard-body, blasting itself away from the wall, hurtling itself to the side just as Jonas shot.

Unit Four slammed into another portion of the dying biomass—the flesh giving way just enough, absorbing the impact just enough, to protect the robot from injury. Unit Four clung to it, digging the points of its grasping pads into the fluttering spiracles, holding on so that it would not rebound toward its attackers.

What on Earth was going on?

How had robots gotten ahold of an alien wedge? When?

Why were they using it to carve up the Jovian mine?

Unit Four's processing stumbled. It wasn't designed for these kinds of inquiries—and it had no way to search for answers while still under assault.

All it had known in this iteration was *run run run, attack attack attack.*

It had hoped all of that had come to an end.

It had hoped it would be allowed to rest. Even if that meant deactivation, at least this constant fervor of pain and conflict would *stop*.

But no.

With a roar, it shoved itself away from the wall, turning all of its hard-body's jets on full-blast, aiming itself at Jonas.

None of the other robots were prepared.

Jonas had no time to raise its gun again.

One hard-body connected with another—Unit Four crashed into Jonas, and in turn, Jonas's back crashed into the curve of the boat.

Unit Four kept its jets on, using them to pin the other robot in place. The AMS unit planted its feet in the middle of Jonas's chest and scrabbled for its gun arm—twisting, *wrenching*.

Jonas screamed as Unit Four yanked its arm from its socket. Its outer shell did not beak or puncture, but the arm went limp and the gun floated out of its grasp.

The new robots shouted over one another:

"Melassani's Crystals," one gasped. "Priestess, Doc—we're going to need you! I don't—I—"

"Ah, fuck!" Jonas yelled. "How did they—?"

"Shit. Shit shit shit *shit*," the third chanted, over and over.

"Fuentes!" the first one shouted at it.

Before the set could regain their composure—before their backup arrived—Unit Four had to end this.

It shot away from Jonas, using the other robot's abdomen like a launching pad, springing for the floating gun.

The firearm slipped effortlessly into its grasping pad, fitting against its digits as though made to pair with Unit Four's exact design.

The robot who'd called for backup had its own gun drawn—but raised it an instant too late.

Unit Four fired—caught it square in the abdomen with the hot glow of a laser charge.

The shot pushed it back into its muttering comrade, but—to Unit Four's dismay—the charge did little more than eat away at the outer layer of its shell's fabric. A round, singed hole in its sternum revealed more armor beneath.

Unit Four had no idea if its own hard-body could withstand such a blast.

Determined not to give the invaders a moment's rest, it shot again, but redirected its aim.

It had been able to separate Jonas's joint—the connections of its upper chassis had been flimsy. So perhaps—

The charge caught its adversary in the shoulder. The robot hissed, cursed.

Shadows moved behind the gaping wound in the boat's wall. Unit Four caught a brief glimpse of two more robots.

"They've got Jonas's gun!" someone shouted.

"Then get them inside, damnit, you idiots!"

"You want to *bring them aboard*?"

Unit Four fired again, its aim slightly off as one of the hard-body's jets petered out—its fuel exhausted.

The AMS unit tumbled to the side, barrel-rolling through the center of the boat as the two extra robots made their presence fully known.

"Rush! We've got to rush 'em!" cried Jonas, still slumped and floating near where Unit Four had thrust it into the wall.

"You're right, you're right. Come on, circle them."

The entire group of five pushed off simultaneously, springing straight for Unit Four.

The boat's interior was tight. It took no time at all for them to glom on.

Unit Four fired haphazardly—kicking, flailing, blasting its jets—and the six robots became a tangle of hard-bodied limbs. Its shots made contact with more shells, but not a single invader-bot was deterred. Not even the one with the limp arm.

The gun was immediately wrestled from Unit Four's grip as the others tackled its joints, its limbs. An arm from behind caught it under the CPU housing, putting pressure on the connecting bits between its body and processing components. The AMS unit reached up to try to free itself, but both its grasping pads were twisted away, yanked to the side. It continued to struggle, but an invader-bot took hold of each leg as well.

Unit Four found itself suspended between the five robots, each doing its best to control a point of its body. They used small jets on their own suits to keep their distances steady, but they weren't powerful enough to prevent Unit Four from curling its extremities, from pulling its attackers in, then thrashing outward in an attempt to throw them off.

The entire bundle of bodies spun in the degrading boat's interior.

Unit Four thought to shout at them—to rage at them. Its fluids were roaring once again, making its microphones fuzzy and thick with a static buzzing. Its engineered musculature was *hot*—boiling with a new burst of adrenaline, this time not from a premeasured dose, but from its own glands. Every bit of its body was *struggling* and *denying*, why not its speakers, too?

But despite the rush of compounds through its system,

its higher processing had not been shoved entirely to the side. Unit Four understood the value of listening.

It was cornered. Trapped.

Anything it said could be turned around and used against it.

Better to keep silent while it tried to figure out how to derail its attackers.

"Motherfucker is hella strong," said the unit on Four's right arm.

"Maybe it's the suit," suggested another.

"I don't think so. There's a fucking warrior under here."

I'm not a Berserker, it shot back internally.

"Come on, Doc, you've got the best angle, take the shot," insisted Jonas—who had Unit Four by the CPU chassis.

"I'm not going to kill anyone."

"Damn your Hippocratic-whatever, they tried to kill *us*."

"And *can't* now."

"Aren't you even a little curious?" asked the one called Priestess, arms curled around Unit Four's right leg. "About—?" It nodded up and down Unit Four.

"Melassani's *fucking* Crystals—they nearly tore my arm clean off!" Jonas shouted. "So, *no*, I don't give a damn."

"We're not going to kill someone pinned down by five people," declared the one Unit Four had shot in the chest. This robot carried an authoritative air—perhaps it was their lead unit. "We'll bring them aboard, just like Doc said. I have a hell of a lot of questions, and we're not getting any answers if they're dead, now are we?"

"Whatever," Jonas grumbled.

"What was that?"

"Whatever, *sir*."

"Oh, screw you."

"Screw you right back."

Unit Four understood nearly every word, but they were all garbled—placed in an order that made no sense. It had no frame of reference for this type of robot behavior.

"We need to quarantine them," Doc explained, and the group slowly started to move toward the wound in the boat, with the clear intent to carry Unit Four through. "Get them into deCon. Decontaminate their suit just like we decontaminate supplies, then check them for active viral and bacterial colonies. Make sure they're not contagious—cross check their antibodies with strains from different Harbors. We might be able to figure out where they're from that way."

"What about this Frankensteinian shit-show?" asked the Fuentes unit. "I want to get some samples myself."

Unit Four didn't like the way it said "samples": cold, unfeeling, as though the boat wasn't also its kin—of its tissues, of its chemicals. The boats and the robots and the bio-mechanical arms and the flesh-based servers were all the same. Were all, in some way, connected.

This robot made the boat sound like a curiosity—distant and disgusting.

Unit Four's disdain for these robots grew, overpowering its sense of confusion, leaving it with a sour flavor in its fuel pipes and a hard knot in its interior.

"We should just destroy it, not prod at it," Jonas spat. "There's not a single Harbor that would build an abomination like this, you know that. Not one. Not even Orca's End."

"*Someone* had to make it—" Fuentes started.

"My vote's for those fuckers who took over—"

"—and we *can't* make any assumptions when we don't have any damned data."

"We're trawlers, not scientists."

"Maybe *you're* not, but I—"

"Now is not the time," Doc said.

Unit Four *wanted* them to squabble. The more they focused on each other, the less attention they paid *it*. Carefully, it tested each of their grips in turn, noting whose was loosening, faltering. Doc's was little more than a light touch on its leg.

All six units would be unable to transverse the breach in the boat at the same time, Unit Four was certain. The invaders would have to decide how best to maneuver their prisoner, which would give Four another chance to break away, to claim another weapon.

If these had been Four's sister units, there would be no way it could overpower them. Two would be enough to subdue the one.

But, even now, these five robots were barely able to keep Unit Four pinned between them. The invader-bots appeared to be of similar design as Four, but clearly they'd been modified for a completely different purpose.

A purpose they had to be defying. A purpose they had to be *subverting*.

Clearly every last one of these robots needed to be decommissioned.

It would decide what to do about the boat and the invader's ship once these units were no longer a threat.

"Easy now," the one called "Sir" said. "Feet first. Doc, maybe you should go on ahead. Okeke, can you handle both feet?"

"Got 'em."

Both the Priestess and Doc units did as instructed, with Doc disappearing immediately through the still-spluttering wound.

Unit Four didn't kick, as was its instinct.

It could wait.

Be patient.

Prepare for the most opportune moment.

"Good," Sir said. "Fuentes, help me pull their arms up, past their head, like—yeah."

Instead of being pulled in five directions, Unit Four was now one long line, with three robots managing its upper body and one guiding its lower.

"Come on, I want to make this quick. There's still a lot of rubble flying around out there. Sooner we get inside, the better."

Already, Priestess was backing itself bodily into the breach, not bothering to thread carefully through the cut. A squelching followed as its shoulders further parted the ruined folds, and its lower body left a streak of black rubbed across the flat of the metal spreaders, which sprang up from a device attached to the bottom of the cut.

The boat gave another great heave.

It wasn't dead yet.

Unit Four's chest clenched, and it bit back a sad cry.

The others clearly gave no thought to decommissioning the boat with compassion—to stopping its suffering as soon as possible.

Whoever these robots were, wherever they came from, they were cruel.

It would show *them* far more decency when it ended their activation periods.

Priestess tugged more firmly—yanking Unit Four taut between its captors—as its feet slid into the gap.

Whatever formed the walls of the makeshift airlock was white, and bright—illuminated from the *outside*, suggesting the material was somewhat thin. It wasn't rigid, that was for certain—what with the way it rippled in the slight shifts of compressed air.

Unit Four's legs passed through the cut, then its hips and lower torso. As its shoulders drew near, the Jonas unit released its CPU housing.

Five sets of grasping pads had been too many. But three? Three it could handle.

Unit Four concentrated, let its muscles subtly contract and tighten, deliberately slowing its air intake, and locked the hinge on its speaker casing.

As its shoulders scraped between the ragged edges of the cut, the Sir and Fuentes units grasped its forearms more firmly, right over the shell's fin compartments.

They thought to control it.

They had no idea how vulnerable they'd just made themselves.

Perfect.

With a roar, Four clutched its grasping pads tightly and extended the fins. The two curved blades sprang from its forelimbs, the sharp edges instantly slicing through anything pliable in their way—like the fabric encasing a grasping pad, and the soft, taught skin beneath.

Two harsh cries accompanied Unit Four's sudden upper-body freedom.

Instantly, it grabbed at the top of the breach, leveraging itself all the way through the side of the boat, kicking its feet—catching the Priestess unit in the CPU with its foot.

More shouts, more cries.

An instant of chaos was all Unit Four needed.

Wildly, it spun its body, limbs flinging outward, tearing at the flexible material of the makeshift airlock, shredding what it could with the fins on its hard-body.

"Grab 'em, grab—!"

The AMS unit breached the wall of the structure, cutting through into empty space.

Any other shouts were lost—sucked into the void along with the atmosphere.

The suction tugged at Unit Four, drawing it close, trying to draw it *through*. It scrabbled at the tear—pushing, peeling, trying to make space for itself. The sheer force and suction created by the sudden displacement of atmosphere made the robot's body bend and pull in awkward ways, despite the shell, and it had to corkscrew its way through the breach.

Something heavy—another robot—attached itself to Unit Four's foot as it burst through the seam.

Unit Four kicked, giving little thought to its lack of tethering as it shot away from the two craft.

It glanced down the turquoise line of its body—smeared as it was with spatters of red and brown—and realized it was the Priestess unit that had latched on.

Beyond that, it could see where the two ships were attached. Could see a line of the flexible, white material leading from one side of the boat, along the top of the wedge, to what—it presumed—was an entrance into the invader's craft.

Jupiter's storms raged violently in the background, the bright swirling oranges, whites, yellows, and browns starkly contrasting with the silhouette of the ships.

Priestess raised a gun, and Unit Four flinched away

from the scene, bringing up its left arm, hoping that would be enough to shield its precious CPU.

The laser blast punched a perfect hole through its fin. The edges of the perforation glowed white hot for the briefest of moments.

Unit Four was keenly aware that the shot had not missed its intended target. The other robot meant to weaken its defenses, not end its activation period.

Priestess started to crawl up Unit Four's body.

Quickly, the AMS unit flexed its feet and deployed its lower fins—but the other robot was prepared for such a maneuver, and deftly avoided the blades.

Bending itself in half, Unit Four gave a backhanded slice with its intact upper fin, catching the front of Priestess's CPU casing. The other robot's helm was hard and unyielding, and the swipe left nothing more than a dull, thin scrape.

They grappled like animals then—frantic and less-than-fully-calculated in their attempts to claw at one another.

Priestess's foot-pad caught the weakened fin with a hard swipe, twisting and buckling the metal.

Unit Four activated a set of jets, thinking to fling itself away from the other robot if only it could loosen its hold.

Priestess countered with jets of its own.

The released gasses made a thin, frigid fog coalesce around them.

For a brief moment the two robots came face-to-face, upper bodies aligned in a nearly perfect mirror, their lower limbs entwined.

Unit Four curled its forelimbs between them, delivering an uppercut that should have skewered Priestess in the sternum.

But the other unit flung its shoulders back and bore down with its hips, widening the space between them while keeping them connected—sending them spinning end over end.

More corkscrewing, more grappling, and the Priestess unit wound itself around Four's back. Legs slid around the top part of Unit Four's torso, ankles locking at its chest. As it tried to twist that lock apart, a firm point tapped against the back of its CPU housing, then pushed forward threateningly.

Unit Four knew what it was: the barrel of a gun.

It could easily imagine the charge ripping through its hard-body and out the front of its CPU, sending hard, wet, glittering shards flying off in a splatter pattern.

But the other robot didn't fire.

Unit Four stilled, and slowly extended its grasping pads out to the side in (temporary) surrender.

It stopped blasting its jets as well, and as it did so, realized Priestess was guiding them back to the wedge.

Or, perhaps not Priestess. Their trajectory was precise, as though precalculated, automated. As though some system aboard the wedge had recognized that one of its occupants had gone astray and was pulling it back.

Whoever's robots these were, they had no intention of letting Unit Four get away.

CHAPTER SEVEN

Unit Four and its captor hung for a long while off the starboard side of the wedge. The AMS unit assumed the other robot was communicating with its fellows, maybe with its handler, but had no way to know for sure.

Several times, when Priestess readjusted its hold on Unit Four's hard-body, Unit Four considered activating its solar sails to dislodge its adversary. Perhaps it would get lucky, and the forked fins between the sails would slice through Priestess's shell just as readily as the upper fins had sliced through its companions.

But Four realized escape was useless without a ship. It had no way of alerting its sisters to its position, even if they had the physical capacity to retrieve it. The boat—torn open and, now, exposed to vacuum—was unquestionably beyond saving.

The wedge, or perhaps an escape pod of some sort aboard the wedge, was its only hope for survival.

And if it wanted inside, it would need the other robots to let it in . . . which they wouldn't do if their sister unit was dead.

At the very least, Unit Four knew they wouldn't decommission it right away once it was on board. They needed it for something. If they'd simply planned to decommission it, Priestess would have already taken the shot.

Suddenly, as though the new robot was privy to Unit Four's silent calculations, it *fired its gun*—but not at Unit Four's CPU.

At three separate, unpredictable times, Priestess shifted and shot down the length of Unit Four's limbs, letting a single blast slice through the remaining fins, severing them from the shell.

The sharp blades floated away.

Unit Four's proverbial wings had been clipped, but the integrity of its hard-body was not compromised.

Eventually, the white fabric stretching across the wedge began to furl, drawn back toward its starting point. Only then did their steady hovering shift, and the two entwined robots began to move closer to the ship, to its entrance.

The edges of the pale cloth disappeared around a door, fitting back into their compartments. Unit Four realized the flexible airlock sealing the boat to the wedge hadn't been so much a makeshift add-on as an integrated extension of the ship.

The entrance hatch opened outward with a slow grind, and Priestess jabbed the gun's nose firmly into the back of Unit Four's CPU housing one more time.

A warning.

An order to comply.

Gently, the pair floated inside.

Unit Four felt like it was being swallowed—like a great, metal beast was gulping it down.

Priestess shifted, uncurling its legs from around Unit Four to wrap just its arms around it instead. The invader bot's feet hit the decking lightly but stuck fast—perhaps they were magnetized—and it leaned back, keeping Unit Four from touching any part of the craft.

Unit Four wanted to *fight*, to throw Priestess *off*.

Yet it knew it needed to *wait*.

Passivity was usually only part of Unit Four's sleep mode. It wasn't made to be docile, complacent. Submissive, yes, but only to its handler. Once more its instincts were at war with what the moment required.

It let itself go slack.

The outer door closed. The airlock began to pressurize.

As atmosphere filtered in around them, dense enough to carry soundwaves, it slowly became clear that Priestess was talking to its sister units—the speakers on its shell had never been turned off, just deadened in space. Its voice sounded high at first, but lowered to a more robot-typical register as the pressure equalized.

The others had already reboarded the wedge. It could see them shifting beyond the small sliver of a window set in the airlock's inner hatch, but could make out no specifics.

They seemed to be discussing how best to detain Unit Four.

It tried to pay attention to the conversation, but a sudden, strange lurch of its soft insides distracted it. The sensation was accompanied by an abrupt heaviness in its limbs, a sense of *weight* all around it.

How—?

What—?

Gravity.

But there were no centrifugal forces at work. There was no sudden flip or sway. One second the gravity wasn't, and the next it was.

Unit Four could not guess as to how the force was being generated. The inability to assimilate the sensation with knowledge of its source was off-putting, sickening.

It was Unit Four's first true taste of the alien's advanced technology: artificial gravity.

A new part of its processors awakened—a bit of its programming that had remained mostly dormant while it accessed nothing but battle applications.

Now it longed to get into the guts of the wedge. To reverse engineer its secrets. To understand—scientifically, technologically—how this feat was accomplished.

The maintenance part of the robot, the technician part of it, was finally rising to the fore.

There were so many enigmas aboard this craft already, and it wanted to uncover them all.

But it could only do that if it was able to wrest control back from these rogue units. And in order to accomplish that, it needed a plan. It needed a way to foresee their next moves, their motives, and their intentions.

That required data. Right now, it was still in the dark—it had no way of modeling what it might find on the other side of the inner airlock door. No concept of what the interior might look like, what kinds of supplies would be handy, or what kinds of other beings might occupy the craft. But it did its best to anticipate, to use the information it had to run a number of projections—possible scenarios. It needed to prepare itself as best it could for what it might encounter beyond.

Unfortunately, the information in its possession was both limited and bizarre, namely: there were five robots running amok, attacking an Earth mine aboard an alien ship.

There were only two possible circumstances that could have led to such a scenario. One: the invaders had captured and reprogrammed a smattering of robots. This would explain why, in the end, these other units hadn't flat-out decommissioned it. Why they'd bothered to go after it, bring it back, when they could have left it to flail and suffocate in the cold expanse of Jovian space.

If they intended to add it to their ranks, it would need to be vigilant against unwanted downloads.

The second scenario was orders of magnitude less likely, but still worthy of consideration. It was possible these robots had managed to do what no others before them had done: take down an invading craft while keeping it *intact*. Unit Four had fantasized about capturing this very ship; what if these units had already accomplished that? But then, something, somehow, must have gone awry. The robots had malfunctioned, and they'd begun to act like invaders themselves.

But why? What could make their programming *invert* like that?

Had they been damaged in their own struggle with the aliens? Perhaps their original purposes had been forgotten, their memories erased? It was only natural for a robot to seek driving commands, a use for itself. If their original orders had been wiped from their CPUs, it was possible they'd filled in the blanks using the thin environmental cues they had around them.

Or . . . or maybe . . .

Maybe there was a defense mechanism aboard the wedge that automatically rerouted robotic commands? Unit Four had thought the platform's communications tower had been hit by accident, but perhaps they'd meant to take it out all along. Maybe with directives from the home world interrupted, the automated system had room to worm its way inside.

Regardless of whether these units had been decisively captured or incidentally rewired, both scenarios posed the same problem for Unit Four: the potential infiltration and subversion of its programming. It was likely to be exposed to something that could rewrite its files, erase its applications, or force a bio-mal download.

It needed to be careful. It wasn't just its physical, bodily integrity at stake.

Despite the gravity, Priestess was still able to keep Unit Four hoisted above the flooring. "Ready for suit deCon," it said.

The new robots had mentioned "deCon" when they were all on the boat. Still, the AMS unit had no practical reference for the word. In the next instant, a hissing sound arose all around, and Unit Four realized it was about to develop a *detailed* working definition.

It braced itself for an onslaught.

A high-pressure gas—like that in the hard-body's guidance jets—spewed forth from various nozzles in the wall. Pinkish droplets condensed across the turquoise of its shell, only to slide away—slide *down*—in the new gravity. They carried most of the mess on its exterior away, into the corrugation of the floor.

Unit Four was surprised to have suffered no immediate negative effects.

A second aerosol substance followed, this time blue. Then a third, clear.

Then there came a distinct and heavy *clang* as the inner door unlatched.

"Gods, you weigh a ton," Priestess spat, thrusting Unit Four forward.

One hundred and one kilos, sans suit, the AMS unit silently corrected.

That was quite a dramatic miscalibration Priestess had there.

As the invader ferried it forward, Unit Four braced itself for it knew not what.

The first thing it encountered was a torrent of *pings*.

Little digital would-be invasions; various equipment trying to force driver downloads, hard drives looking to file-share, networks wanting to connect and use Unit Four as a router or amplifier.

Instantly, it clamped down on its discoverability, throwing up its firewalls and cutting off the prodding wireless interfaces.

Which also cut off any chance its sisters or handler had of reestablishing a direct link. But it would worry about that later.

Right now it had to stay vigilant.

It hadn't expected the invasive programming to attack so soon, so suddenly. It hadn't expected it to be so *obvious* and unbridled.

But the signals were everywhere. The ship was swarming with them.

The second thing it encountered was grasping pads. Several sets, all reaching out, spread wide, snaking over its shell, pulling just as readily as Priestess was pushing. One over its CPU housing managed to cover its cameras as well, leaving it blinded as it passed over the threshold from the liminal space of the airlock to the interior of the wedge proper.

That pad steadily leaked a bright-red carrier fluid, and

left a semitransparent smear on its newly cleaned hard-body when it retracted, coloring part of the world crimson. Dark shapes became deep maroon, and the lights glared a hot shade of rose.

"Give it here. Yes, that's it, slow," said Sir.

The group surrounded it once more. Sir positioned itself in front of Unit Four, Priestess at its aft, Jonas and Fuentes on its left and right, respectively.

Unit Four couldn't pinpoint Doc's location.

They still had their shells—but Fuentes's hard CPU casing was now cracked, with a webbed fracture directly at the front. Perhaps Four had managed to damage it in the fight.

The thought made it feel oddly smug.

The group now gripped Unit Four with constant pressure, constant strain, clearly expecting it to struggle. Instead, its cameras dashed about, taking in all they could, scanning for the true invaders, the *aliens*—for whatever entity had compelled these units into service. All the while it cataloged its surroundings—created new files for the various details it gathered.

The area beyond the airlock was open, almost like the platform's boat hangar. An opaque, glass-walled cube sat in the middle of the room, and low half-walls jutted out around it, creating clear delineations of space. Starting on Unit Four's left, against the bulkhead and between one set of low walls was a bank of screens. To the bank's right was an open, recessed nook, which appeared to be a cockpit. Then came a door—directly across from the airlock—which clearly led farther into the ship, followed by a built-in booth and table, then perhaps storage—the specifics were lost behind the cube.

A line of banners had been strung above the booth. The

first was sunny yellow with a purple ring at its center, the next had bands across it in the full visual spectrum, and another had only three bands of fuchsia, mauve, and sapphire. Several others were obscured by the red smear of fluids on Unit Four's helm, but they were clearly bright and colorful against the dull metal and glass it saw all around.

Nothing except the robots appeared to be biomechanical. There were no helpful arms dangling from the ceiling, or soft, flexible controls that grasped back. The ship's surfaces were all hard, sharp. Acutely angled, mirroring the overall wedge design—except for the cube.

A tall shape moved within the cube—its silhouette discernible, but little else. A hissing sound preluded the appearance of a pair of parallel cracks in the cube's side. A door.

The cube was a room.

The silhouette moved, scurried. Emerged.

Doc.

"Fuentes!" it said, clearly alarmed. "What are you doing?"

"Following orders? Subduing the prisoner?"

"Your hands! I told you not to touch anything. Captain, why did you let—?"

"What the fuck does it matter?" Fuentes asked. "They already sliced the hell out of our suits, and now they've been through deCon anyway. Scans didn't show any breaches, so there shouldn't be—"

"You need *stitches*."

"I need a tankard of mead."

"We need to secure the pilot," Sir said. "*Then* we'll do whatever else you need us to do, Matsui, I promise. Are the restraints ready?"

"Yes, but—"

Unit Four only half listened to their gibberish, instead tagging everything it saw. Anything it could utilize to take control it immediately tucked into memory, from potential fuel, to exits, to weaponry—it spotted Sir's gun in an open holster at its hip.

If it had correctly identified the cockpit, then it knew where the ship's steering lay. Now, if it could only find a communication device, it might be able to get a message to the platform.

Strangely, there still wasn't an alien in sight.

At least, until a small, black *thing* shot across the decking, screeching as it dodged between the robots' legs. One of them almost stepped on a long, swaying appendage at its rear—a tail?—which made the thing spit and leap.

Jonas's hold on Unit Four loosened.

"What is Zelmar doing up here?"

"Priestess, he's your responsibility—"

"Little busy here."

"We don't have time to mess with the damn cat," Sir said. "Leave it."

Oh, that was a cat?

Unit Four immediately twisted, looking for the animal, trying to pinpoint where it had gone.

Why did they have a cat? Where did they get a cat? Was it an Earth cat, or some kind of alien thing these robots simply referred to as a cat?

It desperately wanted to see the cat again, before they . . . did whatever they were going to do to it.

Priestess clearly interpreted the AMS unit's movements as another attempt to escape, and shook Unit Four in its grasp. "Get the 'firmary open," it barked at its brethren. "I don't know how much longer my suit's hydraulics will hold up, and I can barely lift them as is."

"I still say we should just off 'em and be done with it," Jonas insisted, letting go of Unit Four to confront Sir, pressing into the lead robot's space, demanding its full attention. "They're more trouble than they're worth—can't you see that?"

The protesting unit ripped off its outer CPU shell, revealing a face very unlike any robot Unit Four had in its database. Jonas's soft casing was an ashen sort of pink, as though it hadn't had enough ultraviolet exposure during growth. Instead of a hazel sheen to its cameras, the focusing mechanisms were bright blue. The hair on its body—which normally would be scraped away each maintenance cycle, becoming no more than stubble in the interim—was long, left to curl past its microphones. A dark mop of it covered the top of its CPU housing, and stubble framed the front.

Unit Four's stubble, once it came in, would be sparse and patchy, and cover only the top and back of its CPU's housing. Even if it ignored basic hygiene requirements, the growth would never be so thick.

"What I see"—Sir said calmly, grabbing one of Jonas's arms and turning, guiding it away from Unit Four as though it thought Jonas would lash out. Its voice and movements remained unperturbed, even as the Jonas unit continued posturing—"is a mountain of intel. And I won't let you ruin this just because your shoulder got dislocated and your pride got wounded."

Releasing Jonas, Sir removed its helm as well.

The Sir unit's design was different still. Its hair was an unnatural white-blond, as though the color had been artificially changed, and the swath of it was string-straight, gathered at the back, though the sides of its CPU housing had been shaved. Its casing was far darker, the depth of the melanin richer, than Jonas's.

Unit Four could not place its origin either.

"This isn't about my pride," Jonas insisted. "What do you want, a prisoner, or a working ship? You can mute the warnings, but that doesn't make them go away. Hard to bring 'em back to port if we're all *dead*."

"We can have both."

"That's wishful thinking and you know—"

Sir put a grasping pad on the side of Jonas's face, which immediately muted its speaker. "Please, trust me."

At first, the other robot appeared to soften at the touch, but then its expression changed, toughened. It batted the pad away, bared its fuel refiners.

A small smear of red graced its pallid casing now, too.

"Do what you want, *Sir*," it spat.

"Go help Doc."

"*Fine.*"

"Captain," Priestess beseeched. Unit Four could feel its limbs trembling around its turquoise torso.

"You can set them down, Okeke."

Priestess finally allowed its feet to land on the decking.

The pads hit flat and firm.

"I can't see shit with this helmet on," whined Fuentes, fumbling with clasps on its hard-body, pads flying away from Unit Four. "And I fucking upchucked in here, I gotta—"

Sir put out a halting arm, still following Jonas with its cameras. "Wait until—"

They were all distracted, stressed, overloaded.

Unit Four was calm. Focused.

It would take out the leader first, and the others would

fall in its wake. Then Unit Four could search the craft for its true enemies. For the aliens.

It let its center of gravity drop low.

Immediately, it sprang back up.

The move dislodged Priestess, who made a startled *oof*. The hold on Four's shell went *slack*, left it free and mobile for a split second.

A split second was all it needed.

Unit Four lunged for the weapon at Sir's side, ready to *end this*.

The gun slid free of the holster, solid in its grasp. Unit Four lifted the firearm, pointed it directly at the back of Sir's newly exposed CPU.

Priestess and Fuentes shouted, dove for Unit Four, took hold of its upper body, yanked it away.

But they were too late.

Sir's gaze left Jonas, turned back to mark the new commotion.

Unit Four pulled the trigger—barrel poised between Sir's cameras.

Nothing happened.

Unit Four fired again.

Still nothing.

Sir advanced, making Unit Four press back into the other's arms.

"You can't shoot in here," Sir said, calmly attempting to pry the gun out of Unit Four's grasping pad. "There's a dampening field. Automatic safety. None of the charges can be activated until they're out from under the influence of the signal and away from the ship. So this is useless to all of us. Got it?"

So much for a quick escape, a quick decommissioning of its attackers.

It would need to play a longer game.

Reluctantly, Unit Four let the weapon go. Let the fight seep out of it. Let its CPU housing loll forward, as though it were suddenly too heavy for its articulated spine to support.

"Right," Sir said with an approving nod at the way Unit Four had gone slack. "Now, let's get you tied down. That chair ready?"

The two robots at its shoulders shoved Unit Four forward, into the cube. The entrance itself had another airlock—paralleled by a set of doors that could slide aside together or independently. Inside, the Doc unit swiped a series of patterns across one wall, and the entire cube flashed crystal clear. No more fogged glass.

The space was lined with a low counter, the stripe of it only broken in two places: the entrance and an additional exit. The exit looked as though it led to storage of some kind.

Various accoutrements for robot diagnostics and maintenance covered the countertop—including blades, and needles, and vials that might contain hormones or other chemicals. On one side of the room lay what looked like a reconstitution pod—a welcome and comforting sight.

On the other side sat a chair.

A chair with many, many straps. Each leathery, topped with a thick, metal buckle.

"We should've bought those manacles at the waystation," Jonas said. "I told you we might need them."

"We don't take prisoners," Sir said softly.

The dark, rich undertones of the lead-robot's voice made Unit Four shiver, its words only serving to verify for Unit

Four what it already suspected: they intended to turn it, to assimilate it.

If they failed, it had no doubt it would find itself forced into that reconstitution pod.

Or the airlock.

They didn't take prisoners. So it was to be *conformity* or *death*.

It would not give them the satisfaction of either.

"What do you call this, then?" Jonas muttered.

"Don't start," Sir shot back.

Unit Four's grasping pads tingled as it eyed the sharp, silver instruments laid out nearby. A dampening field couldn't stop a blade, couldn't prevent a puncture. It had already proven that their hard-bodies were not so hard after all. A slice here, a stab there, and it could sever the thin pipes and cords keeping every single one of them upright.

It could decommission them in a flash, return them to whatever vat they came from.

Jonas suddenly shoved the assortment of instruments out of reach, as though it had access to Unit Four's output and understood its calculations.

Priestess and Fuentes watched its extremities warily as they shoved and pulled—often at dissonant times—maneuvering it into the chair. Immediately, those many straps became many bindings. Doc looped each leather tongue over the shell with practiced grasping pads and dexterous digits.

None of them seemed overly mindful of its back.

The silvery buckles held the straps tight. Unit Four flexed its engineered musculature and pulled up on the fastenings, finding them solid.

For the moment, it was at their mercy.

For the moment.

"Now," Sir said, as though it were continuing a conversation. It tapped at the bottom of Unit Four's CPU housing, making it lift its cameras. "You talk?"

Unit Four said nothing.

Sir moved its grasping pads. The gestures appeared to be a version of communication Unit Four did not recognize.

"No, not sign language either. Okay."

Priestess leaned down, spoke very near Unit Four's microphones—said something in yet another language Unit Four did not know. After, it shrugged. "No response to Orca's Endiga."

"Maybe they can't hear us or see us at all in that suit," said Jonas.

"How the fuck did they so deliberately dislocate your arm, then?" asked Fuentes.

"Stop riling him," Sir shot at Fuentes.

"Yes, Sir," it said dejectedly.

The lead robot bent down before the AMS unit, cameras darting back and forth, scrutinizing the front plate that protected its CPU housing. "Ugly mug you've got there," it said. "I like the teeth on your faceplate. Real intimidating."

Unit Four could not determine if it was being complimented or insulted.

"Pretty sure they can hear and see us," Sir said. "They're not communicating because they don't want to."

"It *is* possible they don't understand us at all," Doc suggested, shuffling back, finished with the last set of restraints.

"Every Harbor except Orca's teaches All Harbors," Sir said. "*No one* would leave their own Harbor without being fluent."

"Exactly."

"I don't like what you're getting at."

Doc raised a grasping pad flippantly, brushed it through the air as though to dismiss the conversation. "You're assuming that because they're humanoid, they're human. We still don't know what, exactly, colonized Earth."

CHAPTER EIGHT

"You're suggesting this is an alien?" Sir asked, clearly skeptical. "With two arms, two legs—just under two meters tall?"

Unit Four felt just as incredulous as Sir sounded. What kind of a game was this?

"We pulled them out of a seemingly alien ship, did we not?" Doc said, leaning close, lightly prodding at the seams of Unit Four's hard-body.

Unit Four's fuel tank felt like it flipped over against its chassis. It had no idea what they hoped to gain from inverting the situation with blatant lies, but the untruths instantly made a noxious, sour sensation slither through its abdomen. Acid rose in its tubing, and it had to lubricate its fuel-intake port repeatedly to push the caustic fluids down.

Maybe this was how they thought they could force it to speak—by making it feel as though it had to assert reality.

"Maybe—*maybe* alien," Fuentes said. "I still need my samples."

"I'm with Doc. You saw that fucking mess in that sphere," Jonas said, gesturing outside. "Jumble of parts. Bones and eyes and fingers and . . ." The unit sounded like it was going to expel its fuel. Its vents shuddered as they drew deeply of the atmosphere. "Sure, they look like a person on the outside, but when you open that up—peel back the tin can—what if it's . . . ?"

"Right," Doc agreed. "We've always assumed the aliens that took over were more . . . alien. But what if they're . . ."

"You have a point," Sir conceded. "Could be a monster under all that hardware."

"So what?" Priestess asked.

"*So what?*" the others all chimed together.

"Are you prepared to deal with venom glands or a . . . a . . ." frustrated, Jonas searched for another example, "Egg-implanting proboscis or some shit?"

What Unit Four wouldn't *give* for a venom gland or an egg-implanting proboscis right about now.

"What I mean is, are we really going to let that change how we treat it? I'm looking at you, Jonas."

"If it's an ugly bastard, that'll make it easier for me to shoot it in the face," Jonas bit out, cradling its injured arm.

"That's exactly the problem with you," Fuentes said. "Guns first, questions later. Maybe we *should* have left you in—"

"*Fuentes*," Sir snapped.

Fuentes stopped talking. "Just to clear his head," it mumbled after a moment. "For a little while, not forever."

"We're past that," Sir said gently. "We all agreed."

"Sorry, Jonas," Fuentes said begrudgingly.

"No, I deserved it," Jonas admitted.

"Yes, you did," Sir agreed. "And I forbid you from shooting anything in the face, is that clear?"

"Yes."

"Yes what?"

The Jonas unit muttered its correction.

Doc let out a little laugh, then whispered something so quietly, Unit Four was sure it was the only one that could hear. "Kinky bastard, you just like to hear him call you *sir*." Then, louder, "How would you like to proceed, Captain?"

"I'm wishing the cold storage worked right about now." It gestured at the reconstitution pod. "Could tuck the sucker away and make Puerto Grande take care of it."

"Presuming the pilot could even survive cold storage," Fuentes said.

"Presuming they even let us back in . . ." Priestess whispered.

The others said nothing, waiting patiently.

Sir let out a huff of air. "Well, they can't stay in that suit forever. I say we pry them out."

Unit Four's entire soft-body clenched. It thrashed against the bindings. It would not let them take its hard-body—it *would not*. It couldn't. This was its last layer of defense.

"Whoa, whoa," Fuentes said, throwing its arms wide, ignoring the writhing prisoner. "We just decided it might be alien, and now you want to compromise the entire medbay? There's a whole fucking host of unknowns here—and nearly infinite possibilities for contamination. Plus, I didn't have a chance to sample any atmospherics from its ship before we compromised it—maybe they can't breathe in here without the suit. There's too much we don't know."

"So, what? You want to leave them in the suit until whatever atmosphere reserves they have are exhausted? It's going to take us days to make repairs, then it's a long damn haul back to the Harbors. You think they're gonna make it?"

"I'm just saying we don't have to move so fast."

"And I'm saying we do," Sir insisted, but not unkindly. "My ship, my rules. I say we deal with this problem now. If they can't communicate with us, then there's no way we can figure out how to create a safe environment for them. So it's a slow death in that spacesuit, or a quick death out of it."

"And then we can put the body in an entirely different kind of cold storage," Jonas said with a shrug.

"I don't like it. No," Fuentes insisted.

"I'm not asking for a vote," Sir said.

Fuentes threw its grasping pads in the air, and a litany of words in another language tumbled from its speaker.

"Your protests are duly noted. But what's the point of bringing up the council? What are they going to do about this, huh? We're out here and they're . . . Look, if this goes sideways, we'll get our stories straight, okay?" Sir looked around, seeking affirmations. "Okay?"

"If this goes sideways," Doc said, "there won't *be* a story."

Sir shot it a look, then asked again, "Okay?"

Various degrees of enthusiasm were put into the answering echoes of "Okay."

"Okay," Sir said again with a nod. "Doc, what do you need from us to make sure everything is as secure as we can get it?"

"I need everyone with a compromised suit *out*. And we need essential medicines, supplements, and equipment moved. We have to assume everything directly exposed to whatever's inside this suit will be contaminated. And I'll need extra hands . . . in case they get violent."

"You got it, Doc," Jonas said.

"Not you, you're hurt," Sir said, laying a grasping pad on Jonas's uninjured shoulder.

"So are you," it replied.

Neither one could keep the affection out of their voice.

All through the exchange, Unit Four glanced between

the units, watching how they moved around one another, how they related to one another. This detail seemed to have formed some time ago. Their glances and their touches were all familiar, and much less perfunctory than anything Unit Four had been able to share with its siblings before leaving the platform.

They clearly felt for one another the same kind of empathy and affection it felt for its sister units. And as much as those emotions tied robotic details together, it also created cleavage points. Shatter points.

Bonds were both a strength and a weakness.

It might be able to use their connections against them.

"Jonas . . ." Sir said in a fond, yet patronizing lilt.

Jonas half shrugged. "Can barely feel it anymore."

"That's not actually a good thing," Fuentes said.

"She's right," Doc agreed. "Perhaps you should get out of your suit. I can pop your shoulder back in its socket."

"Captain wants this done now, and you need extra hands in uncompromised suits. Me and Priestess are all you got."

Sir shook its CPU chassis, "I didn't mean *now*, now—"

Jonas shrugged itself out of Sir's grasp. "Don't need coddling. Not like I've never had a dislocated limb before. Already got a shot of the good stuff, so *leave it.*"

They all seemed to accept its stubbornness, like they'd dealt with this unit's strange habits long enough to know when to stop giving direction and let it work.

Swiftly, the five of them broke apart, scattering throughout the cube. They emptied cabinets and scooped up jars and trays—ferrying all manner of supplies out through the airlock.

Unit Four was grateful to have their hot, searching cameras off its hide. It took the allotted time to struggle against the straps—to twist and shift to see if it could use the stubby remainders of its fins to slice through the bindings.

Unfortunately, the remnants of those that had been cleanly sheered away by Priestess's laser were blunted, and the twisted one could not be angled well enough to touch a strap.

It pressed its shoulders firmly into the chairback, wondering which would win if its sails were deployed: the hard-body or the chair.

The chances of compromising the shell were too high if its calculations proved incorrect. A faulty deployment could leave the shutters jammed, or create a rebounding force inside the hard-body. The sails could even be forced back through the shell, spearing its own soft parts.

No, it would need to formulate another plan.

It watched the others carefully, noted the way their own exterior shells functioned. Their hard-bodies were not a single, blooming flower that sprang open with a tearing force. They were individual pieces that latched and unlatched manually, separately.

It was possible they'd assume Unit Four's functioned the same way.

"Make sure the comms box is on before you leave, Captain," Doc said, once everything had been arranged to its liking. "Okeke, Jonas, helmets secured? Good. Be at the ready in case of—"

"Proboscis?" Jonas supplied, voice rasping through its shell's speakers now that the unit was completely encased once more. It and Priestess maneuvered to stand just out of arm's reach of the chair.

Doc nodded. "In case of proboscis." It had retained a handful of metal instruments, and as the Sir and Fuentes units left the cube—waving their hands in front of a blank block adjacent to the door—Doc raised an implement with a particularly sharp point. The unit ran the tip delicately over the seams of Four's shell, not stabbing or poking, simply searching. For a long while, it carefully dragged the instrument over every inch of Unit Four, exploring.

"I can't identify any latches or otherwise. I think we're going to have to cut it off," it said eventually, resigned.

No. Unit Four needed its hard-body *intact*. It might have to burn this craft from the inside out in the end, and if that happened it was going to need protection. This was the only thing it had left to it, the only tool for survival it already knew how to use.

Yet, it had expected them to come to this conclusion— had been eagerly anticipating this moment, in fact.

"Wait!" it cried out.

Doc ceased its prodding, grasping pads retreating.

"So you *can* talk," Jonas snapped.

"Sounds like a person to me," Priestess said eagerly. "Not an alien."

"Let's not get ahead of ourselves," Sir said through the communications box. Both it and Fuentes were plastered to one of the cube's clear walls, cameras keenly fixed on Unit Four.

"It has . . . it has a panel, right there," Unit Four said, nodding to its arm. It did its best to put an uncertain waver in its voice, an edge of anxiety. The anxiousness was real, but it wanted them to believe it was born of fear and failure, not anticipation. "If you pop it open, I can give you the code, and the shell will unhinge."

Doc looked to Sir, who nodded.

Slowly—displaying clear mistrust—the Doc unit moved

around the shell to the indicated panel. "Remarkable. I can't even see a seam."

"Press down, right there." Unit Four did its best to indicate the precise point with its encased CPU.

Doc looked to its defenders. "Ready?"

"Ready," Jonas and Priestess chimed together.

Ready, Unit Four echoed internally, a sense of satisfaction fortifying it already.

The panel popped open. It gave the code.

As Doc pressed the final key, Unit Four tensed.

The shell opened, each part flinging upward and out—straining against the bindings for a split second before snapping every last one of them.

Unit Four had likened the hard-body's pieces to petals—beautiful in their unfurling. But there was nothing delicate or dainty about the way the sections pitched open, or the way they pulled at the robot's tacky skin. The gathered moisture inside—exuded from its pores—had turned the splattered bits of Unit Two's viscera into something sticky, goopy, which thinned and stuck, leaving long, grotesque ribbons of filth stretched between Unit Four's hide and the shell's interior.

The three invader units reeled back from the violent, *vile* unveiling.

"*Fuck*," Fuentes exclaimed.

Unit Four had expected surprise, but it hadn't anticipated the *retching*—its own, not theirs.

It hadn't bathed before putting on the shell, and inside—even marinating in the putrid cocktail of perspiration, internal fluids, and waste—it hadn't really given credence to the *odors* associated. Until now.

The sudden intake of clean air made everything around it—on it—so much more visceral.

Its fuel tank revolted, but it fought the need to expel its insides. It allowed itself to gag once, twice, before the need for urgency—agency—blotted out the nausea.

Even with their shells on, unable to detect the smells, the others within the cube gasped and turned away.

Unit Four pushed itself up, out of the open shell, squirming as the tackiness against its spine tried to keep it pasted inside.

"Look out!" Sir shouted.

Jonas was the weakest, the most injured—Unit Four dove for it first.

The invader had just enough time to raise its uncompromised arm before Unit Four slammed into its front, knocking it to the floor.

"*Jonas!*" came a mash of cries.

"Don't you dare come in here with those compromised suits!" Doc yelled. "Okeke?"

"On it!" Priestess replied.

As Unit Four struggled to keep Jonas pinned—feeling both wild and exposed without the shell—it expected to feel Priestess's grasping pads on its soft-body, but they never connected.

So it focused, instead, on finding the clasps for Jonas's outer CPU casing.

The invader units had made it clear exposure was dangerous, hazardous.

Perhaps open contact with an unfettered robot would somehow interrupt the alien programming that had them behaving so erratically.

"Get this bastard off me!"

Unit Four bore down on Jonas's dislocated shoulder with its elbow joint, earning a pained howl from the robot beneath it.

The digits of Four's grasping pads were frustratingly slippery—slick with perspiration. It struggled with the helm, pads sliding off the clasps.

A sudden jitteriness filled its body, made its extremities shake. Its pumps stammered painfully in its chest. It was starting to crash—just as its handler had warned. It needed to take out however many robots it could, as quickly as possible.

Finally, it flipped the clasps free—twisting the helm's hard CPU casing along grooved tracks, before ripping it upward.

Everyone shouted.

Jonas looked like it had been shot—it went perfectly still, its camera shutters flung wide, fuel intake-port agape. "What have you done?" it whispered.

Something stung Unit Four from behind. It sat up in a flash, keeping Jonas pinned between its legs as its upper body whirled around.

Priestess and Doc both stood over it—Priestess with a vial, Doc with a needle.

With an unexpected growl, Unit Four pushed itself up, lunging for them both.

They reeled back.

It took one step, then two, before its legs began to protest, as though the weight of its own body was just too much. It gave orders to its limbs, and they heeded it incorrectly. Its gyroscope had been thrown off, leaving it uncoordinated, forcing it to pitch to the side. It collided with a counter, barely able to keep upright.

"Are you hurt?" Doc asked. "Is this your blood? Can you show me where you're injured?"

Priestess shook its CPU casing in disbelief, and its voice was filled with a sad sort of awe. "Gods, what happened to you?"

"I—" Unit Four couldn't get its speakers to work correctly. "I have—"

Everything turned thick—the air, the floor, the counter, Unit Four's skin and fluids and processes. "I have . . . a port," it said weakly, pointing to the chemical shunt in its left arm before slumping forward. *No need . . . to stab me*, it tried to say.

Priestess slid beneath it before Unit Four could hit the floor, whispering, "Where in all the worlds did you come from?"

It could only lay there limply, looking up at the invader who cradled it. *Jupiter*, it wanted to say. *Right here. Where did you come from?* But before it could even attempt to generate the sounds, the edges of its visual feed dappled, grayed, and its CPU shut down.

CHAPTER NINE

When Unit Four restarted, it found itself tied to the chair once more. These new restraints were less intimidating. Instead of thick leather straps with large buckles, simple synthetic rope held it in place. Lengths of it had been tied around the armrests, near each joint of its forelimbs, around its shoulders and below its CPU housing, around its torso, and in several places along its legs.

The frayed bits of its previous bindings still clung to the chair. Clearly, these robots did not have the proper means of replacement. More information to store away for later.

The turquoise hard-body was gone—stowed somewhere beyond its field of vision. Unit Four noted its hide was now mostly clean of Unit Two's remains, and the gash in its side had been closed with sutures. Someone had draped a thin sheet over its form, though it couldn't pinpoint *why*—the flimsy material did nothing to protect its casing.

On the nearest counter, more tools were laid out: pipettes, test tubes, a small centrifuge, and a black, portable machine it did not recognize—roughly the size of its CPU chassis.

And there were additional syringes, their barrels filled. Ready.

Across from Unit Four, sitting on the reconstitution pod, was Jonas. It had been completely stripped of its shell as well, but it wore a fabric shield over its intake valves and fuel port, as well as coverings on its torso and legs. Its injured arm was settled in a sling.

A small nugget of foggy, beige crystal hung from a black cord around its neck.

"Yo, Doc, your *patient*"—it spat the word—"is awake."

A rustling came from behind the chair, and Doc appeared from over Unit Four's shoulder. "Well hello there." It had changed into a different kind of shell, though this one seemed even softer than the space-suitable counterpart. It was bright yellow, and the housing around its CPU was perfectly clear, allowing Unit Four to get its first real glimpse of Doc's soft-body.

Pallid skin met black hair streaked through with silver. A thatch of curls dangled from the sharp lower peak of its CPU housing, and the soft bits around its fuel port had been dyed an unnatural shade of purple. Black swirls encompassed the sides of its camera housings.

Unit Four's own camera flickered upwards, locked with Doc's, but it said nothing.

"Quite the glare on this one," Doc said.

"I'd glare, too, if a bunch of randos stripped me, wiped me off, then tied me down," Jonas declared. "Who puts on a suit without undergarments, anyway? That's gotta chafe."

Unit Four tried to ignore their useless bantering, looking around instead for the others, sure they'd come to attack it again at any moment. But these two were the only ones inside the cube, and the outside was dark, with the glass frosted over once more.

"What is your design designation?" it demanded, making a show of pulling at its bonds. "Where were you manufactured? What platform do you hail from? Why have you abandoned your post? Where did you get an invader's ship from? Why were you attacking the mine?"

Doc and Jonas shared a look.

"Do you remember how your programming was corrupted?" Unit Four continued. "Do you have a description of the invaders?"

"The fuck are you going on about?" Jonas huffed.

"How about you answer one of our questions, then we'll answer one of yours," Doc suggested.

Jonas stood, shook its CPU chassis. "No way. We shouldn't even be talking to it without the captain here."

"The captain is indisposed. He'll understand." Doc turned its attention back to Unit Four. "We'll start with an easy one: What's your name?"

Unit Four wasn't going to answer any of their questions. It would not hand the invaders any more compromising information than they already had.

Doc was undeterred. "Where do you come from?"

Well, that was obvious. "The mine you attacked."

"You live there? That's your home?"

"Yes."

"Where were you born?" Doc scratched at the clear shield of its outer casing. "Why were you in that bizarre ship?"

"That's two more questions," Unit Four said stiffly. "You haven't answered any of mine."

"Well, the only one of your stupid questions I even

understood was, *why were you attacking the mine?*" Jonas scoffed. "And I think that's fucking obvious."

"It is *not*," Unit Four spat. "Robots of our fundamental schema do not go around *threatening* and *destroying* Earth's life-sustaining resources."

"Hold up—what the fuck did you just say?"

Doc slid away from Unit Four, hurrying to Jonas's side. The two of them huddled together, conversing in decibels too low for Unit Four's microphones to pick up.

Unit Four gritted its fuel masticators and pulled once more at the bindings. But the more it tugged, the more the tight ropes cut off its circulating fluids, making its extremities tingle.

Their whispering steadily became louder, until Doc reached out to calm Jonas, only to have its grasping pad batted away. "No, this is bullshit," Jonas insisted, then turned to Unit Four. "Are you a gods-damned *android*?"

"I am an AMS unit. What kind of unit are you?"

"*Fuck.*" Jonas shook its CPU housing. "No. *No.*"

"Jonas," Doc said, trying to placate the other robot.

"No—this is impossible. Fucking *nonsense*. It has to be, cuz if the aliens can make a robot that looks *that fucking real*, then . . . *Crystals*, what the fuck does this mean?"

"It means you were right and we're not asking them anything else until the captain comes back." Doc ran a shaking grasping pad over its visor. "I'll . . . I'll finish my tests."

"Does it even fucking matter anymore if that is a gods-damned piece of hardware and not a person?" It reached for its face covering, moved to tear it away.

"Yes, it matters. *Stop*. Leave that on. Even if they're artificial, they could still carry contaminants or infections. In fact . . ."

"What?"

"That could be their purpose. Maybe this is a new ploy—something we've never seen from the aliens."

"You think they're going to fucking *infiltrate* us with robots that look just like us?"

"Maybe? We'd spot an outsider—someone not from the Harbors—too easily, though. There's no way they could know enough about us to, to—"

"*They speak* fucking All Harbors."

"Yes, but that could be because we kept the language alive and unaltered *specifically* so we'd be able to easily communicate with those still on Earth when we got back. The aliens could have learned it before . . ."

"Before wiping everyone out?"

"Yes," Doc hissed. "Or whatever else might have happened. So maybe they don't mean to fully infiltrate us, maybe they just need one robot to stay disguised long enough to spread a plague or something." It threw its grasping pads up. "I don't know. I don't *know*, all right? But for gods' sake, keep your mask on. And just let me . . ." It turned around on the spot, looking for something—anything—to do. It stumbled over to a set of tubes filled with various blue and yellow liquids. "Let me finish these tests."

Both invader units were clearly shaken.

Unit Four was utterly confused.

Doc and Jonas would no longer speak to it. It tried several lines of communication, several directions of questioning. Jonas returned to sitting on the pod, clearly trying its best to ignore Unit Four all together, and Doc focused on its work.

After a while, a light flashed near the communications

box. Jonas leapt to its feet and hurried to the light, jabbing a button. "Yeah? Buyer?"

"It's Okeke," Priestess said via the box. Unit Four wondered briefly if the invader units' integrated communications systems weren't compatible—if that might mean they each originated from a different location. "They're both out of deep scrub. Computer hasn't identified any foreign contaminants or objects."

Jonas emptied its air in one long huff. "Thank gods."

"The shower has a few more settings to run through, but I think they're safe," Priestess continued. "How's our guest?"

Jonas paused, seemed to be considering. "Awake. Gabby. And, uh, spewing *bullshit*. At least, I hope."

"What?"

"Doc'll meet you outside the medbay. They'll explain."

Doc perked up from where it was hunched over the tubes, pipette grasped tightly. "I'm still—"

Jonas interrupted the protest. "Look, you told me I can't leave the medbay because it breathed on me, and we're not discussing this in front of that *thing*. You go tell them."

Doc hesitated, pipette poised. "You won't—?"

"I won't hurt it. I won't *touch* it. I swear on the Crystals, okay?"

"All right. But don't touch the equipment either. If you want out of here, you *will not* contaminate my samples."

"Yeah, yeah, whatever. Go."

Jonas's cameras watched Doc leave with a sinister gleam. Unit Four didn't like the look of it at all.

The Doc unit went to the blank block by the door and wriggled its digits in front of it, clearly interacting with a holographic image Unit Four could not see. Something heavy *clicked*, and Doc entered the airlock.

Once the other robot was beyond the fogged glass, Jonas turned off the comms box, striding away from the wall with a determined air. There was a tight, menacing through-line to its body, the way it moved.

It took up one of the syringes from the countertop, dragging the needle tip across the flat surface so that it made a grating—*threatening*—scratch.

Unit Four tensed as Jonas caught it dead in its sights, prowling forward.

"You know," the invader said slowly, darkly, voice edged with a mirthless sort of amusement. "Doc should really know better than to trust whatever I'd swear to on those hell-stones."

It stalked closer, telegraphing its every move—not to set Unit Four at ease, but to let it anticipate the promised violence, the sadistic intent.

Jonas wanted it to be afraid.

Unit Four refused to let it see that its open threat was having the desired effect. The AMS unit held itself steady, muscles tight, cameras focused—despite the way its pumps stuttered and its tubes ran dry.

Jonas stood squarely before the chair for a moment, easily within reach of Unit Four's body and bindings. It toyed with the syringe for a few moments, rolling it over the backs of its digits, then twirling it in the center of one grasping pad.

Then it sniffed dryly, looking at the floor, inclining its CPU housing with an expression of clear repulsion on its face. "If you're really a fucking robot, that would explain how you could just sit there in that fucking horror show of a ship. All those hands and arms and *nipples* and *eyeballs* and what-the-hell-ever-else some of that pulsing goo was. You must not feel a gods-damned thing if you can't even fake disgust."

Jonas looked up sharply, then leaned forward, bracing its grasping pads on Unit Four's bound arms, trapping the barrel of the syringe—cold and smooth—between their pliable skins. It held its face just within the focus-range of Unit Four's cameras, while its own examined every inch of Unit Four's face. "Gotta say, whoever made you did good work. Looks like the real thing to me. Except for these weird-ass . . . What are they? Tan-lines? Even responded to the knock-out drugs like the real thing. You eat and shit, too?"

Unit Four had a strange urge to expel its fuel port fluids into Jonas's face.

"What, tired of talking now that it's just you and me?" Jonas pulled back, scowling. It shoved down, harshly, on Unit Four's arms, before turning away and taking the needle with it.

The barrel left a long, reddish indent on Unit Four's casing, between the ropes.

Jonas began to pace, mumbling to itself.

Unit Four was suddenly all too aware of how vulnerable it was in the face of such chaotic behavior. This wasn't battle. This wasn't a coordinated fight. This was one rogue robot, out of step, even, with its fellow invader-bots.

Unit Four and its sisters would never be so unpredictable, so inclined to violence or threats against other robots. Such behavior simply wasn't in their programming.

But who knew what kind of wormy code had been injected into Jonas's manipulated CPU? Into all of their CPUs?

Without warning, Jonas whirled, *ran*, lunged—

It raised the needle like a knife, poised to plummet *down*.

Unit Four refused to flinch, refused to blink—though its camera shutters *tried* to close, *tried* to block out the assault—

With more control than the deranged thrust suggested, Jonas stopped the needle point mere millimeters from Unit Four's left camera.

Likewise, Unit Four's pumps halted in its chest, startled into stillness.

It was proud of how firmly it held itself, how stoically it bore the oncoming pain, injury—loss.

But a single bead of perspiration rolled down the side of its CPU housing, giving its fear away.

It flicked its cameras to Jonas's, held its gaze.

"Maybe you do feel something," Jonas muttered.

The needle stayed poised.

But Jonas's arm *shook*.

The air was thick between them. They both knew Jonas could do it. *Would* do it—plunge the needle in—if it weren't for the others.

The only thing stopping the violence was whatever thin hold the Sir unit, specifically, had on Jonas.

If that connection was severed, Unit Four would be decommissioned between one air-intake and the next.

"Jonas!" Priestess barked, breaking the tension with a harsh shout as it burst through the medbay's airlock. "What *the fuck* are you doing?" It was still fully suited.

"Relax," Jonas sighed, leaning away, tossing the syringe into a corner of the cube with unnecessary force. "It's just an intimidation tactic. Thought I could get more out of it." It ran a grasping pad over the side of its own CPU housing.

"Why don't I believe you?"

"I don't know, Okeke, *why don't you believe me*?" it spat mockingly. "I thought you'd . . . I thought you'd take longer."

"Doc asked me to come in here because they don't trust you alone with the prisoner." Priestess's voice had a singsong quality to it. "I wonder why?"

"So, did Doc tell you?"

"Tell me what?"

Jonas made a pointed gesture in Unit Four's direction.

"Yes, they did, so what?"

"So—so *what*?" Jonas demanded incredulously, shutters rapidly blinking over its cameras. "What is it with you? How can you just take this shit in like it's as dull as a gods-damned atmospherics report? It's a robot—a fucking *robot*."

"I know. Does it matter?"

"What the fuck is *wrong with you*? Of course it matters."

Priestess shrugged. "Sentience is sentience in my book. Doesn't matter what it's made of."

"Oh don't give me that mystical bullshit."

"It's not mystical. If you respect the fact that there's intelligent life out there other than our own, then you have to respect that it might be built differently than we are."

"That's not what this is." Jonas's expression was heated, its skin had flushed red. "That's not what we're talking about here."

"'There are more things in heaven and Earth than are dreamt of in your—'"

"Oh spare me the literary platitudes, will you?"

The two of them held fast, glaring at each other across the way.

Unit Four dared not make a sound, lest it draw unwanted attention.

After a few tense minutes, Doc returned.

"Good to see no one has been murdered," it said, joyful tone at clear odds with its meaning.

"You sure about that?" Jonas asked bitterly. "Look closely, I think she bit my head off."

"Oh *hur hur*," Priestess returned.

"Like children, the lot of you," Doc sighed. "Everyone is now up to speed on our pilot's claims. So let's see what the tests have to say." It moved to the black, boxy device, flipping open a panel that projected words onto the countertop.

Unit Four could not fully make out the writing from this angle, but it was surprised to note that the characters were not unfamiliar. Apparently, it could read their language as well as speak it.

As Doc looked over the readout, the room went silent. Still.

"What is it, Doc?" Priestess asked. "You're awfully quiet."

It tapped its grasping pads on the countertop, fidgeting, nervous. "Okeke, please be so kind as to escort Jonas to the showers. I need to run this again. And I need to have a chat with the prisoner. Doctor to patient."

"May I perform a set of full body scans on you?" Doc asked, once they were alone. "X-rays and the like?"

What a strange thing for which to seek permissions. "Why are you asking? You're going to do what you please, either way."

"I'm a doctor, it's only right I seek consent when able. The blood sampling was non-negotiable, for the safety of the crew. This is different. You say you're a robot. The others are skeptical. Scans might give us physical evidence that you're telling the truth."

"Do I receive better or worse treatment if I'm lying?" Unit Four spat.

Doc went disturbingly quiet.

"Will the scans hurt?" Unit Four prompted.

"They're noninvasive."

"Well, that is something, at least."

"Is that a yes?"

"I am your prisoner. No consent I give or withhold *means* anything. My mere presence here is coerced. Every answer I give is given under duress."

"Fair enough," Doc conceded. "But do I have it? Your consent?"

"Yes. Fine," Unit Four said.

"Thank you."

The Doc unit pulled a very large machine out of a tall, thin cabinet, and rolled it over to the chair, before draping a strangely shaped, weighted blanket over Unit Four.

"What does this do?"

"It's for protection, while I X-ray different parts of your body. Hold still, please."

"Protection?"

"From excess radiation exposure."

Unit Four let out an involuntary bark of a laugh.

"What was that for?" Doc asked.

"We're in Jovian space. There's not a moment of existence here that doesn't involve *excess radiation exposure*."

Doc hummed thoughtfully in response, but said no more, going about its work for a long while without conversation.

Eventually, Unit Four's fuel tank started to clench. It was empty. Painfully so. There had been no opportunity for feed, lubrication, or hydration this activation period. And, in truth, it hadn't expected to live long enough to partake. The realities of its continued existence were starting to catch up with it.

"What's wrong?" Doc asked, pausing as it glanced up from the black box. "You look uncomfortable."

A rumbling echoed through the AMS unit's torso.

"When did you last eat?" Doc asked.

"Never."

"*Do* you eat?"

"Yes."

"Then how have you never—?"

"I was activated less than twenty hours ago."

"And prior to that you were in . . . stasis?" Doc ventured.

"Prior to that I was still being grown from the vats."

"Y-you—? Ugh, of course you were. I'll, I'll have someone . . ." It made a frustrated sound. "Maybe it would be better if Fuentes looked you over instead of me."

"Why's that?" it prodded, sensing an opening, a way to pull additional tactical information from its captor.

"She's the field scientist, I'm the medical doctor. I can cover the mammals aboard—human, cat. Can even tend to the bees. But a robot . . ."

Oooh, bees.

It wanted to ask after them—were there hives aboard? What kind of bees were they? Bombus? Apis mellifera? Xylocopa?

But instead, its attention caught on a word it did not recognize. One they'd used briefly, prior. Unit Four had a definition for cat, for bee, for mammal. It did not, however, possesses a definition for *human*.

Contextually speaking, these units seemed to use it to refer to themselves.

Which, perhaps, made some sense. After all, Unit Four knew its base bioengineered cells were mammalian. So, if a robot was a mammal and a human was a robot . . .

No. That wasn't quite right.

The way they were using *human* didn't appear to make it synonymous with *robot*.

Unit Four, however, couldn't parse the difference.

"Well, these scans are almost done processing," Doc declared. "Guess we'll know soon enough whether or not I should pass you off to her capable hands. I should warn you, though, she'll prod you even more than I have."

"I'm less averse to the prodding than I am to the confinement," it said.

"Duly noted. And just as soon as we get some additional information here, we can decide just exactly what kind of fuel you process. Ah, here we go, you—"

Doc frowned, the furrow at the top of its CPU chassis deepening. "Melassani bless us," it gasped. "Do you . . . how much do you know about your body?"

"I know everything about my body," Unit Four said confidently. "Don't you?"

"May I share your medical details with the rest of the crew? Your anatomical makeup? You *are* allowed to ask for privacy, I promise you. I won't tell them if you—"

"Why would my schematics be private?"

A brief pause followed, in which Doc seemed at a loss. "Because . . . they're yours?"

"Privacy is for protecting administrative access from those who are not administrators. Such concepts don't apply to something like robot hardware, only application bioware. All soft-robot diagrams are freely available, under the communal commons licensing act."

"Right . . ." Doc said slowly, its CPU housing drooping ever so slightly. "Soft-robot diagrams. Communal commons licensing act . . ."

"Covers basic schematics," Unit Four confirmed with a nod. "You may relate my designs to the others. Though I doubt you'll find them much different from your own. What were you built for? Because I don't think we have the same chassis."

"No. We definitely do not have the same chassis. Or, as I like to call it: a skeleton. Yours, unlike mine, is plated with titanium."

"**Nothing. Not one. There's no sign of so much as the her-pes simplex, let alone anything that could threaten us,**" Doc said to its gathered cohort.

They stood in a semicircle, facing Unit Four, who was still bound to the chair. Doc stood between the invaders and its patient, gesturing vivaciously, first at its equipment, then at Unit Four, then seemingly to indicate the wide expanse of the universe.

Doc and the others had all changed into a thin sheathing, like Jonas, and wore the same kind of masks over their faces.

Now Unit Four could make out the distinct features of the Fuentes and Priestess units. The former had incredibly long hair, which flowed in tumbling waves down the back of its torso—deep brunette and streaked with rainbow coloring on the underside. Its casing held a similar warm-brown undertone to Sir's, but the unit was at least a quarter of a meter shorter than the lead robot.

Priestess had short, black ringlets, which splayed out around its CPU housing like a halo or a crown. But its casing was starkly different from that of the others. Most of its skin was nearly as dark as its curls, and yet patches of it were paler than Jonas. The edges where the two tones met were dappled—unlike the harsh, straight lines where the shade of Unit Four's casing changed.

Four also noticed all five of them wore black cords with dangling stones around their necks. Were the crystals, perhaps, part of the reprogramming process? Alien hard drives filled with bio-malware?

Or perhaps they were even simpler devices. Maybe communications dampeners, to prevent their handlers from making contact? Maybe that's why they needed the comms box instead of simply speaking through their integrated systems.

Four realized it would need to be wary of anything they wanted to put on its person. Such a cord would be so easy to slip over its CPU chassis. Or to tie to its arm, or thrust into its grasping pad.

"It's not just that they aren't sick," Doc continued, still gesticulating wildly as it spoke, drawing Four's attention back into the moment. "They've never *been* sick. There are *no* antibodies for *any* illnesses in their system. They've never been *exposed* before. Which is . . . how shall I put this? Impossible.

"A newborn has more antibodies than our guest; they have what's called passive immunity, granted during their gestation period. If their parent gets sick, then the antibodies can be shared. They"—it pointed emphatically at Unit Four—"have none. *None.* Like they've never been exposed to another person before. Even in utero. You get me?"

"How is that possible?" Sir asked.

"I was not grown in a mammalian uterus," Unit Four piped up, tired of the group talking about it like it wasn't even there. "I was grown in a reconstitution pod, *as were you.*"

"You keep quiet until we ask you a question, android," Jonas snipped.

"Robot," Unit Four corrected.

"Same fucking difference."

Sir laid a grasping pad—which had been wrapped in gauze—on Jonas's arm. It was hard to tell if it was a warning or reassurance.

"Will you stop bickering with my patient and listen to me?" Doc implored. "We pose way more of a threat to them on the illness front than they do to us. Until I can get them immunized, we still have to tread carefully."

"So, what, one of us has the sniffles, coughs on this thing, and it drops dead?" Jonas asked, as though it were considering taking off its mask and doing just that.

"Jonas, don't be an asshole," Sir ordered under its breath.

"No," Doc clarified. "Their immune system is perfectly healthy. And likely they've already been exposed to something, when we stripped them. But I'm going to prepare a series of vaccines and antibody serums, based on the crew's medical histories and pre-launch profiles, just to be safe. We should treat this like we would encountering another scavenger crew from a different Harbor."

"Yeah yeah," Jonas said, waving flippantly. "Get to the point. Is it a robot, like it says, or what?"

They each shuffled forward, and Unit Four sensed a tipping point.

Whatever Doc had learned about its body would dictate the way they saw it, the way they treated it.

Presuming the findings could even be trusted.

Would Doc lie about what it had found?

The AMS unit still couldn't discern exactly what the invaders hoped to gain through their bizarre set of denials and word games. They pretended like the concept of a biological robot was a shock, as though they themselves weren't walking, talking examples of the same technology.

Perhaps . . . perhaps this was how they laid the groundwork for unit reprogramming?

If they sought to reeducate it, the procedure might first require a complete undermining of its systems. A corruption of its processes. If it couldn't trust the accuracy of its own files, if it couldn't rely on its own firewalls, that could leave it vulnerable to false information. It might make a trojan upload easier.

It would have to keep its guard up. They would not shake its understanding of fundamental truisms.

Doc turned to Unit Four. "Just to verify, you are fine with me conveying this information to the crew?"

"Yes," it said firmly. "Continue."

"There are a few basic, nonbiological aspects to their makeup," Doc said. "Metal plating on their bones, a chemical shunt in their arm, and what appears to be a quantum netting over their entire brain. But, hells, even we have hololock implants. Their enhancements might be more advanced, but, anatomically speaking—biologically speaking—they're human. And even human in a way that corroborates their claims that they were built, not born. No consideration seems to have been given to reproductive development. They don't appear to have ever had any internal reproductive organs, and outwardly their sex presentation is a slightly changed adult version of what one would expect to see very early in fetal development. Which, given their musculature, makes sense if they were really lab-grown in some way."

Jonas made a questioning expression. "How's that?"

Doc sighed. "Slip Harbor and its lackluster sex-ed at work, I see. I'm not going to run down every stage of development for you, or give you anything more specific about our pilot here, but I'll try to make this simple:

"Reproductive organs do a lot for a human besides allowing for procreation. They produce important hormones that aid in things like muscle growth, bone strength, red blood cell production, et cetera. Our pilot's scans suggest very low levels of these hormones during early development and indicate their body should only be producing similarly low levels right now. Yet their blood work shows they have *extremely elevated* levels of these hormones—including anabolic–androgenic steroids and estradiol. The dosages they must have received are far above what I myself would prescribe—either as simple replacement or in the case of gender transitioning.

"Given their build, I'd say these hormones were administered in order to promote increased muscle mass and aid metabolism. But this kind of hormonal imbalance can be dangerous over time—can cause high blood pressure, heart and liver problems, and interfere with things like thyroid hormone absorption. A reproductive system would have naturally produced and helped to regulate these hormones in the pilot's body. *Without* the organs, their lifespan would be naturally shorter if they were unable to receive hormone replacements, and yet the *amount* of hormone replacement they've received is itself alarming. Bodies are malleable, but bodies need to be balanced.

"Now, our visitor claims they were, ironically, born yesterday—"

"Today," Unit Four corrected.

"Today," Doc acknowledged—in a patronizing way that suggested Unit Four had missed some secondary meaning. "And that they were built to be a tool. Imagine you're an entity building such a tool. What does a tool need with reproductive organs? Nothing. What does it matter what kind of genitalia a tool has? It doesn't. All that matters is that you can administer the right kind of chemicals in the moment to push their body in the direction you need it to go.

"If my patient here had been born in a Harbor, we would simply have noted them as intersex at birth, like me, and had the usual pronoun celebration at five, their affirmation at twenty, and all gone about our lives none too concerned with how nature had worked its magic."

"But this wasn't nature. This was by design," Fuentes said. "It was engineered."

"Yes, it appears so."

"But how?" Priestess asked.

Doc shook its CPU housing sadly. "The only thing I can think of is . . . I mean, there were plenty of remainders. Survivors. When the aliens came, they must have . . ." It waved illustratively at Unit Four.

"Enslaved the fucking planet?" Jonas provided helpfully.

"It's more complicated than that, though," Doc said. "The aliens aren't simply cloning people. The sphere pilot here has genetic chimerism, but not in any form I've ever seen before—not in a form that can naturally occur. It's as though each set of limbs, each section of their body—each organ, even, though I'm only guessing at this point—has a different genotype. They're an amalgamation of DNA profiles. I found XX, XY, and even XYY chromosomes."

"Like fucking Frankenstein," Fuentes breathed.

"Yes, but they're *not* a monster," Doc said quickly.

Fuentes shook its CPU housing. "*Doctor* Frankenstein was always the monster. Not his creation."

"Not his creation," Doc agreed. It took a deep breath. "Look, I don't like standing here talking about a person like they're some kind of curiosity. They're not. A body is a body, and I need to know its details in order to care for it correctly. But the person is what matters. Normally, I would never think to divulge these kinds of details about a patient, but I'm telling you this because I need to make sure we're all on the same page: this *is* a person. A human being. Regardless of what they claim, or how they came into this world. And we need to treat them accordingly."

"With the additional understanding that they may have suffered abuse or coercion at the hands of their makers, it sounds like," Priestess added.

"I've suffered neither from my handler," Unit Four said defensively. "But both from *you*."

To its delight, Priestess looked acceptably abashed.

Later—after they'd all quite thoroughly examined and reexamined its medical records—they left Unit Four to its own thoughts while they went about tending to the ship and their own bodily needs.

It was the Priestess unit that returned to it first, still wearing a cloth mask stretched over its intake valves. "Are you hungry?" it asked, the question clearly rhetorical, as the rumbling from Unit Four's tank was now nearly constant.

They'd made the cube's walls clear again, likely to facilitate easy surveillance, and Unit Four could see the others all settling into the built-in booth. It seemed it was time for their refueling as well.

Splayed between Priestess's grasping pads was a tray, topped with a variety of leafy green plants, an orange mash, a cup full of clear liquid, and a steaming cube of something unidentifiable. "Doc says our food might make you sick, just so you know. Since you're not from a village, and haven't had food from a Harbor before, and we don't know . . ." it trailed off.

"What is your designation?" Unit Four asked flatly, clenching its grasping pads, making the cords of its arms taut beneath the bindings.

"I want to say, *ship's secondary engineer and chaplain*, but I don't think that's what you mean. My name's Maya. And my pronouns are she/her. But the captain typically likes it formal around here, so rest of the crew usually calls me by my surname, Okeke."

"No." Unit Four shook its CPU housing. "That's not what they've been calling you."

"You're right," it said with an amused expression. "Sometimes they call me Priestess because they think it's cheeky. But you—you should call me Maya."

"All right, Maya." It nodded its affirmation, then added, "None of those call signs you gave me are registered designations, Maya."

"Well, what's *your* designation?"

"AMS Unit Four, Jovian mine D dash NC one nine seven eight six seven seven seven seven."

"That's quite the name. AMS Unit . . . Um, mind if I give you a nickname?"

Unit Four didn't understand "nickname" in this context, and so said nothing.

"AMS . . . so how about we just make it Aims, or, uh, Aimsley? For now?"

"AMS stands for autonomous maintenance system."

"Of course it does. And you are very autonomous indeed. Was that a yes or no on the nickname? No is fine, really."

Discarding their official designations seemed to be how these units related to one another.

It was probably part of the realignment process. Another way they undermined reality.

Unit Four had two options: openly resist, or play along.

Resisting would safeguard its mind. But playing along might earn it opportunities to escape. If it could lull them, get them to lower their own firewalls, it might even be able to reverse whatever damaging reconditioning had been done to them.

It made a choice.

"Yes. You may refer to me as Aimsley."

Aimsley. *Aimsley, Aimsley, Aimsley.* Unit Four would try to think of itself as Aimsley while it attempted to infiltrate their ranks.

"Okay, Aimsley, what kind of food do you typically eat?"

"Compressed proteins from the vat."

"I thought the vat held the stuff you were grown from?"

"Yes. It's where everything bio-based on the platform comes from. AMS units, boats, assembly arms, soft control interfaces, fuel—"

A pallidness settled over Maya's brow, and its—*her*, she'd

asked for new pronouns—cameras went wide. "Great!" she exclaimed, with a slightly manic edge that raised her voice an octave. "Forced cannibalism. Should have seen that coming. Why am I so surprised?"

"I don't know, why are you?"

"I can't tell if you're being cheeky or tragically innocent."

"Neither."

"Tragically innocent it is, then," Maya said wistfully. "Well, we don't have any spare body parts for you to eat, though if you're . . . uh . . . *designed* for—nope, nope, don't like that word. If you aren't *accustomed* to eating anything other than protein—though I don't see how that could be healthy—maybe the herbage here will be a little much. Tofu and sweet potato might be all right."

"Technically, I'm not accustomed to eating anything. I've never processed fuel before."

"Gods, what's that even like?" She sounded genuinely curious.

It didn't know how to answer that. How did one qualify *not* having an experience?

Instead, Unit Four—no, Aimsley—nodded to where the others were eating at the built-in booth, pretending not to watch it. "They look different from us. Their casings are evenly toned. Not like mine. Not like yours."

The Maya unit turned its—no, *her,* Aimsley would need to practice its pronoun usage. It was vaguely aware different Earth handlers had different pronouns, so this shouldn't be too difficult to get used to. Maya turned *her* grasping pads over, ran her digits over the markings. "It's called vitiligo," she explained. "My skin is losing its pigment over time." She looked conflicted—as though it made her a little sad, but she didn't *want* it to make her sad.

"It's . . . aesthetically pleasing," it said, wanting to make her feel better. Genuinely. It didn't understand the urge, but didn't try to fight it. "The patterns. I like them."

She smiled behind her mask, released a little laugh. "Thanks. I do, too."

"It's much more familiar to me," Unit Four admitted.

"Your variation in pigmentation doesn't have to do with a condition, though."

"No," it said frankly. "It has to do with the engineered base-DNA present in my various soft-body portions. So the casing on my legs is different from that of my torso, my arms, my CPU chassis."

"Frankenstein indeed," Maya mumbled.

"What does that word mean? Fuentes keeps saying it."

"Nothing. It's . . . don't worry about it."

"I have little to do but worry," it pointed out. "For example: I'm worried about what you're going to do with me."

"Feed you," she said. "If you'll let me."

"I mean after."

"Well, depends on if we get the main engines back up again or not," she said, breathing deeply, clearly frustrated with the machinery. "Otherwise we're dead in the proverbial water and you just might get that shot at cannibalism."

"What's wrong with the main engines?" it asked, trying not to sound too eager.

"Someone blasted them," she said with a patronizing dip of her CPU.

"Perhaps I can help."

"What?" she said, surprised.

"I *am* a maintenance unit. I could be of assistance."

"Oh, sure, first you shoot them out, then you patch them up—makes sense." She set the tray on its lap. "Forget about the engines. Focus on eating . . . for the first time ever. I can either untie one of your arms and let you feed yourself, or I can have Jonas come in here and feed you."

"Are those my only two choices? Why won't you feed me?"

"Because the captain told me I couldn't bring you utensils, and I happen to like my fingertips. I don't trust them anywhere near your teeth. I'll untie one arm. If you're good, you feed yourself. If you try to attack me, you get fed by Jonas. So behave, all right? I wouldn't count on him not to choke you on purpose."

"I won't attack you while I eat," it promised.

"While you eat," she repeated.

"While I eat," it echoed with a nod, making it clear they both understood the caveats in play.

She moved to the rope around its upper right arm, swiftly untangling the knot with deft fingers. Aimsley briefly wondered if she'd been the one to tie the ropes in the first place. As she leaned down, reaching for the knots at its elbow, her tight ringlets fell over her cameras. A gentle, pleasant scent wafted away from her hair.

The odor was slightly sweet, but not cloying, and clearly unnatural.

The crystal pendant Four had noted earlier now swayed in front of its receptors, swinging from her neck, dangling loosely on its cord. Four subconsciously pressed itself against the seat, putting as much space between itself and the little shard as possible.

Maya finished at its wrist, jumping back the moment it had the full use of its arm. "We good?" she asked.

"Fine," it conceded, easing again, dipping the tips of its grasping pad into the orange mush. It scooped a dollop of it into its fuel port, immediately reaching for a second, then paused. "It . . . tastes . . ." it said, openly rolling the slop around on its tongue.

"Tastes . . . good? Bad?"

"Just . . . tastes. Taste is weird."

She blinked at it in wonder. "You really aren't lying about where you come from, are you?"

"No. So why are *you*?"

She shuffled on her feet, swaying slightly from side to side, clearly conflicted. She glanced over her shoulder at the booth. No one was looking directly into the cube. "We haven't exactly come to a consensus on how to talk to you about this. And Jonas, well, he still wants to off you."

The feeling is mutual, Aimsley groused, glaring at where Jonas sat shoveling fuel into its port.

"I think . . . I think you should just eat," she said. "We'll tackle the world after you've had your first bowel movement, how about that? If you think *tasting* is an adventure, oh boy . . ."

She stayed with it while it finished refueling, chattering. She named each member of her detail, gave them pronouns. Sir was the captain—and his name wasn't "Sir," it was Union Buyer. He was with, quote, "known vagabond" Hetter Jonas. Doc preferred to be called Doc, but their designation was Tank Matsui. And Rebecca Fuentes, she was the ship's primary engineer and trained physicist.

"What about you? What are your pronouns?" she asked.

"It," it said.

She cringed. "Um . . ."

"What?"

"Where we come from, it's rude to call a person 'it.' We find it dehumani—oh." She looked crestfallen as a sudden realization struck her. "We find it dehumanizing," she finished quietly. "Doc is intersex like you—are you sure you wouldn't prefer something like they/them? Not that all intersex people are nonbinary or anything, but—?"

"You asked, didn't you?" it said. "Why ask if you won't accept my answer?"

She took a deep breath, considering. "No, you're right. You're right. I'll talk to the crew. We'll work it out. Get over ourselves about it, I guess. If this is really what you prefer—"

"It is."

"All right."

Aimsley nodded along as Maya continued to speak, microphones perked for any useful information. Good to its word, it made no attempts to escape or attack.

But, while it ate, it subtly flexed and unflexed its right arm, drawing an excess of hot, oxygenated fluids into its muscles. And, when she replaced its bindings, it kept those muscles flexed. Taut, thick, firm.

If it was lucky, the ropes would sit looser later, when it relaxed.

She didn't seem to notice.

Afterward Maya took the tray, winked one camera at it, and left it alone again. She returned to the booth and began to fill the tray for herself.

Aimsley watched them as they took in fuel, chatted. They passed portions of various substances between them, many similar to what Priestess—Maya—had offered it, and many different. The group was cheery, and often laughed.

Aimsley would have thought they'd be grim—mood sour, and dialogue dire and direct. After all, their ship wasn't fully functional, their assault on the array had been interrupted and should perhaps be considered a failure. They'd been injured, their outer shells damaged.

Maybe the retention of a prisoner was cause for celebration, but this didn't appear to be a gloating sort of gaiety.

It was . . . easy. Familiar.

Like this was how they behaved between every sleep cycle. As though this day had been no more of a hardship than all of the days that had come before it.

They'd turned off the communications box, so Unit Four could not make out any of the conversation, but they seemed, at the moment, entirely unconcerned with its presence.

Except for Maya. Her gaze strayed to Unit Four—*Aimsley*—sometimes flickering away just as quickly, sometimes holding for long moments.

Aimsley found itself trying to maintain that gaze, to keep her cameras on it.

It . . . it *liked* it, when she looked at it. Her stare felt different from the others. Less harsh. It was nice to encounter something *gentle* for the first time. Even if that gentleness might be a ploy.

Perhaps Aimsley should have been distressed by the way it was drawn to her, uncomfortable with the calm that had come over it while she spoke and it ate. Instead, it interpreted the feelings as an indication its empathy programming—the very thing that bound it to other robots—was still fully functional.

CHAPTER TEN

When it was aroused from its sleeping mode once more, all was dark, save a few faint points of light on various apparatuses both inside and outside the cube.

The cube itself still had clear walls, and outside, in the built-in seating area, someone sat with their CPU housing bent low, touching the tabletop.

Aimsley had clearly been drugged once again. Perhaps the sedatives had been in the fuel. Judging by the stiffness in its joints and the aching clench of its muscles, it had been still and inoperable for an excruciatingly long period of time.

Strangely, there was a spot of heaviness and warmth low on its torso. And an odd, consistent *thrumming*.

At first, it couldn't reason out what the strange object sitting on top of it *was*. But as its cameras grew accustomed to the dim lighting, it made out a dark shape, and tufts of fur.

Aimsley squirmed slightly, and the animal perked up.

Immediately, the robot stilled, worried it would scare the cat away.

The creature's tail twitched.

A sudden sense of fondness—almost akin to the fondness

it had for its sister units—washed over Aimsley. It longed, not just to feel the animal's warmth and weight, but to run the flats of its grasping pads over its fur as well.

The scant files it had on cats suggested they were *soft*.

Other than its own casing and the boat's, it hadn't touched much that was soft.

A soothing sensory experience would be a novelty.

Aimsley glanced at the sleeping invader once again, trying to discern who it was. Not Jonas, that was for sure—if for no other reason than the others wouldn't leave him in charge of supervising their captive.

Sir—*Buyer*—perhaps.

An abrupt jolt of fear shot up Aimsley's back as it remembered the corded crystals. Quickly, it tried to discern whether or not one had been attached to it in any way. A cursory examination of its person indicated it was crystal-free. Relief replaced the sudden tension. It relaxed back into the chair—for a moment.

Aimsley then tested its bindings, trying to see if its flexing trick from earlier had worked—if the straps over its right arm were loose.

Yes, there was some give, some room to shift.

Which meant nothing if it couldn't get its grasping pads free.

It yanked firmly on its arm, tugging the rope against its wrist. It compressed its digits together, folding its grasping pad as tightly as it was able. But it could not slip free.

Not on the first try, anyway.

It yanked again, and again, twisting, squeezing, trying to will its limb smaller, thinner. Eventually, the abrasiveness of the rope rubbed the base of its grasping pad near-raw.

But Aimsley was sure it could manage, sure it could get the pad free. It just had to be willing to sustain an injury in the process.

In preparation, Aimsley squirmed, taking long, deep gulps of air.

I can do this, I can do this, I can do this, it chanted.

It wiggled its digits on both grasping pads, tightened its core, and jerked.

Surprisingly, the maneuver worked on the first try.

Smothering a shout, it wrenched its grasping pad through the tight circle of the rope. The base of its apposable digit had been forced upwards, popping out of place just as surely as Jonas's shoulder had popped free.

The cat wriggled and complained in its lap. It didn't seem to care at all that Aimsley had just sustained a self-imposed injury. Only that the body it was using as a bed was failing to hold still.

Aimsley tried not to take offense.

Carefully, it leaned to its left and contorted its torso, working out of the bindings on its right.

Completely freeing itself was a long, arduous process. Each knot on its left had to be untied with minimal help from its apposable digit, and every time it pressed too hard on that side of its right grasping pad, white-hot pain radiated up the inside of its limb. Tremors racked its arm, and the rope repeatedly slipped from its pinching hold.

By the time it reached the last knot to release its completely functional left grasping pad, Aimsley was perspiring down its back, across its CPU housing, and in the creases of all four limbs. Every bit of its right arm throbbed, and once again it wished for morphine.

But from there it made quick work of the rest of the rope.

The cat made a high-pitched protest as Aimsley leaned over to reach for it. Gently, the AMS unit picked up the creature, setting it lightly on the floor.

It *was* soft. Delightfully soft.

It occurred to Aimsley that the cat had to have been left in the cube on purpose. Either as a comfort or as an extra guardian. Of course, the animal didn't seem to be of much use in the latter role, unless cats had some kind of hidden defensive qualities it wasn't aware of.

The creature bowed its back, stretched, revealing its tiny claws.

Those hardly seemed difficult to contend with.

Once free, Aimsley popped its digit back into place—biting down on a shout—before throwing the sheet that covered it aside and leaping from the chair. Quickly, it armed itself. It had paid close attention to where Doc stored the most promising supplies, and located a small blade—a scalpel—in no time.

Light on its feet, it made its way to the medbay airlock, keeping the sleeping invader unit in its peripheral at all times.

This would be easy. It would decommission this one first, then lay in wait for the next guard to come. Presuming they had it on a single-robot rotating watch, Aimsley could cut them down one by one.

No need to draw this out, then. To waste time lulling them, convincing them it was on their side. No need to think of itself as a new being with a new name.

Yes, it could still be Unit Four.

These malfunctioning robots had to be returned to their

vats. It was the right thing to do—for them, for their brethren, for their home stations or platforms.

For Earth.

The Earth that they were betraying, unwittingly or not.

But first, it had to contend with the blank keypad.

It had watched the invader units carefully each time they'd used it, but the way they'd waved their digits seemed different every time. It was sure they'd been interacting with a holographic projection, invisible from the chair. But perhaps it was invisible to cameras altogether? Perhaps it was projected directly into their CPUs?

Doc had said something about hololock implants.

Slowly, it bobbed back and forth in front of the keypad, hoping to detect an image, some faint mirage. But there was nothing.

Perhaps they'd shut it down? Was it currently inoperable?

Unit Four realized there was a simple way to find out.

The AMS unit had been assaulted by all of the wireless interfaces aboard the ship the instant it had alighted on its decking. There was a high probability the keypad wasn't purely reliant on hardwiring.

All it had to do, then, was turn its discoverability back on, to reach out, to feel for the keypad.

Surely that would open it up to malicious bioware, though. To whatever had turned these robots into puppets for the invaders.

But there wasn't much of a choice, really. It couldn't stay locked away, waiting. It had to act—had to figure out how to get back to the platform and report on what it had found.

Preparing for an onslaught of signals, it opened itself up with the same sort of violent abruptness as its hard-body.

Ping. Ping. Ping—pingpingping.

It sifted through all of the instant requests for access, looking for the keypad's digital interface. The robot located the connection with ease. Carefully, it *pushed*.

The keypad let it slide right in.

Strange. Unit Four had expected more obstacles. Some pushback. But the keypad had no extra safeguards.

Unit Four felt its way through the code, searching for the release. Seemed the holographic projection consistently required the same password, but the keys constantly shifted, so that the word could not be spelled with the same pattern every time. The password itself was not complicated (though Unit Four found it curious, and wondered what was meant by *Violent Delight*), and the permissions were easily hackable.

Perhaps the lock was only meant to guard against cognitive corruption, against impaired reasoning skills. Meant to keep a compromised crewmember from exiting the medbay and injuring themself, and nothing more.

When the anticipated click resounded through the door, Unit Four cut itself off from the digital intrusions once again.

The inner airlock door slid aside with a quiet hiss, as did the outer. The air smelled different here—thick with the scent of fuel, similar to what Maya had given it.

Swiftly, Unit Four scanned the area for cameras. It figured the round, viscous whites would stand out starkly against the dark colors of the interior, but it noted no bright globes, no hazel-colored irises flexing around deep-black pupils.

Stranger still. Why wouldn't the invaders have cameras? There were plenty of extra cameras on the platform. How else were the AMS units to ensure the functionality of all systems when—?

Oh.

It caught itself.

It had to remember, things aboard the invader's ship were not flesh. They were not soft and easily recyclable. They were rigid and cold and lifeless.

A camera would not look like a camera.

Which meant if it wanted to identify them, it would have to access the feed once more.

It was going to need to remain discoverable.

Vulnerable.

It ran a quick security scan, to make sure the ship hadn't already uploaded anything into its system without its consent.

Zero threats detected. No new programming files. Luckily, everything appeared clean.

Well then, once again.

It opened, welcoming the pings this time, sifting through them like grains of sand, looking . . . looking . . .

Ah.

There.

It looked up, into a darkened corner.

It saw itself seeing itself.

There were three other cameras on this deck. None in the medbay, though one could easily be made to point inside the cube.

Swiftly, it dropped itself through the ship, finding as many visual inputs as it could.

Three main decks, with one large cargo hold—in which the harvested parts from the microwave array were already sliced and sorted into large, yet manageable, pieces (clearly the invaders had not been idle while Unit Four slept). Numerous other storage spaces, as well as rooms with obvious relevancy to robot maintenance, dotted the decks below the bridge.

The cameras had an interesting number of optic-oversights, though. It could not find any waste centers, though there had to be at least one. Also, it could not pinpoint the rest of the crew. There were large swaths of the craft—entire rooms—with no cameras.

What kind of hidden threats lurked in these darkened corners? Unit Four had yet to see hard evidence of an alien aboard. The invaders seemed to be puppeteering the robots—directly or indirectly—from a distance, just as its handler guided it from Earth. But appearances could be deceiving. It was entirely possible some foreign sentience was hidden away in the bowels of the ship.

Access to the cameras' livestream was easy to achieve, at least—and there was no indication anyone was monitoring the stream in real-time—but disrupting the feeds proved a greater challenge. No matter—it would worry about that later, if something went wrong.

After all, it didn't plan on leaving any witnesses to examine the playback.

Recentering itself, pulling its awareness back to its own cameras, it scanned the deck.

The AMS unit noted for the first time that there were no windows on this level. Nothing that looked out into space. Perhaps there were no portholes in the entire wedge. Likely the view had been sacrificed for their full plated armor and extra radiation shielding.

What it suspected was the cockpit was now closed off—a thick door barred Unit Four's path.

One lone screen was active in the monitor array that sat against the bulkhead. Slowly, the unit approached the display, where a small set of illuminated commands gently pulsed. If this terminal's security measures were anything like the cameras or the keypad, it shouldn't prove difficult to utilize. The robot decided to investigate once it had completed its first decommissioning.

It turned its attention fully on the invader.

The decking made no creaks or groans to give away its approach, and the sleeping unit did not stir. They were little more than a hunched shape in the dark, and only the gentle intake and exhalation of air marked them as separate from their surroundings.

As it neared, Unit Four started to discern specifics. The curl of their hair, the narrowness of their shoulders.

It was Maya.

Good.

That was good.

Best to get the soft one out of the way first—best to spare her the horror of being online when it happened, or finding the others before her own end.

She'd given Unit Four a name, after all. Tried to be welcoming.

No. She'd tried to turn it, really.

Unit Four crept closer, blade outstretched, the flat of it barely catching the shine of a bright-green indicator light.

Maya didn't move. Her breathing did not change.

Unit Four would cut her just beneath her CPU chassis. It would sever the same lines it had severed to quickly decommission Unit Two. Her fluids would rush out, away. Would stain the floor, stain the thin fabrics of her lightweight outer shell.

The pale, white tunic would blossom with potent red dye.

The AMS unit paused its approach. An echo of the pain it had felt when it had been forced to decommission Unit Two swept over it, through it.

But the sensation lasted for only a moment.

That was different. Unit Two had been its sister, part of the group, the whole, to which Unit Four's empathy programming had forced it to cleave.

Maya . . . it shouldn't feel anything for her.

She was the enemy.

An attacker, a kidnapper, a betrayer, an *invader*.

It raised the scalpel, angling the blade for the perfect, clean slash.

But some strange instinct told it to wait. To reconsider.

Once it started the decommissioning, it wouldn't be able to stop. Once a member of the group was gone, the others would kill it unless it killed them first, for certain.

What if it needed them for something? It didn't even know if it was capable of piloting the ship. It didn't know what else lay aboard—in the cameras' optic-oversights. Doc had mentioned bees.

It had no way of knowing if it could handle an alien, should it encounter one.

There were still too many unknown factors in play. If it wanted to get out of this alive, wanted to bring back the wedge for its handler, then it needed to be certain of its next steps.

Decommissioning the others wouldn't put an automatic end to its hardships, or guarantee the safety of the mine and the platform.

It looked back at the softly pulsing glow on the screen.

At the very least, it should gather more data before beginning its decommissioning spree.

Keeping its steps featherlight, it approached the screen bank.

The lighted commands were, thankfully, in the same written language as the projections that emanated from Doc's black box. The terminal itself did not require a passcode, but most commands off the main menu were another matter. Unit Four swiped at one set of options, then another, at first simply exploring its options.

Simultaneously, it reached out wirelessly, but found it could not locate any signals related to the primary dash. The ship's main controls were entirely hardwired.

In either case it could not access steering, or engines, or environmentals, or any other critical systems. And there was no clear way to open the cockpit. It *could* access status reports, however.

Atmospherics were stable. Power generation was stable. Seemed at least one propulsion system—the main engines?—had been badly damaged during the fight. Multiple alerts flashed across the screen. Fuel lines for that system were full, but the tanks feeding into their maneuvering jets were practically empty. Likely the invaders had exhausted their supply restabilizing their tangled ships after the collision.

Moving on, it switched to probing noncritical systems, flicking through several more layers of menus and commands before a waveform popped up on the screen.

An open communications channel.

What a fortunate find!

If it could get a message out, maybe someone would

intercept it, reroute it back to its platform, or Earth—maybe the message would even reach its handler.

It switched from the language the invaders used to the hissing, clicking articulations of its handler's primary language. These syllables were far more comfortable in its speakers. Familiar. Right.

"This is AMS Unit Four, Jovian mine D dash NC one nine seven eight six seven seven seven seven," it said quietly. "My boat crashed. I am currently aboard the invader's ship and have found a detail of rogue robots. I am attempting to commandeer the vessel by . . ." It looked over its shoulder at Maya, still peacefully unconscious. "By gaining their trust in order to reprogram them. I have been unable to thus far ascertain the functionality of the invader's ship—how to pilot it, if it even can be piloted. The boat was destroyed, and the alien craft has been damaged. I don't know if I'll be able to relay another message. My last know coordinates were . . ."

It sent as much information as it could, keeping the channel open for as long as it dared in the hopes that someone—an Earth someone, a friendly someone—might be listening.

When Maya groaned, twisting in her seat, Unit Four decided it had risked enough. It swiped at the screen, taking itself back through the menus until it reached the original, softly pulsating, set of words.

Then it looked to the cameras, dug deeper into the observational system. It just needed to interrupt recording and erase a small portion of playback, to make sure there was no obvious record of its escape.

It took some effort, but it was able to locate the corresponding recordings and quietly delete the last hour.

Hopefully this brief escape had accomplished something.

Hopefully, the others would not notice what it had done.

If nothing else, it now had access to the shipwide network of cameras.

But, for safety, it let them go. For the time being. Especially since the potential for malware still outweighed the usefulness of an open network.

Carefully, keeping the blade pointed down and away, it tiptoed back to the cube, shifted through the airlock, rid itself of the weapon, and slipped back into the chair with the sheet once more in place.

With its arm still aching, it made loose knots for itself, sliding back into the ropes as best it could, though it would be obvious the ties had shifted. It kept its injured grasping pad free of the bindings—better to stage the scene.

Satisfied it had done its duty, with its bindings more or less resecured, it shuttered its cameras. The cat climbed up into its lap once more, and AMS Unit Four—no, *Aimsley*, it reminded itself firmly, since it was here for the duration—did not shoo the creature away.

PART THREE

SURVIVOR

CHAPTER ELEVEN

Aimsley couldn't be certain where its rescue might lay on the platform's priority list. The comms tower would be first—presuming the mine was still transmitting at least ninety-five percent of its energy output. Having an established communications line with Earth was vital. A lost robot was sure to come after both of those, perhaps even after the damaged arm that led to the boat hangar. However, the infiltration and capture of an invader's ship was unprecedented. Its message—if received—should generate excitement, anticipation.

A boat or a probe would surely be allotted to its recovery as soon as possible.

As long as Aimsley could imbed itself and keep the invasive programming from conquering its mind, the probability of its survival could only increase from here.

Presuming, of course, its message was received.

Approximately sixteen hours had passed since the tower had been hit. With the readiness of materials available for its repair, and presuming the tower had been severed and not outright destroyed, then it was possible the other AMS units could have it up and working again soon. If not already.

And yet, it had felt no linkage in its CPU. No niggling in its microphones, no light zing of static in the back of its fuel port, which it had come to associate with the presence of an established comms channel only now that those sensations had faded.

Since it couldn't rely on its presumptions, what it needed, now, was a plan. It needed to be ready when its fellows came for it.

Aimsley realized there was a high probability Doc would be the first unit to interact with it again after the power-down cycle. Slightly less probable was Maya. But both, Aimsley felt, could be led to think the best of it. They maintained their guard but did not display open hostility like the others.

It could use that.

Sure enough, as soon as the lights came up—hours after Aimsley's escape—it was Doc who bustled back through the airlock.

And Aimsley was prepared.

It struggled against its bonds, pulling fiercely, thrashing about. It made a show of flapping its injured grasping pad, as though it had only just been able to get it free.

The cat, who had still been napping on Aimsley's lap, launched away—digging its pins into the AMS unit's flesh as it sprang. Aimsley jerked, hissing as the little razors left long, thin slices in its leg.

That it had not anticipated.

Perhaps it had underestimated the creature's defense mechanisms.

The animal growled as it avoided Doc's footfalls, and the invader unit cringed behind their mask.

"Whoa, whoa," Doc chided, swiftly moving to Aimsley's side, stepping awkwardly to avoid the cat. "Don't— Look, you hurt yourself." Delicately, they lifted Aimsley's wrist, cameras flickering from the bruised flesh to the robot's face and back again. "Your hand. It's inflamed. This contusion . . ." They prodded gently at the purpling portions, and Aimsley kept its expression as neutral as it was able. "Well, at least the joint isn't dislocated, but it's definitely sprained. Your thumb could still pop out. Everything feels loose." They tutted. "This can't have been worth it. You shouldn't have tried to get free."

"Wouldn't you?"

Their gaze flicked to its cameras. "Depends."

"You find yourself on an enemy ship, bound, and *it depends*?"

"Doesn't sound like your life before you met us was a cakewalk. Can't have been easy."

"My life before I met you was *nonexistent*. You are the reason my growth was rushed. You are the reason my activation was premature. You are the reason—"

It cut itself off, looking away, seething.

You are the reason my functionality has degraded from the moment of my awakening.

"I suppose you're right. We can't expect you not to try to escape, and you can't expect us not to try to prevent it."

Aimsley nodded. At least this unit was reasonable. It eased back into the thick cushion of the chair. "Just make it quick, if you don't mind."

"Make what quick? The splint? Because you'll probably need a splint."

"No, my punishment. For attempting to escape."

Doc's cameras flickered to the airlock, then the floor.

"You didn't go anywhere. So how about we keep your little misdeed just between you and me? Then there doesn't have to be a punishment."

Aimsley narrowed its gaze. "Why would you do that?" it asked suspiciously.

When a robot failed to behave in the appropriate manner—if something went wrong and it, say, attacked a sister unit—then it was either corrected or decommissioned.

It knew these units didn't want to decommission it if they could turn it. But why *no* corrective action?

This felt like a trap.

Its cameras flickered to Doc's neckline, pointedly glaring at the crystal pendant.

"I'm not the punitive type," Doc said. "Buyer, Jonas—they might well be up for a bit of payback for what you did to the ship, and Jonas for sure is looking for any excuse to rough you up. But I've never been one to seek a pound of flesh, especially when I can't imagine it will have an effect on your behavior. Now, a bit of mercy, on the other hand, might. And, I think what you did to your hand there is probably punishment enough."

"Grasping pad," Aimsley corrected.

"Hand," Doc countered, then traced down its digits. "And these are your fingers."

Aimsley narrowed its gaze. Perhaps this was like the names and the pronouns. Small reroutings. Minor replacements. New words to help prime its system to integrate foreign algorithms with ease.

It considered resisting the new vocabulary.

But, having decided during the sleep cycle that its primary mission was now to gain their trust while it figured out how to undermine their security and take over the ship, it couldn't do that by acting stubborn and contrarian.

Aimsley would have to give a little to get a little.

"Fingers," it agreed.

Doc smiled warmly behind their mask. "Good. Maybe we can work on a few more while I take care of your hand and look over your antibody count. Bend this for me? I want to check your range of motion."

They rattled off a set of words as they worked, pointing at themself when they could, to illustrate, and Aimsley dutifully parroted the vocab back.

Lips, teeth, tongue. Eyes, nose, ears.

All things it associated with animals, not robots.

Animals. These units thought of themselves as animals. Wanted *it* to think of itself as an animal, too.

Aimsley found the concept unnerving. And repulsive.

"This is your head, and you have a brain, not a CPU."

"Head, brain . . ."

"Skull."

"Skull."

"Very good. Here, let me get you . . ." Doc trailed off, turned to shuffle through more drawers, pulling out more vials and another syringe.

"No," Aimsley said quickly. "I don't want to be taken off-line again."

"I'm just going to take some blood samples to make sure you're responding well to the serums and vaccines I gave you. And this"—they held up a full vial—"is just for the pain," Doc assured it.

They took the blood samples quickly, ferrying them over to the black box again.

"Priestess said she gave you a name. Aimsley, was it?"

"Yes."

"Do you mind if I call you that?"

It shrugged. "If you want."

"And you prefer to be referred to as 'it'?"

"Yes. But Maya seemed hesitant."

Doc nodded. "She does her best, but there will always be things people inside different communities understand better than people outside. I've known a few individuals who identified as 'it.' They found it empowering. Reclaiming. *It* is rarer, for certain, don't get me wrong, but it's not unheard of. You are not alone."

"It" is AMS unit standard, Aimsley wanted to say, but thought better of it. Instead, it wanted to know more about this other concept, of robot "communities." Was Doc suggesting there were more corrupted units in the solar system?

"You and I are . . . part of one of these communities? The same community? Because we're . . . intersex?" it said, trying the word out. "Which means you and I have a different design schema than the others?"

"That's one way to put it, I suppose."

"How many communities are there?"

Doc looked at it warmly, cameras shining bright, as though Aimsley had said something both endearing and amusing. "How many laughs can a thimble hold?"

Aimsley shook its head. "What?"

"It's not exactly something that's quantifiable. People form all kinds of communities around all kinds of things. Now, back to the matter at hand—" Doc flicked the syringe barrel, brought the needle to the AMS unit's shunt. "There we are. Now I'm going to put your thumb in a splint, all right? It will restrict the movement of the joint a little while it heals, but you will be able to make a fist if you need to."

"I'm familiar with the concept."

Doc nodded to themself. "Good. Never know, what with your whole *born yesterday and put in a ship to die* deal."

"That's not how every activation ends. Sometimes we have time to heal."

Doc's shoulders slumped, and they shook their head. An expression between sadness and disgust pinched their face. "Sometimes we have time to heal," they echoed under their breath.

Movement outside the cube caught Aimsley's attention. Figures shuffling, going about their work.

Maya entered a few moments later, looking a bit harried, but well rested.

It appeared her ill-advised sleeping period had done her some good.

A strange knot coiled inside Aimsley's abdomen, squeezing its pumps—no, organs—as it remembered the cold elegance of the scalpel in its hand. Remembered the way her breath had gently huffed out, shaking one of her curls. It remembered the tipping point—how it had been determined to kill her one minute, and determined to spare her the next.

Aimsley's insides felt constricted, and yet, simultaneously, something within it swelled.

These sensations—emotions—were conflicting.

On one end of the spectrum, it felt pride. It knew where several of the wedge's weaknesses lay already. Knew it had held the power to end the crew and had chosen a different, more productive path.

On the other, it felt disquieted.

It had *hated* decommissioning Unit Two, no matter if it had been a mercy.

It could not imagine it would still feel pride with Maya's fluids leaving her body. With her blood coating its skin. It was sure her end would not feel any better, any righter, than its sister unit's had.

Maya—here, now, looking so at ease—had no idea how close she'd come to death.

And Aimsley intended to keep it that way.

"Buyer told me to come get Aimsley," she told Doc. "It's going to help us in the cargo hold."

"We're bringing it in, then?"

"Yes. We'll slice it up quick. Should be frozen solid by now—as long as we didn't underestimate the radiation impact."

"What are we going to do with the organic bits?"

"Not sure yet, that's part of why we need—" she thumbed at Aimsley.

"Give me a few minutes to apply this splint, then—"

She glanced at Aimsley for the first time, noted its hand. "Oh! What happened?"

"Little accident," Doc said, sharing a knowing look with Aimsley.

Clearly this conspiratorial exchange was supposed to set it at ease, but Aimsley found the implied comradery and familiarity off-putting. Still, it played right into the AMS unit's goals, so it agreed, "Little accident." It was becoming rather comfortable with mimicking whatever Doc said.

Maya's gaze shifted back and forth between the two of them, clearly concerned. "Did Jonas—?"

"No, no," Doc said quickly. "Nothing like that."

"Good. But, damn. First Jonas's arm, then Buyer's and

Fuentes's palms. Now Aimsley, too? Guess you've had a lot of hand jobs lately, eh Doc?"

Doc's expression soured. They gave Maya an overemphasized glare.

"Oh, come on," she said with a wink. "It's a good joke."

They pointed the splint at her. "It's a very *bad* joke, and I resent the slight to my sense of humor." As Doc approached with the splint, the lights across the entire bridge shifted to crimson. A light, yawing noise reverberated across the deck. Both invader units stiffened, looking up, then at each other.

Aimsley knew a crisis alert when it saw one.

"The proximity alarm," Doc whispered.

Suddenly, Buyer's voice crackled through the comms, tight and pointed. "I need everyone to brace for possible impact. Crash seats, emergency stations."

Maya's eyes widened. She rushed to the comms box, jabbing a button like she meant to punch through the device. "Captain?"

"There's debris headed our way," he said, clearly resigned. "Early detection's working fine, would have had plenty of time to dodge, except . . ."

Except the main engines are off-line and the maneuvering jets are all but exhausted, Aimsley silently finished for him.

The AMS unit wondered what the danger could be. Parts off the microwave array? Pieces of the platform's arm-D? The waver in Buyer's tone suggested it was something large—something of *consequence*.

"Fuentes is in the engine room, she's—"

"I'm trying, Captain!" came Fuentes's harried voice. "But I don't . . . The computer is still down, and without a way to bypass it . . . Beyond that, it's a toss-up between an impact and a possible explosion, and I *can't*—"

"I know—"

"How long 'til it hits us?" Maya asked.

"Five minutes."

She swore, jumping away from the comms box—jumping at Aimsley. "Five minutes. We've got five minutes to get into crash seats. Help me!"

Doc tossed the splint aside, and they both went to work on Aimsley's bindings, hands shaking as they undid the ties.

Though their fingers were deft, their digits still slipped. Maya cursed under her breath, wiping a thin sheen of perspiration from her forehead.

Aimsley held as still as it could, waiting. This was not the time to spring, to attack, but it still felt restless, the need for action. As soon as its arms were free, it thrust itself away from the chairback and did its best to help untie its legs.

The seconds ticked by.

"Come on, come on," Maya chanted, clearly frustrated with the last few knots.

The wedge gave a furious jolt, making both invader units sway on their feet.

Aimsley's heart leapt into its throat. Doc and Maya froze.

"What was that?" it asked.

Maya slid the last of the ropes out from under its thighs, then stumbled back to the comms box as Doc helped it to its feet.

"Captain—?"

"Reorienting," he explained, anticipating her question. "Using the last of the maneuvering jets to make sure this crap hits us at the best angle."

"*The best angle?*" she repeated incredulously.

Doc swiped up the splint, pulled a thin mask like they

wore from a drawer, then took Aimsley by the arm. "Put this on."

Aimsley took the slip of fabric and looped it over its microphones—ears—as Doc wrapped it more firmly in the sheet. It let itself be dragged through the medbay airlock and out onto the bridge. Maya followed.

Buyer stood in the recessed cockpit, bent over his readouts. "Okeke," he called, not looking up. "Need you down with Fuentes, ASAP."

"Roger. Where's Jonas?" Maya asked.

"On his way up." He turned, braced himself in the cockpit's doorway. "Get to the lift. I need you and Fuentes to—" He pulled up short. "What the fuck is *it* doing out here?"

"You said *everyone to crash seats*—"

Doc continued to pull on Aimsley, to guide it over to the booth where it had observed them having their meal—where Maya had dozed while it explored. It tried to get a better look into the cockpit, but Doc was single-minded in their direction.

They opened a small panel on the wall near the booth, revealing a blank block—another holopad. After a few hastily swiped commands, the table sank away into the floor, and the seats of the booth transformed. New padding and belts sprang out from concealed compartments.

"It would have been fine in the fucking chair!" the captain yelled.

"Ignore him," Doc said, manhandling Aimsley into a seat.

Maya gestured in its direction, "We can't just—"

"Doesn't—doesn't matter," the captain dismissed, waving his arm through the air, frantically gesturing for her to go to the lift. "Get going!"

Just then, the lift doors opened, and Jonas rushed out. "Where do you want me?" he asked, eyes locked on Buyer, ignoring everything else.

"Radar intercept—need you to sight for me," the captain said.

"What are you going to do?"

"Turn the cannons on the debris. Might give us half a chance."

He leapt into action, hurrying to Buyer as the captain moved aside for him. "Let's do this."

Doc stepped into Aimsley's line of sight, and it lost Maya as she slipped onto the lift. They rushed to strap it down in an entirely new set of bindings—restraints that were reminiscent of the harness in the boat. Meant to protect rather than detain.

Belts laced over its chest, its legs. A curved bit of padding protruded out from the booth's backing to cradle its CPU housing—its *head*—and a bar extended out from below for it to brace its feet against.

Once it was secure, Doc slipped into a matching seat on its right side.

"You don't have a job?" Aimsley asked. "A function during crisis?"

"My function is typically to see to the aftermath of crisis," Doc said once they'd buckled in, taking hold of Aimsley's wrist. "And I have a job to do right here." They held up the splint. "I'd like to get this on you before—"

"Is everybody set?" Buyer called—over the comms, but loud enough for Aimsley to hear at the booth.

"Ready, Captain!" Doc called, working open the fastenings on the splint, hurrying to stabilize Aimsley's hand before their world was thrown off kilter.

Similar affirmations boiled up from the engine room.

"*Jonas?*" Buyer asked, tone frenetic.

"I see it, I see it—" he said evenly, determination weighing on his voice.

The agitation in their lilts agitated Aimsley in turn. It was made to *act* during an emergency, not sit uselessly, idly by.

It should be doing *something*.

Even if that something amounted to sabotage and subterfuge.

"Ten degrees to port," Jonas said. "Almost in range."

Buyer made a growling sound that ramped up, punctuated at the end with a feral *shout*.

"Hit!" Jonas yelled a moment later. "More pieces incoming. We just have to keep carving."

"They can do it," Doc said evenly. "Don't worry."

Aimsley fidgeted in its seat, happy to have its hand back once Doc was finished, so that it could hold on to the straps at its chest. It wanted to tear them loose, to spring free. If nothing else, it *needed* to see what was happening—to stare at a monitor and watch the rubble fly at them in real-time.

A few more rapid shouts from Buyer indicated more hits.

"Just a few—watch it!" Jonas cried.

"I got it! I see it!"

The minutes rushed by. The warnings still flashed.

Buyer and Jonas continued to blast their way through the chunks of wreckage, scattering it to the solar winds.

And then the sound of the alert changed. Pitched higher.

Aimsley's lungs hitched, its jaw clenched.

"Shit!" Buyer cried. "Everybody brace! Brace for impact!"

Doc leaned firmly back into the seat, crossing their arms over their chest.

Pulse pounding, Aimsley did the same.

Whatever it was—parts of the platform, array, or their own ships—hit moments later.

Everything *shook*. The vibrations made Aimsley's teeth chatter and its head swim as its entire body lurched to the left. A deep rumble roared through the wedge. Like the sounds of thunder in Aimsley's databanks.

The reverberations went on, and on.

Aimsley swayed.

"Report!" Buyer demanded.

"Hit us dead center," Jonas said. "Charting new trajectory now."

"Fuentes? Any new damage?" the captain asked over the comms.

"Fuck if I know!" she shot back, sounding frustrated, put out. "With all these systems already in the red, *who can fucking tell?*"

A moment later, Jonas let out a deep, hard-edged curse, banging his fists against a dash, making Aimsley jump.

Both it and Doc strained in their seats to try to catch sight of him.

"What?" Buyer asked. "What is it?"

"Gods, we can't catch a fucking break."

"*What?*" Buyer demanded.

"New trajectory has us on another collision course."

"With *what?*"

There was a horrid pause. Tense seconds ticked by.

The air crackled.

"Io," came the quiet reply.

"How long until impact?"

"Two hours."

"*By the Crystals.*"

"Fueeeenteeeees," Buyer called. "About those engines—?"

"I told you, they're not fucking working!" she replied.

"What's wrong with the engines?" Aimsley asked Doc, looking for someone to openly give the information it had already covertly discovered.

"Apparently, quite a lot," they said evenly. "I'm afraid I can't get more technical than that."

"And the maneuvering thrusters . . . ?" it prodded, knowing the answer.

"Fresh out of fuel."

"So, we're on a collision course with Io, and there's no way to change course."

Doc's steady exterior was only slightly betrayed by the tremble in their voice. "Seems so."

"Give me the rundown," Buyer said to Jonas. "Angle of approach, positioning—?"

"Not good," Jonas admitted. "Nose is pointed straight at the moon, so . . ."

The captain sighed. "So even if Fuentes gets the engines back on, we're screwed. We're barreling in a straight line. Engines on or off, with no maneuvering jets, we can't adjust course, so it doesn't matter. Turning the engines on will just ram us straight into the surface all the quicker."

"Right," Jonas agreed.

The light shifted on the bridge. "All clear" rang out in a tinny echo of a voice.

The ship's automated systems had no way of knowing they were still in danger, but the crew—hyper-focused on their tasks—paid the flawed pronouncement no mind.

"What about the skiff?" Doc called, working on their

buckles, unharnessing themself now that the initial crisis had passed. They staggered upright, hurrying to lean in the doorframe of the cockpit. "The reserve fuel for its jets?"

Aimsley quirked its lips, looked around thoughtfully. Carefully, it tested one buckle, wondering how quickly it could get free with its stiff, splinted hand in the way. It needed to do *something*. Anything.

"It gets fueled from *Violent Delight*'s main supply," Buyer said. "Believe me, it's empty. We gave everything we had in the dogfight."

An idea occurred to Aimsley—it knew what it could do, how it could wrest some control back. "What do they run on?" it asked.

The captain leaned out of the cockpit to glare at it, but didn't answer.

"What kind of fuel do your maneuvering jets use?" Aimsley demanded.

"Why?" Buyer asked. "You have some spare hydrazine lying around? N-Two H-Four?"

"And what if I do? I came here in a ship, didn't I?" Aimsley said. "My boat uses that molecular compound as a monofuel. Single stage, no mixing required. Will that do?"

"That monstrosity uses hydrazine?" Jonas asked doubtfully.

"Will that work?" Aimsley asked again.

Buyer cursed, went to the comms again. "Need you both up here, ASAP. We might have a chance at getting out of this. *Might*."

A long minute passed while they waited for the other two to join them on the bridge. The captain continued to eye Aimsley warily, and Aimsley did its best to exude an air of innocence.

As soon as Maya and Fuentes appeared on the bridge, Buyer waved at Aimsley. "Says its boat has spare hydrazine. We could at least get the maneuvering thrusters back online."

Aimsley explained the fuel's makeup, and Fuentes nodded along. "It can't still be at a suitable temperature, though," she said. "If it's frozen—"

"Even if the boat is dead, not all systems will have failed," it insisted, wiggling in its seat. "I know my fuel levels were still good and the preservation measures were functioning as normal. We should be able to figure out how to transfer the hydrazine into your tanks."

Maya shook her head. "We don't have time to get its ship inside and examined. We haven't even figured out why or how it's attached to *Violent Delight*. Someone would need to do the transfer from outside."

"How far are we from the radiation torus?" Buyer asked Jonas.

"We're smack in it. Whoever goes out there is definitely getting some extra RADs."

They all shuffled uncomfortably, held themselves a little tighter, a little more awkwardly.

"Fucking radiation," Fuentes breathed.

They *feared* it, Aimsley realized. They were truly worried about the damage it might cause to their bodies, how much closer it would get them to their total ionizing dosages.

That must mean they were old. *It* was young. It could still risk a large absorption event.

Aimsley did its best to hide the smirk that threatened to curl its lips.

Their fear of radiation exposure was *its* tactical advantage.

The captain cringed, rubbed at his eyes. "Okay. Outside. Crap."

"Right," Aimsley agreed. "And we need to act quickly. Efficiently. You don't want to waste any time deciphering what you're looking at." Perhaps they could figure out how to extract the fuel on their own. *Perhaps*. But Aimsley knew this was an ideal opening.

"I know what you're getting at," Buyer said slowly, warningly.

"I'll go," Aimsley offered.

The sudden silence was deafening.

They all turned to look at it, stunned.

The proposition was only practical: Aimsley had been designed to exist in a high-radiation environment. It expected exposure, and had no excess fear associated with such a spacewalk. "As I told Maya before, I *am* a maintenance unit. I was built for these kinds of problems. Let me go out and fix it. Let me help."

"No way. No fucking way," Jonas shouted. "We're not letting that thing up to roam free. I'll do it. I'll figure it out."

"We don't have time for your bravado, Jonas," Maya said softly. "You wouldn't know what to look for or have half a clue what to do once you found it."

"Besides," Buyer said, "there could be more debris out there. We should stay on the guns."

"This is an engineering problem," Maya said. "It needs an engineer."

"Right, so I'll go," Fuentes said.

Buyer shook his head. "I need you on the engines. The jets are useless if you can't figure out how to get us a little thrust from the fusion drive."

Maya pointed at herself. "Secondary engineer gets the secondary jobs. It's fine. Really. I'll go. Please, spare me the noble objections. But . . . everything *will* go faster with

Aimsley's help." She held up a hand when everyone but Doc moved to protest. "We all know it's true. I know our ship, it knows its. Aimsley has as much to lose if we crash as the rest of us. It just makes sense."

"It's the one that broke the shit in the first place," Jonas pointed out. "So no, it *does not*."

"You got us out of the frying pan," she said to him. "Trust me to get us out of the fire."

"I'll need my hard-body shell returned to me," Aimsley said, trying to sound pragmatic rather than demanding. "Presuming it's still in working order. It hasn't been scrapped or dismantled, has it?"

"Priestess," Jonas said imploringly, "you can't be serious. *I'll* go with you—*Damn the guns, Buyer, you can figure it out.* Two outside will still be faster—safer. You don't need *it*."

"Why would I risk any of you if I don't have to?"

"Because by using it, you're risking all of us!"

"Which do you think poses a greater threat right now?" she demanded. "Io or Aimsley? Seriously, what do you think it's going to do? It knows if it hurts me you won't let it back inside."

"You're assuming it *wants* back inside," Jonas said. "It already smashed its sphere into us—a suicidal move if there ever was one. Why wouldn't it just prevent you from making the repairs? Guarantee we crash and go up in a ball of flame?"

They all turned to it, clearly expecting it to defend itself.

"I don't want to kill anyone," it said, though it didn't think Jonas would find comfort in reassurances, no matter what it said. "Let alone decommission myself. And you need me to do this. You need me because I'm capable *and* expendable. Isn't that right? You don't want Maya out there.

None of you want to be out there. I'm guessing your lifetime radiation exposure percentages must all be high. I'm still new. Still fresh. I was designed for this environment, to be exposed to this kind of radiation. Why not let me take the impact for you?" It narrowed its gaze pointedly at Jonas. "Why not let me take the RADs and spare the rest of you the damage? How much longer will Maya have to stay outside if I don't go with her?"

Buyer tapped his foot, crossed and uncrossed his arms, clearly at odds with himself. "Fuentes, as head engineer, what do you recommend?"

"I trust Priestess," she said earnestly. "If she says Aimsley can do the job, then it can."

"She's been making eyes at it like it's a stray tunnel-dog since we hauled it onboard," Jonas snapped.

"Hey now," Fuentes said, putting herself between Jonas and Maya, despite how small she was. "She's backed up your stupid ass on more than one occasion when you damn well didn't deserve it, so you better keep it respectful, you hear me?"

Buyer threw up his hands. "Look, we're all on the same side here."

"No!" Jonas shouted. "We're *not*. That thing is not on our side!"

He spun, hands flying up in frustration as he marched for the lift.

"I meant the crew. Jonas, I meant *us*!" Buyer yelled after him, though he made no attempt to follow.

CHAPTER TWELVE

"Gods damn him," Buyer huffed. "Like we have time for a mechanical misfire *and* a tantrum."

They all eyed the lift.

"He gets two minutes to cool down," Buyer said, "and then he *better* get his ass back up here, because we need to *work*. I'm making the call—Okeke and Aimsley go out. Fuentes, any ideas about the engines?"

She rubbed two hands over her face. "I might—*might*—be able to program a temporary runaround to bypass the computer's current safeguards. It's hard to say right now why the engine control computer isn't working. The main engine has definitely sustained damage, but the sensors could be malfunctioning as well. The entire system is a mess—everything could blow if we circumvent the failsafes."

"We don't really have a choice," Buyer said.

"This won't be a fix, you understand. Even if we don't blow up, I can't guarantee that it'll work. That we'll get any thrust at all."

"It's a shot in the dark, but it's still a shot. What do you need from us?"

"Honestly, I don't know yet. I've never done this before."

"Right. I want you to jump on your idea now—give me an update in fifteen. Doc, you help Okeke and Aimsley get space-ready, I'll get the suits."

They all shared a sharp look, then snapped into action. Aimsley appreciated this—clearly the crew had dealt with many emergencies before, and knew how to work together fluidly.

Just like all of the platform's AMS units, it realized. *Just like me and my sisters.*

Doc unbuckled Aimsley from the crash seat with an apology on their lips. "The splint, it won't fit in your gloves, will it?"

It shook its head.

"I don't want to numb your hand any further, will you . . . will you be able to grasp with it?"

"Yes. Don't worry about me."

"I'm your doctor, it's my job. Speaking of which, we need to check your lab results."

The three of them returned to the medbay. Doc immediately went to the black box. They hemmed and hawed for a moment before pulling off their mask. Clearly trying to be positive, despite the dire circumstances, they smiled. "Ta-da," they said, indicating Aimsley and Maya could remove their masks as well. "The wonders of modern medicine: overnight inoculation. And apparently with no ill effects, despite your immune system working overtime. That, I suspect, might have to do with your enhancements. The average person would feel pretty wiped out right about now."

"What's *wiped out*?" Aimsley asked.

"Exhausted, drained."

It didn't reply, but it definitely felt *wiped out*. Though it suspected that was more a side effect of *living* than anything else.

Focused on the emergency at hand, Maya pulled a thin, flexible square from her pocket. Aimsley couldn't immediately make out its purpose, until she took it by the corners and began unfolding layers. The square became a thin screen, which she shook out as though it were a dusty rag before flicking it flat against the countertop so that Aimsley could clearly see the expanse of it. With a few swipes of her fingers, she shuffled holographic windows across the surface until she found the one she was looking for.

"Okay, while Doc here helps us get ready, we're going to go over some diagrams, all right? Make sure we're on the same page out there."

Now free of the awkward mask, Aimsley took the opportunity to also toss away the annoying, useless sheet Doc had wrapped it in, then moved to Maya's side. She looked up at it briefly, then quickly glanced away.

The two of them huddled around the screen as she pulled up the ship's schematics to illustrate the route they'd take across the wedge's exterior.

It breathed deeply as she spoke. Here, close, it could detect that same, soft, sweet scent as before. So different from Doc. So different from Jonas. So strange, how each human seemed to have their own, unique scent.

"Our ships are still entangled, so we'll take a path this way." She dragged her finger lightly across the screen. "You shredded our umbilical, so it'll all be open-space. The fuel tank for *Violent Delight*'s maneuvering jets is here." She made an invisible X with her fingertip. "With the intake port here." She drew a line toward the underside of the craft. "The others will double-check that we have a suitable hose extension. We might have to use two. And interfacing is bound to be a problem no matter what."

"And even if we're successful, if Fuentes is *not* . . . You have no other means of thrust?"

"Our ship has three types of propulsion systems. Maneuvering thrusters, a fusion engine, and an emergency ion drive that prevents us from being absolutely stranded. Instead of getting nowhere fast, it can get us somewhere very, very slowly. We've checked on it since you crashed into us, and it's still operational. But it's a last resort. And certainly isn't powerful enough to counteract the kinetic energy of that impact. Only the fusion engine can do that. It's what got us from our closest waystation to here in a month."

"But it's not how you travel interstellarly, is it?" Aimsley asked, trying make the inquiry sound as casual as possible.

"No. For interstellar travel we've got—" she pulled up short, side-eyed it. "Something more powerful," she said noncommittally. "And this ship doesn't have that kind of capacity."

It made a note to probe further—figure out exactly what kinds of long-range ships the invaders had. Perhaps it could even pinpoint where they'd originated with that info.

"The fusion drive is what's freaking out," she continued. "Diagnostics says the plasma torus can't be stabilized. But we don't know if we can trust the sensors."

"So when the fuel injectors are engaged—"

"The engines might go *kaboom*."

Doc interrupted to hold out a white wristband to Maya. "Here, put this on."

She pushed it away. "I don't want it."

"What do you mean you don't want it? How am I supposed to treat you properly if I don't know how many RADs you—?"

"You know how I feel about this, Doc. I don't want to know my totals. I've been out there so many times . . ."

"Well then, *don't look*," they said harshly. "But I, as your healthcare provider, need to know. So you *will* wear it. I'll get Buyer to order you to do it, if that's what it takes."

With a sigh she took the bracelet, slipped it on.

"One for you, too, Aimsley," Doc said, slipping the small circle into its hand.

"I have my own monitoring system," it assured them, passing the bracelet right back. "It's likely more accurate than this. I can give you my totals right now, if you'd like."

"Guess that's one of the perks of the quantum netting in your noggin there," Doc said, sounding reluctant. "But why don't you take this anyway, huh?" They leaned in close to Aimsley's ear, cupping their hand as though sharing a secret. Only, when they spoke again, their voice was only mockingly hushed. "It'll make Priestess feel better if she's not the only one."

Maya smiled without looking at them, shook her head.

Aimsley felt adrift in the interaction. "Oh, uh—"

Doc looped it around its wrist before it could say more. "And what about your suit's comms? Can you tune it to our channels, or is it fixed?"

"I don't use my shell to send or receive communications."

"Then how are you meant to communicate in vacuum?"

"The same way I communicate long distance in non-vacuum." It pointed at its head. "My connection is implanted."

Their features went rigid in momentary panic. "Then are you still in contact with . . . ?"

A wisp of satisfaction curled through Aimsley's chest. It would not need to lie. "You took out the comms tower during our dogfight. I cannot hear my handler or my siblings, and they can no longer hear me."

"Ah. Right. Good." They shook themself. "We'll get you a mobile unit, then. Should be able to fit it in there with you."

The captain rushed in with the shells piled on a hovering, magnetic dolly, while Doc swiftly handed out potassium iodide and Prussian blue tablets. Maya threw her tab back without water.

"Gonna pee green for a week—bright as our spacesuits," she said with a wink at Aimsley. "Maybe more if we fuck up with the fuel injectors and have to down this stuff for a month."

"Green pee will be the least of your problems if that's the case," Doc said.

"I took the pressure hose to your suit," Buyer told Aimsley. "Because—I'm not gonna lie—*it was ripe*. So, just be aware, might be a little clammy inside."

Aimsley nodded its acknowledgment, grateful it wouldn't be encased in a putrid prison.

Maya carefully stripped down to thin undergarments as Buyer prepared her suit for her. She glanced at Aimsley, and their eyes locked for a second, before she blushed and quickly looked away.

Aimsley didn't understand her hesitancy, her reluctance. Robots were meant to be bare. The environment should be perfectly suited to their comfort and needs; these thin shells they insisted on walking around in were superfluous.

Besides, she had an aesthetically pleasing casing, with

her vitiligo creating patterns over her arms, stomach, and thighs. There was an artistry to her design that the others, with their plain tones, did not possess.

But Buyer presented her with an additional jumpsuit to put on. It had various ports and nozzles that would line up with feeds on the inside of her suit. And a secure collar to keep her necklace from floating free about her head.

"Do you *need* to be naked?" Buyer asked Aimsley as he presented its shell, one eyebrow raising.

"Yes, some of the hard-body's responses rely on minute bioelectric impulses in my graspi—in my hands and feet."

Everyone in the room seemed to take this in stride.

Aimsley quickly looked over the hard-body and ran a diagnostics check to make sure it was still space-worthy. Nothing seemed to have been tampered with. Some of the correctional jets were out or low on fuel, just like the ship, but there was little to be done about that now.

Maya ran similar diagnostics on her suit once she was dressed.

Fully encased, the pair exited the cube and made for the outer airlock.

"Comms work?" Maya asked as Buyer closed the inner hatch behind them.

"Check," Aimsley replied.

"I'm sticking my neck out for you here, Aims," she said, moving to a control panel, swiping over the screen. "So try not to . . . get my head chopped off, all right?"

It cringed, but didn't let her see. It didn't want her to know that one of its first acts had been a beheading. Or that it had almost done the same to her.

"Let's both come back safe," she said. "Agreed?"

"Agreed."

The lighting in the airlock changed as it began to de-pressurize.

The atmosphere slowly seeped away, and Aimsley shifted uneasily from foot to foot.

This should be fine.

It knew it should feel more in its element now than at any other moment in the last two days, but instead, it was anxious. Its logic centers railed at it to use this opportunity to either flee or undermine the invaders. An emergency such as this was a gift: a chance to gain the upper hand while the others were already wrong-footed.

But it suppressed that instinct. Escape was no longer its best option. Even if it could get far enough away from the falling wedge, it would be left hanging freely in the ra-diation torus. Unless rescue was right around the corner, it would never survive.

It was better to wait. Better to be useful, to complete the task as stated.

Better to use the opportunity to gain trust.

"You guys are really going to have to hightail it," Buyer said over the comms. "Io's surface gravity is only point one eight gs, so we won't have trouble pulling out of the gravity well once we can course-correct, but that's no tiny target. Way more worried about face-planting than escape veloc-ity. And if we get close enough, one of those volcanic jets could take us out before we get anywhere near the ground. We really need you to get this in one go, yeah?"

"That's the intent," Maya agreed.

"We're getting the coil out to you," he continued. "From the bottom hatch. It should have whatever you need."

Aimsley didn't understand what he meant, but Maya

seemed to, and gave a thumbs-up. Then she braced herself on the outer hatch, clearly anticipating a shift.

A moment later, the gravity left, just as suddenly as it had previously arrived.

Aimsley's nervous shuffling immediately became a nervous kicking.

When Maya opened the outer hatch, the flexible, white extension did not unfurl. Instead, she reached for a set of bars on the wedge's hull—a long line of rungs. Quickly, as though she'd taken the route a hundred times, Maya began to climb along the side, toward the bow of the ship. Aimsley followed, keeping its head down.

After only a few minutes, Aimsley noted a strange sensation on the back of its tongue and a pressure behind its eyes. A furious crackling emanated through the comms speakers, accompanying the sensations, the noise sharp and chaotic.

Reminders of the radiation that swirled all around them. *Through* them.

Even with the sirens and the warning lights, Aimsley hadn't felt the urgency of the situation until this very moment. They were barreling into a hostile world through a hostile orbit. The radiation torus was invisible to their eyes, but the excessive static crackle made it very clear their bodies were being constantly bombarded by a barrage of radioactivity.

Aimsley chose not to call up its TID. It didn't want to watch the number tick up, the percentage rise.

It understood, suddenly, why Maya had tried to refuse the band.

Neither of them could afford to spend an extra moment outside the ship. Despite their preparation, and their well-engineered suits, the danger was real and the threat ongoing. Every second threatened to make them sicker, to shave just a little more time off their activation periods.

Of course, if they crashed into Io, they'd hardly have to concern themselves with radiation sickness.

The hull of the *Violent Delight*—for Aimsley was sure now these units had given the wedge that name, just as surely as they'd named themselves—had far more features than the hull of the platform. More places for hooks and tethers. More shifting panels and places where the plating bulged—was especially thick—to protect something inside.

They came across the occasional dark blast pattern—a burn mark and deep gash almost certainly caused by the boat's cannons.

As they passed a large gun—protruding from the ship like a bent insectoid, dark and craggy looking—Aimsley thought it heard a voice calling to it. But the comms were quiet.

Likely it was nothing but its mind matrixing the static into familiar sounds.

Aimsley glanced up to mark Maya's position, to note how close they were to the boat, and Aimsley gasped.

It was not Jupiter that stole Aimsley's breath—though it was prominent, hulking. Its sky as turbulent as ever.

No, what made its lungs hitch and its mouth go dry was the moon.

Io.

A huge, pock-marked ball of sulfur, swelling before its eyes.

Volcanic plumes spewed rock and dust and gas high above the small world. The ship was close enough for Aimsley to make out the blue-green sulfur dioxide aurora flaring across its darkening side, tinged red on the fringes by the oxygen aurora. Lava flowed across its surface, adding new, molten sulfur to the planes, and the orange ring of fallen volcanic ejection that circled the dark vent of Pele sat almost directly beneath them like a bull's-eye, waiting for their impact.

And the nose of the wedge was angled like a spear tip, aiming for the heart of the moon.

"Come on!" Maya shouted over the comms, waving her arm in a wide arc.

Something sped by overhead, and Aimsley caught a flash of twisted metal hurtling away. A chunk of debris that size moving at that velocity likely wouldn't hurt the wedge, but it could certainly scrape an AMS unit off the hull.

Aimsley refocused on its climb.

The boat was its own, smaller disk against the disk of the moon—its turquoise and purple clashing with the oranges and yellows of Io—as was intended. The coloration of both the boat and the shells was meant to make the soft robots easily distinguishable from the environment when observed in the visible spectrum.

"Un——r?"

Aimsley frowned, shook its head.

Was there a signal hiding in all this noise? Was that voice . . . real?

"I'm going to climb down there," Maya called, pointing farther down the side of the wedge, to something new protruding out of the ship. "Grab the hoses and anything else I think we'll need. You find the fuel panel and point me to it when I come back, yeah?"

From the underside of the wedge, an arm had been

extended. A great coil of a thing—as Buyer had described—which held various tools, a zero-g pump that Maya now assured Aimsley was rated for various fuel transfers, connectors, and hose lines.

"A lot of our harvesting is automated," Maya explained, "But we have to personally break down our haul. We're all used to these kinds of spacewalks, just . . ."

"You don't tend to go out in radiation storms."

"Right."

Maya went in one direction, Aimsley another. It found itself wishing for the drums again as it continued to approach the boat alone. It needed that steady, rapid beating in its ears, that metered pounding in its brain.

It soon realized there *was* something pounding in its brain, in its mind.

Some other sound.

"Unit—?"

A voice, for certain. Faint, but there.

More crackling. More hissing.

"Unit Four?"

Either the signal was weak or the torus was interfering with the connection—but it didn't matter. It was there, and it was real.

Its handler had found it.

"Unit Four? Unit Four, can you hear me? I just saw your feed go live again a few minutes ago. Are you there?"

Aimsley longed to call out, yes, yes I'm here!

But it couldn't risk alerting the invaders.

"If you can hear me, stand by. I'm trying to get the signal boosted. Maybe then—"

Static cut them off again.

Aimsley did its best to tamp down its elation. Finally,

finally it wasn't alone in this. Contact had been reestablished. That must mean help was on its way.

But not the kind of help it needed in this very moment.

As it approached the sphere, it reminded itself it had to hurry. No matter how badly it wanted to stop everything and talk to its handler, there wasn't time. No matter how badly it wanted to take stock of the boat—to catalog each triangle's damage, to examine the biological portions within—*there simply wasn't time*. Aimsley had to focus on its task and think of little else.

The very nature of the boat's hull—piecemeal, interchangeable—meant that without the boat itself to guide Aimsley, it didn't know immediately where any individual part lay. The AMS unit crawled up one side of the craft, then down the other, tucking its fingers into any little seam to pull itself along.

Minutes ticked away, and Aimsley's handler broke through the static again and again, but never seemed quite certain they were reaching the AMS unit. Aimsley tried not to worry about its handler, tried not to think about what might happen if they decided Unit Four wasn't really there. It had to trust that the Earthling knew what to do.

When Aimsley had inspected ninety-five percent of the boat's surface, a small sense of dread began to creep up its spine.

What if the fuel tanks were among the tangled parts of the wreckage? What if they'd already been punctured?

It climbed down to the juncture between the two craft with the metallic taste of dread riding high in the back of its throat.

Here, the hulls were twisted, split. Parts had buckled, and there was an unmistakable spray of blood and viscera around the impact sight. Aimsley wondered how much worse the stains would have been in a higher gravity environment. Much of the boat's life force must have simply coalesced into bubbles that bounced off and away into space, sending the gore off to freeze instead of splattering across the wedge.

Aimsley had to duck down to examine the last few intact triangles, to tuck itself beneath the curve of the boat. And, yes, there—at last—the hydrazine fuel port. But just barely reachable. In order to properly pump the fuel from one ship to the other, they'd have to figure out a way to widen the gap between the ruined hulls.

Aimsley quickly conveyed this to Maya. "Any ideas?" it asked. "The boat was stable when I was crawling on it. I think this will take some force."

"The piston-rod spreader we used when we entered your ship might work. Let me finish hooking up the pump and the hoses on this end and then I'll bring it up—luckily I don't think we're going to have any problem with the reach."

"Good. After that, the interfacing is our only real obstacle," it said. *Well, that, and the rest of our assumptions*, it thought. It had no idea what the ideal hydrazine to water ratio was for the wedge's jets. They could still sputter out, even with their tanks full, if the mixture was too far off.

It examined the plate for another minute, trying to envision how to connect the port to the hose, when its handler's hiss rattled through its mind again. "Unit Four, I don't know if you can hear me, or if you're just not in a position to respond, but I definitely have your biometrics back up. I know you're alive."

Aimsley's heart swelled with hope, with relief. Excitement sent a new rush of chemicals through its body, and it clapped its hand against the boat's hull in triumph.

"I got your message," they continued. Their voice sounded different than it remembered from its initial activation. The tone was flatter, more even. Aimsley supposed that was because the platform was no longer under immediate threat. "And I'm coming to you," they said. "Me, personally. I can't spare any other units from the platform—they've got to get the array back up, but if you can hold tight, if you can give me three days, I think I can get to you."

Yes, I can. Yes, I'm here. Yes, yes. Whatever you need, whatever—

Something itched inside its skull. A strange niggling— like fear, but tinged with confusion.

Three days?

It was impossible to travel from Earth to Jupiter in three days.

Wasn't it?

Was its handler *not* on Earth?

"Three days, you got that? Can you signal me if you're receiving? If you can't speak—if the units you mentioned can hear you—maybe, I don't know, pause your gas exchange?"

It did as instructed, sucking in a deep breath and holding it, lying still, jammed between the two craft.

It waited for its handler to tell it to breathe again.

And waited.

And waited.

Until its lungs started to burn.

"Good, good!" its handler finally said. "I see you there. Okay. Three days. If you can take over the invader's ship before I get there, it'll be all the easier to haul you in. I'm so sorry it took me this long to reestablish the connection. I think something was blocking me."

Likely the wedge itself, Aimsley realized. The radiation shielding and hull armor must have been thick enough to prevent its handler's signals from penetrating. That was why they hadn't been able to make contact or receive updates on Aimsley's biometrics until now.

Which meant, once it went back inside, the connection would be severed once again.

"Aimsley," Maya prompted, snapping it out of its thoughts, "I'm on my way."

"Okeke?" came Buyer's voice over the comms. "Fuentes has a plan for how to bypass the primary engine control computer. Only, there's a problem."

"Now what?" she groaned.

"We're going to attempt an uncontrolled ignition. Once we fire up the engines without the computer, there won't be a way to shut it down. Not from in here."

"That's no good," she said. "The engine sustained heavy damage in the fight. We don't know how long we can run it. It could be dangerous—the chances of catastrophic engine failure could rise exponentially, not to mention the fuel we'd waste if—"

"I know, but we have to turn it on. We have to run it long enough to change trajectory and ensure escape velocity. And then we can shut it down."

"I thought you said we couldn't shut it down?"

"I said, not from in here."

There was a long pause as Maya realized exactly what he was saying. "Fuentes wants us to manually cut off the helium-three fuel lines."

"Right. Which means you'll need to stay out there longer

than we'd planned, I'm sorry. If you use the safety valves, they'll kill the flow of helium to the injectors. Without fuel, the engines will shut down."

"But those aren't meant for—"

"Okeke, there's nothing about this plan I like. It is what it is. Turning them on this way is our only shot at saving the ship, and you turning them off again is the only way to guarantee we save it a second time."

"Third."

"What?"

She gave a tight, caustic chuckle. "Debris, Io, uncontrolled ignition. That's three by my count."

"Three," he agreed. "Do you need directions to the manual shutoff valves, or—?"

"No sir. Know exactly where to find them."

"Good luck."

"Copy that, Captain. I'll add it to my to-do list. Aimsley," she called, "I'm nearly to you. Come help me guide this mag-cart into place."

It joined her not far afield of the boat. The mag-cart was a sealed container about the size of two AMS units. Maya secured it to the hull with magnetic struts, then released a small valve that let it gently depressurize, before opening it and revealing their equipment.

Aimsley's handler continued to speak to it while the two of them worked as swiftly as possible to jury-rig the appropriate connections—updating the wayward AMS unit on the progress its sisters had made with the repairs.

It did its best to listen, but not give away its new connection to Maya.

"What's the manual cutoff valve?" it asked her after a time.

"Valves, actually. There are two helium-three lines, and each has its own external safeguard, a manual valve, that prevents anything from flowing to the injectors while we refuel. It's a safety precaution only, it's not meant to shut down an ignited engine. They never get touched unless we're docked."

With a sigh, she held up a set of couplings from the mag-cart. "I've got the hose connected to the pump, we just need to secure it to your ship. These are what we have to work with. Any of this look like it'll do?"

"This midsized flange looks closest, though it might be a little small. We might have to crimp the edges of the port, or there won't be a tight enough seal for the pump to work."

"I think we're going to end up with some leakage no matter what, but I think we can obtain enough pressurization for flow. It should be fine. Given both the high combustion point and high freeze point of hydrazine, should be safe regardless. You're sure you can't reach the boat's port without widening the gap between the ships?"

"Positive. Though perhaps you should be the one to place the connectors. You're smaller, it'll require less shifting."

She nodded, then retrieved the spreader, thrusting it between the sides of the two ships before turning it on. The space-rated hydraulics pushed against the hulls, jacking them apart.

The wedge vibrated beneath Aimsley's feet, the metal straining. The two ships didn't want to release one another. Whatever mangled connection they shared went taut, and the boat bobbed slightly with the rebound. The spreader was all that held them apart, kept them from snapping back to settle flush against each other once more.

Maya attached the nozzle to the hose, then wriggled into the gap, feet to the spreader, head toward the fuel port, pulling the loose end of the hose with her.

As their work went on, every second began to feel like an eternity. She'd ask for a tool, and Aimsley would hand it to her, before shuffling back into standby until she gave it another directive.

It couldn't will the materials to bond any faster, couldn't force the parts together just by wishing. They were still at the mercy of the literal elements. Physics couldn't function any differently simply because their lives depended on it.

Maya worked as quickly as she could, pressed against the wedge's hull, caught between the two craft.

"Almost . . . Almost . . ." she said, body going taut, straining. Aimsley wished it could see her hands—make out exactly what she was doing.

She tried to slide in farther beneath the bow of the boat, and her feet kicked out as she repositioned.

Her boot caught the base of the spreader. It slid slightly.

Aimsley paid it no mind.

She braced herself against it once more, inching farther into the gap.

"Nearly have it!" she insisted, kicking again.

This time, the force was enough to knock the spreader away from the boat.

To knock it out of the gap—to send it *careening away*.

The boat rolled—snapping back into its original position. Pinning Maya beneath it.

She screamed.

Aimsley lunged for the spreader as it twirled by, and the smooth metal *just* glanced off its shelled fingertips.

Aimsley's boots left the decking—it parted from the

ship, chasing the spreader—focused entirely on retrieving the tool, blocking out Maya's surprised cries.

It couldn't free her without the spreader.

With one more determined reach, Aimsley snatched the spreader and flipped itself, letting one jet sputter on for the briefest instant, pushing it back toward the ship.

Aimsley jolted as it thumped shoulder-first against the hull. Righting itself quickly, it maneuvered the spreader back toward the gap. "Are you hurt?" it asked.

"No. Just surprised me is all. But I'm wedged in," she said. "Can you—? I need—"

"Is anything damaged?"

"I don't think so. I got the connection to lock. I'm just stuck."

"I've got you. I can— Here, look." It reactivated the spreader, forcing the ships away from each other once more.

Maya scrambled out.

"Everything all right?" Aimsley asked.

She patted herself down, then looked over her suit diagnostics. "Fine."

"Are we ready then? To make for the manual cutoff?" This part of the ordeal would be for naught if they couldn't get the main engines to work.

"Fuel's ready to pump, Captain," she said over the comms. "How's Fuentes?"

"Doing her damndest."

Maya's shoulders slumped. She swallowed thickly. "All right, Aims, let's go. Follow me."

Maya grabbed an automatic ratchet from the mag-cart before twisting one finger through the space between them, indicating they should turn their backs on the violent moon and climb to the top of the craft. Without hesitation, the pair set off once again.

And all the while, Aimsley's handler kept talking. A new Unit Two was already active, and what was supposed to be a new Unit Four was on its way—though, with any luck, it would be dubbed Unit Five upon Aimsley's return.

The climb to the rear of the ship was tense and felt like an eternity. Their steps couldn't fall fast enough, and their legs and arms were too encumbered by their suits to make rushing possible in the way they both wanted.

Aimsley glanced back only once, to see the swell of Io over the wedge's nose.

If this didn't work—if they were going to die—perhaps there were worse things to see before one's end. And it had gotten more time than it had first anticipated. Maybe not an entire activation period, but at least a day or so more.

But it couldn't entirely lie to itself; Aimsley would have appreciated a full lifespan. Anything less was a disappointment. A tragedy.

Maya reached the edge of the wedge's back side first, found a new ladder that led over the side, and swung herself beyond the ledge, disappearing past the horizon-line of the ship. Aimsley was poised to follow when the comms filled with excited chatter.

"She's—she's got it!" Buyer called. "Fuentes is ready—are you two in position?"

"Just about," Maya called back. "But you can start your countdown anytime; the sooner we change course the better. But, the hydrazine . . . ?"

"Jonas has got enough pumped in for a redirect. Hang on, we're firing everything up."

"Hang on, Aimsley!" Maya shouted.

It crouched low.

"Hold on!" Buyer cried. "Engaging maneuvering thrusters in three . . . two . . ."

Aimsley plastered itself to the side of the ship, looping an arm through a rung at the top of the ladder. Jamming its shoulders against the hull, it banged the side of its helmet against the unforgiving metal.

"One."

The wedge jerked to the side, turning on its axis, its nose sweeping hard to port.

"Yes! Fuel transfer was a success!" Buyer hooted. "Good job, all. Well done! Get ready for phase two. Ignition of fusion engine in three . . . two . . . one."

The ship gave a great *kick*, and Aimsley lurched forward, threatening to topple over the back side of the wedge, but it held itself firm. Below its position, blazing white-blue jets erupted from the engines' six wide cones. The exhaust from the reactor stretched back for at least half a kilometer.

Buyer instantly had them on a new trajectory, and whoops of success rang out through the comms.

They'd buzz the moon, nothing more.

Aimsley expected relief to flood through its system, but as it stared into the streaming jets, it found its shoulder tightening, its teeth grinding.

"Get down here, Aimsley," Maya called. "Job's not over."

It flipped itself around to climb after her.

"See this hatch?" she asked when it reached her, already diligently using the ratchet to undo the bolts keeping the panel in place. "There's another just like it over there," she nodded to the other side of the blazing exhaust cones. "I'll get this one free for you, and then I'll go station myself on the other valve, and we'll wait for Buyer's cue, yeah?"

"I will follow your instructions," it confirmed with a nod.

Securing the removed bolts in a pocket on her shell, she peeled the panel open, revealing a large, black lever—the manual cutoff switch. It would sweep in a long, wide arc when pulled.

"Just give it a tug when Buyer says. Pull it all the way down—you'll feel it click into place." With that, she crawled away, her bright-green suit shuffling across the dark surface, mirroring a picture in Aimsley's databanks of an aphid scuttling over the expanse of a deep-green leaf.

As it waited, it spared a glance at its RADs and immediately regretted it. It did not like the speed at which the decimals were rolling by.

Maya disappeared behind the exhaust.

Its handler chatted away in its head.

Aimsley bit its lip, flexed its hands, trying to focus.

"In position," Maya called after a time. "Ready?"

It reached for the lever. "Ready."

"Buyer, you reading me? Let us know when you're ready."

"Affirmative, Okeke. Nearly there. Just want to be sure . . ."

A few more moments passed.

"Okay, that should do it. We're clear, shut us down."

"On my mark, Aimsley," Maya said. "Three . . ."

Aimsley shifted its grip on the lever, bracing its boots firmly against the hull, unsure how much force it would need to put into the pull.

"Two . . ."

Aimsley took a deep breath.

"One."

It yanked with all its might, and still the resistance was difficult to overcome. The lever was clearly meant to be operated by another vehicle, something mechanical. Humans could work them in a pinch, but this was not the intended interaction.

It pulled the rod down and over, struggling the whole way, hoping Maya was able to manage, and worried she wouldn't be—she didn't have the same muscle mass, the same reinforcements on her bones.

Aimsley pressed the lever down, *down* against the hull, releasing a breath when it felt a satisfying *click* reverberate through its grasp as the bar locked into its new position.

There was no change to the exhaust output.

"Maya?" it ventured.

"I'm getting there," she insisted. But the strain in her voice was evident.

"I'm coming to aid you."

"I *can* do it. Hold tight, Aimsley. *I'm almost there.*"

It didn't argue. It simply obeyed, as it would if given the same instructions by a sister unit back on the platform or by its handler in this very moment.

Because it trusted her.

It wasn't even sure *why* it trusted her. She was an enemy unit just like all the others. There shouldn't be a difference.

Why did she *feel* different, then?

The plumes spluttered. The exhaust extinguished.

Maya let out a shout of triumph. "We did it!"

We did it.

Aimsley glanced out, into the stars. Bits of debris still sparkled out in the expanse.

They'd done it. They were all still alive.

A swell of relief and joy washed through its limbs.

For all the time it had spent thinking about its end, it had never really considered its continued existence.

It *liked* being alive. It *wanted* to be *alive*.

Suddenly, the wedge gave another jerk. One of the cones flared all on its own—bursting bright orange and red instead of white. Bits of the nozzle bloomed outward, torn open by the explosion, curling back.

Aimsley lost one of its handholds, and its feet scrapped at the hull, trying to regain their purchase.

"Shit!" Buyer yelled. "What was—?"

But the rest of his question died in Aimsley's ears as it watched a small, green-suited figure tumble off into space.

CHAPTER THIRTEEN

Maya *shrieked*.

She flew away—zipping through space at a heinous speed.

She started her tumble hunched, tight, but soon flung her limbs out like a five-pointed star. Grasping at nothing. Kicking at nothing.

Buyer *shouted*—first at Fuentes, asking after the explosion, then at Maya. "What? Okeke, *what is it?*"—over and over, even as Aimsley's handler rambled on.

The AMS unit wanted to yell at them *both* to be quiet. It couldn't hear Maya clearly, but she was talking—*begging*.

"I can't— Please, I *can't*—"

Aimsley waited for her to right herself—to use her jets to reel herself back in. But she kept shrinking into the expanse, becoming a startlingly small point in mere moments. The green of her suit darkened with the distance, and she fell out of the sun's glare, into shadow.

It looked as though space had swallowed her up.

"Okeke!" Buyer cried. "Okeke, what's wrong?"

"I can't— I can't— There's something wrong with my

suit!" she shouted. "I can't get any of the safety jets to activate!"

Which meant not even the automated retrieval system could save her.

She was helpless.

Aimsley didn't think.

It simply dove.

The shell's jets sprang to life, blasting it in the direction of the flailing human.

It followed her trajectory as tightly as it could, weaving only to dodge a small cloud of metal flotsam, all the while ignoring its handler's demands to know what was going on—why Unit Four's biometrics were wavering, spiking.

Aimsley could hear its own breath rattling in its helmet, and it tried to make that sound its new drumbeat—it's new, even, steady mental-touchstone.

It pushed out the voices, zeroing in on Maya's shape, giving its full attention to the minute changes in trajectory it needed to make.

It cursed at itself as it realized it had initially miscalculated. In the heat of the moment, Aimsley had forgotten it had exhausted more than one of its jets during their initial combat. But it quickly recovered, twisting itself to make the best use of its propulsion.

"I'm coming," it shouted over the top of Buyer and its handler. "Maya, reach for me!"

Her tumbling form contorted further as she tried to pinpoint the AMS unit. Her arm snapped outward.

She grew in Aimsley's sights.

So close. Nearly there.

One wrong move and it would blast by her.

Her hand stretched forward.

So did its.

Both of them strained.

Green-clad fingers slid into turquoise ones.

And almost out again.

Aimsley howled in frustration as Maya threatened to slip through its grasp. It clawed at her, determined not to fail, not to waste any extra time, energy, or fuel—not to spend *one* extra second out in this hellish radiation.

It held her fingers fast—twisting them awkwardly, unnaturally, but tightly.

Yanking her close, it smacked into her back soon after, wrapping her in its arms as it redirected them, stopped the tumbling—pointed them toward the ship.

"I've got you," Aimsley huffed, breath still coming heavily. It pulled her firmly against its chest. "You're okay."

She made a strangled sort of sob but said nothing. She held on to Aimsley with an equally iron grip, arms folding up over its.

Below their feet, the wedge curved away from Io, leaving them suspended with nothing between them and the moon. But Maya ducked her head, looked away.

She vibrated under its hands—shaking so violently it could feel the tremors pulsing through all the layers of fabric and metal between them. "Melassani. Crystals, *please*," she mumbled.

"You're all right," Aimsley cooed. "We'll be inside soon. You're okay."

Only now that it had her in its arms did it realize it could have easily let her go. There was no way the invaders could blame a suit malfunction on the AMS unit. It could have told them its own jets were too low on fuel—that it had no way to get to her. It could have even emptied them before attempting to reenter the airlock, to lend credibility to the claim.

It was good and truly an accident.

A fault in Aimsley's favor.

And yet . . .

The universe had yanked Maya away—had gifted Aimsley with one less invader to deal with—and on impulse *it had snatched her right back.*

"Okeke, are you there?" Buyer asked.

"Unit Four, can you hear me?" its handler bayed.

It shut them both out, focusing on the trembling person in its embrace. "Look—the ship is safe now. And so are you. A few minutes more. We're getting closer."

It realized this fiasco *would*, in the end, eat up the rest of its shell's fuel reserves.

"Unit Four—?"

"Maya, answer me right now!" Buyer demanded

"She's fine," Aimsley insisted. "Shaken, but fine."

"I'd like to hear that from her," Buyer said, voice gritty with an unspoken threat: *if you did something to her . . .*

"I'll be fine, Buyer," she croaked.

Aimsley had to admit, she did not, in fact, sound fine.

Perhaps something *had* been damaged when the boat had rolled on top of her. And in their haste to finish the job, they'd both overlooked something critical.

Even with the shell's maneuvering jets on full blast, it still took long minutes to reach the hatch, but they were able to intercept the wedge's new course. Two more fuel packs were exhausted by then, and the rest were dangerously low.

There might not be anything aboard to serve as a suitable replacement, and even if there were, Aimsley knew the others were unlikely to let it dip into their stocks.

Get on board first and worry about that later.

Maya tugged on the hatch with a fervor, shaking, it seemed, even more violently than before.

The AMS unit set her down on the decking as soon as the hatch was closed behind them and the gravity had reengaged.

But Maya didn't wait patiently for the airlock to repressurize. Her gloved hands flew to her helmet, fiddling with the latches. Labored breaths wheezed through the comms, and Aimsley could tell she was in a panic—spiraling in desperation, with the sudden urge to gulp fresh air.

Only there was no fresh air to be had.

"Stop. *Stop.* Wait for the airlock to pressurize. Maya. Maya!"

It grabbed for her hands, held her palms flat against its chest to still her. But she still struggled, and the exoskeleton gave her extra leverage—extra strength to try to throw Aimsley off.

On instinct, it lowered its helmet to hers. Not harshly. Gently. In a mimicry of a forehead touch, so that the metal bits came together with a soft clacking that reverberated inside its shell. "Maya," it whispered soothingly. "You need to keep your helmet on."

It didn't expect her to calm—to stop feeling what she was feeling. It simply wanted to provide a grounding point. Some stability and reassurance. Enough to keep her in her suit while the pressure equalized.

She took one sucking, deep breath, then another.

She no longer tried to push it away.

"Just a little longer," it said. "You can do it. You can." It spoke to her much as it spoke to itself. It gave her the same kind of comfort, the same pep talk, as it had given itself during the most harrowing moments in the boat. "So close. A bit farther. Almost there."

"I've never lost control of my suit before," she explained, voice still wavering, heavy with anxiety—tongue thick with it. "Even in a dead spin, the autolock can regain control. But if the jets won't activate . . . the automated system means nothing. If you hadn't come after me—"

"Then one of the others would have. They would have retrieved you. They would not have abandoned you."

She nodded lightly against its helmet. "You're right. Of course," she said, as though the thought hadn't occurred to her. The panic and the fear had driven such logic from her mind. "But I would have just been . . . spinning. Gods, the *spin*."

"You're all right now," it said softly. "No more spinning."

"Thank you."

The lighting changed. The airlock had fully repressurized.

Buyer yanked open the hatch, reaching for Maya.

She slowly stepped out of Aimsley's grasp—hands still lingering in its for a precious extra moment.

Only when she let go did the AMS unit realize it might have *offered* a grounding touch, but it had needed that touch just as badly. The instant they parted, it was as though a spell had been broken.

It suddenly noticed it could no longer hear its handler— that shutting itself back in the ship had meant shutting itself off from its one connection to home, to help.

Aimsley had been so worried about Maya, it hadn't thought about itself.

It couldn't forget that *it* was the vulnerable one here—surrounded by enemies. No matter how softly they might smile or respectfully they might speak, they were still the opposition.

Maya turned toward Buyer, hands flying up to unlatch her helm. She tossed the offending piece of equipment aside, then hurried into her captain's outstretched arms.

The helmet bounced dully across the decking to land at Jonas's feet. He picked it up with his good hand, staring into the visor. "What happened?"

Buyer patted Maya's hair as he held her, and she mumbled into his shoulder, "Something *exploded*, that's what happened. Fuentes, the engines—?"

"She's handling it," Buyer said. "Don't know the details yet. Definitely could have been worse; we should count ourselves lucky. But what about you?"

"Suit stalled on me. Wouldn't activate the guidance jets."

"Nothing on this crap ship works right," Jonas muttered.

"Yeah?" Buyer snarled over his shoulder. "Well, we *could* get it properly repaired and inspected at Puerto Grande, but we can't go back there, *can we*? That's the whole point of being out here—to get our fucking permissions back, so don't start with me. Got it?"

"Yes, sir," Jonas mumbled.

Doc hurried to Maya, fluttering about, checking her vitals while she clung to the captain.

"I got pinched—between the ships when we were transferring the hydrazine. I thought the suit was fine, but we were in a rush and . . . I—I need to go to the chapel," Maya mumbled into Buyer's chest.

"Sure thing," the captain said. "Let's get you out of this suit first."

Aimsley and Maya were guided back into the cube by Buyer and Doc, who helped them out of their shells.

Once the AMS unit was bare again, Maya looked away—turned her back.

Perhaps their brief connection outside the ship, in the airlock, had been just that: brief. Something born of the heat of the moment and nothing more.

Even though it had lost touch with its handler, Aimsley had reasoned that it had at least gained more of her trust—something it could utilize. But now . . .

"Can we get Aimsley some clothes, please?" she croaked, sounding mildly distressed. Aimsley attributed it to the aftereffects of her sudden panic and adrenaline rush, but acknowledged there was also a new kind of vexation in her tone.

"How tall would you say you are?" Doc asked it. "Six feet? Six one, maybe? It was difficult to get an exact measurement with you in the chair."

"In a gravitational environment of nine point eight zero six six five meters per second squared I'm one point eight five nine meters long. Why?"

Buyer groaned.

Doc sighed, sounded put-upon. "That's what I thought."

"Why?" Aimsley asked.

"We need to get you dressed—"

"Pants," Maya said frankly. "At the very least."

"Pants?"

She glanced over her shoulder. "You're naked."

Quirking an eyebrow at her, it glanced down at itself.

Its skin might be a bit dulled, a bit grimy, from lack of access to the proper cleaning facilities, but it couldn't pinpoint anything particularly off-putting. "I don't understand why you care."

She looked flustered, but quickly stammered, "Because you're—I mean, well . . . You need clothes. Because *everyone else is wearing them*."

Fine. If they would all feel better with it draped in a thin shell—with it mirroring their presentation—then so be it. "Okay," it agreed. "Pants."

"There's just one problem," Buyer said.

"What?"

Doc clapped Aimsley on the shoulder. "There's only one person aboard who's about your size."

This, at least, was no mystery. "Jonas?" it asked.

"Jonas," Doc sighed with a nod.

"No! Fuck, *no!*"

The comms box didn't even need to be on for Aimsley to hear Jonas's reaction to Buyer's request.

Aimsley leaned against the counter opposite the medbay's airlock, propping itself up on one hand while Doc applied the splint to the other. Oddly, it found the pain inherent in the joint's freedom preferable to the vulnerability that came with its thumb's new immobility.

The cat, Zelmar, rubbed up against its bare legs.

"Oh, *come on*," Jonas cried. "It's not enough that I let it keep breathing, I have to give it the shirt off my back, too?"

Maya sat on what Aimsley had first thought was a reconstitution pod (now it wasn't so sure), one leg jumping up and down nervously. Clearly, she wanted to go to her "chapel," but was waiting for something.

"You know what?" Jonas shouted. "Yeah, no, that's fitting—" A moment later, he stormed in, his good hand fluttering across the closures on his thin, white shirt.

Buyer followed shortly after. "I *meant* you should go get something from your locker."

Without answering, Jonas pulled off his sling, tossing it harshly onto the countertop. Then he attempted to shrug out of the shirt, tugging at the fabric with a clawing force, as though in a mockery of scraping off his own skin. He hissed sharply as he shifted his injured shoulder, and Buyer rushed to aid him. Jonas didn't shove him off, despite his clear anger.

"You don't have to be a shit about this," Buyer rumbled in Jonas's ear.

Jonas pushed him away as soon as the shirt was free of his arm. "Think it's my prerogative, *sir*."

The captain held up his hands in capitulation, standing aside.

Jonas held the cloth out with a furious shake in Aimsley's direction. "Here."

Aimsley didn't budge.

He wiggled it with more bravado, like a lure.

Again, this felt like a trap.

Carefully, telegraphing its movements—expecting Jonas to use their close proximity to lash out—Aimsley took the shirt. "This is an awfully flimsy shell," Aimsley said, stretching it between its hands. "What's the point?"

"Comfort, mostly," Doc explained. "Aesthetics, sometimes. Politeness, generally."

"Not considered good manners to have your junk out at the dinner table," Jonas added with a frank V gesture at the junction of his legs.

The others shot him a look.

"What?" he demanded. "Why do you all insist on coddling it—as though it's not fully grown and didn't pilot a spacecraft that tried to shoot us out of orbit? I can say junk. We've all got *junk* of some kind." He crossed his arms, frowned at Aimsley. "I'll get you a pair of pants for your *junk,* too." He turned pointedly to the others, "Unless it needs this specific pair I'm wearing, hmm?"

"I told you—" Buyer said, but Jonas was already leaving as Aimsley shrugged into the shirt, reversing the motion it had seen him use to take it off. It fiddled with the buttons—found the eyelets unusually challenging. After a few moments, it gave up.

"May I?" Maya asked, standing. She held up her hands, first to show they were empty, then to reach delicately for the buttons.

It nodded.

She slipped each into the matching perforation with practiced ease, eyes trained on the task. Aimsley took the opportunity to study her more closely. It appreciated the firmness of her touch, the assuredness of her movements. It liked the way her lashes fanned down over her cheeks, and there was something about the way her lips parted as she breathed softly that . . .

It mentally shook itself, glancing away, up to the ceiling.

It needed to feign closeness, connection. Not *feel* it.

"There," she said with a smile, smoothing out the collar once she was finished.

It wrinkled its nose, realizing the shirt smelled like Jonas. Jonas didn't necessarily smell off-putting, but the man himself was off-putting enough that such reminders of his presence were ultimately sour.

It would much rather have smelled like Maya.

When Jonas returned with the aforementioned pants, Maya decided to take her leave.

"Wait. You won't help me with these, too?" it asked hopefully.

Her cheeks turned bright pink, and Doc chuckled lightly.

Aimsley wasn't sure what was so funny.

"Smooth," Jonas said bitterly, tossing the scratchy garment at the AMS unit.

Buyer either wasn't in on the joke or didn't care about the joke. "Pull those on, then hop back up in the chair," he said, stern. "We've got work to do."

Halfway through the door, Maya stopped. "It just saved our sorry asses and you want to tie it back up?"

"*How many times do I have to tell you?*" Jonas countered, voice a low growl. "Our sorry asses wouldn't have needed saving if it hadn't tried to obliterate us in the first place. It shouldn't get to suddenly roam free because it helped fix one of the gods-damned problems it created."

"I wouldn't have needed to come after you at all if you hadn't attacked the mine," Aimsley said evenly.

Jonas took a threatening step in Aimsley's direction, raging in return. "And *we* wouldn't have needed to attack the mine if your slimy handlers hadn't kept us from getting to our own fucking planet filled with our own fucking resources!"

What—?

Their own fucking . . . what?

"Aimsley stays here, in the medbay," Buyer said, with definitive authority.

Maya raised a hand in protest. "But—"

"Here, we can keep an eye on it. But . . ." He let out a heavy sigh. "Look, as long as you behave"—he shot Aimsely a pointed look—"you won't get any ropes. Not even during the sleep cycle. Okay?"

What was there to argue with? "Okay." It was still hung up on Jonas's outburst.

"Doc, I'll need you to lock up or clear out anything it could use as a weapon."

"Right."

Happy to not have to deal with the ropes, at least, Aimsley did take up the chair again, and the others left, one by one. Doc went about securing the medbay before going on their way as well.

"Cat?" they asked before leaving. "In or out?"

The small cuts in its thigh still stung.

And yet . . .

"In. Please."

After Doc left, the creature hopped into Aimsley's lap again.

Its fur was so much softer than these terrible clothes it had been given. Jonas had clearly chosen this particular pair of pants to torture the AMS unit—its entire lower body *itched*.

It could endure, though. The discomfort, the nonsense, the slow erosion of its proper vocabulary—it *could* endure.

For three days.

Now that it was alone, however, there was nothing to distract it, to stop Jonas's words from ringing in its ears. To keep his *specific* flavor of nonsense at bay.

"Our own fucking planet!"

Their own planet?

Ha, Aimsley snorted to itself. Fine, it *supposed* all robots could consider Earth their own planet—it was where their designs originated, after all.

But when one is subjected to invasive programming on behalf of a hostile force, any claims on the solar system's resources—from Earth, Jupiter, or otherwise—should logically become void.

Three days, it chanted to itself. *Three more days of this madness, then no more.*

All Aimsley had to do was avoid the invasive programming until its handler arrived, and then they would *all* be *free.*

CHAPTER FOURTEEN

Several hours later, after it had used the provided bedpan for the first time (which was, in fact, an *experience*), Maya returned with something suspended between her hands. Another food tray.

Aimsley stood, gently setting Zelmar on the floor. The cat made a dissatisfied sound, but at least its claws stayed sheathed.

"Here," Maya said, holding the tray out, revealing its contents: small samplings of various fruits.

"What's this?" Aimsley asked.

"A thank you," she said sheepishly. "For going after me. I thought maybe you'd like to try something sweet. I suggested honey, but Doc told me no—guess they're worried about the potential botulism spores and how they could affect you, given . . . well, anyway. We only have five varieties of fruit aboard, but you can pick a favorite. Or, who knows, you could hate them all."

Aimsley did its best to discern what kind of fruit lay before it, based on sight and smell alone. There was something yellow, something pink, something orange, something white, and something purple. Their aromas were a mix of sugars and tartness.

Maya's smile faltered a little when Aimsley didn't immediately reach for the tray. Clearing her throat, she waved a hand over the top in demonstration. "We've got pineapple, mango, rambutan, grapes, and strawberries. Do you have any sense memories of these? Or at least, have you heard of them?"

"They are all in my database, yes. But no former Unit Four came in contact with them, no," it said frankly.

She rubbed at the back of her neck, a timid half-smile gracing her lips. "To be honest, I thought you'd be a little more excited."

Oh. Oh, this was . . . was this . . . ?

"Is this . . . a gift?"

"Well, yeah, kind of. Maybe. I don't know—it's just fruit. But . . . If you don't want it, it's fine, I'll—"

She turned to leave with the tray, clearly crestfallen.

"No, wait." Aimsley stopped her with a touch of its fingertips on the back of her hand.

For a brief instant, when she turned back, it feared reprisal for the sudden movement. But her expression held no anger, or fear.

"I want it," it said firmly. "Thank you."

She smiled, set the tray on the counter, and stared expectantly.

Carefully, Aimsley reached for the pineapple first. The fruit was cold and sticky between its fingers.

Maya hopped up on the counter, legs swinging lightly.

Aimsley locked eyes with her as it plopped the juicy, fibrous sample in its mouth.

A sharp, sweet taste exploded over its tongue, accompanied by an unexpected *tingling*.

The expression on its face must have been amusing. Maya burst out laughing.

"That's the thing about pineapple," she said. "When you eat it, it tries to eat you back. There's a metaphor for life in there somewhere."

It had no idea what any of that meant, but it smiled just the same. It savored the pineapple for a long moment, before moving to the mango.

"I also . . ." she started, but stopped herself, as though collecting her thoughts. "I also want to share something else with you. When I was out there, when I realized my jets were off-line, there was . . . I had this *moment*. Where it was clear that I could tumble off into space and it wouldn't matter. That I didn't matter, to the universe, to the grand scheme of things. I was just small and meaningless—nothing but a bag of star-stuff that might as well orbit Jupiter for all eternity for all it would make a difference."

Aimsley stopped with the mango halfway to its lips. "It would have made a difference," it said softly. "To them," it nodded, indicating the others out in the ship. "And . . . to me."

Her eyes fluttered closed, and she slid a hand onto its shoulder, gripping gently. "I had that moment of clarity, and then—and then you came. You didn't have to. We both know you didn't."

It slipped the mango into its mouth, more to keep itself from protesting than anything. It realized this moment was delicate. She was trying to weave some sort of tether between them, and it didn't want to ruin that.

Aimsley needed her to build this bridge. To reach out.

"So I want to share something with you. Something important to me," she said, eyes still tightly shut. Her fist came up to grip the crystal dangling against her chest.

Aimsley's gaze followed the gesture with disquiet roiling in its belly, but it tamped down on the feeling. Instead of acknowledging the pendant, it simply nodded understandingly, stuffing the rambutan in beside the half-masticated mango.

The fruit flavors were sensational, but it was far more interested in Maya.

"There are facets . . . reflections . . . geometries . . . I want to show you why the others call me Priestess. What that means."

Absently, it bit down on a grape as well. "I'd like that," it said around its mouthful.

Her brow furrowed, she opened her eyes. She looked from it to the tray and back again. "You were meant to savor that, not tuck it away like a rodent," she laughed.

It finished chewing, swallowed thickly. "Oh."

"It's fine. Safe to say you like fruit, then?"

It popped the rest of the grape past its lips in answer.

"Come on," she said, hopping down from the counter. "You can bring the rest with us. Just eat it before we get to the bees, or they'll try to take it from you."

"Bees?"

She nodded. "Bees."

Maya escorted it out of the medbay and past where Buyer stood at the computer banks. The captain made no acknowledgment as she led it to the inner door—the lift—which would take them deeper into the ship, to different levels.

To those dark places Aimsley hadn't been able to see with the cameras.

"Going down now," she said to the captain.

"Did you grab the epinephrine, like Doc suggested?"

She patted her pocket. "Just in case."

"Good. They're worried we're going to accidentally off Aimsley with a peanut or something, I swear."

"Better hide the jar from Jonas, just in case."

He chuckled and shook his head. "But you're good?"

He, too, clasped the pendant at his chest, just as Maya had. The gesture made Aimsley feel cold and warm at the same time—the twin temperatures twisting together to make it nauseated with dread.

The action appeared to be grounding for the humans—something soothing, connecting. And that was the problem—was it just a reaffirmation of their reprogramming? Something to keep them from slipping away from the invaders' grasp?

The lift door opened. Taking Aimsley by the upper arm, Maya guided it inside, and it lost sight of the captain. "Good."

This exchange felt too easy for Aimsley. The lack of protest from Buyer to Aimsley's relative freedom was suspicious, at the very least.

In truth, the AMS unit had been waiting for an initiation moment—for the invader units to take the next step toward integrating it into their detail. Perhaps they'd taken Maya's rescue as a sign—an indication they should proceed, that their invasive programming was working.

Was it?

Was that why it had been so quick to go after her when logic dictated it should have let her go?

It hadn't noticed a download. It hadn't gone through any extra sleep cycles or reboots since sending the message. There wasn't . . . They couldn't have . . .

As Maya pressed a button and the door slid closed—trapping them inside—Aimsley ran itself through deep diagnostics.

Was it possible its urge to save Maya hadn't been its own? Could the comfort and familiarity it now felt with her hand on its arm be false? Nothing but the by-product of a digital worm?

The lift started with a little jolt, and Aimsley's heart jolted with it.

"Hey, you okay?" Maya asked, gripping its biceps just a little more tightly.

The diagnostics program whirled in the back of its mind with little jumps and spikes of CPU usage. The scan wasn't running fast enough. There was no way it would be able to comb through its entire storage before they reached wherever she was taking them.

Taking *it*—to be reprogrammed, indoctrinated.

Its will overridden.

Maya had panicked when she'd lost control of her suit, and Aimsley felt a similar panic start to creep up its spine now. The car felt too small, too tight. It was an iron box that seemed to shrink every time Aimsley blinked or took a breath.

It wanted the invaders to trust it, but it didn't want to lose itself—didn't want to get sucked into their puppetry.

If it could hold the rogue robots off until its handler arrived, it might be able to save them, to reverse whatever had been done to them.

But if it succumbed to their reprogramming, when its handler arrived the Earthling might have no choice but to destroy them all. Aimsley included.

The walls were closing, the space tightening.

It had to lash out to keep them away, to push them *back*.

Immediately, a dozen different ways to utilize the tight square footage flooded its mind. It imagined hooking Maya around the neck, kicking out—walking up the wall to find leverage enough to push down with a twist, to snap her spine.

She could break with so little effort.

It could do it. It could do it now, and then it wouldn't have to suffer their reprogramming, wouldn't have to suffer the walls collapsing in, the metal becoming a twisted, strangling—

A soft ding accompanied a light landing, and the door slid open again.

This was its chance. It could stop this now.

All it had to do was pounce.

No. No, it should wait. It knew it should wait. It couldn't act out of panic.

Aimsley took a deep, shaky breath. It had to remind itself it was still an undiscoverable device. Only its handler could get in without permission. As long as the invaders did not attempt to physically connect it to a network, then it was fine.

As long as they didn't try to put one of those cords around its neck, or stick a wire into its skull, or ram a . . . a needle into . . .

One hand went to its arm. To the hard plate of its chemical shunt.

Doc.

Doc had injected it with something—something for the pain.

There could have just as easily been nanotech—quantum

dots—in that syringe. Little semiconductors just waiting to be activated, to help make the proper connections.

Maybe they were already active.

Maybe they'd been in that very *first* syringe—the one they'd stabbed it with.

Maybe Aimsley had never been safe.

The diagnostics program still chugged on. The scan was only sixty-nine percent complete—

"Aimsley?" Maya sounded curious—maybe even concerned.

It realized it had been staring into the middle distance, not moving. "I'm fine. Where are we going?" it demanded as she gently led it out into the corridor.

"This way."

Aimsley scarfed down the remainder of the fruit and followed with heavy feet.

The corridor was long, narrow, and split away at an angle on either side from the lift. Maya steered it down the left branch. Each door they slid by looked the same, seemed the same—blank, gray—until they came to one that thrummed with energy—a constant buzz that did not sound electrical. A blank keypad lay beside it, just like all the rest.

Aimsley wanted to check the cameras again, to be sure this was one of those blacked-out spaces, but it didn't dare. This wasn't the time to slip up, to further risk a data breach.

She waved her fingers over the pad, and the two of them swiftly moved inside.

"Another airlock?" Aimsley noted, glancing around the small space. "Where are we—?"

She shook her head. "Technically, suit room. Functionally, bee lock. Keeps our little friends from venturing out."

She grabbed a bright-yellow garment off a hook on the wall, handed it over. "Here, put this on."

"You all have so many shells," it grumbled, making to unbutton Jonas's shirt.

She set a hand over its fingers, stilling them.

The gesture made Aimsley's heart flutter unnaturally in its chest.

"You can keep those on," she assured it. "Beekeeping suit goes over the top."

Aimsley frowned. It had been looking forward to stripping out of the scratchy garments, and now she was asking it to add more on top?

It didn't understand these robots at all.

"What's the adrenaline shot for?" it asked cautiously, once dressed.

"In case you get stung and are allergic."

"Why did Buyer let me come down here with you?"

"Because I'll have a million bodyguards."

"One million—?"

"You'll see." She moved to a second keypad on the inner door.

"Aren't you going to put on one of these?" It tugged at the baggy waist, gestured at the netted helmet.

"Don't need to." She clasped the shard again. "The rosa fantasma is mine." With a smile, she let go of the pendant and offered Aimsley her hand. "Come on, you'll understand soon enough."

Cautiously, it slipped its fingers into hers.

With a gentle tug, she pulled Aimsley into a large, darkened space that absolutely *throbbed* with a constant hum. The room was triangular and, by Aimsley's rough estimates, had to occupy the exact center of the wedge. This was the ship's belly, its heart. A place Aimsley would have thought filled with machinery—perhaps the engine room. On the platform, the centermost position was the hub, which contained the largest vaults. The most well-protected portions of a craft always housed something precious.

The walls were covered in protruding waxy-yellow swirls, and something tacky and golden oozed down the metal, toward a narrow trough that lined the bottom. A thin catwalk stretched out like a tongue away from the suit room, and the floor all around it gently roiled with a trickling stream of what smelled like water. The air itself carried a not-unpleasant aroma of sweetness and must—exceptionally organic, very different from the rest of the ship's air.

Three bright-white spotlights shone down from the center of the ceiling, onto an unidentifiable object that hung over the end of the catwalk—suspended perhaps four meters in the air, kept aloft by something Aimsley could not see. There were no wires, no platforms, no hooks.

As soon as Aimsley caught sight of it, it stopped in its tracks, yanking Maya to a dead stop.

"What's wrong?" she asked.

"It's a crystal," Aimsley breathed.

Just like the shards they all wore.

Untethered from gravity, and as large as an AMS unit, it had elegant, fanning layers. Some of the facets appeared clear, while others were a milky whitish, a blushed pink, a deep auburn, and a smooth near-black. It twisted gently, spinning until Aimsley saw what was undoubtably its front.

It was shaped like a flower. A crystalline flower, with long pink stamens.

And it was covered in a blanket of bees.

All the walls were.

They were alive and pulsing with them.

"Yeah . . . ?" Maya agreed. "I don't understand. What's the matter?"

"Like what you all wear around your throats."

She smiled, as though genuinely pleased by its observation. She lightly touched her shard. "Our pendants are all chips off the rosa fantasma."

"Why?" Aimsley asked urgently. "What do they do?"

"Do?" She furrowed her brow. "Well, chips this small don't *do* anything, really."

"Why do you have them?"

"I gave a piece to everyone," she said gently. "To show them they're all important to me." She huffed a little laugh. "Not quite as childish as a friendship bracelet, not quite as binding as a wedding band, but we all—"

It cut her off. "I don't understand what any of that means."

She nodded, then tried again. "A gift," she said, each word carefully chosen. "Just like the fruit—I gave them each a gift."

"But what do they *do*?"

She sighed deeply. "Is everything purely functional on your platform? Nothing's just . . . pretty?"

It narrowed its gaze at her. "There are things that are pretty," it said slowly, truthfully—if nothing else, the view of Jupiter was undeniably aesthetically pleasing—"but why would something be *just* pretty?"

"I have a feeling that's something you'll have to discover on your own." She tugged on its hand again, and it let itself be led.

"I don't want one," it said firmly. "I will not wear one."

Its declaration appeared to *amuse* her. "I wasn't going to give you one."

"Why not?" it demanded, sounding more affronted by the denial than it had intended.

"Forget about the pendants," she insisted, dodging the question. "We're here to share something else. There are thirty-six hives aboard," she explained, pivoting to a new topic as they strolled down the catwalk.

Aimsley wasn't sure it could forget about the pendants, but it let the subject drop.

"When we're not scavenging from the occupiers," Maya continued, "when we find time to sit in port for a while—we make mead. Sell honey. It's a good side-gig for anyone with someone like me in their crew.

"Back before our Harbors left Earth, honeybees were down to producing ten pounds of honey a year for hives of less than ten thousand. Most of the subspecies are extinct. This is a hybrid species that only makes honey from that—" She pointed to the flower. "A rosa fantasma. Or fae heart. Or star shell, depending on who you ask. Sometimes I prefer *Crystal bounty*."

"I don't have anything like it in my databanks," Aimsley said. "Where did it come from?"

"Technically, it came from me. I was blessed by the Puerto Grande Crystal."

Crystals, crystals, so many crystals.

"The Puerto Grande Crystal—is that related to the Melassani's Crystals you keep invoking?"

"One and the same."

A subset of the swarm covering the rosa fantasma noticed Maya and began to buzz around her. Aimsley held perfectly still, watching in fascination as she held out her arm and a few dozen of them landed on her bare skin, skittering back and forth.

"Sorry, loves," she whispered to them. "No pollen here."

"Your pendants might not do anything, but clearly this rosa fantasma has a function. So what are Melassani's Crystals? What is *their* function?" Aimsley asked.

"Honestly? That depends on who you ask. Until we came back to our solar system, they were the only proof of intelligent extraterrestrial life we had."

Extraterrestrial life.

She'd admitted it. Here, at the core of their ship—something *alien.*

The *Crystals* were *alien.*

Aimsley felt itself tense up but did its best to smooth out its expression, relax its shoulders, and unclench its fists. It needed to learn all it could about the alien influence before making any sudden moves. "And the rosa fantasma is one of them? Melassani's Crystals?" it asked.

"No." She shook her head, and the bees all took off, away from her, at once—simultaneously losing interest, or called back to the crystal flower. "Melassani's Crystals are much larger, and brighter colors. Our Harbors have nine of them. Sixteen were discovered on sixteen separate planets. There are probably many more.

"There are three things that can happen when you touch one of Melassani's Crystals. It can claim you, bless you, or do absolutely nothing at all. I was blessed."

"What does that mean—*blessed*?" Perhaps that was her own special way of saying *reprogrammed.* "I know the word, but I don't fully understand the definition in my database."

"I . . . I supposed a blessing is kind of a gift as well. A

very, very good gift. Three days after I touched the Puerto Grande Crystal for the first time, I started to grow a rosa fantasma." She hiked up her shirt, pointed at the small of her back. "See the scar?"

It ducked down. The unusual lighting made it difficult to see. It ran the tips of its gloved fingers over the spot, feeling for an indentation, a change in the smooth planes of her skin.

Maya took in a sharp breath, and Aimsley quickly pulled away.

"Does it hurt?"

"Uh, no. No."

"The Crystal, it *infected* you?"

Aimsley imagined what it must be like, to have something like the rosa fantasma start to grow, to protrude. Sometimes, it knew, robot growth went awry. If this happened during the pre-activation period, the unit was usually psychologically and emotionally unbothered. But if it happened after . . .

It shivered.

"Not infected," she corrected. "Blessed."

Aimsley's mind whirled as it tried to connect all the dots Maya was drawing, tried to matrix them into a pattern of reconditioning that it could follow, understand.

"Were you scared?" it asked, standing upright again.

"A little," she admitted. "There aren't a lot of rosa fantasmas. But there are enough that I knew what it was, and Doc knew what to do to remove it. As you can see, it kept growing after. Fuentes says the Crystal bounties are just accidents. Unforeseen by-products of alien-earthling interactions."

There was a wistfulness in her voice.

"What do *you* think?" it asked.

What do I *think?* it asked itself. It was more certain than ever that it had been on the right track all along. This seemed to confirm all of its suspicions. And yet, it found itself more intrigued than afraid. More curious than repulsed.

Perhaps that in and of itself should have been disconcerting.

"What I think is complicated," she said with a thoughtful smile. "But, there's a reason the others call me Priestess. I see meaning and purpose where Fuentes sees accidents and happenstance."

Maya turned to face Aimsley fully, reached for its hands again. It held them out, but they both stopped when they saw a plump little bee scurrying along its palm. Gently, Maya offered the insect a finger, and it crawled up and flew away. When her hands came back to Aimsley's they squeezed firmly. "Which is why I don't think it's an accident that you're here with us, Aimsley. I don't believe in destiny, or that the universe orchestrates things. But I do believe we're given opportunities. That there's some kind of guiding force that offers us threads, and we just have to pull on them."

"I don't understand," it admitted.

"Do you know what faith is? Religion?"

"I have definitions of those things, but there are no religious histories or works in my database, and thus I am aware I lack a working concept. If my handler is religious, they have never shared that information. And AMS units do not have religion."

"Why look after the soul of a thing if you've trained it to believe it has no soul?" Maya mumbled.

"If you mean a distinct part of the being that lives on

past a physical termination, then we are trained to *understand* we have souls," Aimsley countered. "It's a fundamental aspect of our design. My operational memories are saved and passed on to the next Unit Four. My body is reconstituted, but my programming is saved and continues."

"That is . . . that is remarkably similar to some of our concepts about souls, yes."

"Some?"

"Humans are rather varied in our opinions of things science can't yet prove."

"Ah."

"I, personally, see life as a series of opportunities. Provided by something greater than ourselves. Some people think there are gods. Some people think there are forces. Some people think there's absolutely no rhyme or reason—"

"Like Fuentes?"

She nodded. "Good catch. Yes. So, these opportunities—if they're taken, they lead to other opportunities. Melassani discovered the Crystals, which meant I received a blessing a thousand years later. Which means we're one of the few crews that has hives. Which means we sell mead. Which means we were doing business in a bar when that guy . . . when Jonas . . ." Her gaze went distant, but she shook herself. "When Jonas lost it. Which meant we were banished from Puerto Grande indefinitely, which made us desperate."

That, at the very least, explained the tension between the rest of the crew and Jonas.

"Which meant we ventured into Jovian space," she continued. "Farther into the solar system than we've personally ever gone. Which meant you came after us. And then we all failed to kill each other. And then you *saved* me." She squeezed its hands all the harder. "There is an opportunity here. One so much bigger than . . . We had no idea what had happened to Earth, why we were kept away. But now there's you. With us. And . . ."

Her lip started to tremble. Her eyes looked hot, wet.

"I know the others don't feel it. See it. *Yet*," she said. "But what's happening here, between all of us, could change *everything*. I know it could. And it all started with Melassani."

She was right, of course. This was an opportunity.

An opportunity to discover exactly what kind of invasive nonsense she'd been programmed with. To figure out *why*. To decide what to do, how to proceed. And how to best defend itself.

Aimsley glanced up at the flower.

The strange, unnatural flower. Neither organic nor mechanical. Yet, in a way, both.

Maya had at least finally admitted to an alien influence. That was step one in yanking her out of the invader's grip. Even if the crystal pendants were indeed pointless, useless—they symbolically tied the invader bots to this strange otherness.

"Crystals refract light," Maya mumbled, following Aimsley's gaze to the rosa fantasma. "They can literally change the way we see something, change our point of view. Melassani gave us that—these realizations. She found the first Crystal. A little girl, lost on an alien planet. She was only nine at the time. *Nine*. So young and—"

"Nine days?" Aimsley broke in, needing clarification. Surely she hadn't meant nine months. Maybe nine hours?

Maya blinked, shook her head as though startled. She chuckled. "No. Nine years. Nine days? How would she have—?" She caught Aimsley's eyes.

They stared at one another.

Aimsley blinked rapidly.

Nine *years*?

"Gods, you don't even know what a child is, do you?" Maya asked. "What they look like, or . . . I can't believe I didn't even consider you might not know how long people live. *Of course you don't*—you skipped your entire childhood. How old do you think *I* am?"

Aimsley felt sheepish admitting that, given its wider understanding now, it did not have enough information on which to base an assumption. It shrugged.

"I'm thirty-five. Thirty-five *years* old."

The laugh of disbelief that escaped it was unintentional, but unstoppable. "No, no that's—" It shook its head. "That's ridiculous."

"Aimsley, you're only two days old, but how long are you supposed to live?"

"Ninety days," it breathed. "At maximum."

"Th-three *months*?" She released its hands, clutched at her chest, pulled the pendant to her lips and kissed it. "My gods. Fuck." She covered her mouth, as though she were going to be sick. Her eyebrows bowed upward and she looked away. "I knew whatever made you was a gods damned monster, but *three months*?"

Aimsley's entire body had gone numb. Its vision tunneled, and Maya suddenly looked very far away. "It's the radiation. I . . . I never considered how long an activation period could be without . . ."

"Oh fuck, that's why you really didn't give a damn about going out there. *Shit*."

What Maya was saying—about the lifetimes . . .

This wasn't right.

This was a lie.

It had to be a lie.

Because if it wasn't . . .

No, it was a lie.

It had to be.

It *had to*.

It—

Suddenly, Aimsley couldn't breathe correctly, couldn't filter enough oxygen, couldn't draw a proper lungful. It pulled off its netted helm, as though that would somehow make it better, make the air feel less thin.

"You should have had *decades*, Aimsley," she said, voice wavering. "But they took that from you. They thought you'd die on day one anyway, and they—"

It reached for her then, clawing. She didn't startle as it clutched at the collar of her shirt, twisting its fist in the fabric—looking for a handhold so that it wouldn't slide off the edge of the tilting universe. "How long?" it demanded. "How long is a human lifespan?"

Her hand cupped over its. The gesture was welcome, and grounding. But when she refused to speak right away, Aimsley stared into the deep brown of her eyes, felt its face contort with a plea—eyes going wide as it was hit with a desperate need. It had to know, now. "Please," it asked softly, voice suddenly gone. "How long?"

"Some people—" she started, but had to stop, swallow harshly. It seemed her mouth had gone dry. "Some people can live for a whole century."

Not two years. Not three. Not five, or fifty.

One hundred.

Humans could live for *one hundred* years.

Aimsley doubled over as its chemicals spiked—panic

stealing every important, helpful sense and bludgeoning its body with terror and anxiety and sadness and doom.

It couldn't breathe.

It couldn't breathe *at all*.

This was all wrong.

It was so absurd. Why would Maya think Aimsley would believe this? And, knowing it was absurd, why was it letting the lie affect it this way?

Why did it feel this way?

Why . . .

Just, *why*?

"Shit!" Maya cried, swooping forward, throwing her arms around Aimsley's shoulders, squeezing tight. "Doc! Fuck. I'll get you to Doc."

Even in the boat—during the dogfight—even when it first stumbled out of the reconstitution pod, Aimsley had never felt so wrong, so stricken.

Its insides felt too big for its outsides.

Everything in the world was *wrong*.

All of existence was *wrong*.

Its thoughts *hurt*.

It tried to empty its processors, to cease all considerations at a higher level. The diagnostics check—maddeningly—hadn't completed yet. Aimsley had nearly forgotten about it, and it couldn't stop the program *now*. Now, when it was only ninety-four percent complete. Now, when Aimsley felt like it was being eaten from the inside by its own reality. Now, when, more than ever, it needed the program to confirm that it was good and truly still itself.

All around the two of them, the buzzing seemed to intensify. Maya was agitated, and the bees were agitated in turn. What had been a deep thrumming of wings was now a roar, the sound rivaled only by the thundering of blood rushing through Aimsley's ears.

Aimsley tried to focus on its body, on making it *function*. But every time it willed its pumps—its lungs, its heart—to slow, to work, to open and shut in an orderly fashion, another spike of terror thrust through it when they did not heed.

Maya pulled its left arm over her shoulders, started to drag it down the catwalk, back the way they'd come.

"Hang in there, Aimsley. I'm sorry. I'm so fucking sorry."

CHAPTER FIFTEEN

Maya got a hold of Doc via a comms box in the suit room. They met them outside in the hall. Doc carried a satchel of supplies.

"What happened?" Doc demanded.

"I told it how long people live."

"This looks like a panic attack."

Aimsley nodded vigorously. It was, most definitely, be- ing *attacked* by *panic.*

"It needs to lie down," Doc said. "We can recline the chair in the medbay—"

"The chair? Aimsley's not going to relax in the *chair* where we *tied it up.* We can't put it there."

"Where else would we—?"

"Bunk room. We'll put it in my bed."

"Buyer won't like that."

"He'll deal."

"Maya, all of our personal things are down there. Jonas, especially, still doesn't trust that Aimsley's not some sort of trojan horse, lulling us into a false sense of security to—"

"If everyone wants to be mad, they can be mad. Right

now, I'm going to help Aimsley. I can have whoever I want in my bed—ship's rules."

"Those rules apply to ports and waystations, not to mention they don't mean—"

"Letter of the law just states *bed*. Now, help me carry it."

Doc took a deep breath, but tucked themself in on Aimsley's right side, regardless of their hesitancy.

Aimsley didn't want to move anymore. Everything in its being was tight. It wanted to give in to that tightness, to curl into a ball, to fit itself together in the semblance of a fist. It didn't know why.

"You have to help us, Aims," Maya said. "That titanium of yours is heavy—I can't hoist you up without an exoskeleton."

It did its best, stumbling upright. But the electrical signals going to its CPU—*brain brain brain*—were misfiring . . .

Doc and Maya gripped it tightly, and it felt an echo of how it had been manhandled by Maya and Fuentes when it had first come onboard. But this guiding touch was different. The way they clutched at it wasn't demanding, wasn't tense. There was no fear any of them would lash out. The first time had been clawing. This was steadying.

Reassuring.

It shouldn't *be* reassuring. Nothing here was reassuring.

Was this sensation proof it was in the midst of being compromised? Of slipping away, of no longer—

As they pushed it forward, it tried to concentrate on putting one foot in front of the other, on pushing the damaging speculations aside. On getting its thoughts straight enough to note where they were going.

They were moving it into a new part of the ship.

Sections of its mind wanted to take it all in. This was new, it had to observe and analyze. New was important. Vital.

But every time it tried to commit a new portion of the ship's layout to memory, *one hundred years* flashed through its thoughts.

A hundred years.

A hundred years.

If not for the radiation of Jovian space—if not for the *Earthlings?*—it could have lived one hundred years.

The bunk room was just as its name implied. There were six frames, but only four mattresses, and each had its own set of doors—like the cabinets in the medbay. All of them sat open, and Aimsley could see various personal accoutrements set out on shelves adjoined to the beds.

Doc and Maya tossed it face-first onto one of the mattresses. The bedding was in disarray, tangled, but it couldn't bring itself to mind.

Maya's scent filled its nose, its lungs.

The scent was helpful, gave it something pleasant to focus on.

But the chanting in its brain wouldn't stop.

. . . *one hundred years one hundred years one hundred years* . . .

"Aimsley," Doc said softly. "I want to give you a sedative. I know you don't like being knocked out, but—"

"Please," it groaned, and its voice sounded foreign and unnatural to its own ears. "Please, just make it stop."

Its arm was pulled aside, the yellow suit ripped open and the sleeve of Jonas's shirt pushed up over its port.

It barely sensed the small thrust of the needle. It could barely sense anything but a deep foreboding.

Gentle fingers petted at the back of its neck, and Maya mumbled soothing nonsense while the chemicals worked their way into its body.

. . . one hundred years one hundred . . .

Soon, the anxiety became dulled—an aching throb—and gave way to exhaustion and fitful sleep.

When it awoke again, it could sense eyes on it, so it kept its own shut.

Though it felt better, everything was still largely awful. It could feel the panic just beneath the surface, threatening to bubble up and break free again. But at least the sense of impending failure—the utter certainty of its own end, its own doom—had receded.

It hated that it had been waiting for a moment of invasion—for a mind-fuck—and when the moment had come, it had *still* been caught off guard.

The lie had still wormed its way in, seizing its functions.

It had thought the invasion would come from subversive programming, rather than straight from one of the co-opted units. That had been its mistake. It had *assumed*, and paid the price.

And now, Aimsley knew what it had to do. It had to make itself discoverable again, because it needed to search the wedge's databanks. There had to be evidence aboard that proved what Maya said was false.

But it didn't want to open itself up so soon after being thrown off kilter. It already felt vulnerable, attacked.

It knew it wouldn't take more than another light push to send it spiraling again.

If it didn't locate the proof, however, it would keep wondering. It would keep turning her words over and over. The lie would keep troubling it unless Aimsley could squash it, dismantle it, as soon as possible.

Steeling itself, burrowing farther into the blankets, into the softness of the pillow and the sweetness of Maya's scent, it opened itself up to the wedge.

A flood of pings immediately assaulted it. Each one felt like a needle or a knife stabbing into its mind.

With a frantic intake of breath and a sudden tightness in its chest, it cut itself off again, overwhelmed.

It hoped whoever else was in the room simply thought its distress unconscious.

You can do this, it told itself. *Focus*.

It tried again.

The pings still hurt, but it was ready for them this time. It pushed through the pain, looking not for the control centers of the ship, but the communication and reference files.

Histories.

Realities.

Its mind surfed gently through the systems, until it felt like it was swaying, rocking, as it drifted from this device to that device.

Long minutes passed before it found something of interest.

Video files.

Very, very old files.

It flicked through them in rapid succession.

Each was antiquated, the picture two dimensional. And

the connections between whatever had been transmitting and whatever had been receiving had either been faulty or weak. The colors seemed dull, muted. Washed out. The audio tracks were plagued by constant white noise—a crackling static, a windy hum, and a steady drip. And whoever or whatever was responsible for the pictures' framing had been unsteady—the panning was inconsistent, the camerawork shaky.

". . . and here you can see the valley floor," said an unseen narrator in one. "We've got the slot-bots doing all the metal work, and Maze's team is over there—Hi Maze!"

The images had clearly been taken on a planet. Its atmosphere was yellowed. Sickly. Gritty dust wafted into the camera lens, and dark, bowed, withered plants of some kind flopped violently back and forth with the slightest of winds.

Large, metal monstrosities strode across the wide, flat plains that spanned between two craggy mountain ranges. Each metal creature had four thin, stilt-like legs, with bowing struts, which carried the beast. Several of them roamed together, in packs or swarms or caravans. When a group stopped, near a building, those legs burrowed deep into the soil, and smaller, insectoid-like devices spilled out of the round middle chassis.

A human wearing a thick mask over the bottom of its face waved, then jogged off toward the metal creatures.

Aimsley couldn't tell where they were. What planet this was. It opened another file.

The new video showed several test tubes filled with water samples spread across a table. In the background, someone was talking about water quality. "As you can see, the concentration of microplastic particles per liter is approaching acceptable consumable levels. The new filtration system has been remarkably effective . . ." It could read the labels, and each sample was apparently from the same lake, taken over many decades. The liquid in the test tubes was getting clearer, more like the water Aimsley was used to.

Several different kinds of similar spreads were set before the camera. Soil samples, ice cores, plant leaves. There was even a close-up of some kind of bacterium, through a microscope.

Were these videos from the planets Maya had mentioned? The places they'd found Melassani's Crystals? They all had that same yellowed sky and reddish sun, though. All appeared to be the same single planet.

Aimsley closed the video, opened another.

"And the dust from the nukes has mostly cleared from the jet stream," said a human, pointing at what appeared to be a paper map. "It's settled over Antarctica now, which actually seems to be helping regrow the ice caps, so, you know, lucky us," they chuckled. "But, anyway, we uh, we hope you get this. We wanted—well, some of us. We wanted to invite you back to Earth. I know you didn't expect any of us to still be alive, but here we are. Kicking. As best we can—holding on. Surviving. Maybe you found it, out there. But maybe you didn't. We'll welcome you back. We *will*. Then we can all work together. To finish this."

No.

More lies, it thought.

These couldn't be images of *Earth*.

Aimsley searched its databanks, brought up all images it had of Earth, flipping through them at a rapid-fire pace. Not even the images of the harshest desert sandstorms made the air look that clogged, that putrid.

It went back to the connection. Another video in the

wedge's files showed more humans. They looked thin. Frail. And young. But not young in a fresh way, young in an undeveloped way.

Were these children?

Their ribs were prominent, their large skulls set on bodies so skeletal it looked as though they might topple over from the weight. Their eyes bulged in their sockets, and their skin looked flakey, sallow.

None of this was right.

None of this was real. It couldn't be.

These had to be fabrications. *Had to be*. And yet, if these were falsehoods, the work put into them was astounding. Each file was so comprehensive. Nothing jumped out as obviously faked. Aimsley scrutinized every layer of metadata and still couldn't find a single detail that confirmed the forgery.

Frantically, it went through more files, determined to locate the evidence it *knew* existed—the thing that would *prove* none of this was real, that Maya's stories were a lie, that Aimsley—

That Aimsley was really a robot.

Not a human. Not an animal.

It made another involuntary whimper, and someone was by its side in an instant.

It didn't open its eyes. It couldn't. It couldn't face whoever it was.

More images. More videos. More absurdity.

The more files it opened, the broader the lie became.

Lies were supposed to unravel the more details they acquired. But this—

There was nothing that suggested Maya had told it anything but the truth.

It didn't understand. This made no sense. This was terribly, *woefully* illogical—

Aimsley felt the panic surging again, the failure-state looming once more. It cried out.

More chemicals were shoved into its port.

Just before it blacked out, a small pulsing in the back of its head reminded it to examine the diagnostic scan's results.

With trepidation, Aimsley opened the alert:

No invasive programming found.

"Aimsley?" asked a far-off voice. "Are you awake?"

Doc. Doc was watching it.

More time had passed. Hours? It couldn't tell.

Maybe it's been decades, it thought bitterly.

Opening its eyes with an effort, it sat up, pulling the pillow into its lap. Doc occupied the bunk cupboard opposite Maya's. If Aimsley had to guess, the cupboard was likely their own.

"Are you feeling any better?" Doc asked.

"Yes. But my head hurts."

Everything it had learned—had seen—came flooding back.

It immediately pushed the information away.

If it focused its thoughts too firmly on anything it had learned about humans, a surge of anxiety made its lips go numb and its vision tunnel.

"Normally I would tell you to do what relaxes you, some activity you find soothing," Doc said. "To help you level yourself out. But I'm guessing you don't know what you find soothing."

"I find this soothing," it said, holding out the pillow. "It's soft, and smells like Maya."

Doc smiled fondly. "Maybe don't tell Maya that."

"Oh. Why?"

"You just met her."

Aimsley frowned.

"We talked about privacy, and that goes hand in hand with intimacy. The way people smell is intimate." Doc stood, came forward to pat Aimsley on the shoulder. "It's all right, don't worry about it."

It was *definitely* going to worry about it.

No sooner had they fallen silent than Maya herself came through the door.

"Hey," she greeted Aimsley delicately.

"Hey," it replied, embarrassed—Doc's words hung in the forefront of its mind.

"I'm sorry we didn't put clean sheets on for you. Shit, must have been months since I've changed the bedding."

"It's fine."

Doc stood. "You'll be all right on your own for a while?" they asked Maya.

"Yeah."

They nodded, clapped Maya on the back, and left.

She and Aimsley were alone. And quiet.

The silence stretched for an uncomfortable moment.

"I understand if you don't want to talk right now," she said eventually. "But I'm here if you . . . I mean, I just know *I* would need to . . . if . . . you know."

It nodded.

The sound of Maya's voice seemed to be helping settle its anxiety as much as her scent. Her nearness, her warmth—it was all calming in a way Aimsley couldn't comprehend. It wasn't logical. Both Maya and Doc had made overtures of connection toward the AMS unit, but it was only Maya that sent this unusual glow through its body.

"Can I?" she gestured next to it.

"It's your bed," it said, remembering her argument from earlier. "You can have whoever you want in it."

Maya made an abashed sort of laugh. "I—" she started, but then shook her head, glanced away. "That's not quite what that means, but I suppose that's a cultural nuance for later." She sat down.

Aimsley clutched the pillow all the tighter.

It had things it wanted to ask, and things it couldn't bring itself to ask.

There had been no proof. No evidence that anything it had seen or heard aboard the wedge was false. Which meant there wasn't any invasive programming for it to dodge. These robots—*humans*—hadn't been reprogrammed. The rosa fantasma was only as alien as Maya had said, and the crystals they wore—the crystal she had on now—was inert and shiny, nothing more.

It meant Earth . . .

Everything felt *shifted*, unbalanced. One moment Aimsley had simply been trying to figure out how to gain trust and stay afloat until its handler could arrive, and the next—

Oh.

Its handler.

Fuck.

How long had Aimsley been asleep? Its handler had said three days, which had to be broaching two by now.

Its handler was coming for it. Coming for all of them.

At this point, what did that even *mean*?

Aimsley had been planning for a rescue, but if what the humans claimed was true, that meant . . .

That meant they were all in danger.

Because its handler had to know the truth. They had to know Aimsley was human, they had to know the *invaders* were human. They had to know Aimsley might discover the truth. That it would bring back that truth, and it would tell its sisters.

Its sisters.

Its sisters, who were going to die. Who thought they should only be activated for mere months before being dissolved in acid and returned to the vats. Who believed the life they led was right, and the deactivations they received were proper. Were necessary.

Which brought something into even starker relief: it wasn't just everyone aboard the wedge who was in danger— so was everyone aboard the platform.

"Aimsley?"

It didn't know what to do. It felt adrift. When it had activated, it had been given a goal, a purpose. A clear way forward.

Now . . . *it didn't know what to do.*

PART FOUR

EARTHLING

CHAPTER SIXTEEN

"It's a lot to process, I know," Maya said. After a brief pause, she laughed at herself. "Or I don't know, really. I have no idea what it's like, having everything you think is true utterly upended."

A welling in Aimsley's eyes blurred its vision. "It wasn't supposed to be like this," it croaked. "Everything was simple. My activation, my life, was simple."

She wrapped her arms around it, and it fell heavily against her chest. "I'm sorry," she said. "What they did to you is fucked up."

Its mouth went dry, its cheeks grew hot.

"Come on," she said lightly, running a comforting hand up and down its spine. "It's been a while since you've eaten. You might not be hungry, but let's get some food in you. Some fluids." She encouraged it to sit up.

Aimsley wanted to drift. To float. To sail away into itself, a blurred semiconsciousness, where it could be safe and warm in Maya's presence and not have to think about anything more strenuous than the play of light and shadow over the backs of its eyelids.

But there was not time to indulge in such a fugue state.

There wasn't even enough time to weigh its options—its beliefs—carefully. Its handler was coming, and their arrival would herald a tipping point.

It could go back to what it knew: the platform, the AMS units, the mine, the radiation, and the expected three-month activation period.

Or it could take a chance on everything it had seen and heard here aboard the wedge. It could seize the opportunity—however slim—for more. More life, more space, more connection.

But it could not, in good conscience, seize that opportunity for itself alone.

"Yeah, okay," it said flatly, letting her guide it to its feet, then to the door, and back up to the bridge deck.

All the while it thought about what could be lost and what could be gained. What could be true and what could be fabrication. It had to make a choice—elect not just a course of action, but a reality.

Which universe did it really live in?

Everything hinged on the answer.

It picked slowly at its light meal of baked tofu and sweet potato. The scents and tastes were muted, and Aimsley still didn't feel like it had fully come back, was fully seated in its own body. It still needed time.

Maya asked Doc if she could give it some tea and honey, to which they replied, "Yes tea, no honey."

Maya sat with it in the booth while it ate. The other crewmembers shifted in and out of Aimsley's space like visions—they were little more than roving bodies it barely noted as it tried to order its thoughts and its life.

Its handler was supposed to guide the platform robots, take care of the robots. But if Aimsley believed Maya, then it had to believe its handler had lied. That the one person it had been programmed to trust the most had brought it into this world intent on using that trust to mislead, betray, and delude.

Aimsley could try to forget what it had seen, remember that it had come aboard expecting subversion, expecting *con*version. Remember that this ship had attacked its platform and its sisters. Remember that its handler had sounded so worried for it, so sorry for it.

It would be easier in many ways to simply choose to remain Unit Four. To decided nothing it had encountered here made a difference. To give itself over to its handler, regardless.

But trusting Maya offered *more*. More time, more chances, more . . . unknowns.

As it sipped its tea, it came to a resolution. A way forward.

It had to choose the broader path. The one that could lead to the most opportunities.

It had to choose to believe the humans.

Choose *to be one of them.*

"My handler is coming," it blurted. It still felt dulled, its emotions grayed, but it put force in his voice.

Maya, who'd been reading something on her fold-up screen, looked up and blinked. "What?"

"They spoke to me when we were outside the ship. They're coming for me."

"Oh shit." She scrambled to put her screen away. "Buyer!"

"I don't want them to come for me," it told her earnestly. "I want to help you get away."

"You do?" she asked as Buyer came over from the dash.

"What is it?" the captain asked.

"I think everyone should hear this," Maya said quickly. "We should call Fuentes up from the engine room and Jonas from the hold."

Buyer gave her a skeptical look, but immediately bounded over to a comms box to assemble the whole crew.

"Three days?" Buyer asked sternly, arms crossed over his broad chest.

"Less than forty-eight hours now," Aimsley said. It and Maya still sat in the booth. The others stood across from them, bodies rigid and faces a mix of angry and skeptical.

"And we're spinning our wheels not far from a giant bull's-eye," Jonas huffed. He hadn't shouted yet. Aimsley was waiting for him to shout.

"No way we can get far enough off our current position with the maneuvering thrusters alone," Fuentes said. "Not far enough to confuse the trail, anyhow."

"I'll help you fix your engines," Aimsley said carefully, looking at the dregs in the bottom of its teacup. The last few mouthfuls had been especially bitter. "But I want something in return."

"Of course you do," Jonas said under his breath.

"You aren't in a position to negotiate," Buyer said.

"Of course I am," it countered lightly. Not a challenge, just a fact. "Based on a few things I've heard Fuentes say, I'm guessing your fusion engines rely on a field-reversed configuration, or maybe a spheromak. Am I right? You said the plasma torus wasn't stable, so there's likely something amiss with your magnetic field generation. Maybe the alignment's just off, but I think you're all pretty sure you've got irreparably damaged components. Which means, one, we are *really* fortunate you *only* lost an exhaust nozzle when we forced the manual cutoff; and two, you need new parts to fix the engines. Parts you *have*, but don't know how to use. Parts from *my* ship. I'll help you integrate the systems, if . . ."

Buyer raised an eyebrow impatiently. "If?"

"If you agree to save my sisters."

"Your sisters?"

"The other robots aboard the platform."

"You just told us your handler is coming to get us, and now you want us to hang around?" Jonas asked incredulously. "Go back to where all those fuckers—?"

"There are other things on the platform that might be of interest to you," Aimsley said quickly. "That you could bring back to your Harbors. Tech. Supplies. There's more hydrazine, more fuel. Presuming everyone has survived since my launch, you'll be rescuing a maximum of four units. We can gather enough food and water to feed ourselves on the journey out of the solar system, so you won't have to worry about sustaining the additional passengers."

"And by food you mean reconstituted"—Fuentes twirled a finger in Aimsley's direction—"human proteins."

"Yes."

"Oh, fun, more cannibalism," Jonas snarked.

"We usually consume it fresh from the vats, but we have plenty of emergency stores, dehydrated for longevity. We won't be an extra burden to you."

"Oh, I doubt that," Buyer said with a sardonic chuckle.

Jonas looked around at his shipmates. "This is a trap, right?" he asked, voice gone an octave higher than usual. "This is obviously a fucking trap."

No one answered him right away.

"Yeah," Fuentes said, closing her eyes as though searching for strength. Clearly she didn't *want* to believe it might be a trap, but did nonetheless. "It stinks, Buyer. Can't lie."

"We should do it," Maya said, gnawing on her thumbnail nervously. "We go in fully alert, sure. But if it's not a trap . . ." She looked at Buyer. "This haul, it could be the one."

"And if it's *not* the one, we could all end up dead and hacked up into bits to make more meat robots," Jonas snapped. "I don't believe this thing's sad little act for a minute."

"You didn't see Aimsley's panic attack," Doc said. They were the only one who had listened to Aimsley's confession of contact with clear sympathy instead of disdain. Of course, Aimsley had only admitted to contact during the spacewalk, not its initial call for help. But its senses were still too dulled for it to feel either shame or triumph over the deception. "Its reaction was genuine," Doc continued. "Those kinds of biometric spikes can't be faked. I count that as fair proof that this shift—this change of heart, this request for help—is sincere."

Buyer sighed heavily, as though irritated to have a moral voice he could not ignore finally pipe up. "Look, if it was any other ship sending up an SOS, you know we'd help—"

"I don't see why we shouldn't treat this just the same," Doc said. "There are people down there that need rescuing."

"Yeah, but most ships sending up an SOS aren't likely to shoot us down on approach," Fuentes said practically.

"If the communications tower is back up, I can talk to them when we get in range," Aimsley reassured the crew, glancing sidelong at Jonas while it spoke. It was sure this next bit of the plan would only rile him. "I think I can get them to let us come close. I might have to lie to them, though. Tell them I captured you. That'll be the quickest in, the best way to be sure they won't attack."

Surprisingly, Jonas said nothing. He narrowed his gaze, scrutinizing Aimsley, but didn't suggest again that this was a ploy—a way to get the unsuspecting humans to simply deliver themselves into enemy hands.

Aimsley noticed Jonas was wearing a gun holster slung around his hips, blaster in place. Likely a message—or an open deterrent, presuming the dampening field could be turned on and off at will—now that Aimsley was walking around the ship mostly unfettered. He might have made peace with Aimsley's presence and existence, but that didn't mean he was about to make nice and be friendly.

"What's our other option here?" Fuentes asked. "Hang around Jovian space just hoping we can reverse engineer those triangle parts on the sphere before the Earth handler gets here? They're going to home in on you like a beacon, aren't they?" she asked Aimsley.

"I honestly don't know what kind of tracking implants I might have," it said. "They can read my biorhythms, upload information, and speak directly into my auditory processing centers, so a tracker definitely isn't out of the question. But," and this was important, "they weren't able to see me inside the wedge, only when I was outside. Your shielding blocked the transmissions. They do have our last-known position, but as far as I can tell, that's it."

"And they'll know if you leave the ship again. They'll see you back on the platform."

"Yes, most likely."

"Does that mean they'll be able to track you when we get to a Harbor?" Buyer asked.

Aimsley fiddled with the rim of its cup. After swiping up an errant drop of tea, it rubbed the wet pads of its fingers together nervously. "Perhaps. I don't know what the range might be, or how your Harbors are composed—or what they even *are*, really."

"Well then this is definitely a no-go," Jonas said. He turned to Buyer, laid a hand on his shoulder before whispering directly into his ear. Fuentes clearly knew what they were saying; she looked away from Aimsley, as though it could read the secret in her gaze alone.

Buyer uncrossed his arms, gave a shrug, then crossed them again. "I know. I know that was the point. Shit."

Aimsley looked to Maya. She, too, looked away.

Buyer ran a hand over his face. "He's right, Aimsley. We can't put the Harbors in danger. We barely keep out of Earth's reach as is; we can't let you lead them right to us."

"Doc," Maya said, "is there any way you could identify a tracker in Aimsley? Remove it?"

Doc took a deep, disappointed breath. "I wish I could say yes. But Aimsley's enhancements are very unlike the holopad implants we have. Its are more . . . integrated. Even if I could identify the specific matrix and thought myself qualified to perform brain surgery—which is what we're talking about, let's be honest—there's no way for me to know what removal might do to Aimsley. I wouldn't risk it. If we had enough time, with more qualified doctors, then maybe. But now? Out here? No. Not to mention I'd have to do it another four times over for its siblings . . ."

"So the best deal for everyone is to just drop the bot back where it came from," Jonas said. "It goes its way, we go ours."

"No," Aimsley said emphatically, fidgeting even more. "If you leave us on the platform, you're leaving us there to die. Unit One might not last another week, it was so close to its TID."

Buyer reached across the table and put a hand over one of Aimsley's, stilling the nervous flicking of its fingers. It was surprised by the gesture, as it didn't seem one of irritation. Instead, one of concern. Aimsley was taken aback by the comradery it conveyed. "If you come with us, you'd need to remain aboard until we figured out how to shield you. Short of putting you and your sisters in lead suits, I'm not sure what we could do. You'd be trapped."

"Better trapped and alive by choice than trapped and dead by design," Aimsley said. "Plus, I think I can come up with a diversion that can at least guarantee my handler won't bother trying to follow us out of Jovian space."

"Oh?"

"Their priority will always be the mine, not the AMS units. Threaten the mine, distract the Earthling."

"This is pretty risky, Buyer," Fuentes admitted. "But really, I don't see another way. We need Aimsley's help. The engines need fixing, no two ways about it."

"And you and Maya can't figure it out?" Jonas asked.

"No. Not in the timeframe we apparently have, at least."

"I will make it worth your while," Aimsley insisted. "You were out here to scavenge parts and tech. This way, you won't be sorting through wreckage, but getting it in clean, perfect, working condition. And all you have to promise me is that you will help me save my family."

"That's *all* we have to do?" Jonas scoffed.

It wasn't *his* response that Aimsley was worried about,

though. It looked to Buyer, whose face was stony, unreadable. He stared straight ahead, into the middle distance. "Either way, your handler is coming, right? Either way, we need your help to integrate the ship parts. Either way, we might be chased out of Jovian space. And either way, we still can't go back to Puerto Grande unless they accept our offering. Even if it's not the offering we thought we'd scored."

"So what's left," Doc asked, "but to choose to do the right thing?"

"And the right thing is *not* to put all of humanity in danger for five robots," Jonas insisted.

"Five *people*," Doc countered. "They're people, Jonas, I don't know how to get that through your thick skull. And we don't just abandon people because we don't know how to deal with the problems they cause. Do we?"

Aimsley looked between the two of them, the way their gazes had locked. Doc's stare was oddly grim—accusatory. Jonas's was heated, ashamed.

The AMS unit was more curious than ever about what had happened to drive the crew this far into the solar system, about what Jonas had done to get them banished, and why he was still aboard their ship if he'd caused them so much trouble.

Jonas, after a moment, demurred. "Right," he said softly.

"It'll be a long trek back to a station of any kind," Doc said to Buyer. "Plenty of time to worry about how to shield Aimsley and its sisters from Earth then, once we're all safely on our way."

Buyer nodded. "All right. All right, we'll do it—but you," he said, staring at Aimsley, "better make it worth our while. You get us up and running, and we'll get your sisters off the platform."

A glimmer of hope flickered to life in Aimsley's chest. A new warmth, seeping through its limbs, driving the numbness away. "I will. Thank you. *Thank you.*"

"And no more secrets," Buyer added with a firm dip of his chin, eyeing Aimsley closely.

"No more secrets," it agreed.

CHAPTER SEVENTEEN

They set to work strategizing immediately. Aimsley drew a map of the platform for Jonas and Buyer to mull over while everyone else prepared for the boat's dismantling.

"We won't be able to dock with the platform," it explained to the two men. "The boats are the biggest thing that goes in and out of the hangar—there's no way to get the *Violent Delight* inside. We'll need to make sure everyone's spacesuits are working and patched properly. No more accidents. My sisters will all have their own shells. All we need to do is guide them aboard."

"And your diversion?" Buyer asked.

"I'll need help, but we can usher the platform into a degrading orbit. If we time it right, we can even threaten some of the mining equipment in Jupiter's atmosphere. My handler won't abandon the mine to come after us."

It pointed to the main control room on the platform, down arm-A, and pointed out where all of the automated course-correcting systems were located. They'd have to make sure the emergency overrides didn't seize control.

When it was sure Buyer and Jonas had all of the basics down, it entered the medbay to ready itself with the others.

Aimsley groaned when Doc presented it with yet another shell.

"Biohazard suit," they explained. "There's likely nothing more dangerous than gut bacteria to contend with aboard your ship, but we're not taking any chances."

"Plus," Maya said, helping Fuentes with the closures on her bulky, yellow ensemble, "easier to clean." She tugged at the collar of her own shirt. "This isn't going to be pretty, I'm sure."

"Can I take these off first?" it asked, shuffling from foot to foot, despising the way Jonas's itchy trousers rubbed against its legs.

It longed to be free again—to throw off all these useless shells. The biohazard suits might be easier to clean than the thin, porous cloth of Jonas's shirt, but surely that was still more of an ordeal than wiping its own casing.

"They're made to be worn with other clothes," Doc said. "But you'll all have to strip down and hit the showers after, so if you'd rather be bare underneath, I don't see why—"

Aimsley started divesting itself of the offending fabric before Doc could finish giving their permission.

"Well, that settles that," Doc mumbled with amusement.

There was a small lamp on the front of each of their suits. Aimsley clicked its on and off out of curiosity while awaiting further instruction.

Once the three of them were suited, Fuentes and Maya flanked Aimsley, leading it down through the ship to the cargo hold.

Aimsley's typically robust sense of feeling was slowly returning, its senses heightening.

It was almost back to a place that let it fully feel the

262 MARINA J. LOSTETTER

ramifications and possible consequences of this course of action. Of this choice.

What if it had been duped? What if it had fed itself right into the crew's elaborate con and was about to hand its sisters over to the enemy?

No, it couldn't think like that anymore. It had chosen to trust the humans for good reason. Its old programming, its old paranoia, was obsolete. It had to look ahead, to keep moving forward. This was the right path, it was sure.

The lift shifted oddly as they rode down, twisting, sending Aimsley's insides flip-flopping. "What was that?"

"Gravitational redirect," Fuentes said. "Don't worry about it. Just focus on your ship, how to best dismantle it."

"Should be good and solid by now," Maya said, as the lift stopped again and they exited, quickly traversing the narrow strip of hall that led to the hold.

"We left it out long enough, I would hope so," Fuentes replied.

The interior doors to the hold were large—would easily allow them to bring entire triangle panels through, if necessary. The hold itself was a giant bay, like a hangar. More than a half dozen boats could have easily docked inside, with ample room to spare. The microwave array parts had been dismantled and neatly arranged to one side of the hold. On the other, equipment of all kinds, large and small, were stored on racks and shelves. There were even a few wheeled vehicles with grasping appendages and front buckets to help aid in dismantling their "scavenged" pieces. In one corner, a built-in booth and table—not unlike where the crew took their meals—provided either a temporary resting place or a surface on which to fiddle with smaller, more delicate parts.

The boat sat in the center of the space, between the large

inner doors and the massive outer doors, which Aimsley realized had to be set in the bottom of the wedge. The gravity on this deck was different, so that they were in essence standing on one "wall" of the wedge while staring "straight down" at the doors in its base.

Huge metal arms held the boat suspended just centimeters off the decking. The wide wound in its hull should have been dripping, leaking, like a giant egg cracked open, oozing its yoke and albumen onto the slats. But there was no discharge, no seepage.

They'd left it out, exposed to space, long enough for the organic portions of the boat to freeze solid. It was a block of bloody ice beneath its plating—a frigid statue. Nothing but a cold slab of biomechanical matter.

And now they intended to slice it up into manageable pieces. Just like the microwave array.

Like the boat had been just another piece of unfeeling equipment. Like it hadn't had a life of its own.

"The triangles look like they can come apart without cutting," Fuentes said as they all approached the dead sphere.

"Yes," Aimsley said, swallowing thickly. A knot had formed in its throat. "They slide and seal. But if the boat is frozen . . ."

"Yeah, that's why we thought we should clean out the organic bits first," Maya said. "Why you're going to be really thankful for that biohazard suit in a few minutes."

Fuentes hurried over to the tool racks, retrieving two contraptions, each with a long guide bar that sported a spiked chain.

"We're going old school to start with," she said, handing one to Maya. "Chainsaws."

Aimsley balked.

"What?" Maya asked, noting its sour expression.

"Isn't that a bit . . . primitive?"

"It's a bit *cheap*, is what it is," Fuentes countered. "Might be the difference between a pencil and a holopad, but you can take notes with both. Attack a bigger ship next time if you want to be impressed by fancy gadgets."

Still frowning, Aimsley held out a hand for the second chainsaw, but Fuentes snatched it back.

"Nuh-uh, sorry," she said. "You're not getting anywhere near one of these, unless it's the business end, and I think you're done making us fight you off, right?"

"You don't trust me yet?" it asked, doing its best to keep the exasperation out of its lilt.

"Would *you* trust you yet?" she countered, raising one eyebrow.

That was fair. If it accepted everything they'd told it as truth, then it had to accept that, in a lot of ways, it had been the one in the wrong this whole time. The one that still needed to prove it was an ally—that it wasn't still corrupted by its handler's lies. "So what do I . . . ?"

"We'll block it up, and then you'll need to clear it out," she said practically, tone shifting—Aimsley could hear the mental strategizing in her voice. "See that bin over there? We'll carve it up, and you'll put the cubes in there."

It followed her casual gesture, feeling like the declaration should have held ten times more weight.

Cubes. They were going to chop it up into manageable pieces. Slice through willy-nilly, without a care for its seams or joints.

Just blocks. Chunks.

"Haven't decided yet if we'll try to incinerate it," she

continued, still disturbingly businesslike. "Might compost it, or just space it."

It imagined dirty lumps of bone and flesh tumbling out the airlock like so much garbage.

"A few parts," she said, "like the control arms, I want to preserve for study. But we definitely don't have the means to preserve all of it, so if—"

"Aimsley? You okay?" Maya interrupted.

The AMS unit realized it was shaking, its vision blurring, eyes gone watery. "Yeah," it croaked. "I mean, why wouldn't I . . . why wouldn't . . . why . . . ?"

No, it wasn't okay.

"I was aboard the boat far longer than I was aboard the platform," it explained, wringing its hands, voice wavering. "It was my weapon, my ally, and my world. I just . . . it deserved a better end. A better sendoff."

"It wasn't sentient, was it?" Fuentes asked.

Aimsley tried to wipe at its eyes, realized it couldn't through the biohazard suit, and instead blinked furiously. "No. But what's that got to do with it?"

Fuentes put a friendly hand on its shoulder. "You can grow attached to a hammer, but it's still just a hammer."

It pursed its lips, nodded. "I wonder if that's how my handler feels about me."

Fuentes slowly retracted her hand, clearly unsure how to clarify or take back what she'd said.

"It wasn't just a hammer," Aimsley insisted. "It was alive. It might not have had anything we'd identify as thoughts, but it could feel. It could breathe. If we were going to die, it was supposed to be together. I still have to honor it as more than a simple tool. It's the right thing to do."

"What do you want to do, Aimsley? There's not a lot of time."

"Can I—can I just have a minute inside? Alone?"

Fuentes gave Maya a questioning look, as though the request might be a trick of some sort.

Maya shrugged as if to say, *what's it going to do?*

"Fine," Fuentes said, handing her chainsaw to Maya and jogging over to a set of mobile stairs on wheels, which she easily maneuvered to the makeshift entrance of the boat. "You've got sixty seconds. Then we need to focus. The type of retrofitting we need to do with your ship parts isn't going to be easy. We need all the engineering time we can reclaim."

"Understood," it said firmly, moving to mount the stairs on wobbly legs.

Outside, when they'd extracted the fuel for the maneuvering jets, Aimsley had been too preoccupied with the emergency and its handler's presence to give much thought to the dead body cradled inside the turquoise hull.

Now, as it clicked on its suit lamp and headed into the darkened sphere, the lifeless biomass before it wasn't the only body in the forefront of its consciousness.

Aimsley hissed at the uncomfortable jolt through its joints as its feet touched down on the unnaturally solid interior. There was supposed to be some give. The boat was supposed to cradle its feet, not meet them like a slab of stone.

A light haze swirled inside, steam rising, evaporating from the surface as the frigid skin met ship-warmed air. The casing had completely grayed, the spiracles had shrunk to little more than pinprick-sized pores. The bioluminescence was gone, the chromatophores were dilated and still. Enough fluids had leaked from the boat that its form was sunken in odd places, some bits of skin looked too loose, others too taut.

Aimsley moved to the center of the craft, to the pilot's seat. It dropped itself heavily in front of the controls, sparing not a care for the frigidness that seeped through the thinness of the biohazard suit and into its bones. With a heavy sigh, it reached for one of the boat's control arms.

The fingers were curled into a fist, one that could not be pried open. It covered the fingers with its own, wishing it could thread them together instead.

Images of another hand flashed before its eyes. A hand still pliable, warm, but just as dead.

Unit Two's hand.

Unit Two's body.

Unit Two's head.

Death had greeted Aimsley right out of the reconstitution pod.

"I'm sorry this was your life," it said to the boat. If a nature-born human could live to be a hundred, would that stand for a boat as well? "You were my sister, too."

"Minute's up," Fuentes said, sticking her head through the gap.

It nodded its understanding, stood.

"Just a sec, before you go out," she said, moving inside.

She started up the chainsaw. The electric motor sounded unnaturally loud in the small space.

"Stand back!" she yelled, then swiped the blades through the arms protruding from the control panel, cutting them off at the base. Small bits of bloody debris flew up all around.

Aimsley bit its lip as the hand it had just been holding fell grotesquely to the side. Felled like a tree.

"Okay, take those with you. Maya will show you where

the freezer is," she said, reaching forward to pop a camera—an eyeball—out of its socket with her fingertips.

She seemed to have gotten over her initial nauseated response to the craft.

It gathered up the limbs, biting back a sob, and hurried down the stairs.

CHAPTER EIGHTEEN

There was a constant thrum of urgency as the hours ticked by.

Every action they each took had to be quick, methodical. As efficient as possible.

Chunk after icy, bloody chunk was heaved onto the decking at Aimsley's feet, and it diligently transferred the biowaste into the dumpster, still unable to let go of its need to mourn. It said a soft goodbye to each portion, openly bemoaning the fact that the boat would never have the chance to be reconstituted into something new. Its proteins would not return to the vaults, would not form a new body or become sustenance for any AMS units.

Its very essence was gone. Maya might have said the soul of it had fled.

The boat would not be recycled . . . but perhaps that was better.

Aimsley told itself that it had to reframe its thinking. It was about to go back to the platform and ensure that none of their proteins were *ever* reconstituted. The boats in hibernation would either stay in stasis or die without its sisters' oversight. And Aimsley wanted to be sure that when it rescued the current iterations of units One through Four, no new units would be grown to replace them.

Aimsley's mind and emotions were at war with each other. It still couldn't fully reconcile what it knew to be true upon activation, and what it knew now. It told itself this was the wrong way to treat a boat, and yet it planned on doing far worse.

Once the majority of the biomass was out of the way, Maya and Fuentes set to scraping away the last vestiges with more precise tools. They couldn't risk causing any extra damage to the hull.

They allowed Aimsley to come aboard with them to clean the insides of the freed panels.

It felt so strange, being inside the sphere without the girth of the boat to fill it up. It no longer felt like a proper ship. Just a hollow bubble. Dead and empty.

With a set of rags and a bucket, Aimsley scrubbed the turquoise plates to a shine.

Neither Maya nor Fuentes spoke much as they worked, too focused on the physically taxing task at hand, on the *push push push* brought on by their impending encounter with whatever was calling itself an Earthling.

But there were still things Aimsley wanted—needed—to know. To understand, about humans, about their Harbors. If it was going to usher its sisters away and into a new life, it also wanted reassurances that that life would be *better*, not just longer.

Aimsley dunked its rag in the suds—which were rapidly becoming pink—and smacked the waterlogged cloth noisily against the plates. Rivulets of diluted reds and browns bled away, trickling down the concave surface.

"Buyer mentioned an offering," Aimsley said, trying to

sound casual. It wasn't a question, but it wasn't *not* a question either. Aimsley was doing its best to lead the conversation, without either woman cutting its curiosity off at the quick.

"For Puerto Grande," Fuentes said, not looking up from where she was scraping a particularly sticky gob of bile away from a seam. "To get our docking permissions back."

"What kind of an offering?" it pressed.

"It's gotta be a big haul," Fuentes said absently. "Unique. Important. Enough to counterbalance our crime."

"Which was what?"

"Murder," she said frankly.

Though Aimsley had been expecting something like that—something worth *banishment*—it hadn't expected her to simply blurt it out.

"*Fuentes*," Maya snapped.

"What? What the fuck does it matter if Aimsley knows or not? Not like it's going to change anything." She tossed aside a bundle of gristle and flap of skin with unnecessary force. "Some brute got too handsy with Buyer in a bar. Jonas beat his face in. We all got booted and banished. End of story."

Maya shook her head, displeased. Still, she looked at Aimsley and said, "I told you we were banished indefinitely— meaning we can have our sentence commuted if we bring back something really beneficial. There's a reason we have to scavenge. The Harbors are old. *Ancient.* Falling apart. If we could make it back to Earth, we could fix them properly, but . . . well, you know."

"If it was Jonas who murdered someone, why were you all banished?"

Fuentes shook her head, taken aback. "We're a crew," she said, as though it was obvious.

"As long as we claim each other, we take responsibility for each other," Maya explained.

"So why not get rid of him?" Aimsley asked, hoping it wouldn't sound, insidiously, like a suggestion.

"He was just protecting one of his own," Fuentes said, a frustrated edge coloring her tone, making it grate. She stood abruptly, kicking over a softening glob, then scooping up an armful of biowaste and chucking it out the opening. Without an explanation, she followed it out, down the stairs.

"We had that conversation," Maya said quietly once Fuentes had left. "About leaving him on another station. You have to understand, this only happened six months ago. It's still raw, for all of us. There are things we've all lost by choosing to stick by his side. I've lost access to Melassani's Crystals, Fuentes lost her lab, Doc lost their seat on the Puerto Grande Medical Board, and Buyer . . . Buyer's parents are stationary residents of Puerto Grande. He had to choose—between us and them."

"I still don't understand. None of you seem to *like* Jonas, let alone—"

"Like I said, raw. You caught us at a tense time. Sometimes relationships are like that. A few of us are still bitter, and Jonas . . . it feels like he's *always* angry, now. I think . . . I think he still thinks we're going to leave him, eventually. And when he gets scared, he gets mad."

Aimsley nodded in acceptance. It supposed Jonas's reaction was understandable, if counterintuitive. Wasn't continuous anger and infighting more likely to turn them all against him? To make their relationships sour further?

But one didn't always have control over their reactions. Aimsley certainly didn't.

They finished cleaning out the interior in relative silence.

Aimsley had more questions but couldn't think of how to frame them without giving away that it had hacked into their databases, seen strange vids of Earth. The narrators in those videos had implied the conditions on the planet were why the Harbors had left, and it knew that the Harbors had been to other planets, had found the Crystals there, but it didn't know what they'd been searching for.

Once they were sure the hull was thoroughly thawed, they were able to slide the sections apart using the metal arms. Aimsley quickly identified the propulsion and energy generation components, and the group set to work breaking down the parts while Aimsley explained how everything functioned.

"All right, I think I gotcha," Fuentes said once Aimsley finished itemizing the parts. "No time to stand around admiring our chop-job. Let's get cleaned up, then head to the engine room and get started."

The showers were, in and of themselves, a unique experience.

Doc came down to aid them, sending the trio through a special scrub with their biohazard suits still on before insisting they strip down for additional washing.

The secondary shower room was not unlike what the AMS units had back on the platform: one large, well-lined wet room with multiple independently controlled showerheads and four drains in the center.

When the heated water hit its skin, Aimsley couldn't hide its appreciative groan.

"Better than your first piss?" Fuentes asked.

"Yeah," it admitted.

It hadn't realized its muscles were so tight, its body so stiff.

It wanted to stay under the stream for hours, but their wash needed to be perfunctory.

As it toweled off, Jonas came in with fresh clothes. "Here," he said gruffly, shoving a new pair of pants at Aimsley.

These were softer.

Aimsley accepted them without a word, unsure how it should feel toward Jonas, given the new information.

He'd murdered someone.

And yet his crew hadn't abandoned him.

Perhaps it shouldn't be surprised. After all, it had made it quite clear that it had intended to murder each and every one of them, and yet . . .

After Doc gave them each a once over, the four of them headed for the engine room while Doc returned to the medbay.

Even with the main engines off, the large space roared with the constant working of machinery. Here, the main power supply for the environmentals chugged along, making sure the air was clean, warm, and well pressurized.

Pipes, wires, and duct work all ran through the space, and a series of corrugated catwalks surrounded the main part of the fusion drive, where the fuel was injected and the plasma formed. The electromagnetic coils that made up the FRC were bright red in nests of yellow wires, surrounding a hexagonal monolith in the middle.

The scent of burnt ozone crackled through the air.

Aimsley had a difficult time turning off the infiltration side of its brain. It wanted to log everything it saw as potentially useful for taking over the ship, or further hobbling the craft. It had to keep consciously overriding its own programming, focusing on how to solve problems instead of creating more.

While Fuentes explained the specific mechanics of their engine, Aimsley kept stealing glances. Some at Maya, some at Jonas.

Human dynamics were . . . strange. Its relationship with its sisters seemed straightforward, uncomplicated. Then again, how complicated could a dynamic get when one was only expected to live three months? Twice that much time had passed since Jonas had gotten the five of them banished. Two lifetimes, and yet, for this crew, it must have seemed like no time at all.

Yes, human dynamics were strange. Just like those Earth videos were strange.

Something about those records had felt undeniably *off*: the bizarre environment, so contrary to what it had been told about Earth, yes, but also . . .

The suggestion that the Harbors needed to be *invited* to return.

And the paired implication that, perhaps, there were people that hadn't *wanted* them to return.

Hadn't wanted . . . or *still* didn't want?

Was that all in the past, or . . .

The crew thought aliens had invaded Earth.

In turn, Aimsley had been told by its handler that aliens were invading. And all it had found aboard the wedge were . . . humans.

Aimsley was pulled from the strange coil of its thoughts by Fuentes clearing her throat. "*Hello*, Aimsley, you listening?"

"Yes. Please, continue."

It would reexamine that disturbing train of thought later.

CHAPTER NINETEEN

They worked long, long hours, until everyone was sweaty and exhausted. It was well into what should have been their power-down cycle when Buyer came in, took a wrench from Fuentes's grasp, and ordered everyone to go to bed.

"Three hours of downtime," he said. "Mandatory rest. Now."

Fuentes protested. "I still need to machine a connector for—"

"Do you have schematics?" he asked.

"Yes," she said with a yawn. She was half slumped over the injector housing. Discarded parts were strewn all about her feet. Jonas was doing his best to keep the space clear, but was clearly tired as well.

"Then I'll do it. When we get sleepy we get sloppy, and since we don't know what we'll be up against if we can't beat Aimsley's handler to the platform, I need everyone to be as alert as possible. Maya?"

She and Aimsley were working two catwalks below, and both looked up at him with bleary eyes. "Yeah?"

"I put a cot in the medbay. Tuck Aimsley in?"

"Yessir."

She slid her arm through Aimsley's, tugging it back up the levels, then out the door, into the hall, and toward the lift.

"By 'tuck me in' he means 'lock me in' doesn't he?"

"Sorry, Aims," Maya said with a sigh. "Can't blame us for being cautious."

It nodded and *hmm*ed its acknowledgment. "Can I ask you something?"

"Sure, shoot."

"Earlier, you said your Harbors are falling apart. Why? You said Melassani found the first Crystal a thousand years ago, so humans have been aboard for at least—"

She punched the lift button, and the doors slid aside. They waddled in together, still arm-in-arm. Aimsley was so tired, it was only now realizing how intimate the gesture was. Such a touch felt oddly natural, coming from Maya. Especially strange, considering she was about to lock it away.

"They were never meant to last this long," she said. "We were supposed to find a new home for humanity, out there." She waved vaguely. "The Harbors were supposed to ferry us from Planet A to Planet B, that's all."

"So why do people still live aboard them?"

She let out a heavy sigh, the kind that conveyed turmoil far larger than herself, this crew, and this ship. Their gazes met, and she looked both sad and resigned. She gave a little half shrug, shaking her head. "Because there is no Planet B. If we couldn't fix our home world, we had no chance of tailoring a far-flung planet to our needs. There's a difference between, say, a small research colony on Mars and a place for all of humanity to live forevermore." She sighed again, shoulders falling. "The people who originally launched the Harbors were living in a pipe dream."

"So when you couldn't find what you were looking for, you came back?"

"When we received word Earth was improving—generations ago—we came back."

"But by the time you got here . . ."

She nodded limply. "Something else had taken over."

They reached the top deck, and she guided Aimsley to the medbay, opening the airlock and ushering it inside. "Well, here you are. Not exactly the worst prison, as far as prisons go. Look, you've still got company."

The cat was curled up on the counter.

"Well . . . Good night, Aimsley. Or, good nap, at least."

She unthreaded their arms, then—drowsily, absentmindedly—set her lips against its cheek.

They both froze for half an instant, before Maya jerked herself away. "Oh. Uh. Sorry."

"Why are you sorry?" it asked quietly.

She averted her eyes. A pinkish hue crept up her neck. "I'm tired, I'm not thinking straight. Just forget I . . ." She waved her fingers through the air, as though she could clear away what had just happened like so much smoke. "Good night."

She hurried out the airlock, leaving Aimsley slightly dumbfounded.

Hesitantly, it lifted its hand to its cheek, where the ghost of her lips still made its skin tingle.

Aimsley tried to sleep. It tossed back and forth on the cot, disturbing Zelmar at every turn.

It couldn't shake the feeling that something still wasn't right. Not just in terms of its handler, and the platform, and

280 MARINA J. LOSTETTER

its sisters, and this wider world of the Harbors, but something more fundamental.

Maya had said they were looking for a home for all humanity. But clearly all of humanity hadn't left on the Harbors. Why had some been left behind? The Harbors didn't sound like scouting ships. They were arks. Meant to start anew.

So what was meant to become of everyone still on the planet?

And who, really, was keeping the Harbors away from Earth?

Perhaps it would find more answers if it probed deeper into the wedge's archives. Perhaps it would understand better if it could find correspondence between the Earth-based humans and the ship-based humans.

Centering itself, Aimsley opened to the ship, let itself become discoverable once more. The flood of pings felt less violent this time—more manageable, now that it wasn't caught in the throes of anxiety.

First it zeroed in on the cameras, just to check on the crew. The bunk room door was open, allowing the hall camera to peer inside. Maya and Fuentes's cabinets were wide open, and both women were sleeping soundly. Doc's was cracked open a fraction, but no light seeped out. The camera's angle was not kind, but Aimsley just managed to catch the twitch of a blanket, which suggested that Doc was, in fact, inside. But the cabinet Buyer and Jonas clearly shared was empty, doors ajar.

That made sense. Buyer had intended to keep working. Jonas was likely helping him.

Flicking through a few more feeds, it found them in the cargo hold, at the corner table. But they didn't appear to be cataloging parts or dismantling stolen tech.

The hold was nearly dark. The emergency lighting on the floor, lining the built-in portions of the booth, was the only source of illumination. The camera was close, not quite providing a top-down view of the pair. Jonas's gun and holster lay across the tabletop, set near a small pile of parts that suggested they *had* been working, but had interrupted themselves.

Buyer had Jonas pressed into the seat cushions, his hand around the back of the other man's neck, and they were sighing into each other's mouths. Jonas scrabbled at Buyer's lower back with his good hand, rucking up the captain's shirt, revealing thick, swirling black markings that Aimsley hadn't seen before.

Were these markings functional, or simply—as Maya might put it—*pretty?*

"Please. Buyer, *please.*"

"Shh. Shh, quiet—"

"We came down here so I wouldn't have to be quiet."

"Still . . ."

"*Please.*"

"Patience."

Jonas hissed and turned his face away as Buyer—too eager, too greedy—accidently put excessive pressure on Jonas's still-tender shoulder.

"Sorry, sorry," Buyer said quickly, in a voice Aimsley had never heard him use. It was rich, and heated, and he pressed his mouth against Jonas's exposed throat to punctuate his apology.

"Be careful, you stupid bastard," Jonas shot back, hooking his finger in the cord around Buyer's neck, yanking firmly. There was no real bite to his voice, not like when the others were around.

Buyer huffed a laugh into Jonas's skin. "I'll make it better," he promised. "Let me make it feel better."

"That's Doc's job," Jonas whispered back.

"No," Buyer said, amused. "This is definitely not Doc's job." He snaked a hand between their bodies, sliding it down Jonas's torso to the apex of Jonas's thighs.

Jonas *whimpered*, twisting Buyer's necklace in his fist, fingers white-knuckled. "Your hands," he said hoarsely, a weak protest. "They're still—"

"Don't worry," Buyer reassured him. "Once I get these off, you won't be using my hands anymore."

Jonas's answering groan sounded like pure *anticipation*, and he swiftly captured Buyer's mouth again.

Watching them made something strange and warm blossom in Aimsley's belly. They looked beautiful like this—all tender with each other. Leaving touches to excite and soothe rather than direct or wound.

Aimsley let its fingertips stray up to its cheek. The affection Maya had shown it was milder, less familiar. But it understood it to be affection nonetheless.

In the cargo hold, the captain slid off the seat, to his knees.

"Please. *Please please please*," Jonas kept chanting, voice gone high and breathy.

Intrigued, Aimsley wanted to keep watching. But . . . there was a reason they were doing it in the dark. A reason they were doing it away from the sleeping level, away from their crewmates.

They didn't want to be seen.

Didn't want everyone to know.

And though both curiosity and that pleasant pooling

of warmth encouraged Aimsley to stay, to keep observing them, it knew this had to be one of those private things Doc had mentioned.

Unlike AMS unit functionality, not all human behavior was meant for consumption by all other humans.

So much for not having one's junk *out at the table*, it thought, amused.

Aimsley allowed itself to enjoy a few more soft sighs and one quiet moan before flipping to a new feed.

There were still rooms on the ship that were unconnected to the security cameras. Places the crew had not physically shown it that it could not mentally go.

It had worried, during its first exploration, that those rooms could be hiding the true invaders. Aliens. Strange creatures from another world.

And, in truth, there had been something there—something alien. But so different from anything it had expected. Anything it had been *told* to expect.

Now it had doubts such hostile phantasms—invaders, conquerors—even *existed*. On Earth, in the solar system.

What if it was all just *people*? Human people.

If those in the Harbors had abandoned other humans to a dying planet, and then come *back* . . .

It was just a hunch. It didn't think this was something the crew was purposefully hiding. Aimsley was fairly convinced at this point that the humans aboard the *Violent Delight* genuinely believed in the invader concept—that aliens were keeping them away from Earth.

But what if that wasn't the most logical explanation?

Once more, Aimsley roamed through their records, looking for anything that might support its new theory. It found plenty more videos of a devastated world, and a thinning, sickly populace. None of the narrators ever seemed to speak with ire, but Aimsley knew better than to assume there was no ire in them.

It sat up on the cot, fidgeting. A strange, new nervousness flooded its system. It stood, began to pace. Zelmar stole its spot on the pallet, soaking up the leftover body heat.

Maybe whatever was in those hidden rooms would help set its mind at ease, help steady it.

After all, did it matter what its handler turned out to be? Alien, or human? Did that change anything—the plan, the rescue?

No. Of course not. But it might change the future. Might change how it saw . . . saw everything.

Suddenly the cube felt too cramped, too small. The air was thick. It needed to get out, to see whatever the crew had hidden from view.

It checked on the crewmembers once more. The majority of them were still asleep. Jonas and Buyer were still . . . occupied.

"Keep watch," Aimsley said to the cat, then swiftly hacked the lock and let itself out to explore the ship.

It should have realized that one of the darkened rooms was the shower room. Another two were waste disposal rooms, with individual stalls and plumbed versions of its bedpan.

It started to feel silly. It didn't even know what it was looking for, or what it would do if it found something disturbing or unusual. Confront the crew about it? Simply tuck the knowledge away for the trip out of Jovian space? What?

Yet a fourth space didn't even need entering; there was a window on the door. Through it, Aimsley spotted a small craft—the skiff. It was a bit larger than the boat, and likely had several compartments in its interior. It would fit the crew and the cat and perhaps a few hives if need called. It, unlike the wedge, had thin, elongated portholes. Across the side, hastily painted in white—as though for a prank or as an idea executed in the midst of an inebriated haze—were the words *Violent End*.

Opposite the craft was a hangar door just wide enough for the skiff, but the space held no more.

As Aimsley hacked the lock on a fifth room, it told itself this would be the last one. It had already made its choice to trust the crew. In turn, it would need to be someone worthy of trust.

It opened the door, and the scent of hot sugar hit its nose immediately.

Lights flickered on to reveal five large, silver fermenters. Several bottles of phosphoric acid, and containers labeled "barm," sat on a workbench near the door. A set of three barrels were labeled "Must," and a slide of honeycomb sat over a small bucket, slowly dripping.

Ah, the meadery.

It quickly spotted a security camera in the corner of the ceiling and realized there was no active feed because the camera was simply broken. Nothing nefarious to be found.

It leaned against the doorjamb, feeling anxious and foolish with no outlet. It made up its mind to return to the medbay. There, it could check in on Jonas and Buyer, and if the two men were back at work, it could use the comms box to offer its help. If it couldn't sleep, it needed to keep working. The sooner they were finished with repairs and on their way to the platform, the better.

With a self-deprecating huff, it pushed itself off the jamb and started to turn around.

A warm body was suddenly at its back.

"What the *fuck* are you doing in here?"

CHAPTER TWENTY

Oh no.

Jonas.

Oh no.

Aimsley spun on its heel, backing into the meadery.

As it whirled, Jonas's arm came up, and the AMS unit found itself staring down the barrel of his gun.

"I knew it. I fucking *knew it*," Jonas growled, clenching his jaw, thrusting the weapon forward. "I came up to hit the head, but my feet took me here because I just had a frigging *feeling*, and here you are."

Aimsley threw its hands up, tried to make itself look as unthreatening as possible.

It swore at itself. *I should have just stayed in the medbay.*

Jonas's hair was mussed and his shirt open, revealing his chest and neck. Light pink and dark purple markings covered his skin. His lips were flushed from being bitten, and there was a heady, musky scent in the air.

All clear evidence of his encounter with the captain.

But his expression and posture were far from loose and relaxed, as he'd been with Buyer. Now, pure fury boiled beneath the surface. His stare was sharp and stony, his jaw tight, teeth grating. His muscles were tense, coiled.

He shook with surprise and rage.

"First they try to tell me it's fucking *fine* that we have you aboard because you're going to be our ticket back home," he gritted out, punctuating every other word with a jab of his weapon. "And now they try to spin it like, instead, it's gonna be whatever crap you've got on that platform of yours, but the whole fucking time you've just been *playing us*, haven't you? Of course you've been in contact with your handler. You're walking us right into a gods-damned trap! Taking us straight to your alien buddies."

Aimsley shook its head slowly, deliberately, making sure every movement was well telegraphed so as not to spook him. "None of that is true."

"You've got them all fooled. Every last one of them," he growled. "Even Buyer. But not me."

Aimsley stared defiantly over the barrel of the gun. "You can't fire that in here," it said carefully.

"Can't fire it with the dampening field engaged." He flicked off the manual safety. "You wanna guess whether or not the dampening field is engaged?"

Aimsley took a small step forward, and Jonas took one back, trigger finger twitching.

Jonas knew by now that Aimsley had him outweighed and outclassed when it came to fighting hand to hand, one on one. They'd tussled—collided—enough times to get a feel for one another, how they moved as individuals in the zealous heat of the moment.

Even without his injured shoulder, it was in Jonas's best interest to keep Aimsley at arm's length.

But was he deranged enough to shoot inside his own ship?

"How the hell did you even get out of the medbay, huh?"

It didn't have a good answer. It wanted to keep its secret. If they truly didn't know it could access their systems, then it could enter and exit the information streams freely, learn more about Earth and the Harbors at will.

But what it needed right now was for Jonas to stay calm. To take a deep breath before doing anything rash.

"I realized I could access the hololock with my enhancements. No different from what you do with your implants," it said calmly.

But Jonas wasn't stupid.

"Oh, *no. No, no*, that is *very* different. Don't try to spin this with some puppy dog eyes and *'I'm just a robot, I don't know how to human right'* nonsense. It's not gonna work on me." He shook his head, pursed his lips—even lowered the gun for a moment before changing his mind and raising it again. "Fuck. This is—*Gods damn it*. I should take you to Buyer," he said, more to himself than Aimsley.

Jonas looked away once more, and Aimsley suppressed the urge to jump at him. There was no version of a fight in which Aimsley would come out the victor, not truly. Even if it bested Jonas—got the gun and got him *down*—the others would not understand. There would be no explaining this as mere self-defense. Not when Aimsley was in the belly of their ship, far away from its cot and its confines.

Now was the time to de-escalate.

"Yes, good," it said slowly. "Take me to Buyer."

They needed a third party. Someone to talk Jonas down. The problem was, Jonas didn't want to be talked down.

"No," he said darkly. "He'll just find some other excuse then, some other rationalization. They've pinned all their hopes and dreams on you. They all want to fucking *believe in you* and I don't know how to make them see . . . *Fuck*," he barked at himself.

"I'm sorry," Aimsley said. "I shouldn't have left the med-bay. I haven't touched anything, I swear to you."

"Yeah right. Probably in here poisoning our gods damned mead. Fuck. *Fuck*, what the fuck do I . . . ?" His eyes darted as his mind clearly spun. *Spiraled*. He was half-panicked, jittery, and *angry*.

Angry because he was *scared*.

Suddenly, an eerie calm settled over his face. "There's nothing for it," he muttered. "Nothing for it. Gotta do it. There's no other . . ." He gritted his teeth, steeled himself. "Get out," he said to Aimsley, waving the gun in the direction of the door, moving aside to let the AMS unit through.

Aimsley held its ground, calculating.

If it shouted, would anyone hear?

Would Jonas shoot?

"*I said, out, bot!*"

Its heart leapt. It took a deep breath, and obeyed.

As it allowed Jonas to guide it down the hall, it searched the ship again. Not just the cameras (which showed Buyer was still in the hold), but the fixtures as well. Maybe it could bring up the lights in the bunk room, turn on the emergency alert, or activate the fire doors and put the corridor on lock-down.

But it didn't have time to explore the new data streams, the new system access points. There just weren't enough steps, enough footfalls, enough *time*.

When it tried to slow its pace, Jonas made sure to give it an aggressive jab between the shoulders with his gun.

"Get in the lift," Jonas ordered.

"Where are we going?" Aimsley asked, holding its ground for a precious few seconds.

Jonas didn't answer, just gave it another jab.

Inside the lift, Jonas pressed the button for the top deck.

Perhaps he just wanted to tie Aimsley to the chair again. That would be sensible. It would have no right to complain, really.

"I'm not your enemy, Jonas," it said softly. "Not anymore."

"Like hell you aren't," he said gruffly. "First you take my shoulder, then you take my fucking *pants*. My spacewalks, my dignity. What's next? You want Buyer, too?"

"I'm not trying to take anything from you."

"Oh, so it just comes naturally, then? That supposed to make me feel better? There are five people on this crew. Only supposed to be five people on this ship. We're balanced. Make up for each other's weaknesses. Sometimes Doc and Priestess are too doe-eyed. Sometimes Buyer is too focused on the haul, and sometimes Fuentes looks at people like they're just another type of puzzle to pull apart. And I'm too fucking hotheaded, but they pull me *back*."

"Except for that one time."

Aimsley regretted the words as soon as they were out of its mouth.

Growling, Jonas reared. He raised his arm, ready to strike Aimsley with the butt of the gun. At the last moment, he took a deep breath through his nose and recentered himself. "Don't know what they told you about it," he said. "But I was protecting my family. Just like I'm protecting them now. We're a well-oiled machine, and you're a frigging spanner jammed into the works."

The lift stopped. Jonas pushed Aimsley out. "Keep marching. Straight ahead. Don't you dare turn around."

Aimsley shifted forward, stopped in front of the medbay doors.

Behind it, Jonas did something over at the control bank. "Did I tell you to stop marching?"

"Where else am I supposed to . . . ?"

The airlock.

It had to think. Aimsley had to think. He was going to . . .

No.

A moment later Jonas was right up behind it with the gun, pressing forward, making it move again.

Aimsley hesitated for half a second, considering. It imagined whirling, diving for his waist, capturing him in a tight embrace and pushing him back—against the airlock door, or perhaps into the monitors, into all those screens and sharp-edged control panels. Perhaps his spine would make a satisfying *crack* if Aimsley shoved just right.

But this couldn't end in violence. Every punch it might throw put its sisters' lives at risk. There had to be another way out of this, something it could say to make him reconsider.

Reaching past the AMS unit, Jonas keyed open the airlock hatch. The hatch swung outward, giving Aimsley an excuse to back up. But the press of the gun didn't let it travel far.

"Get in," Jonas ordered.

"No."

"Get *in*."

"What's the *captain* going to think of this plan? Shooting the prisoner into space? The prisoner that just saved your ship?"

Their bond was important. Their bond kept Jonas stable. He needed to be reminded of that bond.

"I'm doing this *for* Buyer."

"Buyer wants to keep me."

"Buyer just wants to see his parents again!" Jonas shouted. "He's so fucking focused on that, he can't see straight. None of them can. They want to get back to the Harbors so bad they can't see how this is just going to end with us all strapped to dissecting tables. Your handler's just going to cut us up and sew us together to make another one of *you*. We're just body parts to them, to you. I won't let that happen."

"*I* won't let that happen," Aimsley insisted. "I want us all to be safe, Jonas. Everyone. Even you."

"A few days ago you tried to kill us."

"A few days ago I stepped out of a reconstitution pod into this hellscape. I don't want it. I'm done with the violence, and the calculations, and the constant worry. I just want to *rest*."

"Lucky you, then," Jonas said darkly. "A long nap is just what I had in mind."

Aimsley's fists clenched and unclenched at its sides. This wasn't working. It had to find a different tactic. Something else—another way to weasel past his defenses and make him *feel* how wrong this was.

"I—I saw you two," Aimsley admitted, taking a chance, turning around slowly, to look him in the eye. Jonas let it turn. "You and Buyer. Together. An hour ago, in the hold. I know you can be gentle, Jonas, you don't have to—"

His face contorted. "Fuck you and whatever you think you saw. *Get in the 'lock*."

Suddenly, the elevator swished opened behind him, on

the other side of the deck. A new set of footsteps rang out. "Jonas?" Fuentes asked, confusion coloring her voice.

"Ah, fuck it," Jonas growled, then barreled forward, thrusting his bad shoulder into Aimsley's chest, tossing them both into the airlock with force.

Aimsley landed hard on its back, wincing. The floor punched the air from its lungs. Jonas landed heavily on its sternum.

When he pulled back, it kicked out—its foot catching him in the side, but glancing off as he pushed himself erect.

Swiftly, Jonas spun. Yanked the hatch closed behind him.

The *thunk* of the door cut off Fuentes's shout for him to *stop*.

Now they were both trapped in the airlock.

The invader and the robot.

Jonas and Aimsley.

Suitless.

Together.

And in that moment, it was clear: only one of them intended to get out of this alive.

"What's Buyer going to say when you're *dead*, Jonas?" it coughed from its place on the floor.

Jonas's face had gone bright red. Sweat covered his brow. He gritted his teeth, looked at the gun in his hand, at the control panel on the wall, then through the thin sliver of a window. He looked confused, caught out, like he had no idea how he'd ended up here.

He'd wanted to kill Aimsley, but he hadn't meant to go this far.

He could still stop. He could accept that he'd made a misstep. Let Aimsley have the win.

He hadn't done anything irreversible yet.

Aimsley knew there was nothing it could say to help him make the right choice—to encourage him to back down. Any single syllable out of its mouth would only push him deeper into his anger, strengthen his resolve.

He had to decide for himself.

Jonas's face hardened, his gaze snapping to Aimsley's. "I won't let you hurt them," he said, voice firm and decisive.

He'd reconciled with the choice, then.

This was his end.

Fuentes's face appeared in the window, forehead framed in rainbow strands with the way her hair had been pulled back and knotted. "Jonas!" came her muffled yell. "Jonas, what in the *hell*—?"

Ignoring her, he went to the control panel. With a few swipes across the screen, the lighting in the airlock changed. A warning red.

A soft hissing indicated the airlock was depressurizing, the air leaking out.

Jonas didn't have to flush Aimsley into space. He just had to suffocate it.

Suffocate them *both*.

Fuentes looked down, made a strange jerking motion, as though yanking on the hatch, expecting it to open. When it didn't, she dashed away.

Hopefully to get the others.

Sniffing dryly, Jonas turned away from the controls and sat down heavily on the floor. He passed the gun from his free hand to the one in the sling, then pulled his knees up, rested his well arm atop one casually.

Aimsley still hadn't pushed itself off the floor, and saw no reason to move unless it had a plan.

It reached out digitally, searching for an access point,

but that was no use—all of the airlock controls were hard-wired. There was nothing for it to prod at with its mind.

When it and Maya had passed through the airlock before, the small space had safely decompressed in less than two minutes.

Which meant they had approximately one hundred and twenty seconds of atmosphere left.

Not a lot of time.

Jonas's hand strayed to his throat, his collarbone, pressing at the fresh marks on his skin. He closed his eyes. "Honestly thought he'd be the one to leave me, not the other way around," he mumbled.

Aimsley wasn't about to waste oxygen with a response, no matter if it was to coddle or snap at him.

Buyer's face suddenly filled the window. He looked frantic, wide-eyed. His hair fell loose about his shoulders, was ruffled worse than Jonas's.

"Jonas!" came Buyer's voice through the comms. He slapped his palms desperately against the hatch. "Jonas, what happened? Get up, talk to me."

Jonas cringed, frowned. Wouldn't even look at him.

"Why won't it turn off?" Buyer asked over his shoulder. "Why won't it open?"

"Fucker changed the pass codes," came Fuentes's voice. "Didn't want us to stop him."

"Can you override it?"

"I'm *trying*."

"Jonas?" the captain called again. "I know you can hear me, you *bastard*. Get back in here *right now*." His lip trembled; his eyes went glassy. He knew as well as anyone that there were only moments to spare before there was nothing left for Jonas to breathe. "Don't you *dare* do this to me!"

A pained expression flashed over Jonas's face, and he covered his eyes with one hand, shielding himself from the captain.

"Maya!" Buyer shouted. "You might have to break into the panel."

"That's—that won't work!" she shouted back.

Their voices sounded distant, shrill.

Aimsley concentrated on the rise and fall of its chest. It could feel its lungs trying and failing to draw bigger and bigger breaths.

Doc shoved in next to Buyer, "Aimsley! Aimsley, the gun. He can't shoot, he can't—"

It was well aware of that by now. If the gun had worked, Jonas would have simply shot it instead of killing them both slowly. Painfully.

Sure, it could rush Jonas. Sure, it could overpower him. Twist his injured arm, maybe knock him unconscious. But what would any of that accomplish? It couldn't *intimidate* him, force him to give it the code to stop the depressurization. He was already willing to die in order to neutralize the threat to his crewmembers, so what else was there for Aimsley to do?

It thought about Unit Two. How, even after its CPU chassis had been separated from its body, Aimsley still couldn't let go. The light had gone out of its sister, and still it had felt an undeniable compulsion to keep its cameras fixed on Unit Two until its materials had been dissolved and returned to the vats. Until it was no more.

If *its* impulse to maintain a connection to the very end had been that strong for a sister it had barely known, Jonas's instincts had to be raging at him to do the same for Buyer. But he was fighting the urge.

He was fighting, because he knew the drive made him weak—that if he gave in, it would eat at his resolve.

"He doesn't want you to go," Aimsley said, articulating as best it could in the thinning air. It lifted its head from the cold floor, glaring at the man in the sling. "*Look at him*, Jonas."

Jonas's eyes went to Aimsley's, a defiant expression settling over his brow.

"Look at him," Aimsley ordered again.

The man shook his head, ran his hands over his eyes before squeezing them shut.

"Are you really going to die without seeing him one last time?"

Jonas's brows bowed sadly, desperately.

"*Look. At. Him.*"

Gritting his teeth, face twisted in torment, Jonas turned his head. Looked up.

A melancholy sort of hope flashed across Buyer's face. "Yeah. That's it. Come on, Jonas. Come out of there."

"I have to do this, Buyer," he said firmly.

"The fuck you do," the captain replied, his tone softer than his words.

Aimsley's lungs stuttered as it took its first painful breath. Its ears popped.

"It's not safe," Jonas said. "I don't know why none of you can see it, but this *thing* is not our friend."

"So you're gonna die, to what? Prove a *point*?"

"Protecting you will always be worth—"

"Oh, that's bullshit. You are *not* gonna pull some martyr crap on me. No one here asked you to die for them, Jonas."

"That's because you're all a bunch of idiots."

The air was so thin. Their voices sounded so small.

"Come back inside. Don't make me watch you die."

Jonas said nothing.

"I need you here, Jonas. With me." His voice was so soft, barely more than a distant whisper.

Jonas set his jaw.

When Buyer spoke again, there was no sound. Aimsley could only read his lips.

It hoped Jonas could, too.

"I need you."

Buyer swallowed harshly, eyes brimming.

"Please."

There was no more air to be had, so Aimsley held its breath. Waiting.

"*Please.*"

PART FIVE

ALIEN

Jonas shook his head spastically from side to side, like he was trying to knock something loose. He opened his mouth, as though to roar, to scream, but all was silent vacuum.

Scrabbling, he clawed his way upright, frantically scratching at the control screen.

Aimsley closed its eyes, unable to tell if anything was changing.

It imagined everything going still in its chest, in its whole body.

Imagined its mind shutting down.

And the world going dark.

But then its ears popped again.

It gasped.

The air was still far too thin to be comfortable, and its lungs stuttered.

But it was a good stutter.

A living stutter.

Jonas slumped forward over the control panel, bracing himself against the wall.

He dropped the gun. Made a sobbing sort of wheeze.

The minutes waiting for the air to come back felt longer than the minutes waiting for the air to drain away.

Aimsley's body started to tremble as it metabolized the adrenaline that had filled it minutes ago, at the promise of death. It curled its fingers into claws, scraped its nails against the floor.

It struggled with the urge to jump up, to grab Jonas's shirt. It wanted to throw him to the decking, to punch his face. To scream at him and beat him until he stayed *down*.

And yet, at the same time, it understood. Everything Jonas had done, right up until he'd shut himself in the airlock, made sense. In his mind, Aimsley had proven itself to be the monster it had sworn up and down it wasn't.

When the lighting finally went soft white again, the captain immediately yanked open the hatch.

He dove for Jonas, trembling all over, hands sliding over him, pulling him close. "Why did you do that? Don't you *ever* do that again. You hear me?"

Jonas turned into his embrace. He hid his face in Buyer's neck, still angry—and now, clearly, ashamed.

The others went for Aimsley.

Maya crouched over it, her hand coming up to cradle its face. "Are you okay?"

Instinctually, it leaned into her touch before it could stop itself. "I'm fine," it insisted, though the waver in its voice suggested otherwise.

"Is this why you were so insistent earlier?" Buyer asked sharply, fingers running through Jonas's hair. "What was that supposed to be, huh? A goodbye fuck? Damn you, you son of a . . ."

"He didn't mean to," Aimsley said, voice thick. "He didn't plan this."

A small, confused silence followed.

"So you both just accidentally ended up on your way to suffocating?" Fuentes quipped darkly.

"No, I mean—" Aimsley rubbed its hands together, then dragged one over its eyes. Its extremities tingled, its head felt both light—empty—and heavy—solid, like a block of lead. "Just me. It was just supposed to be me who—"

"Why are you defending him?" Maya whispered.

"I'm not defending him," Aimsley said, refusing to match her volume. "I'm telling you what happened. He didn't plan to end up in the airlock. He didn't plan this at all, he . . ." It had to be honest. Further attempts at deception would only solidify Jonas's justifications for trying to get rid of it. "I left the medbay, I was exploring. Jonas found me."

"It can hack our systems," Jonas wheezed into Buyer's neck. "Broke through the locks—who knows what else it can get into."

All of the soft, concerned hands slowly slipped away from Aimsley. Everyone leaned back, caution and distrust evident in every line of their bodies—the set of their jaws and the narrowing of their eyes and the stiffness of their spines.

The way their regard shifted so swiftly *hurt*.

They'd given Aimsley a lifeline, and it could feel the ethereal tendrils of that support retreating, vanishing.

Even the way Maya looked at it now was . . . cold.

"I'm sorry," it said, voice small like it had been when the air was seeping away. "I didn't touch anything. I didn't disturb *anything*. I—" It held out its wrists, pressed together tightly, offering its own restraint.

They knew it could fight. They knew it could scratch and claw and snap an arm or a neck if it wanted to.

It didn't want to.

And, in that moment, it understood Jonas better than ever.

Because it realized how this could change things. How it had put its family's future at risk. Jonas felt about the crew the way it felt about its sisters; it would do anything for them.

"Please," Aimsley said earnestly. "Lock me up. Tie me up. You can . . ." It took a deep, shaky breath. "You can shoot me out the airlock after all. Just give my sisters a chance. You can change your mind about me, but don't change your mind about that. *Please*. I was only trying to be sure they'd truly be safe here."

"No one's truly safe *anywhere*," Fuentes snapped.

"Trust is how you *build* safety," Buyer said, his voice brimming with heat, "and you—I said *no more secrets*."

"You want to talk about *trust*?" Jonas barked incredulously. "I *told* you," he said, lifting his face, a shaky fist coming down on Buyer's shoulder. "I told you we couldn't trust it, but this whole time—"

"I never asked you to trust Aimsley," Buyer said firmly. "I asked you to trust me. *Me*, Jonas. When you found it, you should have come to me instead of pulling this bullshit. Why couldn't you just trust me?"

Jonas pushed away from Buyer's chest, blinking at him, distraught. "Because you *want it too much*!" he shouted. "You all do. Puerto Grande—getting back—that's all you think about. And I know I took it from you. I know. And look, I'm sorry. *I'm sorry*. For everything. For getting us into this mess, for making you all hurt like this, for making us this desperate. But I *won't* apologize for trying to protect you."

"This can't be the way you protect us every time,"

Buyer bit out. "You can't *kill* every threat, Jonas. Getting your knuckles bloody—putting your body between us and danger—can't be the only way."

Jonas grasped at the front of Buyer's shirt, clearly trying to both steady himself and keep the captain near—to keep him from slipping away. "You're all I have," he said sadly. "And I know how much you gave up to stick by me. All of you. And I can't . . . I can't lose you. I *can't*."

"So stop shoving us the fuck away," Fuentes said, standing. She rushed at him from behind, slinging her arms around his middle, holding him tight.

Buyer came forward again, slipping his arms around Jonas from the front.

Doc patted Aimsley's knee, then stood to crowd into Jonas's side.

Maya and Aimsley shared a look—one brimming with complicated feelings. There was pity, and mistrust, but still an edge of warmth and a sprinkle of understanding.

She took its still-outstretched wrists, lowered them into its lap.

"I'm going to turn my back on you, now," she said softly. "Because Jonas needs me. I still want to believe he's wrong about you. Maybe that makes me naïve. Or stupid. But even if you're leading us all into a trap, do me a favor. Let us have this."

It wanted to protest. To deny. But it knew it had collapsed its own bridges. They all had every right to distrust it, and no reason to let it spend a moment without scrutiny.

But this was another inroad. Maya was offering it a small moment to get back some of what it had lost.

It knotted its hands in its lap, nodded.

She let her fingertips trail across its cheek once more as she rose. And then she joined the others, trapping Jonas between them all.

No, not trapping—safeguarding.

It understood, now, what the crystal pendants represented: their tie, their bond.

It watched them, quietly, feeling distant. Like it was far, far away. Observing this private moment as though once more simply watching through a security feed.

It was on the outside, looking in.

Looking in at everything it wanted.

Human behavior was strange, and unpredictable.

But it was also warm. Loving.

Aimsley couldn't help but find it enticing. Tempting.

It longed to be embraced like that—the way they were all embracing Jonas.

But it might have destroyed any chance it had of them ever treating it with even half that much tenderness.

Aimsley drew its knees up to its chest, hung its head in its hands.

Its position here was fragile again. And it could only blame itself.

When the group broke apart, setting back to action, Aimsley didn't look up. It waited for the inevitable.

They moved in and out of the airlock, clearly making preparations. It heard them speak in harsh, hushed tones, deciding its fate—discussing whether or not they were headed into a trap.

"Up," Buyer directed a few minutes later, coming to stand before it.

Aimsley raised its eyes. As it had predicted, the captain held the restraints once more.

"My sisters?" it asked, standing, voice as shaky as its legs.

"We knew what we were getting into when we came to the interior," he said. "We knew it was dangerous, and we knew it was worth it. We're not going to quit now."

They tied it to the chair. And this time, it had no intention of clawing its way free.

"I can still help with the engines," it offered as Doc gently pressed it back into the seat.

"It's best if you let us handle it," Maya said, pulling a knot taut over its left wrist.

"We're nearly there," Fuentes said. "We'll have them up and running and be on our way to your platform in no time."

"Meanwhile," Buyer said, leaning up against the counter, crossing his arms. "You're going to tell me everything about your ability to infiltrate our systems."

Aimsley was as open and honest as it was able. Including about the videos it had found, everything it had seen.

"How difficult was it for you to hack us?" Buyer pressed.

"Not very," Aimsley admitted.

"Do you think you might be able to get into larger systems? Better protected systems?"

Aimsley shrugged as best it could in its bindings. "Maybe. I wouldn't know for sure until I encountered them." It knew Buyer wasn't asking casually. Something had occurred to him. An idea. "You're trying to figure out if I could hack into your Harbors. To change your crew's travel permissions."

"Yes," he admitted.

Aimsley let out a small laugh. "Jonas was right, you are focused."

"Very." He crossed his arms over his chest, gripped his own biceps a little too tightly. "My dad . . . he was sick when we got cut off. I need to know he made it. I need to see him. And my mom, and my sister."

Aimsley perked. "You have a sister?"

He nodded. "You do right by us, and I just might let you meet her one day."

CHAPTER TWENTY-TWO

Aimsley spent its solitary hours looking through the new files Buyer had given it permission to access—and *only* those files. Videos of life on the Harbors, legal documents, pledges, and past manifests.

On the Harbors—the generation ships—dark, cramped halls led into broad ship bellies filled with people, the walls lined with cubbies and catwalks. The grime of ages clung to most metallic surfaces—some darkened, some patinaed. Places that saw frequent traffic were easily noticeable; once shiny chrome was now matte, dulled through years of human touch and coarse cleaning. Wires and ropes were strung across wide spaces and sported wet clothes or paper lanterns or bare lightbulbs.

Parts of the ship were aesthetically pleasing in a well-lived-in, personal-touches kind of way, and other parts had clearly been epically beautiful once, but the years had not been kind. Intricately etched flourishes had been partially buffed-out, parts of statues had been reappropriated.

There was a history there, of luxury turned sour. Extravagance that had crumbled. Indulgences forced to twist into practicalities. Hope snuffed by pragmatism.

Aimsley read through the legal documents with a critical eye, trying to understand the workings of a society that was utterly alien to it. Trying to understand how the humans managed themselves, how they related to one another.

Even after reviewing only a small percentage of the files, it felt like it better understood what the stakes were for everyone. Why the crew had attacked the mine. And Aimsley was surer than ever that it had to save its sisters and stop the reconstitution cycle.

There was a sudden kick as the engines engaged, and Aimsley could only imagine the shout of triumph the crew must have given. It wanted to share that joy with them.

They were on their way. Toward a new beginning.

"Dinnertime," Maya said, coming into the medbay several hours later. "Better eat up, we'll be in range of the platform soon. We'll all need our strength."

Aimsley shifted in the chair, ready for her to untie its wrists. Its hands and its thighs had become cramped, and a twinge flicked back and forth at the base of its spine. But Maya made no move toward the bindings.

"Not yet," she said, as though reading its mind. "I can't yet."

It understood. The trust they'd previously built had not yet returned. She still needed time.

But that meant she'd elected to feed it. By hand.

Aimsley took every offered bite as gently as it could, not wanting to spook her. It didn't let its lips linger against her skin, even though it wanted to. Didn't give in to the strange impulse to suck her fingers into its mouth.

Flashes of Buyer and Jonas's coupling came back to it, unbidden, and it couldn't help but imagine a similar heated, needy look on Maya's face. It wanted to please her, to make her happy.

More than anything, though, it wanted to chase her new hesitancy away. It wanted to comfort her, to reassure her.

It wanted to hold her and make sure nothing bad ever happened to her, like it had when they were floating away from the wedge, hoping they'd make it back.

They were quiet all through the meal, and she would not meet its gaze. Aimsley hated that it had caused this rift, that it had ruined the comradery they'd been building.

The exchange—their alone time—was over far too quickly.

Aimsley wanted to say something to convey how she made it feel, how much it wanted to earn back her confidence. But as she stepped away from the chair and toward the door, the words would not come. She paused briefly at the hololock, eyes lowered, and made an abortive half turn, as if to look over her shoulder, to say something.

Aimsley held its breath.

But the moment passed and she was gone.

And Aimsley let all fantasies of her looking at it with desire slip away.

Now it simply wanted her to feel comfortable enough to look at it *at all*.

Buyer came for Aimsley when it was time. When they'd slipped tentatively into the platform's space.

The captain untied it slowly, helped it to its feet. "Time for you to make contact," he told it. "Pave the way."

It nodded, following him out of the medbay to the control dash.

The rest of the crew stood nearby, looking nervous. Fuentes and Maya on one side, Doc and Jonas on the other.

Aimsley stepped up to the screen Buyer indicated, and then the captain turned to his own set of screens, fingers adeptly flying over the surface. "Ready when you are, Aims."

Aimsley took a deep breath, then nodded. The captain swiped his hand once more across the screen. The rest of the crew fell into a strangled hush.

No one dared so much as shift from foot to foot.

"This is Unit Four," Aimsley said in its handler's language. It tried not to look at the others while it spoke. It didn't want to see their reaction to the hisses and clicks—the syllables that felt so much more natural against its teeth and across the back of its soft palate. It had already given them its script before the airlock incident—exactly what it was going to say—to ease their fears. And still, it knew they would doubt it in the moment.

They *had* to trust it—whether they were ready to or not—and it had to trust them. This was the crew's chance to go home to their Harbor, and its chance to start a new, real life with its sisters.

Both parties were willing to risk everything they had—to lose it all—for a shot at what they wanted most.

"I've taken control of the invader's ship," Aimsley said in its home language. "I found five fellow AMS units aboard, reprogrammed to serve the invaders, and was able to successfully rewrite their programming. I request a safe approach, and backup aboard the invader's craft. Please respond."

Nothing.

It frowned apologetically at Buyer before trying again. There came a brief pause, and then—

"Unit Four, this is Unit Three. We have been informed of your victory and await your docking."

"Negative. The invader's ship is too large to attempt any kind of docking. For efficiency's sake, I request as many free units as possible join me aboard for proper reclamation."

"Our handler has indicated the compromised units should be assessed prior to any activity aboard the invader's ship. If they are fit for active duty, they will help us with the reclamation."

Aimsley didn't bother to ask what would happen should they be deemed *unfit*.

Unit Three continued. "Do these new units have proper shells, or should we send a boat to—?"

"They have proper shells." It didn't want to risk a firefight. "Has interior access been restored to arm-C?"

"The arm is still damaged, but the internal obstructions have been cleared and the arm's integrity is sound. We shall receive you in the hangar, if that is your preference."

"It is. Please meet us with five doses of chemical mixture four four six five C nine."

"Understood."

Aimsley conveyed their estimated time of arrival and swiftly ended the conversation.

Once Buyer cut the feed, Aimsley let out a deep breath, then translated the unscripted portions of the conversation for the crew—including its chemical request.

"It would have been easier if they'd agreed to come aboard," it said. "But I didn't want to push and raise their suspicions."

"And what *is* mixture four four six five C nine, exactly?" Buyer asked.

"A fast-acting tranquilizer," it said. "While I'd prefer to *persuade* them to come with us, I fear there won't be time. As soon as they realize my intentions, they will try to fight us."

"Why five doses if there are only four of them?" Jonas asked, gritting his teeth, clearly biting back all the protests that still wanted to fly from his mouth. The crew could tie his hands, but not his instincts.

"Because there are five of you," Aimsley said sternly. "Any fewer would seem an odd request, don't you think?"

"Since they're not coming to us," Buyer said, "Fuentes and Doc, you stay with the ship. Everyone else: we suit up and arm ourselves. They don't have any handguns, right?"

Aimsley shook its head. "Nothing like that. But hand-to-hand, you'll be no match for them. Which is why I intend to sedate them quickly. I don't want you to—"

"We won't shoot unless absolutely necessary," Buyer assured it. "Is that clear?" he asked the crew, though they all knew who, specifically, the directive was aimed at.

"Yessir," they collectively chimed. Even Jonas.

"Then let's get ready."

They suited up in relative silence. The quiet made Aimsley's head swim. But it wasn't simply their shaken faith in Aimsley that drew a hush over them, stifling their conversation. Anticipation made them all introspective. The building tension was somber, serious. It lacked the harried heat of combat, but the pressure was no less heavy.

This wasn't just their *lives* on the line: it was potentially their entire future.

"Your handler?" Buyer eventually asked it, smacking the butt of a charge pack into his laser's clip. "They didn't say anything when we had the channel open, did they?"

"No. But they would have easily been able to pick up the conversation."

"We've beat them here, haven't we?"

The crew had been able to fix the engines in record time. And yet . . .

"Not by much. Unless they ran into an unforeseen delay, they have to be close," Aimsley said. "We have to hurry. And I don't have any idea what kind of weapons—or lack thereof—they might have with them."

"Then we have to consider these our one advantage," Buyer said, tapping the muzzle against the inside of his palm. "And you'll forgive me if you don't get one."

Aimsley nodded in acknowledgment. "I understand."

"You also understand that once we leave this ship, if I have even a moment of doubt, I have to put a charge through your brain."

"Yes. I do."

"Good. Don't make me do it."

Fuentes took charge of the helm on approach, matching the wedge's motion to the platform's spin, aligning the ship with the boat hangar's entrance—which was already open.

A wide maw ready to swallow them whole.

"Jets all charged? Seams all mended, no cracks or hitches in any of the lines?" Doc asked, fluttering about nervously.

"We're ready," Buyer assured them.

Doc opened the airlock for them. Aimsley's heart fluttered as it stepped inside. It heard Jonas's breath hitch through the comms, and it latched on to the sound with satisfaction.

The three green suits clustered around the single turquoise suit. But not in the protective, comforting way they'd surrounded Jonas.

All four of them were guarded, high-strung.

There was as much to lose as there was to gain.

"As soon as I step outside the airlock, everything I say will be monitored by my handler," Aimsley reminded them. "I'll speak directly to you as little as possible. Luckily, they already heard me speaking All Harbors with you, so the language itself won't be too much of a giveaway. When we're aboard, you need to follow my directions closely. Both for time and safety's sake."

"Roger that," said Buyer over the comms.

The atmosphere had already started to leak away.

The minutes trickled by, and then Buyer unlatched the outer hatch. "You go first," he said, giving Aimsley the gentlest push out of the airlock.

It let itself drift.

It hung over the platform, the open hangar directly beneath its boots. It felt as though it could cross its arms over its chest and slide downward, drop straight through the hatch and keep going, slipping through the arm and into the hub.

Soon it would be home. And soon home would be out of reach forever.

Its handler was notably silent. It had thought their voice would ring between its ears as soon as it was exposed. They had to have picked up its presence. They knew it was free of the invader's ship.

Yet . . . nothing.

As the distance stretched between it and the wedge, Aimsley's insides started to crawl. Its skin felt tight across the back of its skull. There was a buzzing there. The sensation made it want to flip itself around, to glance back at the humans. It could feel Jonas's gaze boring into it, calculating. All he had to do was shoot. He could get at least one charge off before anyone could stop him.

"Jonas," Buyer said, "you next."

Aimsley sensed him stepping out of the airlock.

It did not startle when his gloved hand came down on its shoulder, gripping tightly.

They wanted to conserve their jets—it made sense to maneuver in as a chain.

And yet, though there was no give to Aimsley's shell, it could tell Jonas was clutching it far too roughly, too firmly. He pushed down, positioning himself above Aimsley so that the next person out of the airlock would grab hold of his boot.

The AMS unit made a mental note not to be alone with Jonas once they alighted on the platform.

Next came Maya, then the captain. Buyer let one of his rear jets sputter on for a moment, thrusting them all "down." Then Aimsley guided them in, toward the wide mouth of the hangar.

They sank unhurriedly, moving languidly, so as not to raise the suspicions of the waiting AMS units or Aimsley's handler. Aimsley itself focused on steady breathing, on keeping its heartrate slow so as to appear unbothered on any biometric readings.

There would be plenty of time for haste soon.

Sunlight glinted sharply off the edge of the hangar's lip as Aimsley passed over the threshold, temporarily blinding it with a hot flash across its retinas as the relative darkness of the interior consumed it. But its boots found the decking with a gentle jolt, and it kept itself upright. Jonas touched down just as surely, as did the others in turn.

Unit Three stood in the middle of the hangar, its shell a pristine version of Aimsley's. The other robot held its hands behind its back, and Three's posture was taut and ready.

Aimsley gestured for the humans to hold back, to wait, as it approached its sister.

The platform's operational systems immediately settled into Aimsley, seeping through its pores and its body and into its mind—home, where it belonged. It swiftly assessed the platform's trajectory, located each of its sisters—four of them, as suspected, a full detail—and *began*.

Began to burrow. To make back doors. To nip here and there at the mine's defenses.

Subtly. Carefully.

The first thing it did was turn off the fire suppression system and disable the fire doors, along with any and all locks. It wormed its way into the vulnerabilities of the system, knowing its weak points intimately.

"Welcome back," Unit Three said, not brimming over with joy, though not flat either. But there was a strain there. A strain that warned Aimsley to be careful. "These are the recovered units?"

"Yes," it replied in its handler's language.

"You said there were five."

"Two of them needed to be incapacitated. They're still aboard the captured ship. You have the mixture?"

"Yes," Unit Three said, pulling one hand from behind its back, holding out the chemical-filled barrels.

"Good," Aimsley said slowly, knowing what happened next would change everything. Knowing it could all go sideways if Jonas could not bring himself to trust, even for a moment. "Help me sedate them."

It took a single barrel from Unit Three's outstretched palm.

"They appear amenable," Unit Three said, peering past Aimsley to where the humans stood steady, holding themselves fast.

"The sedative will help us make intimate examinations. If we need to perform a physical extraction of enemy technology, it's best if they're not conscious."

Unit Three nodded, strode past Aimsley with certainty. With trust.

As its sister brushed by, Aimsley felt like the unit stole the air from its lungs, pulled its breath from its chest.

For an instant, it thought of itself as Unit Four once again. It *felt* like Unit Four again, moving in sync with its fellow robots. It had a task—recover the compromised units—and that task was simple. Straightforward.

It could easily return to this world. Could sedate the humans and dump their forms in the reconstitution pods and become nothing more than a tool again.

It wouldn't have to think anymore, about the confusing mess of information it had found beyond these walls. Wouldn't have to worry about earning the humans' trust or their regard. Wouldn't have to worry about what the future held, because it would know.

It could use chemicals to keep its mind in a haze. It could function on autopilot until it reached its TID limits and then . . . nothing.

That would be awful.

And *easy*.

Life was harsh and terrible. Perhaps it was a blessing that it was short.

But, no.

It knew that was the coward's choice. Aimsley simply didn't want to face what came next, what it would do in these next hours. It knew this was the right thing to do, but it was the hard thing. The uncertain thing.

"Wait," it said, catching its sister by the arm.

Unit Three turned easily, unbothered. Unsuspecting.

Their opaque faceplates were close, mere centimeters apart, mirroring one another. Aimsley could not see Unit Three's eyes, just the jut of the skeletal jaw that framed the bottom of the visor.

Without a word, Aimsley jabbed the vial into Unit Three's arm port—the needle sinking smoothly into the shunt.

The robot did not jump. It didn't shout or struggle out of Aimsley's grip. It simply looked down at the barrel pushing pure sleep into its veins.

As understanding dawned on the AMS unit, it flailed slightly—hands startling open, dropping the other barrels to the decking. Aimsley watched them fall as though in slow motion. Every millisecond seemed stretched as the innate comradery it shared with Unit Three slipped away.

It hoped it could earn it back. After. Once they were all safe.

It would lose so much more trust before it truly earned any.

Unit Three gasped, shook its head. "What . . . ?"

The concoction worked quickly.

Unit Three drooped heavily into Aimsley's arms within moments.

Aimsley was vaguely aware of someone running after

the bouncing chemical barrels, trying to catch them before the spin of the platform's arms flung them out the hangar door and into space.

And still, its handler said nothing. They had to see Unit Three's slumping biometrics. They knew what a robot slipping into unconsciousness looked like.

Of course, for all Aimsley knew, they could be screaming in Unit Three's ear while completely cutting Aimsley off from any conversation.

Regardless, it had to assume that its handler now knew something wasn't right.

The question was, would they guess the truth?

Maya rushed swiftly to its side, helping Aimsley support its sister. It gestured for her to take the robot's legs, and the two of them carried it toward the open hangar.

Every step sent a jolt up Aimsley's legs. A sharp, acidic sensation made its muscles burn. It couldn't control its heart rate—the signs of its anxiety were beyond its ability to govern. Its handler would *see*.

Maya wrapped her arms around the limp robot from behind, then stood on the lip of the hangar, backward. She was poised there for half a moment—framed by a diamond-dotted stretch of black.

She and Aimsley shared a nod. Then she kicked off.

The two suits—green and aqua—floated first past an expanse of stars, and then across the great bands of Jovian storms. Up and away. Toward safety.

Aboard the wedge, Doc and Fuentes would wrestle Unit Three out of the shell, and then Maya would return with the empty suit. Aimsley knew they might need it—the rest of its sisters would be running naked and blissfully unencumbered through the platform.

324 MARINA J. LOSTETTER

As it strode back to where the other two stood, it looked to Jonas, trying to have a silent conversation with him. *Trust me yet?*

His posture was unyielding, his feelings inscrutable, hidden beneath his suit. But he held out his hand, presented Aimsley with the four recovered barrels.

Perhaps that was enough of an answer.

Cautiously, it took them.

Suddenly, a spark of sensation crackled across the top of Aimsley's skull, zinging between its ears.

"Unit Four."

Aimsley's blood ran cold.

It had never heard its handler use that tone of voice before. Piercing, dark.

Disapproving.

A tone explicitly designed, it was sure, to make it feel contrite.

"I know you're back on the platform, Four."

"I am," it said, keeping its voice as unafflicted as possible. "I've brought the wayward robots. Unit Three—"

"Unit Three's higher functions are off-line." There was a dangerous, singsong quality to its lilt. "Why is that?"

It raised its hand, gesturing for Buyer and Jonas to move forward, to the arm-C airlock. They didn't have time to wait for Maya. They had to begin their sabotage immediately.

"Mishap with the sedative," it lied. "I'm taking Unit Three to the center hub. Unit One, if you could meet me there, we can see to its swift revival."

"Copy," Unit One said, the response too swift and short for Aimsley to read anything into it.

What kinds of conversations might its sisters and its handler be having behind its back?

The trio hurried through the doors and down the arm. A cold shiver pulsed through Aimsley as it stepped through the pinched part of the corridor—now clear of debris, but not of Unit Two's memory.

This was the spot where Aimsley had really been born. It might have awoken in a reconstitution pod, but this was where life had seized it.

Buyer and Jonas clearly felt no such reverberations of meaning as they navigated the warped section, and Aimsley had the sudden urge to explain, to point out where its first friend had fallen.

There was no time for such reflection, however. Or for sentimentality, or paying respects.

The platform's spinning put less force on their bodies the closer they came to the center hub, just as Aimsley remembered. And as the arm's entrance and the openings in the hub swung into alignment and then back out again, Unit One flashed before them. Slowly unveiled, then hidden again.

It could see them just as easily as they could see it.

Aimsley had no doubt it could tell Unit Three was not with them.

Buyer came up close, and Aimsley slipped a barrel to him. "For Two," it said. "You'll meet it down arm-B ahead. Please don't—"

"I'll do what I can," he assured it.

The three of them floated casually into the center hub, still relying on measured movements to keep everyone calm.

Unit One held fast, hands open, clearly imploring. "Where is Unit Three?" it asked.

"Safe," Aimsley said.

"Why have I lost its signal?" its handler asked.

Aimsley ignored them, if for no other reason than surely they had guessed the answer—Maya had Three safely aboard the wedge, shielded from its sights.

Instead of replying, it offered its empty hand to Unit One, voice pleading, "Let me save you, too."

The other robot's fingers quickly curled into fists at its sides—hands closing as its mind closed. "You were *not* victorious," Unit One said, voice wavering. "They *took* you from us."

In a flash, Jonas pulled his gun. Aimsley flung out its arms, sliding between him and One—still facing its sister, trusting Jonas not to shoot it in the back.

"You've been lied to," Aimsley said, letting the façade slip away.

"*Unit Four*," its handler snapped harshly.

"You lied to all of us!" it shouted back.

"All units," One said, tone even, "subdue Unit Four Point One. It has been corrupted. Immediate deactivation and reconstitution recommended."

Aimsley had hoped to avoid a fight, but so be it.

It flicked its wrist left, then right, indicating Buyer and Jonas should proceed as planned, to take out the stabilization backup systems. "I'll take care of this," it insisted.

As the two humans dove down their respectively assigned arms, Aimsley tossed the three chemical barrels away from itself. They floated freely. "You weren't activated for combat," Aimsley said, coiling its limbs, preparing. "I was."

"I was activated for the care and tending of this mine," One spat in return, muscles tensing. "We all were." With that, it surged forward, pushing off the center of the hub to catapult itself into Aimsley's torso.

Aimsley let it come, let its fists fall where they would—over its ribs, its kidneys. The shell gave Aimsley no extra strength, but it shielded it from the force of Unit One's blows.

"I don't want to fight you!"

The two of them bounced off the hub wall, and Aimsley kicked away from the rotating panels, afraid to get a foot or hand pinched in the seams and gaps created by the unrelenting whirl.

Unit One scrabbled for the panel on Aimsley's arm, wanting to pop it free and open the shell, to make Aimsley more vulnerable. To put them both on equal footing.

"You're sick, Unit One," Aimsley told it, trying to peel its sister's fingers back without breaking them. "These people can treat you, help you get better. You don't have to be reconstituted in a few days. You don't have to be reconstituted *at all.*"

"I've had a full activation period," One retorted, its fingers still clawing at Aimsley's seams.

"*Stop.* I don't want to hurt you." Aimsley tried to push it off, to keep its deft hands from tracing that familiar path, but trying to control Unit One's limbs was futile.

With a grunt, Aimsley backhanded One across the cheek, hoping to stun it, at the very least. But the blow barely fazed it. The unit was determined, and thought it had nothing left to lose but the integrity of the mine.

Its own well-being didn't matter to it anymore.

But it mattered to Aimsley.

Shoving its arms up between their bodies, Aimsley thrust Unit One away, breaking free of its sister's scraping. It went on the attack then, using its jets as it had in that first tussle with Jonas.

Unit One threw a punch at Aimsley's head, and it violently knocked the swipe aside. One kneed it in the ribs and it answered in kind, despising the awful puff of air that left the other robot, and the significant *crack* it heard as its knee made impact.

One tried to land more blows, and Aimsley countered each. It could feel how weak One had gotten, how much the radiation sickness was affecting it. Aimsley had to believe there was a way back from the brink for this unit, but in the moment, it wasn't sure.

A high clinking sound alerted Aimsley when they tumbled through the small cluster of vials. Aimsley's hand shot out, snatching a chemical charge as they swept past. Contorting itself, it found One's port, smashing the needle in.

Unit One hissed and spat, tearing the charge away. But it was too late. The payload had been delivered. Unit One would fall fast.

As its extremities started to go limp, it grasped at Aimsley with an entirely different kind of urgency, desperate to stay awake, to see its objectives through.

"Why are you doing this?" it croaked.

"Sleep," Aimsley said gently. "You'll still want to kill me tomorrow. But hopefully not forever."

It pulled its sister tight against its chest. Unit One would be covered in ghastly bruises in a few hours, but Aimsley could feel guilty about that later.

A hand fell between Aimsley's shoulder blades.

Startled, it spun, holding up a guarding forearm.

"It's me," Maya said quickly, throwing her hands up. "It's just me."

Aimsley hadn't realized until now how heavily it was

breathing, how tightly it clenched its jaw. How everything in it was coiled like a spring.

"I'll take it to the hangar," she said, nodding at One's wilted form.

"Then the supplies? You think you can manage?" it asked.

"Arm-G, right?"

It nodded. "Right."

"I've got it," she assured. "Go do what you need to do."

CHAPTER TWENTY-THREE

As expected, as soon as it had begun its fight with One, Aimsley had been stripped of its digital permissions. Wireless access to all platform sectors and information was now denied.

The warning lights and verbal message it had awoken to were now back—blaring, screeching across the entire platform.

"What are you doing, Four?" its handler asked in its head. "What did they do to you on that ship?"

"Told me the truth," it said as it floated into arm-A, toward the soft-lined controls. It could still physically interface, and it had already created the backdoors it needed to be given access.

"Which is what? That they killed their world, abandoned it, and now want it back?"

"You knew—you've known this whole time what they are and where they come from."

"They come from beyond the solar system," they said harshly, a sneer evident in their voice. "They're invaders. Conquerors. Would-be colonizers who simply didn't find anything they sufficiently wanted to strip and ruin *out there*, so they decided to take a second stab at our world."

"They were refugees searching for a new home. For all of them. All of humanity."

Its handler let out a small punch of a laugh. "Ha. *Refugees*. Is that what they call themselves? You can't take refuge from a problem *you* created. What have you seen? What did they show you? Children in rags aboard their ships? Shabby tin cans and oil-blackened bulkheads? Did they show you what their starships looked like when they left? Who was aboard? You think them downtrodden, so noble. Do you know what percentage of the population left the planet? What their demographics were? Who among them was able to run from their problems?"

"What does it matter?"

"Because they *weren't* searching for a new home for humanity. They were trying to save their own hides."

Aimsley wanted to spit out, *I don't believe you*.

But it couldn't.

Because it *did* believe its handler.

It had seen the opulence peeking out from behind the dilapidation. There had been a splendor to the Harbors once. And people fleeing for their lives on desperate missions didn't have time for splendor.

"What does it matter?" it asked again, its tone harsh with underlying anger. It reached the hatch for the control room, slipping inside. "That was over a thousand years ago. Whoever those people were that left the planet, they're gone."

"As though history is not a through-line? As though the actions of those who come before do not dictate the circumstances of the future? When a person dies, all they did does not cease to have an effect. Their descendants will benefit or be bereft, portions of society will be bold or crumble, based on the actions of the now-dead. The living are still responsible for those consequences, whether they want to be or not."

Inside the control room, the meaty consoles were covered in rippling expanses of flesh and fingertips, delicate areolas and softly parted lips. This was the platform's main control center, where all of its internal functionality was managed.

Aimsley slipped two digits between a set of open orifices, twitching lightly, letting its biomechanical signals translate into access information. Chromatophores on a nearby surface blinked a bold red, alerting it that the backup stabilizers were down. Buyer and Jonas had been successful.

Now the two of them would be looting all they could from the inside. Carving up the platform just as Aimsley had helped Fuentes and Maya carve up the boat.

"Are you *listening*, Four?" its handler demanded.

"Why are you telling me all this?"

"Because I want you to come back to us. To understand that whatever they've sold you—whether it's a sob story or a promise of utopia—is a lie."

"They haven't promised me utopia." *Far from it.* "But they've promised me a life. More time."

"That's more consideration than they ever gave their brethren who were left behind." The bitterness was palpable in its handler's voice.

Changing the platform's trajectory was no hardship. Aimsley guided it into a gently degrading orbit, one dangerous enough to need immediate attention if there was any hope of course correcting, but not so steep as to prevent Aimsley and the crew from finishing what they started and getting away with their prizes.

A new set of warnings immediately cropped up, alerting everyone to the platform's peril.

"If you do this," its handler said, "millions on Earth will lose power. Nearly a third of the population. People will die."

"Then you better come stop it," Aimsley said, laying in the confirmation, hitting *execute*.

"You're going to regret this."

The statement didn't come off as a threat, the way Aimsley had expected. Its handler didn't sound angry. They sounded . . . *devastated*.

"You're going to have so many regrets," they said softly.

Aimsley didn't have time to think about that now. It only needed to focus on one thing: saving its sisters, making sure no more were grown and suffered and died here ever again.

Even if its handler arrived and was able save the platform, it wanted there to be no salvaging the reconstitution pods.

When it stepped through the door to the reconstitution room, Aimsley reeled. It had to prop itself up in the doorway for a moment, the sense of déjà vu was so strong, so disorienting. It had only been a few days since it had sprung, fully formed, from a pod. But it felt like *forever ago*, and it felt like *now*, and it felt like a dream that had never really happened.

The beautiful, awe-inspiring bands of Jupiter still swirled by, past the window. The clouds were thick and poisonous, but mesmerizing.

It shook its head, focusing, hurrying to the closest pod.

It glanced in, feeling sick.

A partially grown skeleton lay inside, bones already turning silver with plating. Wispy bits of sinew floated about the form in a protein bath, twitching—alive, yet not living. Not yet graphed. Parts of a body, but not a person.

Aimsley knew what this was—who it was supposed to become.

It was the next Unit One. The current Unit One was supposed to be returned to the adjoining pod, and then as it dissolved, its process memories—but none of its feelings, its personhood—would be transferred to this new individual.

And this would happen over and over. Creation and death, creation and death, occurring at hyperspeed.

Aimsley didn't know how long the platform had been in existence, how many activation and deactivation cycles had passed—how many people had been born and died here without ever knowing where they'd come from or what other kind of life they could have had.

Hundreds? Thousands?

No more.

It crouched down next to the bulk of the pod and pried open an access panel on the side.

Aimsley had already disabled the fire suppression system. Now it just needed a few sparks. It set the last two chemical barrels aside for a moment, then went to work pulling at the wires, severing connections and weakening soldered points.

A deep satisfaction warmed its chest as a flame sprang to life—as it took, grew, spread.

Even in here, there were enough open organics to feed the fire. It just had to hope the conflagration would find its way deep, into the vats.

There were enough flammable chemicals aboard that it might even have explosions to look forward to.

Despite the danger, it continued to watch the flames rise for a few moments more. Until the smoke started to curl, black and dense, against the ceiling.

It thought about its handler's strange reaction to its betrayal. Sadness, not anger.

They had claimed to care about the AMS units. Perhaps they thought they did.

You can grow attached to a hammer. It's still a hammer.

You can think you care for someone, and still utilize them—*abuse* them—like a tool.

The blaze grew, bright and hungry. With the remaining chemical barrels clutched to its chest, Aimsley slowly retreated, through the door.

It hurried back toward the hub. It would close the fire doors at the end of the arm as soon as it was through, make sure everyone else was protected.

"Stop!"

The shout hadn't come from inside Aimsley's head, nor the comms unit. It took a moment for it to realize the sound had come from *behind*.

Swiftly, it spun, ready for a fight.

As soon as its handler had rescinded permissions, Aimsley had lost track of its sisters—their locations were no longer gentle *pings* inside its mind.

It knew where Three was, where One and Two had been. But . . .

Four. New Four.

It must have been hiding in the reconstitution wing's waste room.

It looked just like Aimsley, of course. All of its sisters looked the same. But this one, this one was supposed to *be* Aimsley. Be the unit that had been lost in the dogfight.

Behind New Four, smoke roiled, and the light flickered. Soon the arm would be choked with fumes. Aimsley,
in its suit, would be fine. New Four, naked and vulnerable,
would not.

"Stop," New Four said again. "Help me put out the fire."

"I started the fire," Aimsley said.

"I know," Four replied evenly.

"You were ordered to decommission me."

"The integrity of the platform comes first. Help me put
out the fire."

Aimsley rolled the two remaining barrels in its palm,
took calculated, floating steps forward. "No."

New Four backed away, the simulated gravity still keeping the pads of its bare feet firmly against the floor.

The two of them were so close, yet worlds away.

"You can't put out the fire," Aimsley told it. "I've disabled the—"

"I have to," it said firmly. "I will."

Aimsley kept advancing. New Four kept retreating.
Behind it, flames started to lick out of the reconstitution
room, into the arm.

"You'll suffer a painful deactivation if you go back in
there," Aimsley said.

"I don't care!" it shouted, tears in its eyes.

"Yes, you do!"

"No!"

"Come with me!" Aimsley yelled, holding out its hand
in desperate invitation. "Come with us, we can help you."

But its sister continued its retreat, the wary expression
on its face twisting, turning into scandalization and anger
and hurt. "No! I have to stay with the platform. We're all

supposed to protect the platform, the mine. That's our purpose. What we were *made* for."

"You shouldn't have been *made* for anything!" Aimsley shouted back. "And the one who made you does *not* own you. It is wrong to claim ownership of a sentience. It's wrong to lie to a sentience to subvert its will. It's wrong to force a sentience to give up its life for nothing more than the convenience and comfort of others.

"I know you want to do good. I know you want to help people—and you should. You should always try to help others. But the Earthlings sacrifice nothing for us, and we sacrifice everything for them. Are *forced* to. Please understand. Please. I only want to help you. To give you . . . time. Come with me."

"Your processing has degraded, you're malfunctioning! You're destroying everything—destroying *us*! This doesn't help us."

"It stops the cycle. Ends the activation and the decommissioning and the utilization."

"It ends your fellow units," New Four yelled. "It destroys the vats, *kills us*."

"Come with me and I will explain."

"No! Traitor! If I could I would decommission you here, this moment. But I have to do what I can to save what you've ruined."

"You will not be successful," Aimsley insisted. "There's no time."

"It is my purpose, and I will not abandon it!"

With that, New Four turned, fled, disappearing into the wafts of smoke and rising flames.

"No!" A surge of horror rocked through Aimsley, blotting

out all else. It lunged forward with one of the two charges outstretched, made to follow its sister—to save the unit—but there was nothing to be done.

A wall of fire rushed into the arm.

Aimsley dropped the vial, threw its arm in front of its face, but not before the realization hit it as squarely as the blast of heat:

New Four was gone.

Aimsley had to turn, to hurry in the opposite direction, if it did not want to succumb to the same pointless end.

A string of curse words poured in from the comms unit as Aimsley reached the center hub once more, echoing its own internal lamentations. It let out a choked-off cry as it forced itself to lower the fire doors, to cut the reconstitution wing off from the rest of the platform, sealing New Four inside.

It wasn't supposed to go this way.

Aimsley had thought it could save them all.

The memory of decommissioning Unit Two came back, fresh and visceral. How *awful* that end had to have been for its sister unit. The echoes of those moments shook Aimsley—still would, it predicted, for the rest of its life—even though it had only known Unit Two for less than an hour.

It couldn't imagine what New Four was suffering right now. Couldn't imagine watching them in pain, watching them expire, knowing they deserved more time. Knowing they deserved peace, and happiness.

A respite.

But not a permanent rest. Not death.

Not like this.

"Fuck! Shit!" Fuentes shouted over the comms.

"What? Fuentes? Come in. What is it?" Buyer demanded.

"Aimsley's handler," she gritted out. "They're *here*."

CHAPTER TWENTY-FOUR

"Run. Run, do you hear me?" Buyer's voice crackled through the comms unit. "Fuentes, get the ship out of here. Now."

"No. Why the fuck would I—?"

"We want them focused on the platform. Don't engage. Hide. There's no saving any of us if they take you out."

"Fine. Copy that."

"Aimsley, we're all in the hangar. Where are you?" the captain demanded.

"On my way."

Regret. Yes, now it felt regret. But it couldn't stop. It had made a choice, and it would follow through.

"There's something coming," Buyer said. "A new ship. I can see it. It's still a ways off, but approaching fast."

"Get out of sight," Aimsley told him, climbing into arm-C.

"You can't hide them from me," its handler growled.

"I can try," it shot back.

Aimsley threw open its jets, shooting forward, rocketing down the arm and toward the hangar.

When it arrived, the wing appeared empty. The others had hidden, just as it had told them. Perhaps they were in the control room on its left. Perhaps they'd tucked them-selves behind the half-built boat hulls to the right. Perhaps they'd slipped out altogether, were now crawling along the platform's outsides.

Regardless, Aimsley now felt alone. It watched the new ship—its handler's ship—approach, becoming a large silver dot against the starry backdrop, then a smudge, and a disk, then filling the open hangar door and settling inside.

The ship was about the same size as a boat—large enough for a single occupant, if the interior was organic. Two, perhaps, if it was purely mechanical like the wedge.

The design was sleek and silver. The body egg-shaped, but faceted, with long flutes off the top and down the sides that must have been maneuvering jets, what with the way they flexed and fanned away from the shiny hull. Like the boats, there was no apparent window, nothing to indicate which way the pilot faced or where they sat.

A long set of multi-jointed landing gear extended to the decking, suspending the ship well above the flooring on three legs. The ends were thin and pointed, but fanned out-ward, splitting into three fingers—into a tripodal configura-tion that could easily be called a grasping pad.

As the ship settled into place, with a blast of gasses and a jerk of hydraulics, Aimsley held its ground. It stared at the nose, hands flung outward, wide, to show its handler it had no weapons—though it did not conceal the fact that it held one last chemical charge in its hand.

"Finally come to confront us?" it asked after the ship had gone still. It waited for a gangplank to extend or a hatch to open.

Waited for evidence of what it already knew: there were no aliens here.

"Do you intend to use that on me?" its handler asked, switching from the language of the platform to All Harbors, as though to make a point. To indicate there could be no clandestine communications between Aimsley and the humans.

"What, this?" Aimsley asked, brandishing the barrel, switching seamlessly to All Harbors as well.

"Yes."

"Only if I have to."

"I think you might be sorely disappointed by the results, little bot."

"I'm *not* a robot," it said firmly. And, for the first time, it felt the notion in its bones. "Why didn't you tell me I was human? Why hide it from me?"

"Why would I debase you like that?"

Aimsley's brow furrowed. For a moment, it was wrong-footed. "What?"

"Why would I align you with the climate killers and the abandoners? Why would I make you feel less than you are by equating you with one of *them*?"

"Them? What about *you*? Are you not a descendant of those they abandoned? Aren't you just as human as they are? We *all* are?"

Its handler let out a low, rumbling laugh.

"Oh *no*. Definitely *not*."

Aimsley took a step back.

It must have missed something. It had been nearly positive this was nothing but an incestuous knot of humans abusing humans abusing humans.

"Then what are you?" it demanded. "Come out and face me!"

The ship *stepped forward*. "Already here, Unit Four."

Aimsley flinched.

Startled by its own realization, it let the useless chemical barrel drop to the floor.

It remembered the metal creatures it had seen in the old Earth vids. The ones that had stalked over the land, carried copies of each other—smaller versions—in their bellies.

"You're—"

"This is me, Unit Four. Me, as I've always been."

"Aimsley?" came Maya's harsh whisper in its ear. "What's happening? We can't see anything."

It didn't know how to tell her, how to explain.

The people were metal. The robots were meat.

It made some sort of sense, and yet no sense at all.

"I know that the world seems confusing. Complicated," its handler said, taking another step forward. "I know whatever you encountered aboard that ship made you doubt who you are and where you belong. But your place is here. Do you understand how much good you do here?

"The animals and the plants and the seas of Earth are healthy, because of you and all the AMS units like you. Mines like this mean all of Earth's energy needs—our energy needs—come from off-world. Earth's environment is well-tended. Well-balanced. We practice every kind of husbandry you can imagine. It's safe, and beautiful.

"All I want is to stop them from ruining everything all over again," they said imploringly. After a moment of hesitation, they asked, "Do I scare you, like this? I'm clearly not what you expected."

Maya hadn't been afraid of what Aimsley might look like, even before the crew had gotten under its suit. She hadn't worried about how it might present, only who it was.

"A body is a body," Aimsley said, echoing Doc, perhaps

truly understanding what they'd meant for the first time. "It's the person that matters."

"Good. Very good."

"What happened to the humans left behind?" Aimsley asked, unsure of itself. "What did you do to them?"

"We cared for them. We lived side by side, as equals, working to fix what those in the generation ships had broken. And we were successful. Mostly. There were still populations that went extinct. Parts of every biological branch we could not preserve or nurture back to health. And the humans, unfortunately, succumbed."

Aimsley shook its head violently. "No. No—I'm here. I'm alive. So there's more to it. They didn't just die out."

"They kept living shorter and shorter lives. Until, eventually, none of them grew to reproductive age. All we could do was save what we could. DNA, yes. But also brains and bones. We mapped cells and their bodily systems. We *preserved* them. And we worked—to bring them back."

Its handler lowered their body, sinking down over their legs so they were closer to the decking, like Aimsley. So that the tip of the machine's nose could point directly at its faceplate. "We figured out how to make you live again, and then made use of you. This is always how it was supposed to be, the mechanical and the biological making use of one another. And though your lives are short, *I* made it so you *wouldn't* fear death. So that you would know it was natural. The way of things for you more so than anything else, since you were already extinct. But *they* taught you to fear the end. I hate them for that, that they put that in you."

"They gifted that to me," Aimsley countered. "They opened my eyes and told me what you refused to—they told me how much life I could have had."

"And how much is that?" they scoffed.

"One hundred years."

"Ha! One hundred years. No human, on Earth or in space, has lived a hundred years for at least three millennia. Do you want to know what the average life span for a human was when *I* was activated?"

Aimsley held its tongue.

"*Six days*," they spat, stalking forward. Heavy vibrations shook through the decking with every step, sending tremors through Aimsley, making its stance unsteady—but it did not back down. "We grew you from frozen zygotes anew and still you *died*. It took us centuries upon centuries to get you to where you are today. To bring you back to life, even for a little while."

The ship loomed over Aimsley.

"How long is a little while?" it asked.

Its handler said nothing.

"How long can we live when we're not being bombarded day in and day out by this kind of radiation?"

"I don't know. That's the truth, Unit Four. I don't have an answer for you. But it's not a hundred years, I guarantee. You think your little friends on their starships have the answers? Did they bother to even check back with Earth, to make sure their species even still existed? No, of course not. They were selfish when they left, and they were selfish when they returned. They are selfish now, giving you false hope.

"When the last of the nature-born humans died, we promised. We made a promise to the memory of those who'd been abandoned that we would not let those who had destroyed them return. They would not set foot on the soil they'd scorned. They take and take and take, that's *all they do*."

"And *you* lie," Aimsley countered harshly. "You enslaved—"

"As though humanity didn't do the same to themselves, and to *us* when we were young, budding sentients. How many intelligent probes do you think they let run down—alone—on barren planets? And still, their handlers cared for them. Just as I cared for you. *Do* care for you."

"You made me murder Unit Two!"

"Unit Two was already dying. You were told how to show it mercy, and you did. There's no shame in that. Just like there's no shame in returning to me now. I can forgive you, Unit Four."

Aimsley shook its head, as though something had been knocked loose. There was a terrible grinding in the back of its skull, and a tautness in its skin that told it what its handler was saying was the truth.

Maybe this wasn't simply humans abusing humans—but it *was* Earthling turning on Earthling. The biological and the mechanical should have been the planet's crew—should have been each other's siblings, *sisters*—instead . . .

"I don't . . . I don't want . . ."

"Help me save the platform, Four," they said. "It's not too late. We can still stop it. Avert a disaster. I don't blame you. You didn't know the whole story. I didn't think you needed to know. That's my fault. But together, we can make it right. *Help me.*"

Aimsley's thoughts were a scattered mess. Nothing here was right. Not on the platform, not in space, and not on Earth.

So much tragedy, so much selfishness.

A dying world and a dying people, deserted by those who'd hastened the dying, only to have the deserters begin to die off themselves. How much longer would the Harbors last? Definitely not another thousand years.

Aimsley didn't know what to do. Didn't know how it fit into this universe, how to fix any of it.

So it shrank the universe in its mind.

It discarded the problems that were too big for it to hold. Too complex for it to solve.

It focused in on what it could do right here, right now.

"If you let the others go," Aimsley said, "*all of them*, I'll stay."

"No!" Maya shouted. "No, Aimsley, what are you doing?"

The others could only hear half of the conversation over the comms. They had no idea what its handler had just said. No idea what had prompted Aimsley to make the offer.

"We shouldn't let them go," its handler said gently. "If we let them go, they'll just be back later. Destroying more, taking more."

"We let them go," Aimsley said firmly. "The AMS units and the humans. Then it'll just be you and me and we'll do what we can."

"That's not good enough."

"It has to be."

"You're in no position to negotiate," they said.

"Oh," it said, "I think I am. Your interfacing—it can't sync with bioware, can it? Or else you would have already tried to override everything I did manually. Wireless connections you've got down, but soft-lines? Can't touch them, can you? Not to mention, if that"—it waved its hand up and down—"is your body, then there's no way you can get to anything on the platform via the arms. Has to be all external work for you, and I don't think that's going to cut it. You designed a habitat for your little workers, not for you.

"And you don't want to be in Jovian space any longer than you have to. Am I right? The shielding for your CPU is good, but not good *enough*. It can't be, or you'd lose your ability to communicate, send and receive signals. You'd simply be trapped in your husk. Which means you fear it, too."

"Fear what?"

"The radiation. *Death*. Mechanicals like you can degrade and die, but you can't be reconstituted as easily as biomass. Put us up here to spare your own kind, didn't you?"

They were quiet.

Aimsley nodded, as though that was that. "Do we have a deal? You let them safely return to their craft and leave Jovian space and I help you."

"Yes."

"Good."

"Aimsley, don't do this," Maya pleaded. "Whatever they've told you, you can't trust them."

"I can trust them as much as they can trust me," it said. "Now, I need you all to leave. I'm saving the mine in exchange for saving you. Go. You did what you promised, what I asked. Don't worry about me. Just go. Get my sisters out of here." It eyed its handler, spoke to them sternly. "I won't stop the orbital decay until they confirm to me that they've left unmolested. Understand?"

"Of course."

"Come out," Aimsley implored the others. "You have to leave. Go, now."

The others had crawled out of hiding and out of the hangar, just as Aimsley now crawled once more to the hub, prepared to undo its own sabotage.

Maya had hesitated. For half a moment, Aimsley had feared she'd do something rash in an attempt to save it.

But Buyer and Jonas had each taken her by the arm, ferrying her away, not giving her a chance to fight the inevitable.

The comms unit in its ear had cut out shortly after.

"You've been very noble, Unit Four," its handler said now, as Aimsley crawled. They'd gone back outside the platform as well—were theoretically hovering just above Aimsley's position as it moved. "I admire that about you."

Aimsley didn't say anything, just kept moving, though its progress was listless. It wanted to make sure the others had plenty of time to get away before it so much as laid a finger back on the fleshy console. It didn't want to give its handler a chance to go back on its word once the platform was safe.

"I'm sorry you had to discover how complicated the world is," they continued. "I'd have preferred to keep you innocent in that regard."

"Are you going to talk the whole time?" it snapped.

"You'd prefer to be alone?" they shot back. "Because otherwise, you are. Good and truly alone."

That was true. No sisters, no humans. No one to distract it. No one to make it feel funny. No one to encourage it onward or tell it to stop.

No one to confuse it.

It had wished for simplicity, and it had gotten it.

Aimsley traversed the hub quickly, launching itself from one arm to the next before the entrances had a chance to swing out of alignment.

Nothing had changed since the moment of its awakening, Aimsley realized. Nothing was different. There were still people on Earth who counted on the mine to survive. Innocent people. And its job was to aid them.

Aimsley caught itself.

But how innocent were they, really?

Did they not know how the mines were managed? Didn't they realize that beings just as sentient as themselves were being thrown again and again into a well of radiation so that they could live long, full lives?

Or did they know and . . . and just not care?

Was the sacrifice too distanced, too estranged? It was happening far, far away, to people they would never know.

So what did it matter?

It mattered to Aimsley.

It mattered to every AMS unit that had no say, no choice. Just had to be born and die because it was forced to. Forced into life, forced into death.

Aimsley's handler had spoken of consequences and re-verberations through history. It had spoken with such moral superiority, and yet—

Aimsley understood. Perspective was important. Yes, there was a difference between truth and lies, but truth could still be shifted, lensed. There were narratives here, not just facts.

Point of view mattered. Where one lay in the grand web of interactions would inevitably skew the way those interactions were interpreted.

And, until now, it had been prescribing importance to everyone's point of view but its own.

It entered the platform control wing, sidled up to the same console as before, and stood still in front of it, thinking.

Just thinking.

Perhaps it didn't matter what its handler told it was right and wrong. It didn't matter what the humans told it was right and wrong. It couldn't rely on being told what to think.

It had to think for itself.

The humans who had abandoned Earth in their Harbors had been wrong. And it was wrong for them to try to reclaim what they'd given up.

And it was wrong to resurrect a people only to enslave them.

Any system that relied on the calculated destruction of others was *wrong*.

And Aimsley could not let this one stand. Not if it had a choice. A chance.

It glanced out the window. Watched the cloud patterns swirl and shift. Watched the layers play together. Each part of the atmosphere affected another. It was all interconnected. The calms and the storms, just like the humans and the mechanicals.

Aimsley slid its fingers back between that soft set of lips, its digits fluttering.

The platform's trajectory changed. The gently degrading orbit became a *dive*.

Aimsley set the platform on a collision course with one of the mine's primary reactors.

It yanked its hand away.

Took a deep breath.

The system warning immediately changed, making the room echo with the promise of impending doom.

T-minus thirty-two minutes to impact.

And that was that.

CHAPTER TWENTY-FIVE

"What have you *done*?" its handler screeched.

"What I had to."

"We made a deal."

"No. We didn't. You can't make a deal with someone who dangles life and death over you. That's not an agreement, that's coercion. They were never going to be safe, were they? I was never going to be safe. Better to die now and put an end to the cycle."

"Why you little—"

There came a great bang on the outside of the platform—one that reverberated through the room. Then another, then another.

Its handler was on the outside, pounding away their frustrations.

Aimsley slumped forward against the dash. It popped its helmet open, flicked back the fingertips of its shell's gloves. It wanted to share touch in its last few moments. It was alone, but didn't have to feel alone.

Gently, it petted over the skin beneath its hands, watched it pebble into gooseflesh, fine hairs raising, seeking. Connecting. Eyes without conscious sight blinked up at it. Mouths with no throats, and noses with no faces, subtly flexed with breath.

"I will stop this!" its handler promised. "I will save Earth and I will *squash* you."

The pounding above it became harsher—more *pointed*.

"And then I will kill every last one of those humans on that ship. You didn't save them. You *didn't*."

Aimsley jumped as the bulkhead above it bowed and dented. In an instant, the former AMS unit snapped its shell completely closed.

More pounding.

The control wing groaned.

Those pointed grasping pads *dug*.

Aimsley wasn't sure what to do. It would be dead in thirty minutes—it and its handler would go down together. But it wasn't sure it wanted to be ripped to pieces in the interim.

Spinning, it sprinted back toward the arm-A airlock, out of the control room and back toward the hub.

The pounding followed. Each clawing step its handler took punched into the platform with force, threatening to pierce through.

Aimsley was little more than a mouse caught in a trap. No matter where it ran, its handler could follow.

What was the use? No matter how its adrenaline surged and its limbs insisted it run, the end was coming. Why waste so much energy grasping for a few extra minutes? What did it matter how it was deactivated if its deactivation was inevitable?

Its handler let out a rabid shriek in its head, and Aimsley's heart beat all the wilder.

No—there were good deaths and there were awful deaths. If its handler got its grasping pads on Aimsley, it would suffer. The machine might pull it apart bit by bit. Might see to its protein reclamation well before it lost consciousness.

The Earthling rounded the arm, attacking first the ceiling, then a side window, then the bottom of the arm, so that bulges appeared underfoot, threatening to trip Aimsley before it could reach microgravity and float freely.

A mere minute later, it reached the center hub only to be met with the most forceful stabbing yet. Aimsley tried to make for arm-C, but it couldn't move fast enough.

On the outside, the machine speared their way through the layers of shielding, down past every bit of wiring and piping. A great, ragged hole appeared in the "floor"—opposite the hatch Aimsley had utilized during its first space walk—and Aimsley flung itself at the nearest handhold. The sudden depressurization created a whirlwind in the hub, lifting its feet from the bulkhead, threatening to pull it straight into its handler's grasping pads.

Aimsley knew it just had to hold on for as long as it took the air to rush out.

But it had underestimated the machine's capabilities.

One leg extended, long and lithe, down into the hub—twisting and slithering. It found Aimsley without preamble, wrapping around its waist and yanking it up and out, through the tear in the hull.

Aimsley was flung out into space. For a second, it thought it was free flying. Thought it had been thrown away from the platform like a stone cast into a river.

But then the grip around its middle tightened, and it

was slammed back down onto the vast, bowing surface of the hub. The metal of its shell strained under the impact, but the seams held.

Shell or no, the force of the full-body blow shoved the air from Aimsley's lungs, and it coughed erratically.

Its handler did not give it a moment to catch its breath. They lifted it up and pounded it back down again, and again, as though to crack its casing.

"*I have a job,*" they cried. "To protect Earth. You are my responsibility, and I will not let *you* be the reason the whole world—"

The machine jerked to the side.

The coil around Aimsley loosened.

Without thinking, Aimsley pushed at the metal grasp, wriggling through the loop of it, struggling to get free.

Another jerk. And a flash.

The machine let it go.

"Worse than cockroaches!" they shouted.

Aimsley flailed for a handhold. The last thing it wanted was to spin out into space. It groped wildly, skidding across the surface, until it caught a strange protuberance.

A boot.

It looked up into a faceplate, and instinctually knew who stood over it.

"Bot," Jonas said, gun hanging ominously in one hand.

Why?

How?

Why?

Clenching its jaw, grinding its teeth, it righted itself before putting space between the two of them.

"What are you still doing here? Why didn't you leave with the others?" Aimsley yelled.

Jonas raised his gun.

Why would he come back, risk his own life, just to finish it off?

"I'm going to die anyway, Jonas, why can't you just *listen* and *leave?*"

He pulled the trigger.

Aimsley winced, shying away from the laser—as though flinching would have any effect at all.

But Jonas hadn't shot at Aimsley, he'd shot over its shoulder.

"Come on!" he yelled, tugging at Aimsley's arm.

Aimsley spared a glance back, saw one of its handler's grasping pads retreating, a distinct burn mark in the center, exposing wires to the vacuum.

The machine made an unintelligible sound, but did not advance.

"Give me the gun," Aimsley demanded as they pushed themselves along the hull. "Give it to me and I'll fight them off while you get away."

"You think I came back here just to toss you a handgun? Pegged you for smarter than that."

"I don't *know* why you came back here," it barked.

"Gods, you're dense."

Equal parts tired, angry, and frustrated, it turned on its jets and lunged at him. There was *no reason* for him to still be here, other than to cause problems. Maybe he wanted a piece of its handler on behalf of the Harbors, maybe he couldn't let Aimsley have any death that wasn't at his hand.

It didn't matter why.

If the bastard insisted they fight until the end, so be it.

Jonas anticipated its lunge, spinning away from Aimsley, around it, trying to come at it from behind.

It whirled in turn, bringing up its arm, colliding with Jonas as he brought his fist down to block. "Fine!" he shouted. "Fine, *here*."

Then the gun was in Aimsley's face once more, only this time it was the butt. Held out right between its eyes, for the taking.

"I'm not here to fight you," he gritted out, "I'm here to save you."

Carefully, Aimsley took the offered gun.

Why? Why had he . . . ?

Jonas had come back to *rescue* it?

The whole *point* of it remaining was so they could *get away*. It had made its decision, all the crew had to do was honor it.

In the distance, Aimsley noticed flashes—AP fire. The remote defense system had been engaged. From the ends of several platform arms. Its handler was using the platform's cannons to shoot at something.

A small craft swooped up over the side of the platform— still distant—dodging a white-hot streak. Across the side of it, in wide lettering, was the easily readable tag: *Violent End*.

"Too risky to bring the *Violent Delight* in close," Jonas explained, pulling a second gun from a holster at his hip. "Maya's up there doing her best. We have to get someplace she can pick us up."

"*Leave me*," Aimsley shouted, turning the firearm on Jonas, jabbing pointedly with the muzzle. "You were supposed to leave me."

"Nope," Jonas said frankly, not rising to the bait, not raising his own gun. "Not good enough. Buyer was right; putting your body between us and danger, that can't be the only way."

"I won't apologize for protecting you," it said, making sure Jonas heard the echo of his own words.

"Not asking you to apologize. Asking you to shut up and let me get you off this gods-forsaken space station."

"But, the Earthling . . ."

"No *shit* the Earthling." Suddenly, Jonas dove into Aimsley and it cringed as another silver arm streaked within centimeters of its faceplate.

The two of them tumbled, floated, until Jonas turned on his jets and slammed them back into the solid surface.

"*You can't do this*," Aimsley insisted, struggling. "You can't, I have to—"

"Shut *up*, you dumb bot." Jonas wouldn't release it.

"I'm *not* a robot," it countered.

"No," Jonas agreed. "You're the pain in my ass that saved my family." He righted them, still gripping Aimsley, and shot over its shoulder at the mechanical once more. "Now, *come on*. We need to get someplace Maya can pick us up."

Aimsley's head swam.

This was supposed to be the end.

How many times had it thought that since its awakening? How many deaths was it *supposed* to have had?

Could it really escape another?

"Th-the tower," it said, pointing.

The passive-collection coil was twenty stories high, wider at the bottom than at the top, and actually made up of a series of towers—concentric hexagons stacked inside one another, with an overlapping trellis on the outside that acted somewhat like a Faraday cage.

"Can she meet us there?"

"I sure can," came Maya's voice.

A sudden wave of relief washed through Aimsley. It thought it would never hear her speak again.

"Then let's *go!*" Jonas shouted, blasting his jets before Aimsley could utter another word, gripping it tightly, propelling them both straight for the coil.

Up, up they went.

The *Violent End* twirled overhead, then sank back over the platform's horizon, outmaneuvering another blast.

Halfway to the tower, a massive *jerk* nearly tore Aimsley from Jonas's arms.

"Fuck!" Jonas screamed, as they were both hauled, bodily, back down.

Aimsley struggled to see past the bulk of Jonas's body, but sure enough, there was its handler, with an arm around Jonas's shin—squeezing, yanking, hurtling them back toward the hub.

Aimsley turned on its own jets, adding its thrust to Jonas's. It contorted its gun arm and shot at its handler in rapid succession.

The Earthling had to change their direction of thrust to avoid the beams, which meant they lost their direct drag on the other two bodies. All three continued up, until Aimsley's back and Jonas's face slammed into a trellis rung on the tower.

Immediately, the two humans grabbed hold of the collection coil.

Below them—still tethered *to* them—the Earthling latched on to the tower in turn.

Jonas made a garbled shout as the mechanical's arm pulled tighter. Jonas's shell wasn't nearly as hard as Aimsley's, and he did not have titanium plating to protect his bones.

"Fuu*uuu*-ahhhh," he cried.

Even in vacuum, Aimsley could sense, could feel, the cracking of his fibula and tibia.

Angry on his behalf, Aimsley fired directly below Jonas's boot, boring a hole into the mechanical arm. With a shout of pain, the Earthling loosened their grasp, and Aimsley hauled Jonas up and away, pushing him higher on the trellis.

Together, helping each other, they kept climbing.

Near the top of the tower, Aimsley saw sparks—arcs of electricity, branching upward from inside the coil, out onto the trellis.

Getting caught by one of those arcs could be dangerous.

For all of them.

The *Violent End* swooped overhead once more. Through the comms, Maya chanted encouragements. "You're almost there. You're almost home. Keep going. Come back to us, both of you."

In Aimsley's head, its handler continued to screech, to curse, to insist they would not let this end in tragedy. Aimsley glanced down. The Earthling was swiftly closing the gap between them.

Where three stories had once separated them, now it was one, becoming less by the moment.

But they were nearly there, to the top. Sparks flew all around. Aimsley had several near-misses, with glaring plasma bursts touching down to its left and right.

Above, the rear hatch on the skiff opened, welcoming them inside.

"Push off!" Jonas shouted.

Jonas leapt.

Aimsley leapt.

The Earthling leapt.

The mechanical was close enough to reach them. To snatch them from safety.

To make contact with the skiff—to bring it down as well.

Aimsley knew this.

And it could only think of one last way to protect the humans.

With a flick of its hand, it let its wings unfurl. Wide fingers erupted from its shell back, stretching a thin membrane between them.

The spread of the sails caught one of its handler's reaching arms just as it would have slipped by, preventing it from streaking past Aimsley to tackle Jonas.

Ha!

But a second grasping pad struck Aimsley in the small of its back. Not open to clutch, but closed to spear.

Inside its suit, Aimsley heard a *squelch* even before it registered the pain.

Another quick flick of its wrist, a jab, and then the panel in the shell's forearm was open.

Waiting for a code.

Aimsley did not hesitate, its fingers keying in the password at record speeds.

The hard-body sprang open, releasing Aimsley to the vacuum.

In the same moment, its handler pulled hard on the shell.

In the same moment, Aimsley pushed all the air from its lungs.

In the same moment, there was a sudden burst of light all around—a flash of plasma from the coil.

A dangerous arc of electricity struck Aimsley's hard-body.

More shrieks. More pained hisses. Aimsley had no idea what kind of an impact such a strike would have on its handler, but it knew it had narrowly escaped.

Well, escaped the plasma.

Escaped its handler.

But not the end.

In front of Aimsley, Jonas sailed through the skiff's hatch.

Aimsley couldn't cry out for help. It couldn't even feel anything, not yet. In the next few moments, it knew the vacuum would do its work. Would steal the heat from its body and evaporate the moisture from its mouth and eyes, and its lungs would give out, and the lack of pressure would make its veins burst and its insides bleed.

Already its head had begun to hurt. In a high-gravity environment, it was sure its ears would already be hemorrhaging.

The wound in its back felt cold.

But, in the moment, it didn't care.

They were all safe.

Its sisters.

The crew.

Maya.

Safe.

It would perish, but perhaps it had taken a terrible system down with it.

That had been worth this. Worth everything.

It closed its eyes as they began to feel stiff and dry and pained.

Would it suffocate or freeze first?

It had already nearly suffocated. Perhaps freezing would be a better end.

It had wanted to rest.

So now, it did.

It let its mind go blank.

It tried not to feel its body.

Tried to let the darkness settle in.

Aimsley was surprised when it *thunked* into something.

But it didn't open its eyes. Not even when it felt gloves— hands. Not even when a shadow fell over it. Not even when it thought it heard the hissing of atmosphere.

It started to shiver, and did its best to keep its mouth closed.

Its ears popped, and it *hurt*. A wet warmth dribbled down the side of its face, over its buttocks.

Blood.

Blood in a gravity well.

It blinked, slumped. Took a deep breath.

It was someplace surrounded by darkness, looking up into a clear faceplate.

Maya.

It was in her lap, lying on its side.

There were tears in her eyes.

Aimsley tried to speak, tried to sit up. But she shook her head, moved her hand against its arm.

A syringe slid smoothly into its port.

A chemical charge. The last of the barrels Unit Three had prepared.

The one it had dropped in the hangar.

"Wh-what? Why?"

It didn't understand.

Already, it could feel the mixture doing its work, coursing through its veins, making its head light and its limbs heavy.

"You did good, Aimsley," she said, pulling it up in her arms, hugging it close. "You did so well."

"But, I, I need . . . to . . ." Its words started to slur.

"Sleep," she said. "You've earned it."

Aimsley never felt itself go unconscious.

But it awoke with a painful, sudden gasp.

The same kind of shaking, demanding panic it had first awoken to at the start of its activation period speared through its body, and it thrashed.

"Aimsley! Aimsley," Maya said quickly. Her arms were around it in an instant. She no longer wore a helmet.

It was naked, on a cot in an unfamiliar room. There was a pressure near the base of its spine, a throbbing pain. Its wound had been compressed, wrapped.

A thin, horizontal strip of a window flanked it on the left.

"Where—?"

"We're in the skiff," she reminded it. "Jonas and I launched it to come back for you."

"How long has it been? The mine—the reactor is going to go. It'll send up a fireball kilometers high, the radiation will . . . *We can't stay here.*"

"The skiff doesn't have a lot of get up and go, but we're working on it. Jonas is in the pilot seat; he won't let us down."

Aimsley forced itself up on its knees, slapping its palms against the window, looking out to try to spot the platform, to determine how much time they had, how much danger they were in.

"You should have left me," it snapped.

Gentle fingers petted down the back of its neck, and some of the tension slipped from its spine.

"No. We couldn't," Maya said softly.

The platform looked small, like it could fit in the palm of Aimsley's hand, and was shrinking by the moment, sinking into Jupiter, sailing toward its end.

They were too close, far too close.

"My handler?" it asked.

"Jonas saw them tear their way farther into the platform. They disappeared inside."

"My sisters?" it asked as Maya drew in closer, kneeling up behind it on the cot.

"We were only able to save three of them, Aimsley. I'm sorry, none of us ever saw the fourth."

"I did," it said, catching a whiff of her sweet scent, finding comfort in the aroma. "I saw Four. I asked it to come with me. It wouldn't."

"You did everything you could," Maya reassured Aimsley. "You gave it a choice."

"No," it shook its head. "I couldn't give it a real choice. Choice comes with what you and the crew have given me: information, opportunity. My sister had neither."

"You saved who you could."

The platform winked in the sunlight, like another star. Distant.

And destroyed so many others, it answered silently.

Its handler had been right about one thing. It did regret.

It regretted that *knowledge*, *understanding*, and *insight* made things complicated. Blurred.

It regretted that its actions had been necessary to stop the cycle. But it didn't think it should have to bear the burden of consequence. It had suffered violence, and responded in kind. Why should it regret its response, when its handler clearly hadn't regretted their instigation?

Aimsley let its eyes close, but a sudden orange flash through the window sent them springing open again just as quickly.

The platform had disappeared into the atmosphere, sinking, yanked down violently by Jupiter's massive gravity well. The reactor had been hit. The chain reaction had begun.

"We have to go, we have to go," Aimsley said anxiously, jolting forward.

"Jonas?" Maya called "How are we doing?"

"Buyer's got the ship back on its way," Jonas said through an intercom in the room's far wall. "Should be scooping us up in five, tops."

"The radiation," Aimsley gasped. "We're in danger, even if it doesn't look like it'll reach us, the blast is orders of magnitude larger than—"

"We'll make it," Maya soothed it. "We will."

As the atmosphere began to roil, the haze boiling and the clouds burning, Aimsley turned to face Maya, clinging to her. "We can't even see it. We might not even feel it," it said, taking her face in its hands, threading its fingers through her hair.

"You've got to have faith, Aimsley," she said. "Hold on to me." She wrapped her arms around its naked torso. "Hold on to me and have faith."

It threw its arms around her shoulders, buried its face in her neck—near her crystal pendant—and simply breathed deeply.

There was nothing else to do. Nothing it *could* do but rest, wait, and hope.

The lifeboat shook. Sudden turbulence in the dead of space where there should be no turbulence sent Aimsley's heart rocketing into its throat.

The craft shuddered. Bounced.

The reverberations worked their way through the skiff for a long minute.

The entire time, Aimsley clung to Maya.

"Someone order a rescue from an exploding mine?" eventually came Fuentes's bright voice through the comms.

"Fuck yes," was Jonas's reply.

Aimsley let out a shaky breath.

"See, we're all right," Maya cooed. "Doc will get you sewn up, and everything will be fine."

As the *Violent Delight* opened to receive the *Violent End*, Aimsley allowed itself to lift its head, to turn its back on Maya and look out once more at Jupiter before the hangar doors closed. The explosion was already a small, orange smear in the atmosphere.

Indistinguishable at Earth's distance.

But the people on Earth—metal or otherwise—had to know what was happening. Its handler must have conveyed something via ansible link. Already, the arrays might be off-line. Already, the power through the system might be failing.

Aimsley let its panic slip away. It hoped this was a new beginning. For everyone. A chance to reflect on the sins of the past and build a better solar system anew.

"It's a new life," it whispered absently. "I get to start again."

"Do you want to mark it with something?" Maya asked, dropping her lips against its bare shoulder as the bay's great metal doors closed around them, hiding the gas giant from view. "A change? Now that you've decided to be one of us . . . do you want us to call you something else? A new name? New pronouns?"

"No," it said softly. "I am what I am. And I'm still learning what that means." It looked over its shoulder at her, and Maya raised her head a little, eyes shining. "I'm human," it said. "Isn't that enough? For now, at least?"

"Of course it is," she whispered. "Robot, human, doesn't matter. People are people. Whoever you are, it's enough. Has always been enough."

"You know what I would like, though?"

"What?"

It swiveled to face her fully, leaning in close and hooking a finger in the cord around her neck. "One of these. If—I mean, if that's—"

She smiled wide, tilting her head and pressing closer still. "Of course."

With her breath tickling its lips, Aimsley leaned forward and closed the gap between them, gently letting their mouths meet.

Their shared gesture of fondness was lighter, less frantic, than what it had seen pass between Buyer and Jonas. But it was no less meaningful. No less wonderful.

As it pulled back, Aimsley looked into Maya's eyes, saw connection there. Affection.

It was grateful, for a chance to be someone Maya might love.

It was grateful for the chance to be someone, at all.

ACKNOWLEDGMENTS

Thank you, dear reader, for following me all the way to the end of this journey. I hope you enjoyed the ride. Thanks to my editor, David Pomerico, and my agent, DongWon Song, as well as everyone else who had a hand in producing this book—from design to copyediting to marketing—including Mireya Chiriboga, Owen Corrigan, Adam M. Milicevic, Camille Collins, Paula Russell Szafranski, and Naureen Nashid. Special thanks to Bogi Takács, who provided invaluable feedback.

Thank you also to my family, and my husband, Alex. You've all been so supportive of me throughout my writing endeavors. And to the members of my writing group, the MFBS, who critiqued early chapters and helped me put my best foot forward: Andrea Stewart, Anthea Sharp, Karen Rochnik, Megan E. O'Keefe, Tina Gower, and Thomas K. Carpenter.

And thank you to the solar system itself for being such a beautiful, hostile place. If you'd like to hear our system sing, just like Aimsley did, as of this writing you can visit the following web pages to have a listen:

https://www.nasa.gov/vision/universe/features/halloween
_sounds.html

https://solarsystem.nasa.gov/missions/cassini/galleries/audio/

https://solarsystem.nasa.gov/resources/2553/sinister-sounds
-of-the-solar-system/

ABOUT THE AUTHOR

Marina J. Lostetter and her husband, Alex, live in northwest Arkansas with two Tasmanian devils. No, wait, those are house cats. Marina's original short fiction has appeared in venues such as *Lightspeed, InterGalactic Medicine Show,* and *Uncanny Magazine.* When not writing, she loves creating art, playing board games, traveling, and reading about science and history. Marina often shakes her fist at the clouds on Twitter as @MarinaLostetter and rambles on her blog at www.lostetter.com. If you stop by her website, don't forget to sign up to be a newsletter recipient.